T0013722

Praise for Dianne ̶ ̶ ̶ ̶ ̶ ̶ ̶ ̶

A Newlywed's Guide to Fortune and Murder

"The Agatha Award–winning author of *A Lady's Guide to Etiquette and Murder* is adept at misdirection. Witty British conversation and social history as viewed by an American will continue to appeal to fans of Victorian mysteries."
—*Library Journal*

"A pleasant combination of Victoriana and murder."
—*Kirkus Reviews*

"Numerous plot twists, well-drawn characters, and immersive details of the life and times in turn-of-the-century Victorian England distinguish this historical cozy."
—*Booklist*

"Well-placed clues keep the reader guessing without making the ending either too obvious or too incredible. This is a fun summer read."
—*Historical Novel Society*

Books by Dianne Freeman

A LADY'S GUIDE TO ETIQUETTE AND MURDER

A LADY'S GUIDE TO GOSSIP AND MURDER

A LADY'S GUIDE TO MISCHIEF AND MURDER

A FIANCÉE'S GUIDE TO FIRST WIVES AND MURDER

A BRIDE'S GUIDE TO MARRIAGE AND MURDER

A NEWLYWED'S GUIDE TO FORTUNE AND MURDER

AN ART LOVER'S GUIDE TO PARIS AND MURDER

Published by Kensington Publishing Corp.

A Newlywed's Guide to Fortune and Murder

Dianne Freeman

KENSINGTON
PUBLISHING CORP.

www.kensingtonbooks.com

KENSINGTON BOOKS are published by

Kensington Publishing Corp.
119 West 40th Street
New York, NY 10018

Copyright © 2023 by Dianne Freeman

This book is a work of fiction. Names, characters, businesses, organizations, places, events, and incidents either are the product of the author's imagination or are used fictitiously. Any resemblance to actual persons, living or dead, events, or locales is entirely coincidental.

To the extent that the image or images on the cover of this book depict a person or persons, such person or persons are merely models, and are not intended to portray any character or characters featured in the book.

All rights reserved. No part of this book may be reproduced in any form or by any means without the prior written consent of the Publisher, excepting brief quotes used in reviews.

All Kensington titles, imprints, and distributed lines are available at special quantity discounts for bulk purchases for sales promotion, premiums, fund-raising, educational, or institutional use.

Special book excerpts or customized printings can also be created to fit specific needs. For details, write or phone the office of the Kensington Sales Manager: Attn.: Sales Department. Kensington Publishing Corp., 119 West 40th Street, New York, NY 10018. Phone: 1-800-221-2647.

KENSINGTON and the K with book logo Reg. US Pat. & TM Off.

First Kensington Hardcover Edition: July 2023

ISBN: 978-1-4967-3168-5 (ebook)

ISBN: 978-1-4967-3165-4

First Kensington Trade Paperback Edition: June 2024

10 9 8 7 6 5 4 3 2 1

Printed in the United States of America

A Newlywed's Guide to Fortune and Murder

Chapter One

April 1900

"You are right, Jarvis. We couldn't fit so much as a hatpin in here." From the edge of the attic, I peered through a haze of dust that floated in a patch of sunlight at what had to be generations of Hazelton castoffs—old trunks, boxes, and furnishings, both assembled and in pieces, covered with sheets, which in turn were covered with dust and even more boxes.

"Where did it all come from?" I glanced at Jarvis, our butler. He was exactly my height, and I caught him in profile. Apart from a hawkish nose, the surface of his face was quite flat, until his lips curved in a smile, pushing round cheeks up and forward.

"When Lord Brandon took over the house," he said, "most of the old earl's furnishings were sent to the attic, as were Lord Brandon's things when Mr. Hazelton moved in."

"Then Rose and I moved in with our things, and more furniture was relegated to the attic." Mr. Hazelton—George—was my husband of two months. Rose was my eight-year-old daughter. For at least two generations, this house had been home to the heirs of the Earl of Hartfield, but the last heir, George's elder brother, Brandon, had moved out when he inherited the title and the earl's townhome. Since the next heir, Brandon's son, was only ten years old, he would not be needing this house for several more years.

George had taken over the lease on the house a year ago, and I had moved in when we married. I'd just spent the past hour searching for a room to claim as my office. The third floor was a schoolroom and bedchambers for Rose and Nanny. George had sacrificed a bedchamber next to ours to create a boudoir and bath for me, something of a surprise wedding present. I needed a place to work but felt a bit guilty attempting to lay claim to yet another space. And moving furnishings from that space to the attic was clearly out of the question.

I glanced at Jarvis. "Any ideas?"

"Why, yes. I do have a location in mind." Jarvis had a voice like the rumble of distant thunder. It gave his words a gravitas that had made me trust him from our first meeting—even if there was mischief in the hooded eyes that looked back at me.

"Do tell."

"Allow me to show you." He made for the narrow staircase and preceded me down to the third floor, where we passed through a baize door that took us through the sunlit nursery and the schoolroom. Rose, however, took her lessons with her cousin at my brother-in-law, the Earl of Harleigh's home. Our steps echoed through the mostly empty room. I wondered if I could close off a corner for myself up here. But Jarvis led on.

I followed him downward to the main floor, wondering where this mythical location could be, until he stopped at the open door to my husband's library, and I realized what he was suggesting. "No, no, Jarvis. This won't do."

"You asked my opinion, madam, and I believe this is the perfect place."

"The perfect place for what?"

I peeked into the room. George stood and leaned over his

desk to see what we were doing hanging about in the doorway. His dark brows rose with curiosity, and the genial curve to his lips tempted an answering smile to my own.

"It's nothing, darling," I said. "Don't mind us."

"But I must hear the answer." George had come around the desk to the doorway and leaned his tall frame against the wall. "What is this the perfect place for?"

"It's the perfect place for a cup of coffee," I said and glanced over his shoulder. "I see you have a pot at the ready."

His gaze darted to the butler and back to me. "You needed Jarvis's opinion on the matter?"

"What?"

"He said you asked for his opinion."

"You misunderstood," I said.

"Just a figure of speech," Jarvis said at the same time.

The butler and I exchanged a glance. "I'll just fetch another cup," he said before turning on his heel and nearly sprinting away.

"What the dickens are the two of you up to?" George watched me through narrowed eyes as I brushed past him on my way to the guest side of his desk and took a seat.

"Just looking for a likely spot where I can set up my own office and allow you to use yours in peace." The library had been carved out of what had been an enormous drawing room. With doors on two of its walls, one could access it from the drawing room or the hallway. Bookcases covered a third wall, filled with George's law tomes, some volumes on horticulture and travel, the works of Shakespeare, and two cricket bats. Two wingback chairs framed the window overlooking the back garden. George's desk backed up to the wall of books. I'd been using it for the past two months, while he recovered from being shot shortly after our wedding. While a gunshot wound wasn't something one would expect a proper British gentleman to sustain, George was no ordinary gentleman.

It had been a great relief to learn the bullet hit him in the upper arm and wasn't fatal. He had recovered quickly, though he still lifted weights to regain the strength in his arm. Actually, he'd built more muscle in his arms and shoulders, to the point where he had had to take his suits to the tailor for alterations. I heartily approved of his new look, though it would always be his crooked grin and the twinkle in his green eyes that made my heart flutter. Along with his ability to make me feel like the most beautiful woman in the room.

In truth, I was tall—almost as tall as George, slender enough that a good corset could make me fit for any fashion, and fortunate to have thick, dark hair. Otherwise, I was quite ordinary— pert nose, average complexion, and blue eyes. Oh, and an American accent. But in London, Americans had become rather ordinary, too. Nevertheless, in George's eyes, I was a goddess.

He rounded the desk to take his seat, and I noticed the open newspaper. "Anything interesting in there?"

"Nothing interesting enough to compete with you." He folded the broadsheet and set it aside, giving me his full attention and the benefit of that crooked grin.

"A very clever answer," I said.

"I must be clever to keep up with you. You'd never suffer a fool for a husband."

"Certainly not a second time. Though I suppose I wouldn't have called Reggie a fool, exactly."

George lifted a brow. "Philanderer? Wastrel? Ne'er-do-well? Good-for-nothing?"

Reggie was my first husband. He and my mother had decided that his family's title and our family's dollars were a perfect match. Our marriage had had no effect on his bachelor ways. Ten years after our wedding, he'd died in the bed of his latest lover. Consequently, all of those words fit him. In my opinion, anyway.

I placed a hand over George's. "He was also Rose's father."

He smiled. "Yes, yes, but I like to think she takes after you, my dear. However, for Rosie's sake, I shall refrain from speaking ill of the man."

Jarvis popped in with a coffee cup, and George filled it for me. "What are your plans for today?" he asked.

"Tea with Viscountess Winstead and her family."

He grimaced and faked a shudder. At least I thought it was fake. "Why would you do that to yourself?"

Augusta Ashley, Viscountess Winstead, was an extraordinarily cantankerous older woman, the type of person I would not normally seek out. But her husband's family owned a neighboring estate to Harleigh Manor, my late husband's country home, where I had spent much of my marriage and all of my mourning period. Lady Winstead had been in residence during most of the latter, and while I wouldn't call her pleasant company, compared to my in-laws, she had been a welcome relief. And she'd been kind to Rose.

"Lady Winstead has asked me to sponsor her niece for presentation to the queen."

"Just her presentation? What does that involve?"

"Not a great deal—ordering the correct gown, practicing a court curtsy, and learning how to back away from Her Majesty while wearing a nine-foot train. And, of course, spending an afternoon at court."

"Why isn't Lady Winstead presenting the niece herself?"

"I'm sure she would if the family weren't still mourning her husband's death. Don't you recall Lord Peter passed away right after Christmas? None of the family will be taking part in social events for another seven or eight months."

He raised a brow. "But the niece will? Does she have a name, by the way?"

"Katherine Stover. She's related to Lady Winstead, not Lord Peter." I frowned. "It seemed like a good idea at the time. You were still recovering, and I needed something to do with myself. But Miss Stover was delayed coming to town from Devon, so we missed the queen's first drawing room. The next one won't be until late this month, and with the family in mourning, they may ask me to take on more than just the presentation and actually organize her social season."

"Is that a problem?"

I gave him my sweetest smile. "I was hoping, now that you are fully recovered, we could make plans for our wedding trip." A family emergency had put an end to our original wedding trip. To make up for it, my father had gifted us with a large sum of money, but George had been surprisingly squeamish about using it.

"Yes, well, a wedding trip will have to wait just a bit longer, I'm afraid." He gave me a sheepish grin. "I've accepted an assignment, and I'm not sure how long it will take to accomplish or where it will take me."

My disappointment was momentary, and easily overcome by the delight I saw in his eyes. George did "something" for the government, the Home Office, to be specific, but that was as much as I knew. "That is wonderful news. I felt you were fully mended, and it seemed to me you were becoming restless. Can you tell me anything about your assignment?"

"I'm to investigate the disappearance of a rather unusual and valuable artifact." He waggled his eyebrows. "I can't really describe it further."

"I see. Something old, then, I'd imagine."

He laughed. "I cannot say."

"Everything is such a secret." I let out a tsk. "One would think that you could at least confide in your wife."

"Don't take offense. I can't tell you, because they haven't told me what it is yet."

"Then I suppose it's just as well that I'll have an assignment of my own. When do you begin?"

"I plan to meet with my contact today to find out what he knows of the matter. I ought to be leaving now."

"All I have to look forward to is tea with Lady Winstead," I said.

He grimaced. "I suspect your assignment will be much more onerous than mine."

Eager to meet with his contact, George left almost immediately. I dealt with some correspondence, reviewed the week's menus with our cook, enjoyed an early afternoon walk with Rose, and was just readying myself for my engagement with Lady Winstead when Jarvis brought a visitor's card upstairs to my dressing room.

I took it without moving my head, since Bridget, my lady's maid, had my hair firmly gripped in one hand and piping hot curling tongs in the other.

"Lady Esther is here?" I asked, though since her card was in my hand, the answer was obvious.

"Yes, ma'am. I put her in the drawing room while I determined if you were at home."

I considered for a moment if I wanted to be at home to Lady Esther. Though she wasn't quite as unpalatable as Lady Winstead, to deal with two such women in one afternoon was to ask a great deal of my patience. Still, Lady Esther was not one to call for the sake of calling. I consulted the clock on my dressing table. There was time enough. "I shall see her."

"Very good, ma'am."

Jarvis left to inform the lady I would be down directly, and Bridget finished my hair faster than I would have liked. Thus, there was no reason for me to linger in my room except to gather my fortitude. I drew a deep breath and ventured down to the drawing room.

Though I'd moved into George's house, the drawing room was exactly as I'd have furnished it. A long, narrow room, it had dark oak floors, paneled walls painted a warm ivory, and three distinct areas that flowed from the dining room to the

back garden—tea, games, and conversation. The elderly Lady
Esther was seated in the last of these, by one of the doors that
opened to the garden. The deeply cushioned club chair nearly
swallowed her up. Not that she was petite. She was of average
height but remarkably thin, which made all her angles—shoulders,
elbows, hips, even her cheekbones and chin—look pointed and
somehow dangerous. Her tongue was indisputably the sharpest
instrument in all of England.

"Good afternoon, Lady Esther," I said upon entering the
room. "How kind of you to call."

"And how kind of you to receive me." She rested her hands
on her walking stick and smiled.

I froze in mid-step. I'm quite sure I'd never seen the woman
smile before, though she occasionally bared her teeth. This was
different. This smile appeared genuine, and while not exactly
engaging, it made her look almost approachable. It took a moment to gain my bearings.

The smile slipped into a scowl as if it couldn't do so quickly
enough. "Stop looking so shocked," she snapped. "I can be
pleasant when I've a mind to—when I'm around someone
worth the effort."

Ah! There was the woman I'd grown accustomed to. I took
a seat in the matching chair on the other side of the window.
"Goodness, are you saying I am worth the effort it takes for
you to be pleasant? I'm flattered."

"You are meant to be." She narrowed one eye. "Though I
was not entirely sure flattery worked with you, I suspected it
wouldn't go amiss."

Instinct told me to be wary. "What is it you are hoping to
achieve?"

"I wish to join you for tea."

"I'm so sorry, but I'm expected at the Ashleys' for tea. In
fact, I should be leaving soon."

She rapped her stick on the floor, causing me to draw back.

"I'm aware of that," she said. "I wish to join you. Lady Winstead is an old friend of mine, and I heard you are considering sponsoring her niece. I want to accompany you, in part to ensure that you take her on."

I couldn't say what surprised me more—that Lady Esther knew my business or that Lady Winstead had a friend. And, of all people, it was Lady Esther. Apparently, what they say about birds of a feather is true. "What is your interest in this matter?"

"I simply wish to make myself useful."

Her lips curved upward again. The woman was clearly up to something. However, since she'd asked so directly, it would be very ill-mannered not to invite her to join me. I supposed I'd find out eventually just what she was plotting.

When she was ready to tell me.

"Well, if we're to be on time, perhaps we should be off now."

We took Lady Esther's carriage, and from the moment I sank into the soft leather seat, she kept up a stream of chatter—about the weather, an upcoming ball, and the differences between my neighborhood of Belgravia and Mayfair, where we were headed. Every time I attempted a word—*rap, rap, rap*—she tapped her wretched stick on the floor of the carriage and interrupted me. If I spent much more time with her, I'd be in danger of developing a twitch.

We were almost to the Ashleys' home before she drew breath. I leapt on the opportunity to change the subject. "How long have you known Lady Winstead?"

"A good fifteen years now. I met her at her wedding to Lord Peter. She didn't take part in society when her previous husband was alive."

That was because he was a banker and not of the aristocracy—the same reason I had required a sponsor to bring me into society prior to my first marriage. Yet here was the very proper, blue-blooded Lady Esther seeking the company of both of us. Interesting.

"Were you a friend of Lord Peter then, before his marriage?"
She slanted a glance at me. "Before his second marriage,
you mean? No, merely acquaintances. His first wife didn't
suit me, but Augusta and I struck up a friendship upon our
first meeting."

"I'm surprised she didn't ask you to sponsor Miss Stover."

Her countenance turned to stone. "Are you quite serious?
I'm far too old for such tomfoolery."

We'd come to a stop. A quick glance out the window told
me we were at the Ashley residence. The groom jumped down
and opened the door for us. I watched as Lady Esther stepped
spryly out with just a light touch of her hand on the groom's.
Though I found it hard to believe she considered herself too
old for anything, I wouldn't be at all surprised to learn there
was indeed tomfoolery involved in this situation.

The Ashleys were a prominent family in society. Lord Peter,
the late Viscount Winstead, had been quite the gadabout up to
and well after his first marriage fifty-some years ago to Mary
Sinclair, the fourth daughter of Lord Pomerance. Ever the duti-
ful wife, Lady Mary had given the viscount two sons before she
promptly died of scarlet fever. Lord Peter, as usual, had been
off exploring some archeological sites in Egypt, and the boys
had been safely shielded from the disease by their nurse, so
Lady Mary had left this earth causing the least amount of inconvenience to her family. It's doubtful any of the Ashleys had
given her another thought.

With two sons, Lord Peter had felt the title was secure and
had remained single for more than thirty years, leading one expedition after another in Egypt and Sudan, until he'd become
famous for finding the most interesting and exciting artifacts at
his extensive excavations. Then he had surprised everyone
when, at seventy years of age, he made a different but possibly
more treacherous trip—down the aisle to the altar at St. George's.
He'd married Augusta Fairweather, the childless, and very

wealthy, widow of a banker. The lady herself had already attained her sixtieth year and enough wealth to live out the rest of her life doing whatever she pleased. That she chose instead to enter the married state once more had made the match something of a double surprise.

Particularly to his children.

The wedding had taken place fifteen years ago, and people still speculated on the reasons for the match between the outgoing, adventurous aristocrat and the always ill-tempered commoner.

Since Lord Peter had spent a mere handful of months in England with his bride during the length of their marriage, my guess was money.

Lady Esther and I were led into a large open drawing room with dark paneled walls, where I was not surprised to see several Egyptian artifacts, including an obelisk clock in the corner and an enormous vase on a bronze pedestal, both heavily carved with Egyptian motifs. It did come as a surprise to find all the Ashleys gathered around a low tea table. I supposed after four months of mourning, any visitors were a welcome relief.

Two members of the family I knew well. The late viscount's second son, Simon, and his wife, Violet, who always referred to themselves as Si and Vi, had been chums of my late husband. They rose from their seats on the sofa and greeted me like an old friend.

We were not old friends.

Regardless, I took Vi's hands when she offered them, and kissed the air near her cheek. When she released me, Si took my hand and offered his condolences. It took a moment for me to realize he was referring to Reggie's death, which had happened more than two years ago. They hadn't come to his funeral, and I supposed this was the first I'd seen of him in the intervening time.

They were as near to a matched pair as two unrelated people

could be. Both were blond and blue-eyed, though now that they'd reached their forties, Si's hair was thinning and Vi had dark shadows under her eyes. Their faces bore a matching set of lines, making me wonder if they were still engaged in the exhausting effort of entertaining the Prince of Wales.

"Lady Harleigh."

I repressed a sigh and turned to face Jonathon Ashley, who drew in a dramatic gasp and momentarily covered his mouth with his hand, displaying a signet ring on his little finger. "My mistake. It's *Mrs.* Hazelton now, isn't it?"

His voice was as unctuous as I remembered it from more than ten years ago, when he had hoped to offer me marriage. Mother had put an end to that hope quickly. I returned his smile.

"And I am now *Viscount* Winstead," he continued. "Isn't it amusing how our fates can change in a heartbeat?"

Since it had been his father's heartbeat, or the lack of one, that changed his fate and put that ring on his hand, I was rather appalled by his use of the word *amusing*. Typical Jonathon. Thank heaven Mother had rejected him as a suitor for me.

He had to be about fifty. Also blond, but with dark eyes, he was stockier and wore a mustache and a neatly trimmed beard. It would be difficult to find two brothers so completely opposite. One wanted nothing but amusement, while the other didn't know the meaning of the word. Jonathon had married young and lost his wife perhaps a dozen years ago. One presumes she died of boredom.

He introduced his son, Andrew, a young man of about seventeen, the image of his father but with darker hair and no whiskers.

I was taken aback when my gaze landed on Lady Winstead. She was dressed appropriately in an afternoon gown, with her white hair styled up and away from her lined face, but her brown eyes looked empty, and her mouth drooped open as she slouched in a convalescent chair, wheeled up beside the short end of the tea table. She lifted her head in response to our greetings, tightened her grip on her teacup, and coughed gently, causing her shawl to slide off one shoulder. Though she was well into her seventies, I hadn't expected her to look so fragile and ill.

Lady Winstead fixed her gaze on Lady Esther and appeared to be attempting speech. Before she could force words to her lips, her hand holding the cup trembled. She stretched out her arm, as if she wanted to place the cup on the table, but dropped it instead. Lady Esther and I jumped back as the tea splashed to the floor, joined in the next instant by Lady Winstead, who slipped, boneless, from her chair, making no attempt to break her fall.

Heavens! Had the woman just died?

Chapter Two

A younger woman, who had been sitting next to Lady Winstead, slipped to the floor and around the legs of the tea table to place her fingers along the matron's neck. Since her expression showed relief, I assumed she found a pulse.

At least she had the presence of mind to take some action. The rest of us looked on in horror.

Then I felt the sting of Lady Esther's elbow in my ribs. "Do you intend to watch this like some drama in the theater?" Her words, and the jab, roused me to action.

I sank to my knees as Lady Winstead regained consciousness, and stopped the young woman, as she would have helped the invalid to rise. "It might be best not to move her," I said. "She may have injured herself in the fall. We should call a doctor."

"I'll fetch her nurse," she said.

"I thought you were the nurse," Lady Esther muttered.

"That's right," Lord Jonathon said. "Neither of you would have met Miss Katherine Stover yet."

So, this was Miss Stover. She looked a bit younger than her

twenty-eight years. I took in large brown eyes with brows that currently slanted in and downward as she scrambled to her feet and cast an angry glare at the Ashleys, who still remained in their places, as if nothing were amiss.

"Forgive my manners," she said, swiping a fallen lock of dark hair from her shoulder, "but introductions must wait until I've seen to my aunt." She then hurried from the room. I glanced over at Lord Jonathon to see him scowling at her back.

I liked her already.

"There goes your charge, Mrs. Hazelton, should you choose to accept the role of sponsor." His words were polite enough, but his smirk hinted at hostility. I wondered if she was not a welcome guest in his home. She was not related to him, after all. With Lady Winstead's obvious infirmity, he might well have thought someone else ought to take on the responsibility of housing her.

I slipped Lady Winstead's head onto my lap, hoping it would prove a better cushion than the polished wood floor. When I took her hand, her fingers closed gently around mine. I wondered what had debilitated her to such a degree. I'd last seen her four months ago at her husband's funeral. Other than looking as though she lacked sleep, she had seemed quite hale and hearty for someone who had lived for three quarters of a century.

I glanced at her stepchildren, who, while they appeared uneasy, had yet to lift a finger to help Lady Winstead. "Miss Stover's dedication to her aunt does her credit," I said, wondering if any of them would take the hint.

"Oh, she is indeed dedicated," Vi said as she and Si reseated themselves. "With Kate around, we could easily dispense with the nurse."

"Miss Stover is not here to act as nursemaid." Lord Jonathon leveled a glare at his brother's wife. "She is meant to make her curtsy to the queen, then find herself a husband."

Lady Esther did nothing to hide her outrage. "This conversation is both unfeeling and ridiculous in light of the circumstances. Will one of you not send for a doctor?" Her tone turned the question into a command, but still none of them reacted until she tapped her stick sharply on the floor.

Lord Jonathon held up a hand as Si Ashley came to his feet, presumably to do Lady Esther's bidding. "We'll wait on sending for a doctor, if you please. At least until Nurse Plum has had a look at her. She's been tending to our stepmother these past months and is familiar with these episodes."

"Nurse Plum is very good with her," Vi Ashley said quietly to Lady Esther. "She'll have your friend up and about in a trice."

"Perhaps some tea," Andrew Ashley suggested.

"She was drinking tea when this happened," Lady Esther snapped. The words *you fool* remained unspoken, but we all knew she thought them.

I cradled the lady's head as best I could. Her pulse felt quite slow beneath my fingers, but it remained constant. I gently blotted the moisture from her face with my handkerchief and saw one eyelid strain to open. When it finally succeeded, her gaze conveyed unadulterated fear. My own heart began beating faster while I cooed inane words meant to give her comfort.

After what felt like a lifetime but was probably mere minutes, Miss Stover returned, accompanied by a middle-aged woman with a sturdy build and graying hair, dressed in a pale blue shirtwaist and skirt with a white apron—the typical uniform of a nurse. Without a word to any of us, she knelt on the other side of Lady Winstead. The dowager's other eye opened, and she began moving her head. Nurse Plum ran practiced hands over her patient's limbs, declared her fit to move, then lifted her back into the convalescent chair. In the face of such efficiency, I simply moved out of her way. Miss Stover stood behind the nurse, wringing her hands.

Once she had Lady Winstead settled in her chair, the nurse nodded to Lord Jonathon. "I'll take her up to her room now."

He gestured his approval, and she wheeled her patient out to the hall.

I turned back to my companion, ready to suggest we leave the family alone, but Lady Esther was clearly of a different opinion. She seated herself on the sofa and gestured for Vi to pour her a cup of tea. "What has happened to her?" she demanded of the room at large. "Has she suffered some sort of seizure or illness?"

The proper etiquette in such a situation was to proceed as if nothing had happened so as not to make one's host feel uncomfortable. Lady Esther often threw manners out the window, but her aggressive tone made it sound as if she were accusing the family of neglect. I took a cup of tea from Vi to fortify myself against whatever unpleasantness might ensue.

Lord Jonathon came to his feet, his expression tight. "My lady, we are and have been providing all the care our stepmother could want, and I resent any implication to the contrary. Now, if you'll excuse me." He gave her the slightest of bows and stalked from the room.

Si and Vi exchanged awkward glances.

Andrew cleared his throat. "I'm sorry your friend is not as you remember her. Her health has been failing over the past months, though admittedly, she is having rather a bad day today."

"I assure you," Si added, "she is getting the best of care."

I could sense the harrumph vibrating in her throat, but to her credit, Lady Esther made no such noise. "What exactly is her condition?" she asked in a more moderate tone, which made me easy enough to take a sip of tea.

"The doctor has put it down to grief," Andrew said.

I snorted and immediately covered the lower half of my face

with a napkin. My nostrils burned from the hot liquid. While I blotted my lips, I could see Lady Esther was ready to explode at this explanation. I dropped the napkin to the table and stood. "I believe we have taken enough of your time, wouldn't you say, Lady Esther? We should be off."

My words were enough to distract her. "You have not had a chance to speak with Miss Stover yet."

"She is clearly distressed at the moment. I shall send over a note, arranging to meet with her at another time."

Si, Vi, and Andrew followed my lead and came to their feet, leaving Lady Esther no choice but to comply—grudgingly. The family made haste to ring for the butler, who brought our things and showed us to the door. I didn't take a steady breath until I'd gotten the elderly woman out of the house and back to her carriage.

She kept up her sulky silence until we were underway. "Grief." She growled the word. "Have you ever heard anything so nonsensical?"

A spouse wasting away from grief was not unheard of, but it seemed difficult to believe in Lady Winstead's case—for most of their marriage, she and her husband had lived on different continents. I couldn't completely discount the possibility, but Lady Esther knew her friend far better than I.

I turned to her. "Is it not possible? Does Lady Winstead not grieve the loss of her husband?"

"Not to the point of self-destruction." Her jaw tightened, as did her grip on the walking stick. "They were hardly Romeo and Juliet. He wanted money. She wanted status. Of course, she would have grieved her husband's passing, but she would have carried on. That's what our sort do. I don't know what's happening to Augusta, but that family is up to something nefarious."

Our sort. Interesting. Lady Winstead married into the aristocracy, but like me, she had solid middle-class roots. On those grounds, Lady Esther would never consider us of the same sort as her. Would she? "What do you mean by our sort?"

She waved a hand. "Those of us who do what we must and get on with it. We aren't fanciful. We don't turn our lives into poetry or drama. We simply go about the business of living. That is who Augusta is, not someone who would waste away pining for the past. She might miss that past, but she would move on."

"Then what do you suppose has happened to her? Do you believe if she was ill, her stepchildren wouldn't take care of her? That they would let her die? That sounds rather fanciful to me. If one's fancy leaned toward the macabre, that is."

"I'm not entirely sure what I believe them capable of." She looked me up and down as if taking in my value. "Here are the facts as I know them. There is no love lost between the late viscount's children and their stepmother. They objected strongly to the wedding, but once it took place, they were happy to accept an improvement to their allowances thanks to Augusta's fortune."

"Few people turn up their noses at a gift of money." George being one of those few.

"Quite true, and for those gifts, they tolerated her," she continued. "Now, the last time I saw Augusta was at Lord Peter's funeral, where she was understandably downcast but not stricken with grief. She spoke of leaving in the new year to travel abroad for six months and of finding a home of her own upon her return. She asked me to call on her the following week, when she'd tell me more precisely where she'd be staying, so I could visit her if I chose to do so." Lady Esther raised her brows in question. "Does that sound like a woman who would curl up in a chair in her room and die of grief?"

It did not. In fact, it sounded exactly like the Lady Winstead of my memory. But dealing with the death of a loved one was very different before and after the funeral. One is kept well occupied before that cvent and left quite alone with one's sorrow afterward. I said as much to Lady Esther.

"I have lived long enough to have experienced that myself. As has Augusta, which is why she made those plans to travel, and why I encouraged her. But do you know what happened when I called on her a mere five days later?"

She didn't bother to wait for an answer, because, of course, I didn't know.

"I was denied entrance."

She ground out the words from behind clenched teeth, as well she might. I'd wager no one had denied Lady Esther anything she'd demanded in her entire adult life. I must have shown the appropriate astonishment, for she continued her story.

"The butler told me she was unwell and not at home to callers. I'm sure you can imagine that I protested."

I could imagine her throwing a tantrum. It was surprising the butler had survived such an ordeal.

"He then escorted me to a sitting room, where Jonathon Ashley finally attended me. He gave me the same cock-and-bull story about some illness and her need to remain undisturbed. I reminded him that I was her dearest friend and wished to see her, but he was unmoved."

"Is it not possible that she really was ill?"

She waved her hand impatiently. "She is never ill."

"She certainly is now."

"I agree, and that's what has me so worried. Do you know why I insisted on coming with you today as soon as I learned where you were headed? They have not let me see her in all this time. I fear they are keeping my letters from her, as well, since most of them go unanswered."

There was no dismissing her concern for her friend. I'd never seen the stoic woman in such a state of distress. "You said most of your letters. What has she said when she does reply to you? How does she explain her circumstances?"

Lady Esther tightened her gloved fingers on the walking stick. "She has only recently begun to answer them. And I will admit, much of what she says doesn't make a great deal of sense. I cannot betray her confidence by telling you everything, but I can tell you she is afraid, and she has asked for my help."

Her words brought to mind the fear I had seen in Lady Winstead's eyes when she collapsed, but I could not dismiss her physical condition.

Lady Esther placed a hand over mine. "I know what you are thinking but are too polite to admit. Though I don't for a moment believe she is dying of grief, there is no denying she is deteriorating from something. I need to find out if her step-children are causing that deterioration. I cannot imagine they will allow me back in that house, but you will be there, and I know you are highly observant. All I ask is that you observe them, and Augusta, and tell me if my concerns are justified."

"You are making them sound like the Borgias," I said, though I was beginning to wonder about them myself. "Is there nothing you can tell me about her letters and what she suspects?"

"There is nothing in her letters that will help you more than your own eyes and ears. I do not ask this lightly, but I have a suspicion you are quite well versed in this type of investigation. Am I wrong to think so?"

She was not wrong, and she knew it. Last autumn her nephew had been the subject of one of my investigations. She'd been helpful at the time. Perhaps I owed her the favor.

"That is a subject upon which I'd prefer to keep my own counsel," I said. "But what if I find nothing nefarious happening in that house?"

"I trust you will do your best and I'll be satisfied with the information you provide. She is my friend, Frances. She asked for my help. This is the least I can do for her."

Could I really say no?

"I can make no promises," I said, "but I shall do my best."

Chapter Three

⟨❧⟩

Once back at home, I retreated to George's library. While I considered the entire house as ours, one did need one's sanctuary, and I felt this was his. This was where George might keep confidential information for his work with the government, and I would hate to intrude on his privacy. At some point, I had to sort out a spot for my own office. Perhaps the boudoir off our bedchamber would suffice. In the meantime, I carried out my correspondence and small business matters from the guest side of George's desk.

I drew a sheet of paper toward me and contemplated my dual assignments. They at once overlapped and conflicted with one another. In sponsoring Miss Stover, I was doing a service for the family. In my other task, I was spying on them.

Lady Winstead had requested my assistance more than a month ago, in early March. Her letter had been clear and concise. The writing itself might have been done by a secretary, but the content must have come from the lady's own mind. A second letter, coming perhaps ten days later, had told me of Miss Stover's delay in the country and the necessary postponement of her presentation until the queen's second drawing room. That letter had come from Vi Ashley, which made me wonder if Miss Stover had been corresponding with Vi or Lady Winstead. Based on what I had seen today, Lady Winstead did not appear to be capable of any sort of communication.

Perhaps something untoward was going on in that house. I was now nearly as curious as Lady Esther, but I had to remember my first assignment. I penned a note to Miss Stover, requesting she call on me the following day to discuss the plans for her presentation. Then I rang for Jarvis.

"Yes, sir," he intoned as he stepped through the doorway. Upon spotting me at George's desk, he blinked. "Forgive me, ma'am. I assumed it was Mr. Hazelton who rang. May I assume this means you plan to set up office in here?"

"No, Jarvis. I simply haven't found a suitable place to attend to my own business yet." I handed him the note. "Would you have someone deliver this to Miss Stover at the Ashley residence in Mayfair?"

"Of course, ma'am, and may I ask if you are at home for Lady Fiona? She has just called for you."

Lady Fiona Nash was George's sister and my good friend. "I can always make time for Fiona. Is she in the drawing room?"

"Yes, ma'am."

"I'll go to her right away. Will you be so good as to see to tea for us?"

"Very good." He took a few steps to the door, then turned back. "May I also suggest there is plenty of space in here for a second desk, if it would suit you and Mr. Hazelton to share this room."

"You may indeed," I said, coming to my feet, "but you take quite a risk in doing so. I might be happy to share it, but Hazelton might loathe the very idea."

"Were we discussing two other people, I'd never have mentioned it, but with you and Mr. Hazelton, I'd go so far as to suggest a partners desk." His lips tweaked up just a bit, and I wondered yet again if our starchy, extraordinarily efficient butler had a mischievous side.

"A partners desk, you say? That's an interesting possibility."

"I reckon it would serve you both well."

Jarvis exited into the hallway while I opened the door to the drawing room. "Good afternoon, Fiona. How lovely to see you," I said while closing the door behind me.

Upon actually seeing her, I stopped short. She sat in the chair Lady Esther had used earlier, but the late afternoon sun peeking through the south-facing doors shone like an aura over Fiona's head—her hatless head. There were few women of my acquaintance taller than me. Fiona was one of them. She reveled in her height and often added several inches with elaborate coiffures and hats. Today her chestnut hair was twisted back into a knot at the nape of her neck, and she wore no hat at all. Wisps of hair framed her narrow face, and her usually fair skin was quite flushed.

Fearing something was terribly wrong, I was beside her in an instant. "Fiona, what happened?"

She clutched my hand. "Miss Peabody is leaving me."

"Miss Peabody?" The name stumped me for a moment. I lowered myself onto the chair next to hers. Who in Fiona's household would be a miss? Then I remembered. Though Fiona's son had gone away to school a year ago, her daughter, Grace, was only six months older than Rose. Miss Peabody had to be her governess.

"She left this morning, with no warning at all," Fiona continued. "Just a note on my desk telling me she was going home to marry."

"I see. Tell me, does Miss Peabody usually style your hair?"

She let out a tsk. "Of course not. You know I never let anyone but Jonesy touch it, but there was no time to do anything this morning. I had to go after her."

"Miss Peabody? Do you mean to say you followed her? Where, and for what purpose?"

"I most certainly do. I followed her to the train station to stop her." She pressed her palm to her cheek. "Thank heavens I caught her in time."

I still couldn't get past the idea of Fiona speeding to the station to catch her former employee. "In time for what?"

"To negotiate with her, of course. It's not as if she were getting married this afternoon. I needed her to work with me on this wedding business." She took note of my stunned silence. "Just wait until you are in need of a qualified governess. They aren't exactly thick on the ground."

"I suppose I may be in need of a governess sometime soon. We rather exhausted Nanny's area of education once she taught Rose to read and write, and some rudimentary mathematics. Now she studies with her cousin and his tutor, but when Martin goes off to school in a few months, Graham will let the tutor go."

Her eyes lit. "A few months, you say?"

"In the autumn. September perhaps."

"That might work out perfectly. Miss Peabody is to be married in August. I don't know what she was about, running off to make her arrangements now."

She was likely thinking how much there was to prepare. "Explain to me how this works out."

"We join forces," she said. "Grace and Rose are close in age. I'll need to replace Miss Peabody. I shall provide accommodations. Between the two of us, we could offer an excellent salary, and I think the girls would enjoy their lessons more if they took them together."

"I'll need to consider it, Fiona. My education consisted of a string of tutors—one for history and geography, one for Italian, another for French. Well, the list is endless. I'm not sure what kind of education a governess would provide."

"Not as good as yours, I'm afraid," she said with a frown. "It would be difficult to find one woman with an aptitude to teach in all those disciplines—except you, of course. Good heavens, what sort of future was your mother preparing you for? The diplomatic service?"

"She wanted me to be conversant on any topic and in multiple languages. All the better to attract a husband." I chuckled. "At least she thought so."

"Well, a governess would teach a broad range of subjects. I'm certain we could find one who could teach the girls French or Italian, but probably not both. Give it some thought. If you find Rose isn't learning as much as you'd like, you could always send her on to Queen's College or some other school in four or five years. Meanwhile, a governess could prepare her for that." She came to her feet. "But don't take too long. As I said, a good educator is not easy to find."

When Fiona was leaving, she reminded me of our engagement for an afternoon at the home of Cornelia Dawson later that week. "She is to have actors from *Florodora* to entertain us," she said. "Have you seen the play?"

"Not yet, but we are to attend tomorrow's performance."

"You will love it, I'm sure. And do not forget my birthday gala is this week, as well."

I assured her we would both be there to celebrate her birthday and closed the door behind her. Alone again, I returned to the library and set about making a schedule of all the tasks Miss Stover and I had to complete before the queen's drawing room. I was still working on it when George returned home. I checked the clock on the desk when I heard his footsteps on the drawing room floor. Six o'clock already.

"I thought I might find you in here," he said upon entering the room. He swooped down to drop a kiss on the back of my neck, then draped a long leg over the desk next to my chair. "How was tea with Lady Winstead?"

I let out a grim laugh and told him about Lady Esther calling and insisting she go with me to the Ashleys. Then I ran through the rest of the story, up to the point where she asked me to spy on the family.

"I must say whatever is happening to Lady Winstead, it seems very odd," I continued. "She was supposedly stricken with this illness four months ago, when the family refused to let Lady Esther speak with her. Yet she was completely lucid when she wrote me only a month ago. Today she barely took notice of us, then fell out of her chair into a heap on the floor. If her condition is due to illness, it's a very strange one indeed."

George rubbed a hand along his chin. "Interesting," he said, staring out at . . . nothing.

"Why is that interesting, and what are you thinking?"

He shook himself from his trance and glanced at me. "Can you keep a secret?"

I huffed. "After all our time together, you need to ask?"

"You're right. I should keep it to myself."

"What?" Though I knew he was teasing, I was insulted, nonetheless. "You know I'm the soul of discretion. I demand you tell me this secret immediately."

"The missing article I'm to find belongs, or rather belonged, to the Ashley family."

"They are having a very busy week."

"Indeed. If Lady Winstead is not in her right mind, do you suppose it's possible she's simply placed it somewhere her stepson can't find it?"

"Though I can't be certain, it seems to me that Lady Winstead is more physically incapacitated than mentally. What exactly is this article? Unless, of course, you can't tell me."

"On the contrary, it could be helpful for you to know." He came to his feet and drew me to mine, then moved us over to the chairs by the window. A cool breeze fluttered the gauzy curtains and brought in the slightest scent of cherry blossom.

"You know, Lord Peter was a great explorer of sorts. An Egyptologist, I believe he was called. He headed several archeological excavations in Egypt and Nubia and made some advances in dating the items they found."

"Of course," I said. "He was quite famous."

"And he had a rather extensive private collection of Egyptian artifacts, which he bequeathed to the British Museum."

"Is one of the artifacts missing?"

"Not exactly. What's missing is his journal in which he documents and provides the provenance of all the items in his collection."

"That sounds important, but are you sure Lord Peter meant to provide the journal as well as the artifacts?"

"I met with his solicitor and the executor of the will. It's clear he wanted the journal to go along with the collection. The museum director is quite keen to have it. He says the collection is far less valuable without that journal. Now that you know what it is, is it possible Lady Winstead put it somewhere and has forgotten about it?"

I laughed. "Like your golf clubs?" I gestured to the bag in the corner of the room. "Assuming this journal wasn't locked up, she might have done so a few months ago. At the moment, I don't think she's able to move about the house without assistance."

George chose to ignore the latter part of my response. "Frances, those clubs are an essential part of my work process." He stood and walked over to his golf bag, pulled out a club, and lined it up as if he were addressing the ball. He snuck a peek at me. I rolled my eyes.

He returned his gaze to the clubhead. "Lord Peter's executor said all the antiquities included in the bequest were delivered to the museum a week ago, without the journal. The director contacted Lord Jonathon, who admits he removed the journal from the collection to read it the evening before everything was delivered, and neglected to lock it up. It appears to have been stolen from his desk."

I tapped my fingers on the arm of the chair. "Based on what I saw of Lady Winstead today, I'd say she couldn't be responsible for moving it. However, I don't know how long she's been like this. Was anything else missing? Did he check with the other members of the family?"

"He thought his brother, Simon, had been talking about the collection at his club, so there is a chance it was a professional thief."

"Why would someone want to steal a journal?"

George rolled his hands, flicking the club face back and forth. "Something written by the famous Lord Peter might be quite valuable. But there's also a chance it isn't missing at all."

I raised my brows. "Do you think the viscount simply doesn't want to hand it over?"

"That's what I'm meant to find out."

"How are you to do that? Jonathon is unlikely to admit he wants to keep the journal for himself."

He turned the club upside down and let it slide through his fingers until he held the head like a cane. "I'm not entirely certain what I'll do, but I have no intention of accusing him of theft. At least not yet."

"Do you mean to tell me your golf process has failed you? The answer didn't appear on the head of that club?"

"Very funny. Usually, I'd take a full swing. That's why I have so much space in here." He moved to the open area of the room and lined the club up with an invisible ball. Then he drew the club up and back, paused a beat, and swung through with a swoosh. He gazed off at the wall for a moment, as if he'd really struck a ball and it was flying down a fairway somewhere. Slowly, he lowered the club and turned back to me. "It truly does help me to concentrate, but let's put that aside for now."

I'd put it right next to my thoughts of moving a second desk in here.

"Your discovery of Lady Winstead's condition, and Lady Esther's suspicions, has made this case much more interesting. For the moment, I may just wait and see what you turn up."

"I'm unlikely to turn up Lord Peter's journal."

"No, but the more you learn about the family and how they do, or do not, get on with one another could lead me to a motive for the theft. It's likely someone in the house took it. If you keep your eyes and ears open while you are there, you may find my suspect for me." He grinned. "I always knew a wife would come in handy."

"I shall do my best."

George tapped the club on the toe of his shoe. "Just be careful. Don't ask too many questions, and if one of them arouses your suspicions, for heaven's sake, don't let on."

"I promise to be very much on my guard."

He caught my gaze and held it. "I know better than to ask you to back out of your arrangement, but if you feel yourself in any danger, that's exactly what you should do."

Chapter Four

❧

"I'm afraid I can't stay long, Mrs. Hazelton."

Those words didn't make for an auspicious beginning to our meeting. Miss Stover wore a determined expression as she stepped into the drawing room and handed what appeared to be a warm but decidedly unfashionable cloak to Frederick, our footman. This gave me a chance to review her morning gown—simple and gray, the neckline, sleeves, and skirt declaring it to be a few years old. Not as bad as I'd expected.

I came to my feet and extended a hand to draw her into the room. "At least you are staying long enough to remove your cloak, so I'll try not to be completely offended."

She paused mid-step and brought her gloved fingers to her lips. When she lowered them, her mouth was twisted in a comical grimace. "That was terribly rude, wasn't it?"

I waved a hand to the sofa, and she seated herself. "It could be construed that way, particularly by someone who doesn't know you well."

Miss Stover's maid had followed her into the room and stopped just a few feet away, hovering beside the arm of the sofa.

"Frederick, would you show Miss Stover's maid belowstairs, to the common room?" It occurred to me, belatedly, that it might be Frederick himself that had her clinging to Miss Stover. Well over six feet tall, he was a strapping young man who looked as if he could tear lesser humans in two.

The maid, on the other hand, was quite small, somewhere between thirty and forty, with an olive complexion and dark, tight curls under a sensible felt hat. Her coat must have been a recent hand-me-down that hadn't been altered yet, and she seemed almost lost inside it. She looked more confused than frightened when she furrowed her brow and glanced at Miss Stover.

"Miss?"

"It's fine, Aggie. I'll call for you when I'm ready to leave."

That ought to have been the end of it, but the maid remained standing in my drawing room even after Frederick strode to the door. "I was told to stay with you, miss," she said, revealing a broad Yorkshire accent.

Katherine Stover glanced from me to the maid. "That's not how it's done, Aggie. Please go with the footman."

Frederick returned to the single square foot of floor the maid appeared determined to hold, and gestured to the door. She frowned but preceded him out of the room.

"Aggie must be as unschooled as I am in how to behave in company," Miss Stover said. "I apologize for both of us."

"I took no offense, Miss Stover. If you are going to make mistakes, it's best if you make them with me rather than, say, the queen."

"But I would nev—" She caught my eye. "You jest."

"Indeed. Even during your presentation, you're unlikely to speak with her. But I assume you truly are short of time, so we shall have to be efficient." I already had a pot of tea on the table. After inquiring about her preference, I made small talk with her while I prepared our refreshments.

It was the smallest talk I'd had in some time.

"How is Lady Winstead today?"

"Better, thank you."

"Are you excited about your presentation?"

"Not really."

"Have you plans for any entertainments while in London?"

"None."

"Though they can't socialize, one of the Ashleys could take you around town to see the sights."

"I'd rather not."

I handed her the teacup, then declined to release it once she closed her fingers around the saucer, forcing her to meet my gaze. "You are wasting our time, Miss Stover," I said. "I asked you to visit me so we could become acquainted. Thus, my questions. Your answers have made me wonder why you are here at all. And I'd appreciate more than a one- or two-word answer. You seem to have no interest in making your curtsy to the queen, no interest in London at all, for that matter." I parted my fingers and allowed her to take the cup.

She had the grace to look uncomfortable. "I am making a hash of this, aren't I?" She set her cup on the table, laced her fingers together, and gave me an earnest look. "I do want to be presented to the queen and take part in London society, as my aunt wishes. I'm terribly grateful she's given me this opportunity and grateful to you for your willingness to guide me. However, my aunt is far more ill than I knew when she and I corresponded, and I dislike being away from her for any length of time. I consider her health more important than my presentation, but I seem to be the only member of the family who does."

That was a reasonable answer. Anxiety over her aunt could excuse any lapse in her manners. So could living with Si and Vi for five days, not to mention Jonathon, the pompous and patronizing new viscount. Now that I thought about her living situation, it was hard not to sympathize with her.

"They did seem less than concerned about her," I said. "Perhaps they've become used to her condition."

"They certainly seem to be." She spoke quietly, as if she were tired.

"Preparing for your presentation doesn't have to be a long, drawn-out process, and aside from one or two visits to the modiste, most of it can be done from your home."

Her gaze turned curious.

"I, too, am concerned for Lady Winstead. She was my neighbor when I lived in the country and was kind to me and my daughter. I am pleased that someone in the house shares my concern. I shall try not to claim too much of your time."

Her lips twitched. Goodness, was she about to smile?

"She was kind to you?" Both her brows and her tone rose at the end of the question. "Aunt Augusta?"

I smiled. "The lady has her moments. My daughter was particularly fond of her."

"I believe those moments are very rare. I must add that I appreciate your kindness on my behalf."

"You are very welcome. Now, let us make the most of this time, shall we? Before you leave me today, I'd like to know a bit more about you—your pursuits and interests. What have you been doing in the year since your father passed?"

"I'm afraid there is not a great deal to tell you. I was nurse to my father for the last three years of his life. Aunt Augusta invited me to London frequently during that time, and if I was able to arrange care for my father, I came. Perhaps once or twice a year."

She took a sip of her tea and seemed to be contemplating. "As for pursuits, I enjoy a quiet life—reading and gardening. I am well suited to a life in Devon, where I'm from."

It was beginning to sound as though she was in London out of duty only. Surely, she had to be planning to live with Lady Winstead.

"Once my father passed, my aunt invited me to live with

her," she continued. "I had little other choice. But my father's house needed to be sold, his affairs settled, and quite frankly, I needed the quiet of Devon to mourn his passing. I visited my aunt a few times, but I admit, I dragged my feet a bit and took a full year to get all that business settled. I arrived here last week and fully intend to follow my aunt's wishes and make myself presentable for the queen. With Aunt Augusta's health as it is, I've not been able to learn what she had planned for me after that. I do not flatter myself that her stepchildren will offer me a home with them."

She should certainly depend on them as little as possible. I was about to say as much when I heard a noise—was that a sneeze?—from outside the open door to the hallway. Miss Stover looked surprised, as well.

"Hello?" I crossed the room to the doorway. "Who's out here?"

By the time I reached the hallway, Frederick had Aggie by the arm and was leading her to the baize door that led to the servants' stairs. "Sorry to disturb you, ma'am," he said.

Odd, but since Frederick had things under control, I returned to the drawing room and Miss Stover's questioning gaze.

"It was your maid," I told her. "She seems unduly concerned for your well-being."

"Aggie is not my maid. I believe she was employed as Lady Winstead's personal maid. She might have been sacked, but she's managed to make herself useful to the Ashleys." She pursed her lips. "Lord Jonathon insisted I couldn't travel alone and sent her along with me."

"Has she been part of the household for some time?" I asked.

"Fifteen years at least. She came along with Lady Winstead."

Miss Stover and I finished our tea and made a schedule for the coming week. Though I dropped the subject of the maid's strange behavior, I couldn't help but wonder if she was spying on Miss Stover. If the viscount insisted the maid accompany her today, it wasn't much of a reach to wonder if she was spying under his orders. But why?

Bridget confirmed my suspicions later that afternoon. "Strangest servant I've ever come across," she said. "Her mistress is occupied, and she finally has time to take a seat, put up her feet, and have a nice cuppa, but she kept vanishing. Can you imagine?"

We were in the elegant dressing room George had added to the bedchamber we shared. Bridget boggled her eyes in the mirror of my dressing table as she made some minor adjustments to my hair. "I was working on some sewing, and she was meant to be taking her tea at the table. Every time I looked up from my work, she was gone. Either outside the drawing room or on her way there. I was getting close to tying her to the chair."

"What reason did she give you for sneaking around like that?"

"Just checking on Miss Stover, she said. As if the miss wouldn't ring for her if she needed something."

Bridget finished up and left me just as Rose walked in, wearing her riding clothes, her usually glossy hair a mass of brown tangles. I didn't have to ask where she'd been.

When my late husband died, his brother, Graham, became Earl of Harleigh. He and his family moved into Harleigh Manor, and with nowhere else to go, I spent my year of mourning living with them. Rose and her two cousins, Eldon and Martin, became good friends. After I moved to Belgravia, taking what was left of my money with me, Graham had little choice but to sell the country manor and take up residence in Harleigh House in Mayfair. Eldon, the older of the boys, was away at school, but ten-year-old Martin and eight-year-old

Rose had their lessons with a tutor at Graham's home. And several times a week, they ended those lessons with a ride in Hyde Park.

I gave Rose my seat and took up the hairbrush. She winced before I even drew it through her hair. "Try to remember to plait your hair before your ride next time. It will keep it from tangling. Did you at least win the race?"

She shook her head. "I rode Pierre today. He misses me when I ride one of Uncle Graham's horses. The groom exercises him, but that's not the same." Pierre was Rose's pony and her constant companion since she was five years old. Since Eldon left for school, Rose had been riding his horse—except on those days she missed her Pierre. It wouldn't be long before she outgrew him, and I'd have to find a new home for the pony and a horse for Rose. And a place to keep him. I pushed that problem to the back of my mind.

"Do you remember Lady Winstead, dear?" I asked, dividing her long hair into segments with my fingers before tackling the knots with the brush. "We used to call on her when we were in the country."

"She lived in the house with all the Egyptian things I wasn't supposed to touch," she said. Rose squeezed the atomizer on my perfume bottle and Guerlain's Rococo à la Parisienne filled the air with flowers. "She always let me touch them, anyway," she continued. "I liked her."

I chuckled. That might be the first time I'd ever heard those words in association with Lady Winstead. "That bottle may not be Egyptian," I said, gesturing to the perfume, "but consider it untouchable, as well, if you please. You're too young to wear scent."

She settled back in her seat and let me continue with her hair. "Why did you ask about Lady Winstead?"

"Oh, yes. I saw her yesterday. She lives in town now, and her niece has joined her. I'm to present her to the queen."

"Why doesn't Lady Winstead present her?"

"She isn't feeling well lately, and she's in mourning for her husband."

Rose frowned at me in the mirror. "I hate being ill. And sad."

"I'm sure she does, too."

"Will you see Lady Winstead again soon?"

"Possibly tomorrow." I stopped brushing her hair and met her eyes in the mirror. "Did you wish to join me? It will not be particularly amusing for you. You might visit with Lady Winstead, briefly, but mostly we'll be going through Miss Stover's wardrobe."

Rose's eyes widened. "Does she have a presentation gown yet?"

"We still have to order one."

"I want to go with you!"

I lowered the brush and gaped at her. "Are there no lessons tomorrow?"

She pulled a face and shook her head. "Martin and Uncle Graham are going to visit Eldon at school."

Ah! She was at loose ends and needed something to do. "I'd be happy to have your company, but I warn you, even if the day becomes tedious, you must stick it out."

"But I can visit with Lady Winstead?"

"If she's well enough, yes, you may."

"Did I hear someone say she *wanted* to visit Lady Winstead?"

George leaned against the doorframe, his arms crossed and a look of incredulity on his face. "Good heavens, Rosie. You are quite singular in that desire."

I wagged a finger at him. "Lady Winstead always treated Rose with kindness, so of course she remembers her fondly. And Rose will certainly brighten her day."

Rose bounced up from the chair and made George bend down for a hug. "I think I'll ask Frederick if he'll cut some flowers for me to take to her," she said before bounding out of the room.

"I should probably remind her to walk like a lady, but I hate to spoil her fun." I leaned into George when he put his arms around me.

"Don't," he said. "She has years to act like a lady. Let her enjoy being a little girl. Let *us* enjoy her being a little girl."

"That would be perfectly fine with me, but I fear she's growing up. Lady Winstead isn't the only thing about tomorrow that interests her. There's also Miss Stover's presentation and her presentation gown and gowns in general."

He shuddered. "Too soon."

"Agreed. Perhaps we can divert her attention with a horse."

"What?" He pushed me back to look into my face. "I assume you can explain what a horse has to do with anything."

"She's growing too old for Pierre."

"So we'll have to provide her with a horse? Where will we put it? We've only just enough room for the carriage horses. Do you know how much a horse costs? Do you know how much one eats?"

"I have no idea, as you well know, but clearly you do. Riding is an excellent pursuit for Rose, it's good exercise in fresh air, and it's a social activity, as well. And with my father's money, I assume we can afford it."

"Your father's money," he muttered. "Must we discuss that now?"

My father had given us a significant sum as a wedding gift. It was meant to be used for a honeymoon, but it was enough to support us for an entire year, educate Rose, board her pony, buy a new horse, and board him, too. The trouble was that the amount was also large enough to make George uncomfortable.

"My family is American," I said. "We don't leave everything to the firstborn son. Therefore, much of my father's fortune will eventually come to me. If he wishes to give some of it to us now, what could be your objection?" I followed him out to our bedroom, which was almost in darkness now that the drapes hand been closed, and moved to the bedside table to turn up the gas lamp.

George wandered over to the bed and plunked down on the fluffy coverlet. "I don't know that I objected exactly."

"Didn't you?" George, the poor dear, had clearly forgotten the conversation we'd had upon receiving the bank draft—if one could call it a conversation. "As I recall, you slammed your hand on the table, turned a most frightening shade of purple, then bellowed, 'It's as if the man thinks I can't support you!'"

He leaned back on his elbows and struggled to repress a grin. "I find that a gross mischaracterization. Am I to just sit here while you malign me?"

I leaned against the bedpost. "What exactly did I get wrong?"

"I have never bellowed before in my life."

"You did then," I said with a chuckle. "Then you stomped about the room, not heeding a word I said as I tried to make you see sense."

He narrowed his eyes. "How did the conversation end?"

"I poured you a glass of whiskey and placed the bank draft in a drawer for discussion on another day."

George sat up and pointed a finger at me. "That," he said. "Let's do that again."

"Not this time." I stepped in front of him and took his hands. "You knew my father had a large fortune when you married me."

"Yes, but I thought he'd suffered a financial setback."

I shrugged. "It was temporary. Should I have made you aware of that?"

"Well . . ."

"His fortunes could turn again, you know. Tomorrow. Next week. At any moment that bank draft could be rendered worthless, and I could become a pauper."

He gave me a wry look. "Fine. I feel a bit ridiculous, complaining about marrying into a wealthy family. It's just that I'm rather proud to have always supported myself."

"I understand, darling."

And I really did. Self-sufficiency was something George and I shared, though I had not quite reached the point of self-support. I occasionally fell back on the small fortune my father had set aside for me upon my first marriage. He had recognized my first husband as the wastrel he was and had wanted to ensure I had some money of my own, since my dowry had become Reggie's property.

After Reggie's death, I was fortunate to have funds that my brother-in-law, the new Earl of Harleigh, couldn't touch. I was soon to learn it wasn't enough to live off, but that was where my status as the Countess of Harleigh came in handy. I found if I sponsored young ladies for the London social season, their mothers would thank me with a gift—often money. Miss Stover's presentation at court could produce a similar result.

It was hardly steady work, and quite hush-hush. I couldn't ask for payment. It was simply understood that my efforts would be rewarded. Someone of my rank was not meant to earn her living. Like George, I was meant to marry or inherit a fortune. He would be considered rather an odd duck not to jump at my father's largesse.

He heaved a sigh. "Your father is very good at what he does. I'm sure his fortunes will flourish, and we'll be forced to accept gifts of money from time to time."

"Yes, darling. He's an absolute monster, forcing money on us like that."

"I take your point," he said. He raised my right hand to his lips and pressed a kiss on it, then repeated the act with my left. "I have an inkling that I'm being just a wee bit unreasonable about this topic. But I'm not quite prepared to change my mind yet."

Interesting. "That indicates you might be prepared to do so in the future."

"At some unspecified date, perhaps."

"I'll hold you to that."

"I'm sure you will." His expression was one of relief. "Now, how was your meeting with Miss Stover?"

"She's an interesting woman." I dropped his hands and seated myself at the writing table against the wall, turning the chair to face him. "It seems she, too, is worried about her aunt. The Ashleys, on the other hand, seem to have some concerns about Miss Stover. She was accompanied today by a very nosy maid, at the viscount's insistence. If she'd behaved like an ordinary maid, I'd say he was just watching out for her. But in this case, it was more as if she'd been instructed to watch Miss Stover, as if he suspected her of something. Perhaps of stealing a journal? Have you learned anything new?"

"Me?" George studied his fingernails. "I planned to wait for you to solve this case."

"Yet I can tell by the look in your eye, you have information."

"It isn't much. I stopped by the British Museum and spoke to the director about the Winstead collection." He raised his brows. "That's what it's meant to be called, by the way. Apparently, Lord Jonathon told the director he had a couple of outsiders in his household he's watching. Thus, your observation that he has his eye on Miss Stover is spot on. She can probably look forward to his watching her every move. So can the nurse."

"He suspects both of them of stealing the journal?"

"I don't know that for a fact, but they are both outsiders. Everyone else in the household is family or trusted servants, so it wouldn't be surprising."

"Did the director give you a full report? Do you have suspicions of your own?"

"I have many suspicions. Jonathon Ashley's claim in particular. He left the journal on his desk, and, poof"—he snapped his fingers—"it disappeared."

"That does seem rather careless of him."

"Wasn't it? If I'm to believe him, I, too, would suspect someone in the household. It would be far too coincidental that a thief happened to break in at such an opportune moment."

"I take it you don't believe him."

He rolled his eyes, stood, and began to pace. "I suppose I don't disbelieve him. It's just awfully convenient that something Lord Peter safeguarded for years goes missing the day before it's meant to be handed over to the museum."

"The rest of the collection was handed over, was it not?"

"Everything but the journal. The artifacts themselves are possibly priceless to a collector, yet they were safely delivered. However, without the journal, which provides the details of each relic and its provenance, they become, if not worthless, at least far less valuable."

"But why steal the journal? Without the artifacts, wouldn't it be relatively worthless?"

"One would assume so, but it seems it's valuable to someone. I'm inclined to think that someone is Jonathon Ashley, but it's just a hunch." He spread his hands. "I'm not quite sure what I'm dealing with yet."

"That makes two of us."

Chapter Five

I called on Miss Stover with some trepidation the next afternoon. Whether that was due to the potential criminal activity in the household or how uncomfortable the rest of the Ashley family made me, I couldn't say. I was in a rather difficult position. Lady Esther wanted me to observe the family and their treatment of Lady Winstead. George wanted me to watch them, with the hope of flushing out a thief. The situation made me rather jumpy, and I now regretted having Rose with me. But I'd promised her, and I had already applied the knocker to the door.

The butler, who, I had learned, was called Fuller, opened the door and bowed me into the entry hall, which was really rather magnificent. It was two stories high, paneled in dark wood but made brighter by the white marble floor and the light from the tall window above the door.

"Miss Stover told me she was expecting you, Mrs. Hazelton, but she is currently entertaining a gentleman in the drawing room."

The smarmy look on his face spoke volumes. First, he was

not a supporter of Miss Stover. Second, she must be "entertaining" said gentleman alone. Third, he was delighted to be able to tattle on her to someone.

Bother! It appeared I was needed to break up a tête-à-tête between Miss Stover and an unknown man. Under such circumstances, Rose should be elsewhere.

"If Miss Stover is expecting me, I'll go right in. In the meantime, my daughter would like to call on Lady Winstead. Would you be so kind as to escort her?" I placed a hand on Rose's shoulder. "Lady Rose is well known to Lady Winstead."

His expression softened immediately. "Of course, madam. I'll be happy to take the young lady up."

I was surprised he didn't nudge me with an elbow and wink. I reminded Rose that Lady Winstead was ill and that if she wasn't awake or didn't feel well, Rose could return here and wait for me. I didn't like the idea of sending her to visit the woman at her bedside but considered it the lesser of two evils.

Rose, completely unconcerned, followed Fuller up the grand staircase. I turned to the drawing room doors. The closed doors. No wonder Fuller had been scandalized. Devon might not be the center of society, but Miss Stover still ought to have known better. I didn't bother knocking but walked right in. Miss Stover glanced at me in surprise.

She was indeed entertaining a gentleman. An extremely handsome gentleman in his mid-thirties, perhaps. They stood face-to-face before the fireplace. He, too, turned when my heels tapped against the polished wood as I approached them. Unlike his companion's, his expression was one of mild curiosity and warm geniality. The second one might have been an assumption on my part. He was slightly above average height and broad shouldered, wearing a gray morning coat. He held his silk hat in one gloved hand, allowing me to better appreciate the mass of blond hair that fell in waves to his collar. His nose was straight, his lips were full, and his eyes sparkling.

His free hand was holding Miss Stover's—until she yanked it away, that is.

I took all this in, in the length of time it took to cross the room. "Good morning, Miss Stover. I hope I'm not interrupting?"

"Of course not, Mrs. Hazelton." Her hands floated uselessly in front of her. "Mr. Montague is just leaving."

"Indeed, I am," he said.

Heavens, his voice was like silk.

He smiled at Miss Stover. "We seem to have lost track of time."

"I can see how that might happen, Mr. Montague," I said.

"Yes, well, thank you for calling, sir." Miss Stover's voice was overly loud. "My aunt will be sorry to have missed you."

"Oh, if you are here for Lady Winstead," I said, "I believe she's awake and receiving company. Perhaps a footman can bring her down."

Neither of them responded.

I glanced from one to the other. "I would hate for you to leave and not see her."

"That would take some time." Miss Stover gave the man a penetrating look. "Didn't you mention you were running late?"

"That's right," he agreed and flashed a devastating smile. "I must be going." He gave us each a nod and let himself out of the room. I waited until the front door closed before speaking to Miss Stover.

"Rather strange that he called for Lady Winstead, then left without seeing her."

Her hands fluttered about until she clasped them behind her back. "I suppose it is, now that you mention it."

"How do they know each other?"

"I'm sure they met at one gathering or another."

"Do you mean here in town?" I paused and brought the man's image back to mind. "No, that's not possible."

"Whyever not?"

I released a sigh, already tired of playing this game. "Miss Stover, I may not know everyone in London society, but a man that handsome would not go unnoticed. I would at the very least know *of* him, so kindly tell me who he really is and why you were behind closed doors with him. You can't honestly expect me to present you to the queen and introduce you to society if you plan to take no care with your reputation."

She drew in a sharp breath—not quite a gasp, but dramatic, nonetheless.

I held up a hand before she could speak. "Spare me any histrionics. Who is he, and why were you closeted with him?"

Her shoulders slumped. "He really is Mr. Montague. He's a friend from back home in Devon. He is in London on business, and he simply called to see how I was faring. I didn't realize that was a crime."

Huh. With men like that in Devon, I can't imagine why she ever left home. "It isn't a crime. It isn't a problem whatsoever—until you close the door and meet with him alone. I'm sure Lady Winstead or Lord Jonathon would be happy to see you entertaining a guest, just not in such a clandestine manner."

"It was all very innocent, I assure you."

"He was holding your hand."

"He was shaking my hand. Nothing happened between us. He was simply about to leave."

"Yet you lied to me when I asked about him. What would you have done if Lord Jonathon had seen you?"

"If I'd seen what?"

A glance over my shoulder showed Jonathon Ashley hovering in the doorway. Bother! One advantage of having the doors closed is that no one can slip up and overhear your conversation. Unfortunately, we'd left them open after Mr. Montague had left. The viscount glanced around the room, as if looking for evidence of untoward behavior, and the frightened look

Miss Stover gave me led me to wonder if Mr. Montague was something more than just an old friend from Devon. One of us had to say something.

"Well, I hate to tell tales, sir, but in this case, I believe it's necessary. I caught Miss Stover in your library, fairly hanging off the ladder in an attempt to reach something on the upper shelves."

He scowled. "Indeed, Kate, had I seen you, it would have taken me aback. Next time ring for a servant to assist you, or better yet, why bury your nose in those dusty old books? There's nothing on those upper shelves of any interest to the feminine mind."

The color returned to Miss Stover's face. She owed me for this.

To my surprise, the viscount indicated we should be seated, then took the chair next to me. "I'm glad to have this moment with you together to discuss your plans for Kate." He stopped speaking abruptly and glanced from her to me. "Now that I say her name, I can't believe you are still Miss Stover and Mrs. Hazelton to each other. Are you two not friends yet? Or at least conspirators?" He wiggled his fingers up close to his face.

"Since we will be working closely together, we are sure to become friends. And if I am correctly interpreting this" — I imitated Jonathon's finger motion — "I can assure you we are not casting spells or whipping up love potions."

He smiled — condescendingly, of course. "Yes, well, ladies must have their secrets, but I would like to know what your plans are."

That came as a surprise. I'd thought my presence here was all Lady Winstead's doing — with perhaps a bit of help from Vi. "I'm here today to review and advise Miss Stover on her wardrobe. We shall visit the modiste tomorrow for her presentation gown. We can discuss any further clothing needs with Madame Celeste at that time, too. I know the family is in mourning, so I shall plan a soiree for her on the evening of the queen's drawing room."

I expected Jonathon to thank me for going to the extra trouble of entertaining on Miss Stover's behalf. Instead, his lips drooped with disappointment.

"That doesn't sound like much of a social season," he said.

"Social season?" I turned to Miss Stover, who gave me a helpless look.

"I appreciate any effort Mrs. Hazelton makes on my behalf," she said.

"I'm sure my guests will in turn invite Miss Stover to their entertainments throughout the season," I added.

He grimaced and sucked in a breath between his teeth. "Do you really think so? After all, at twenty-three, she is older than the girls she'll meet at her presentation. I don't know that she'll find allies, or comrades in arms, if you will."

Twenty-three? I cast my gaze at Miss Stover and raised a questioning brow.

She glanced down at her lap, where she twined her fingers together. "I'm afraid it's worse than that," she said. "My aunt likely lost track of the years, but I am actually twenty-five."

He frowned. "As old as that, eh?"

I stared at Miss Stover, knowing her age to be twenty-eight. The small lie only made me more suspicious of her. And Mr. Montague. What was she, or they, up to? My attention diverted, I missed whatever the viscount had just said. Something about helping Miss Stover.

"I'd say your concern is misplaced, sir." I glanced at Miss Stover and sighed. "At her age, she is a little older than the other unmarried ladies being presented, but that is no matter. If people come to an entertainment held in her honor, they will most definitely invite her to their events, no matter her age or whether she is a social butterfly or a wallflower." I turned to the subject of our conversation. "I don't know you well enough,

Miss Stover, to judge if you are one, the other, or somewhere in between, but you will have invitations."

Her expression seemed to indicate satisfaction, so I turned back to the viscount. "Are you expecting something more?"

"I am expecting her to receive an offer of marriage."

The bald statement took me by surprise. A glance at Miss Stover, who looked for all the world like a hunted animal, told me she hadn't anticipated this answer, either. "That is something that is always up to chance," I said.

"But her chances would improve if you were to arrange introductions, would they not?"

"If you are asking me to sponsor Miss Stover for the season, I'm afraid I must decline. I don't know if I will even be in town for the whole of it, and I have other obligations to fulfill." I gave him a smile to take the sting out of the rejection. I doubted Miss Stover felt anything but relief.

He let out a huff. "Is that not what you were hired for?"

I ought to have slapped him right then and there. Though I repressed that urge, I couldn't stop the small gasp that escaped me. "I was not *hired* to do anything, and I resent that implication. Your stepmother asked if I'd do her the favor of sponsoring her niece's presentation to the queen. She asked me to use my status and connections to benefit Miss Stover. That is what I am doing."

He raised his hand, as if I had made his point. "And for that favor, she is compensating you."

"She has done nothing of the sort."

"But she very likely will—with a gift of some sort. I simply wish to renegotiate your terms. I don't know why you are so disagreeable about this."

Not only was the man the worst sort of boor, but he also had to be completely thick. How dare he talk about paying me for my services, as if I were his tailor or haberdasher! What if he spoke about it to someone else? Had he no sense of discretion? If he didn't know any better, it was high time he learned.

"There will be no negotiations. There are no terms. I am doing a favor for Lady Winstead. If she chooses to show her appreciation with a gift, that is her prerogative, as it is if she chooses to do nothing. To suggest anything else is an insult to both of us."

I came to my feet and strode to the door, nose in the air and spine straight, just as my mother had taught me. Miss Stover had better follow me, for there was nothing that could induce me to return to that room to retrieve her.

As it happened, it was Lord Jonathon who followed me to the entry hall. With his hands clasped behind his back, he stepped so close, I could feel his breath on my face.

"I don't care what your arrangement is with Lady Winstead," he said in a hushed voice. "I want her out of this house. If it happens through marriage, all the better for her. But make no mistake about it, she will be gone by the end of the season."

I watched him stride across the marble tiles of the entry hall and around the corner, wondering if he meant Miss Stover or Lady Winstead. Or both.

Chapter Six

ᔕ

I stood in the entry hall, seething. And not only over the insult to me. Katherine Stover had been in this house a mere six days. What could she possibly have done to earn the viscount's ill will? So much that it sounded as if he was prepared to throw her out into the cold, so to speak. I had no idea what her resources might be, but if she had any at all, she might be better off on her own. I certainly didn't relish the prospect of dealing with Jonathon, but with Lady Winstead in ill health, and Vi seemingly out of the picture, I might have no choice.

I hoped Miss Stover did.

My wait in the hall was a matter of seconds. Miss Stover peered out from the drawing room doors.

"He's gone," I said. "It's safe."

She stepped across the marble floor and up to my side, her hands clasped in front of her, gazing down at her shoes. "I believe I'm somewhat to blame for the viscount's lapse in manners. I'm sorry you had to put up with that . . . display."

"We are all responsible for our own actions. He chose to be rude. It is no reflection on you."

She gave me a half smile.

"Having said that," I continued, "he did seem unduly hostile. Have you had a disagreement? Is there bad blood between you?"

She twisted her fingers. "In a way, there is some antagonism between us. It began when I rejected his marriage proposal."

Ah! This was an interesting turn of events. "Well, that makes two of us."

She released a short, mirthless laugh and shook her head.

I knew I ought to go up to Rose. I'd already spent more time down here than expected, but if I had to work with this family, it would be helpful to gain as much knowledge as possible.

But not while standing in the entry hall.

The door to the library, right next to the drawing room, stood open. It was a little less likely someone would wander in and disturb us there, but we'd have to be quick. I drew Miss Stover by the arm into the room and closed the door. "Now that you've mentioned it, I must have the details," I said. "When did he ask you? What exactly happened?" My questions were terribly intrusive, but since she had brought the subject up, one could assume she'd be willing to speak of it.

"It happened the day before you came for tea. He had just learned you'd been asked to manage my presentation. That evening, after dinner, he asked me to marry him."

"And you said no."

"I suppose I ought to have given the idea some consideration, but I have no admiration for the man, and I'm certain he does not admire me. I didn't relish the thought of spending the rest of my life with him trying to change me into the type of wife he wanted."

In my opinion, she had assessed that situation with remarkable accuracy. There was something to be said for having a bit of maturity when one is faced with making such a momentous decision. Her age was one reason the viscount likely thought she'd jump at his offer, even if he thought she was twenty-three. But we could discuss that little white lie another time.

"He must place some value on you, or he wouldn't have proposed marriage."

"Hmm, I assume that value comes from his belief that my aunt will leave me some money in her will. He'd just as soon keep it for himself as see it go to some other man."

"Surely, his father already left him the bulk of his fortune."

"Perhaps the bulk of it was not enough for him."

"Perhaps. Has he made you uncomfortable since you rejected him?"

"He has pretended it never happened. This was the first time I've heard him admit he would like to see the back of me."

I made a face. "You heard that, did you?"

"It doesn't bother me," she said with a toss of her head. "As long as my aunt wants me here, I believe I have a home."

This placed a different light on Jonathon Ashley's suspicion of Miss Stover as having stolen the journal. Any accusation he made might be due to his resentment over her rejection of his proposal.

"Speaking of your aunt, if it's permissible to visit her in her bedchamber, I'd like to check on her. She's been with Rose since I arrived here, and may be growing weary of chatting with an eight-year-old."

"It's the only place one can visit her," Miss Stover replied. "Let me take you up."

At the top of the staircase, we turned right and stopped at the first room, where she knocked on the open door. I took a step forward and glanced inside. Rose sat on the bed next to Lady Winstead, who was still in her convalescent chair and dressing gown, a blanket draped over her lap and her white hair woven into a plait that trailed over her shoulder. She was clearly more alert and looking better than the last time I saw her. Admittedly, it would be difficult for her to look worse.

The room was large but warm and stuffy. Heavy draperies covered a window in the wall opposite the door. The only light came from a lamp on the bedside table. I've never seen a less cheerful room.

"Look who I brought to visit with you, Aunt."

Lady Winstead glanced up at Miss Stover's announcement and gestured for me to come inside, which I did. Miss Stover waited for me at the doorway.

Nurse Plum stood at the ready against the wall beside Lady Winstead's chair, wearing her nurse's uniform, sturdy shoes, and a look of disapproval. If I had to summarize her in a word, I'd call her capable.

When I approached, she brushed past me, leaving the scent of lemon and bergamot in the air, then stepped around the bed to busy herself at the table near the window. I placed a hand on Rose's shoulder and spoke to Lady Winstead. "I see you are reacquainting yourself with Lady Rose. I'm pleased to find you looking so much better today, ma'am."

If I thought the compliment would garner a smile, I was mistaken. "I have consulted a mirror this morning, so I must assume I looked quite wretched when we last met. But I am feeling more myself today, if that's what you mean. I understand I was quite unwell recently." She narrowed her eyes and peered at me as if she were in need of spectacles. "Were you here?"

"Yes, ma'am. I was here to meet Miss Stover. You had us all worried, but it appears the doctor has taken good care of you."

She frowned. "I don't recall a doctor. Just Nurse Plum. She is all I need."

I turned to Nurse Plum, who watched us from across the room. "Did no one send for a doctor?"

The nurse stiffened her posture. "Lady Winstead recovered quickly. Her heart and pulse returned to normal. At that point, we decided there was no need for the doctor. But as you see, she is doing well today."

She was vastly improved, but I wouldn't go so far as to say she looked well. Her eyes held a dull look, as if we'd just wakened her from a deep slumber. Her movements and speech were slow and cautious. I wondered if she'd had some sort of seizure. She ought to see a doctor, but I doubted my opinion would carry any weight.

"Lord Jonathon said you were used to dealing with these episodes," I said to the nurse. "Has she collapsed like that before?"

Nurse Plum looked surprised. "No, she has not. I can only assume he meant I was used to treating Lady Winstead. If I thought a doctor was necessary, I would have insisted on calling for one."

I returned my attention to Lady Winstead. "Lady Esther will be happy to hear of your improvement," I said. "She was very concerned for you."

"Was she? How strange. I haven't seen her for months." Lady Winstead fussed with the blanket, pulling it up higher.

"I understand she's called on you several times," I said. "In fact, she was here with me Monday. "Don't you remember?"

The older woman narrowed her eyes, as if trying to concentrate or focus her thoughts, but she was clearly confused. "Esther was here? What a shame I missed her."

I didn't know quite what to say to that, since she had only barely missed falling at the other woman's feet.

"Are you a friend of hers?" she asked.

"Yes, I suppose I am." If Lady Esther could be said to have friends.

She attempted to extend her index finger but wagged her

whole hand at me instead. "Make sure she comes back. There's much I have to say to her." She drew a heavy breath. "I can't bring it to mind now, but I'd like to speak with her sometime."

I'd been so engrossed in observing Lady Winstead, I hadn't noticed the nurse approach until she placed a gentle hand on the lady's shoulder. "That's enough for now, ma'am," she said. "You will tire yourself."

Lady Winstead already looked exhausted. I took Rose's hand when she slipped down from the bed to her feet. "Your nurse is correct, ma'am. We mustn't tire you, but I shall return, and we'll chat again."

Once Rose said goodbye, the nurse wheeled her charge closer to the bed and we backed away. With some difficulty, I tore my gaze from Lady Winstead and left the room.

Miss Stover waited outside the door. I introduced Rose, then asked her, "Is your aunt always like this?"

With a gesture, she led us down the hall to the next bed-chamber. "Sometimes she's worse, sometimes a little better, but yes, since I arrived, she's been either ill or confused. No one else in the house takes any notice of it, so I believe her illness must have progressed slowly over the past few months."

We entered her bedchamber, similar in size to Lady Winstead's. It was well appointed, with an east-facing window. Either Lady Winstead had chosen it for her or Miss Stover hadn't always been considered an unwanted houseguest. Then I recalled Jonathon Ashley's proposal. She had probably been welcomed to the household until her refusal.

"I'll just fetch my gowns," Miss Stover said, stepping inside her dressing room.

I waited by the entrance, where I could speak with her and still keep an eye on Rose, who had seated herself at the dressing table. "Was that the last time you saw her?" I asked. "A few months ago?"

"A little longer. I visited for a few days at Christmas. My aunt was quieter than I remember her. Understandable since her husband was clearly dying. I stayed long enough to attend the funeral. Even then, she seemed to be in possession of her faculties, and I never saw her collapse as she did yesterday."

"Do you know when she last consulted with a doctor?"

Miss Stover had been moving clothes from one shelf to another. Upon considering my question, she stopped and turned around, then gave me a curious look, reminding me that I didn't know if she could be trusted.

"Forgive me," I said quickly. "I am no doctor myself and ought not interfere in her medical care."

She stared at me a moment longer, then nodded and moved farther into the dressing room. "I'll bring the gowns right out."

As much as I disliked the idea, if I were to gain answers to Lady's Esther's questions, I'd likely have to deal with the new viscount. Bother. Fortunately, I could put that task off for the moment and indulge in something much more to my liking spending his money. At least, I assumed either he or Lady Winstead would be paying for Miss Stover's wardrobe.

Rose brightened at the prospect of gowns. With my daughter on hand, I hesitated to inquire further about the handsome Mr. Montague, so we might just as well turn our focus to clothes. "Yes, Miss Stover, let us see what you have."

"What I have is the perfect wardrobe for spring in Devon some three or four years ago." She pulled out three gowns, carried them into the room, and draped them across the bed. They were autumnal colors, bronze, gold, and red. I'd forgotten momentarily that I wasn't working with a girl, but with a woman of my own age. I moved a sleeve here, shook out a skirt there, calculating what alterations would be needed.

"You are mistaken, Miss Stover," I said. "These gowns would also be perfect for London." I turned to catch the surprise in her expression before I continued. "Three or four years ago. My modiste will be able to bring them up to date easily. Skirts are narrower, as are sleeves. She can replace some of the trim." I frowned. "I was hoping to spend more of the viscount's money."

Her stony expression finally cracked as I surprised a laugh from her. "Well, I assume I'll need more than three gowns."

"Oh, this is the extent of your wardrobe?"

"You'll need much more," Rose said.

"I do have a walking dress and a carriage dress that are more up to date, but for evening entertainments, this is all I have."

I placed one hand on her shoulder and the other over my heart. "You have made me very happy, Miss Stover."

"Then perhaps you would call me Kate?"

"As much as I dislike the idea of agreeing with the viscount, we will be working closely enough that we ought to be Kate and Frances. Now, we shall have to purchase at least three more evening gowns, wouldn't you say, Rose?"

She bobbed her head. "And don't forget the presentation gown."

I turned from Rose to Kate. "Something you are likely never to wear again."

"Never?"

"Her Majesty has very strict requirements for these gowns, and they are not at all fashionable, but the good news is they contain a great deal of fabric, so you will be able to have it remade at some point." I frowned. "The bad news is they are usually white."

Her body sagged. "Must it be white?"

"Madame Celeste will know for certain, and I have another authority on such matters. I'll consult with her, too. We might get away with cream or blush, either of which should suit you better."

She straightened and gathered one of the gowns in her arms. "We visit the modiste tomorrow, then?"

"Yes," I replied to her back as she returned the gown to the dressing room. "Be sure to bring these three gowns with you."

She made some reply, but the sound of coughing in Lady Winstead's room prevented me from hearing her. The coughing subsided, and Kate returned momentarily.

"What was that you said?" I asked.

"I have some tissue in the dressing room. I'll wrap them up to take with us." She took the other two dresses and disappeared into the dressing room again just as the coughing started back up. I waited patiently for a minute. Apparently, Kate couldn't hear what I assumed was her aunt's distress.

"Where do you suppose Nurse Plum is?" I asked Rose, who seemed prepared to rush to Lady Winstead's aid. When I heard a wheezing sound in addition to the coughs, I could wait no longer and left the room to check on the viscountess. Rose followed closely behind me.

The lamp had been dimmed, and the room was in darkness when I peeked inside. I could barely see Lady Winstead, lying flat in bed, still coughing and struggling to sit up. Nurse Plum was nowhere in sight.

"Let me help you," I said and moved to the side of the bed, then slipped an arm around her back. She was slight enough to lift with ease. Rose gathered the pillows to prop up behind her.

Lady Winstead drew one steady breath. Then another. Finally, her breathing sounded easy enough for me to step back. No sign of a wheeze or cough, but her eyes had watered in the process. "That was uncomfortable," she said.

"I should imagine so. May I fetch you a handkerchief?" I asked.

She let out one more cough. "Yes." She waved a hand. "In that bureau."

I crossed the room to the bureau that stood near the door

and opened the top drawer. I'd guessed correctly. Folded hand-kerchiefs took up one side of the drawer. I grasped the one on top, which seemed to be wrapped around something. Of course the item tumbled to the floor. I turned up the gas on the lamp atop the bureau and bent to retrieve the object.

Tossing it into the drawer, I got a good look at it. Heavens! I was quite confident I'd just found Lord Peter's missing journal. It must have been my astonishment that distracted me, because I never saw Kate enter the room until her hand slammed the drawer shut.

Chapter Seven

⟨~⟩

While I was startled and a bit confused, Kate looked completely unnerved. She snatched the handkerchief from my fingers and took it over to her aunt. Lady Winstead blotted her eyes as Kate checked her pillows and jerked the sheets up around the older woman's shoulders. Rose looked on from the side of the bed, while Kate fussed long enough for Lady Winstead to shoo her away.

"Rose, please stay with Lady Winstead until Nurse Plum returns," I said. Then I turned to Kate and tipped my head toward the door. "Shall we?"

She followed me with a heavy tread back to her room. Once inside, I made sure to close the door; then I faced Kate, folded my arms, and waited for an explanation.

"Thank you for taking care of my aunt," she said, attempting a smile. "The gowns are ready for tomorrow, so I suppose we're done here."

She had to be joking. "We most certainly are not done here. Tell me what you know about that item in Lady Winstead's bureau."

Her face went blank. "How would I know about Lady Winstead's belongings? Unlike you, I don't snoop around in my aunt's drawers."

"I'd advise you not to take that tack. You were frightened when you realized I'd seen it. 'It' being what I'm sure is the journal Lord Jonathon believes to have been stolen."

The surprise on her face made me realize what I'd said. Stupid, stupid, stupid! I wasn't supposed to know anything about the journal or the theft. I might have gotten away with leaving here today and telling George where to find it. I gave myself a mental kick. Too late to take the words back now.

"How do you know the viscount thinks it's been stolen?"

"I'd prefer you answer my question first."

She took a step closer to me. "Are you with the police?" she asked in a hushed voice. "Special Branch or something like that?"

She couldn't possibly be serious. I moved to the bench at the end of the bed and indicated she should take a seat next to me. I'd made a grave misstep in letting her know I recognized the journal. I'd have to tread very carefully from here on out.

"I'm quite sure we both know that was Lord Peter's journal, which rightfully belongs to the British Museum."

"It does?"

I stared at her for at least twenty seconds before she dropped her gaze. "I believe you took it from the viscount's desk and hid it in your aunt's bureau."

"It might have been my aunt who did it."

"But it wasn't, was it?"

She tightened her lips into a thin line.

"For goodness' sake, you can tell me about your part in this or I can bring Lord Jonathon in here to ask the questions. Which do you prefer?"

She stared down at her hands, folded in her lap. It was rather cruel to threaten her with the viscount, but I saw no other way. I was not leaving this room without an answer. She finally glanced up at me. "You're really not with the police?"

I shook my head, and she released a sigh. "I was hoping you were. I took the thing, hoping Jonathon, Lord Jonathon, that is, would contact the police. That's why I hid it in my aunt's room. He never goes near her."

All of which told me exactly nothing. "Why did you want him to contact the police?"

"How well do you know the Ashley family?"

"Don't turn this around. I am asking you the questions."

She held up a hand. "I'll answer you, but I just need to know this first."

"Not very well," I said. "Si and Vi were my late husband's friends, not mine. I know Jonathon Ashley well enough to avoid him whenever possible, and Lady Winstead enough to know she has a heart under her crotchety exterior."

She gave me the ghost of a smile. "Lady Winstead is difficult, to say the least, but she was fond of her brother, my father. She's been very kind to me, as well, and I'd like to repay her." She drew a deep breath. "You asked me what I know about my aunt's health, and here it is—I suspect someone is poisoning her. I don't know who, but someone in this house."

I certainly hadn't expected that bit of information, and the surprise must have shown in my expression, because she lifted a hand to forestall any protest. "I know that sounds fanciful or melodramatic, but I saw her in much better health not four months ago. We have been corresponding over that time, as well. I can show you her letters. They are witty, sometimes acerbic, and definitely in her hand. To look at her now, I'd find it hard to believe she could control a pen. Yet her stepchildren say she has been this way for months. You have seen her. Is she anything like the woman you remember?"

"She is not. It was quite a shock to see her yesterday, but there are many medical issues that might explain her condition. It does not mean someone is poisoning her."

She let out a groan and came to her feet, gesturing wildly with her hands. "I have asked them about her medical condition. They put it down to the natural effects of aging. I've asked them to bring in a doctor to examine her, only to be told to calm myself. The Ashleys tolerate my presence here . . . barely. I understand that they don't want me poking my nose into what they see as their business, but I honestly fear for her life."

I resisted my instinct to tell her to calm down. She did seem to be unwelcome here, at least by Jonathon, but that may have nothing to do with her asking questions about her aunt. George had said Jonathon suspected she'd taken the journal, and it turned out he was right. "It's also possible that the viscount resents you coming here and stealing from him."

"I did it so the Ashleys would call in the police. I've been trying to come up with a way to help my aunt. If I go to the police and tell them my suspicions, what could they do? I am a guest here. I have no authority or proof. But if they come here to investigate a theft and interview us, I can plead my case. They can see her for themselves. Surely, they will do something about it." She resumed her seat beside me. "If Jonathon reported it stolen, why haven't they come?" Her eyes narrowed. "And how do you even know about it? You say you are not with the police, but you clearly know something about the journal."

I didn't answer immediately. She sighed and lowered her gaze to her hands. Now that she'd stopped speaking, they lay dormant in her lap. What had I gotten myself into? I honestly couldn't dismiss Kate's claims as nonsense. After all, Lady Esther was worried about the viscountess, too. The family had even denied her access to her friend. But in their defense, Lady Winstead might truly be ill. She might have suffered an apoplexy or some such thing that damaged both her mind and body, and the family wished to keep that information to themselves. I was about to suggest as much to Kate when she raised her head and I saw the despair in her eyes.

"You won't answer my questions, because you don't believe

me." She stood and crossed to her dressing table. After opening the center drawer, she collected some papers and brought them to me. "Here. You will see from the dates these are my aunt's recent letters to me. Tell me they could have been written by the woman in the next room."

"I don't want to examine your personal correspondence."

"Please. It's the only way you will believe me."

I opened one letter, and my eyes were drawn to a specific sentence. "She thought someone was stealing from her?"

Kate slipped into the seat beside me and glanced at the letter. "She noticed some jewelry missing. I'd forgotten about that."

"But couldn't she simply have misplaced it?"

"Read on. She kept the jewelry she wore most frequently in a locked drawer in her dressing table. When she looked for it, it was gone. She suspected Jonathon took it. I don't know if she ever confronted him about it."

"Once his father passed away, wouldn't the family jewelry have gone to Jonathon, as the current viscount? He may simply have moved it elsewhere for safekeeping."

Kate raised her brows. "This jewelry was from her prior marriage. It doesn't belong to the Ashley family. Even if it did, he had no right to break into a locked drawer."

I returned my attention to the letter, which confirmed her claims. "Are you certain this is your aunt's handwriting?"

"She's written to my father and me many times over the years. I'd recognize her hand."

This was not a letter that Lady Winstead could have written, or even dictated, in her current condition. It was clear and concise and written in a steady hand just a month ago, about the same time I'd had my correspondence with her. What had changed in that time?

"How long has Nurse Plum been part of the household?"

"Five months or so, I'd guess. She attended Lord Peter until he died. She may have left for a short time, but if so, she returned quickly to care for my aunt, who my cousins say was suffering from grief." She noted my frown. "You can see why I am concerned. For all I know, Nurse Plum is responsible for Lord Peter's death."

"Is she the one you suspect of poisoning your aunt?"

Kate opened her hands helplessly. "There is no one in this house I do not suspect. I've been here a handful of days and have only just begun to realize something is very wrong. I don't know where to begin to investigate. There's no one I can trust. My aunt does take laudanum, or rather, Nurse Plum gives it to her. There is a large bottle on her dressing table. It has barely diminished since I've been here, so it seems the nurse administers only small doses, perhaps only now and then. But after yesterday, I believe either the nurse or someone else in this house gave her a very large dose, one that might have killed her. I was so concerned about her that I spent last night in her room. And you saw for yourself she is much improved today. What am I to believe but that someone is drugging her, or poisoning her, for the purpose of stealing from her?"

I had to admit she was making a reasonably good case. But what was I to do about it? "If I am to understand you, you stole the journal to force your cousin to bring in the police. Then you planned to tell them of your suspicions about your aunt and her family. And you presumed the police would arrest one of them?"

She twisted her fingers restlessly. "Perhaps. I'm not entirely sure what they could do. But why haven't the police come? Hasn't Lord Jonathon notified them?"

"I know a little about that. Lord Jonathon is in rather a ticklish situation. The journal was bequeathed to the British Museum by the late Viscount Winstead, Lord Peter. It documents all the artifacts he obtained on his expeditions and also left to them. The museum is eager to have it. Jonathon, for whatever reason, did not immediately turn it over to them. Then it went missing. It's the British Museum who contacted the authorities, not Lord Jonathon. While I'm somewhat connected to the investigation, I am not part of it. However, they are rather single-minded and want only what belongs to them. I doubt they will have any interest in what may be happening to your aunt."

"But you must—"

I placed my hand over hers. "I will make some inquiries and see if anything can be done. May I take the journal with me?"

"I'd rather keep it here. As you said, the people at the museum only want what is theirs. If I give it to them, the investigation is over, and they have no incentive to help my aunt."

What she was too polite to say was that she didn't trust me, either.

"We'll leave it for now, but at least hide it a little deeper in that drawer. In the meantime, keep a watchful eye on Lady Winstead, but be careful not to accuse anyone or get in their way."

"Thank you," she said. "I can't tell you what a relief it is to have someone helping me."

Which wasn't exactly what I was meant to do. I hoped George wouldn't be too upset with me. But I had found his journal. Even if I wasn't bringing it home, that must count for something.

Chapter Eight

꩜

George was not upset with me. At least not for discovering the journal. "I can't believe you didn't just bring it home with you," he said. "I was counting on you to complete my assignment, you know."

We were in our bedroom, readying ourselves for an evening out with my aunt, Hetty, and her gentleman friend, Herbert Gilliam. Actually, Bridget, my maid, and I had already finished my toilette, but George had returned home only recently, so I leaned against the bed while he stood before the mirror. His valet, Blakely, inserted the studs into his white shirtfront.

Blakely was a good head shorter than George, but it was a very attractive head indeed—adorned with reddish brown hair that dipped into a wave across his forehead. He also had dark brown eyes. Dare I call them soulful? Indeed, I would. I'd also call him wiry, as opposed to thin. Watching his hands attaching George's shirt studs made me think they'd be better applied to playing a piano or performing surgery. But that was just my fancy. I'd asked him once if he'd ever played the piano. He and George had had a jolly good laugh at the very thought of it.

"I don't know how I could have brought it home, dear," I said. "It's not sized for slipping into one's pocket. It wouldn't have fit in my bag, and I had no coat to drape over it. Considering that Jonathon Ashley must be scouring the house for it, I doubt I could have carried it out without him, or someone, noticing."

"I hope it's still there when you go back. If the girl stole it once, what's keeping her from taking it again and hiding it elsewhere? What makes you think you can trust her?"

"Well, that's the other problem, isn't it? She only just barely trusts me. For all she knows, I could have walked off with Lord Peter's priceless journal, never to be seen again."

Blakely adjusted George's white tie and took a step back, which put him beside me. We both crossed our arms and admired his work.

"He looks perfect, Blakely, as always."

"Flattery will get you nowhere," George said. "You ought to have brought the journal home."

"I was complimenting Blakely's work, not you."

"Flattery always works on me, ma'am." The valet grinned, his dark eyes sparkling with amusement. He was a charming devil, and I wondered for the umpteenth time if he and Bridget might become a couple and leave us behind as they pursued a hotel empire or some other business. Both were energetic, hard workers, and I knew Bridget, at least, had a wide ambitious streak.

"That's enough from you, old chap," George said as he crossed the room to me and held out his arm. "We may have a late evening, but there's no need to wait up for us."

I took George's arm and let him lead me downstairs. "We're a bit early," I said. "We're expected at half past seven."

"That gives us time for a drink before we leave, and you can tell me more about Miss Stover's suspicions." I'd already relayed almost everything she told me, so I suspected what he wanted to know was why I believed her.

We entered the drawing room, and George let go of my arm to pour us each a glass of brandy. I settled into the sofa facing the back garden.

"I have to admit that the difference between the Lady Winstead I saw Monday and today was vast. Monday she couldn't even hold herself upright in a chair, and today she was just a bit foggy. Well, very foggy. Still, if Kate truly did spend the night in her room, she may have saved her life."

"Assuming someone was trying to harm her." George joined me on the sofa and handed me a glass. "It's possible she's ill."

"If so, why didn't one of the Ashleys send for a doctor after what happened to her? I saw her letter to Kate in which she claims someone has stolen her jewelry. She never leaves the house, and the family are even keeping her friends from her."

"Only Lady Esther," George said.

I threw him a sidelong look. "How many friends do you suppose she has?"

He nodded in concession, and we both sipped our drinks.

"I'm only saying Kate's concerns are plausible, in my opinion."

"And?"

"And Lady Esther has asked me to find out what is happening with her friend. Kate's assessment of the situation may be correct, but I hesitate to tell Lady Esther until I feel more confident."

He frowned. "What do you propose doing, and how much will I dislike it?"

"Let me admit to Kate that I know who is investigating on behalf of the museum and convince her to give me the journal. I'll continue to work with her toward her presentation and keep an eye on Lady Winstead. If she knows I want to help her aunt, she may be more cooperative in the investigation. If we find out she's been lying to me and she stole the journal, intending to sell it, then you can have her arrested, and I will be your witness."

George held my gaze. "We'll take this day by day. If it appears you are in any danger, you'll leave the house immediately, with no argument, and not return."

"That sounds perfectly reasonable."

"Then I agree, and by the way, I get to determine if the danger exists."

I flapped my hand dismissively. "Fine. How much danger can I be in watching over one elderly woman?"

Dinner with Hetty and Gilliam was both delicious and lively. And convenient. We dined at Hetty's house—formerly mine—which was just next door. The chandelier glowed overhead, and there was a fire in the hearth, which made the small dining room perfectly cozy. This was the first time Hetty had hosted us for dinner, and my former housekeeper and cook, Mrs. Thompson, had outdone herself with the menu. Hetty had done the same with complementing wine choices.

Aunt Hetty's beau, Herbert Gilliam, owned and managed a theater in London and another in Paris. He'd been gone all week, preparing for the opening of a new play in his Paris venue, and was full of amusing stories of temperamental actors and last-minute problems with costumes and scenery. That he joked about such potential disasters, where another manager might complain vehemently, spoke to his love of his chosen profession.

He and Hetty had been keeping company since November, and I had come to the conclusion that he was quite the perfect match for her. She could never tolerate a man who had no purpose in life, but one who was dedicated to his business to the exclusion of all social activity would bore her to tears. Gilliam had the perfect balance: a successful businessman with an ability to enjoy life to the fullest. He was forty years of age, with closely cropped dark hair, a sturdy build, a mustache that curled upward at the tips, and hazel eyes, which always softened when he looked at Hetty.

Hetty was half a head shorter, all womanly curves, dark, wavy hair, and warm brown eyes. She was also very wealthy and had recently celebrated her fifty-first birthday. A woman of less confidence might wonder if Gilliam's interest was truly of a romantic nature or of a financial one. Frankly, any woman might wonder. Hetty had wondered. But not for long. It was Gilliam who had given her the confidence to trust his intentions, and I couldn't be happier for both of them. I had never seen her so gay as when she was in his company, and he put up with any number of obstacles, which included various members of my family, in order to spend time with her.

Together, they were delightful company.

"What play are we seeing tonight?" George asked. Though we'd finished our meal of sole, filet of beef, and sautéed spring vegetables, we remained at the dining table, nibbling on cheese and fruit.

"It's a musical." Gilliam refilled our wineglasses. "*Florodora.* I'm sure you've heard of it. It's playing at the Lyric."

"I have," I said. "But I thought Hetty told me the two of you have seen it already?"

Hetty laughed. "This will be our third time."

"A consequence of my occupation, I'm afraid," Gilliam said, with a chuckle that made his mustache bounce.

"Checking out the competition, are you?" George asked.

"Something like that. I'd love to stage the production in my Paris theater. The chorines would be wildly popular, but I can't decide if the lyrics would translate well."

"The chorines would be a smashing success in any theater and in any language." Hetty leaned back in her chair and held her hands before her, as if presenting a picture. "A sextet of beautiful young ladies all in pink ruffles, singing and brandishing parasols in time to the music."

"What they're wearing and brandishing is unimportant," I said. "They need only be beautiful young ladies to be a smashing success."

Hetty winked. "You could be right, but in this case, I think the music and . . . dancing, if you wish to call it that, helps."

"No *Florodora* girl could compare with you," Gilliam said very earnestly.

"Is that what they're called?" I asked. "*Florodora* girls sounds so exotic."

"In the play they are actually the English girls visiting the Island of Florodora, but they have taken on a life of their own beyond the play itself," Hetty said. "You'll understand when you see the show."

"Well, I do hope you decide to stage this musical in France, Gilliam. I'd love to cross the Channel and see one of your productions in Paris," I said.

"I keep asking Hetty to join me there." Gilliam raised his brows and reached for her hand.

Hetty took his hand, but she didn't respond to the hint. Instead, she turned to me. "We have been monopolizing the conversation all evening. How have you been occupying yourselves this week?"

I was quite certain George didn't want to discuss his investigation, so I told them about Miss Stover's presentation and her and Lady Esther's concern over Lady Winstead. I regretted it immediately as it brought a more somber tone to our jolly group.

"I hate to say it, but they might well be correct," Hetty said. "It's not uncommon, at least in America, to use laudanum to control an elderly relative. Sometimes those not so elderly. Husbands have used it to keep a wealthy wife placid, serene, and at home, while they go about spending her fortune."

George and Gilliam had drifted into a conversation of their own, so I was alone in my stunned disbelief. "Common, you say? How could they get away with such a thing? And how do you know about it?"

She gave me a look of confusion. "Are you not familiar with Nellie Bly and her articles in the *New York World*?"

"I've heard of Nellie Bly. I know she's a journalist, but what were these articles?"

She considered me for a moment. "Perhaps they were published when you were still too young to have an interest in such work, or your mother might have kept it away from you. Nellie Bly infiltrated the insane asylum on Blackwell's Island in the late eighties. She reported on the horrible conditions and the women who suffered them, many of whom were clearly not insane, at least not when they first arrived." She boggled her eyes. "A few months locked up in such a place could certainly drive one mad."

"If they were mentally fit, how did they end up there?" My shock at her revelation caused me to speak loud enough to draw the gentlemen's attention.

"They became"—Hetty fluttered her fingers—"inconvenient to their families. A husband might find his wife unmanageable, or perhaps he just wants to be rid of her but doesn't want to go through the trouble, expense, or scandal of a divorce. He passes a few coins to a doctor, and suddenly she's suffering from female hysteria and must be locked up for her own benefit."

Gilliam choked, and George's wineglass froze halfway to his lips while he stared at her in horror.

Hetty spread her hands apart. "Have none of you heard of this?"

"I haven't," I said. "I thought the practice of dropping an inconvenient wife off in the country and leaving her there was bad. Locked up in an asylum for the insane, those women would have been better off if their husbands had simply shot them."

Hetty blinked. "Well, that would no doubt be an awful life, but I like to think where there's life, there's hope."

"Considering this happened in America, and Lady Winstead's husband is dead," George said, "how do you see this as applying to her case?"

"It's not just husbands," Hetty replied. "Children have been known to do this, too. If the mother is in possession of a fortune and won't release it to them, laudanum can make her much more amenable. If they keep the woman drugged, they can take over her finances. In your Lady Winstead's case, the family are also giving her friends reason to believe she's been ill, so they'll stay away from her. If they keep the woman isolated, they can keep her under control."

"Your knowledge of this is very unsettling," Gilliam said, pushing his plate aside and eyeing her suspiciously.

She patted his hand. "I promise you it's only through reading. There's one positive note in that they probably don't intend to kill her, though I suppose that doesn't make a significant difference, does it? Dead or alive, they're likely to have her fortune at some point." Hetty paused, then brightened. "Unless she's left her money to someone else. Then they'd do everything in their power to keep her alive so they can continue living off her."

George and I frowned at each other while we considered the possibility. "Wouldn't the new viscount already be in possession of the family fortune?" I asked him. "Lord Peter could not have willed it away from his son and left it to his wife. Or could he? After all, he left all his relics to the British Museum."

"It would be highly unusual to disinherit his heir," George said. "Lord Peter's executor might be willing to tell me how his estate was settled since I'm looking into the theft of the journal. However, we ought not to get carried away in painting the Ashleys as manipulating monsters. There's no reason to assume they have done anything to Lady Winstead. Laudanum is very addictive. She might have started taking a few drops after Lord Peter died, increased her dose over time, took it for too long, and now cannot stop herself. Her situation may have nothing to do with the stepchildren."

"I'm not looking forward to telling Lady Esther either version of those stories." In fact, the very thought had me pushing my plate away.

Gilliam put his hands on the table and leaned forward. "I'm curious about one thing," he said. "If you learn that someone in the family is drugging her with laudanum, what do you intend to do about it?"

"That's a very good question," George said. "I'm not certain there's anything we, or rather Lady Esther, can do when all we have are suspicions. The Ashleys have a nurse attending her. They are her family. I don't think we have any standing to interfere unless we have actual proof."

"I don't know what sort of proof we can find," I said. "I hope this is all just the product of an overactive imagination on the part of Miss Stover."

"And Lady Esther," George added.

We left shortly thereafter and took Hetty's new carriage to the theater. The Lyric Theatre was not as lavishly appointed as Mr. Gilliam's, but our box was quite comfortable, and the view of the stage good, if distant. Hetty and I took the front seats, with George and Gilliam directly behind us.

"Did you happen to bring your opera glasses?" Hetty asked once we were settled. "I seem to have forgotten mine."

I pulled my pair from my small bag and handed them to her.

"Thank you, dear. Do let me know if you need to use them yourself."

I assured her I could see quite well just as the curtain rose. Thanks to Hetty, I was familiar with the play and settled in to enjoy myself. The music was lively, and the wit ran long. I tried to imagine how Lady Holyrood could be portrayed by a French actress. When the character Angela introduced her six dearest friends, I leaned forward in my seat.

It couldn't be.

I leafed through the program in my lap and in the darkness tried in vain to read the names of the actresses playing the English girls, or *Florodora* girls, as Gilliam had called them. In frustration, I nudged Hetty's arm, then frantically waved my hand until she placed the opera glasses in my palm, never tearing my gaze from the stage.

George leaned forward and whispered into my ear. "Are you well?"

I ignored him and put the glasses to my eyes. Scanning the stage for the face I thought I'd seen, I hoped I'd been mistaken. Finally, I found her again, and through the glasses there could be no mistake.

The first *Florodora* girl, Miss Daisy Chain, was actually Miss Katherine Stover.

Chapter Nine

I barely slept a wink all night, thinking of how I would confront Kate in the morning and wondering how she could possibly explain herself. Unfortunately, pounding my pillow and pondering the situation aloud kept George awake, as well.

"This has me questioning everything the woman has said to me," I whispered in the dark. "Is she even Lady Winstead's niece? Is she deceiving her and the entire Ashley family?"

"For what purpose?" George asked, attempting to cover a yawn.

"Money, what else? Perhaps she hopes to be named in Lady Winstead's will."

"If she's not Lady Winstead's niece, how would she have even known the woman was ill, let alone dying?"

"I don't know. Maybe she was acquainted with Nurse Plum and found out about her patient. No, that's not possible." I rolled to my back and plumped my pillow again. "Lady Winstead and the Ashleys have seen her before, so Kate must be her niece, but just knowing she's an actress makes me feel that she's created this entire drama from nothing. Now I think she must have stolen the journal, with a plan to sell it."

"The only buyer would be the British Museum, and I doubt she'd have the nerve to sell it to the rightful owner. I agree you should speak with her about her acting career, but the fact that she has one doesn't mean everything she told you was a lie."

I sighed heavily, and he rolled over to face me, giving up on sleep for the moment. "First of all, something is happening to Lady Winstead. You said yourself that you thought she'd dropped over dead the first time you saw her," he said.

"That's true. And, quite honestly, Kate seems to be the only one to care, aside from Lady Esther and myself. But what if that was just a display of her acting?" I gasped. "What if she is the one dosing Lady Winstead with laudanum?"

"Though it's possible, we don't know that yet. It's good to be suspicious, but it's far too early to decide that she is the culprit, if one exists. Further, we know the viscount was in no great hurry to get the journal to the British Museum in the first place, as if there were some reason he didn't want to hand it over. It wasn't until they pushed him that he claimed it was stolen."

"But it was stolen. Kate took it. That whole story about attracting the attention of the police on behalf of her aunt sounds so implausible to me now. How could I ever have believed her?"

"Frances, she might have been telling you the truth."

"How can I believe her when she's deceived me?" Looking into his eyes, I finally noticed, even in the darkness, how tired he was. I stroked his stubbled cheek. "I'm so sorry to keep you awake." I fluffed the coverlet and pulled it up to my chin. "Let's forget about this now and get some sleep."

With a groan, he sat up. "No, we might as well talk this out now. You keep thinking of Miss Stover as Lady Winstead's niece, and as such, you expect her to behave according to her station."

"I suppose I do. Is that wrong?"

"Who is Lady Winstead, or rather, who was she? A banker's

wife. Before that she was a woman of a middle-class family, as was her brother, who, I would imagine, never gained the wealth his sister did."

"That's true. Kate is a young woman of limited means. She probably never had any expectation of her aunt supporting her until recently. In fact, we don't know if Lady Winstead does intend to do so."

"Exactly, so why shouldn't a young, resourceful woman attempt to support herself by becoming an actress?"

"Because she is being presented to the queen. I am presenting her. What if word gets out that she's part of the cast of *Florodora* and can be seen nightly in the role of Miss Daisy Chain? The queen would be furious, Kate would be ruined, and the Ashley family would be embarrassed. I would be embarrassed."

George chuckled as he shook his head. "Other than the presentation, I assume you have no objections to a woman of Miss Stover's means working as an actress, or at any occupation."

"None at all, but she should have told me."

"You said yourself, just a few hours ago, that she barely trusted you. It's not as though you are being completely forthcoming with the people you are investigating, including Miss Stover. That's how it goes. If they knew you were checking up on them, you couldn't do your job. Unfortunately, you've forgotten the people on the other side of the investigation—for lack of a better word, let's call them the suspects—will also try to deceive you. You can't trust them, but neither do you want to alienate them. You must encourage them to trust you."

"How?"

"Carry on as you have been. I can't see that you have anything to lose in telling Miss Stover that you saw her in the play tonight, or last night, as I believe it is now. If you keep her secret, you may gain her trust, and I'd like her to trust you enough to allow you to bring that blighted journal home. Keep in mind, just because she's an actress doesn't mean she isn't concerned for her aunt's welfare. Chances are you are both working on the same side in that matter."

"But she can't continue acting if she plans to enter society."

"Tell her that. See what she has to say for herself."

"I suppose I could do that. Just because Lady Winstead wants her to have a presentation doesn't mean Kate does. And I suppose that doesn't mean she's lied to me about everything. All right, that's how I'll proceed."

Those were the words I repeated to myself all morning, as I waited for a reasonable hour to call on Kate. We were meant to meet with the modiste today, but that appointment was still over two hours off, so I lingered at the breakfast table longer than usual. That was where Fiona found me when she came to call.

"Good morning, Fiona. I've eaten already, but I can have something brought up for you—or just tea, if you prefer it to coffee." I held up the carafe.

"Coffee will be fine, thank you." Fiona placed her bag on the table and slipped into a chair. She was dressed in emerald green today, with a narrow and very vertical hat with a plume of the same hue.

"I'm surprised you made it through the doorway," I said, staring at the hat.

She lifted her hand to her head. "I didn't break the plume, did I?"

I laughed and poured her a cup of coffee. "I'm only teasing. You had plenty of clearance, and I do like that hat. It's a bit conservative for you, don't you think?"

She patted the back of her hair. "It is informal. But if you like it, I'd be happy to take you to the lovely little shop where I found it. Robert and his secretary are working on final details for my birthday gala. I was told to stay in my boudoir or leave the house, so I'm looking for something to do with myself. Please tell me you aren't busy."

"I'm afraid I am." I explained about sponsoring the niece of Lady Winstead. "We are scheduled with Madame Celeste today to choose her presentation gown and some other gowns for the season."

"Lovely! Invite me to join you. We shall have all the joy of designing a wardrobe and none of the expense."

"I'd like nothing more than to have your company, but I'm afraid I must have a serious conversation with Miss Stover first."

"Speaking of serious conversations, have you had a chance to speak with George about the future of our children's education?"

"I haven't found the right moment yet."

"Is he still grousing about your father's money?"

"Just the part about accepting it," I said. "I suppose I understand his position, but it makes mine difficult."

She studied me for a moment too long.

"What is it?" I asked.

"You may not fully understand how George feels in this matter." She took a few leisurely sips of her coffee, clearly debating what to tell me. Finally, she gave me her attention. "Do you remember my aunt Julia? She chaperoned us a few times when my mother wasn't available."

"Yes. A lovely woman. She lived with your family at the time, didn't she?"

"She did, though it wasn't much of a life. Her situation wasn't like your aunt Hetty's. She was a good dozen years younger than my father. By the time he became head of the family, she had already turned down several offers of marriage and rather came with the estate. Social life and what would be deemed a suitable marriage didn't interest her. She wanted to travel, to write, to paint. In her mind, a society marriage would put an end to those dreams. Unfortunately, with my father in charge of her life, she still couldn't attain them."

She sighed. "All of us children, well, George, Brandon, and I, could see she was miserable stuck in the country, but my father thought he was protecting her."

"Of course he did. Your father was a kind man."

"Indeed, but he had control of her life. She had a comfortable place to live, but she was so unhappy living a life someone else chose for her. On his death, Father settled a small annuity on her. Brandon doubled it when he became head of the family, and insisted she must do as she pleased from that day forward. She left the next day, and as far as I know, she is still traveling the world. We receive a letter from her now and then, but it's difficult to keep up a correspondence with her since she keeps moving."

I tapped my fingers on the table, wondering what she was getting at. "Perhaps I'm taking the wrong lesson from your story, but isn't this a situation where a bequest set her free?"

She paused for a moment, then laughed. "I suppose you're right, but by that time, George was already making a life of his own. I, too, was married and gone. All we recall was how Julia was kept from her heart's desire because my father controlled the purse strings. I'm certain that's what George remembers. But you are right. Perhaps reminding him of how Brandon's generosity gave her another chance will show him that accepting an inheritance does not always come with strings attached."

We chatted on for another half hour or so. At least Fiona did, while I mused about their aunt Julia. Hers was not simply a case of he who has the money rules the roost. There were also tradition and social pressure involved. George and I were beyond that. We were partners. He couldn't imagine that I or my father would use my father's fortune to control his actions. Could he?

Finally, I became aware of the time. I would have to collect Kate soon and said as much to Fiona.

"I won't pry, but once you've had this conversation with Miss Stover, you'll be off to see Madame Celeste, correct?"

"I believe we will." There was a chance Kate would tell me to go hang and we'd drop the presentation all together. But it was only a slight chance. "Why? Are you thinking of meeting us there?"

"That's exactly what I was thinking. Wouldn't that be diverting?"

She was right. And I did want to spend as much as possible of Lord Jonathon's fortune. Fiona's taste was different from mine, and with both of us there, Kate would have rather an original wardrobe. The prospect of an enjoyable afternoon made my immediate task seem less dreary.

"Yes," I said. "That is an excellent idea. Our appointment is at one o'clock."

Fiona smiled. "I'll be there ten minutes before one."

I wish I could have been as enthusiastic as Fiona about my afternoon, but in truth, I was very hesitant to continue working with Kate. That she stole the journal was indisputable, and now I felt somewhat foolish for believing her explanation. Was she telling me the truth, or was she just a good actress? I'd do my best to follow George's advice and take everything she told me with a large grain of salt.

I didn't believe Jonathon would try to foist Aggie on us. Kate wouldn't be alone, after all. But just in case, I brought Bridget. I could always argue that she'd serve the same purpose. I took it as a good sign when I was greeted by Andrew Ashley rather than his father. He was in the hall when the butler opened the door.

His youthful good looks became more engaging when he

smiled at me. "Mrs. Hazelton. How good to see you, though I suppose you are really here for Kate, are you not?"

"Indeed. She and I have an appointment with the modiste today. Is she about?"

The young man collected his hat and gloves from the butler. "I know precisely where she is—in with Grandmama. Kate is beside herself because Nurse Plum is late." He tipped the bowler he'd just donned. "I, too, am late for an appointment, or I would see you upstairs myself. Sadly, I must leave that honor to Fuller."

He bid me good day and stepped around me and out the door. Fuller invited me to follow him to Lady Winstead's room. With Nurse Plum late, it could take longer than anticipated to collect Kate. I glanced at Bridget, who seemed to sense the problem.

"Shall I wait in the carriage, ma'am?"

I agreed, then repressed a sigh and followed Fuller to the stairs. I was spending more time in Lady Winstead's room than in the public areas of the house. "I was under the impression Nurse Plum lived in," I said as we ascended.

"Yesterday was her half day, ma'am," he replied. "She generally spends that night at her home."

"Of course." It made sense that the nurse would have a home of her own. Lady Winstead had become her patient only sometime within the past few months. She must have lived somewhere before that.

Fuller knocked at Lady Winstead's door and stepped aside for me to enter the dimly lit room.

Kate was seated in a chair near the bed, where Lady Winstead lay. Her skin was almost as white as the sheet pulled up to her chin, but her chest rose and fell in a steady rhythm.

I moved to Kate's side. "Is your aunt unwell again?"

"She's a little better now." Kate spoke without looking up.

"I had difficulty waking her earlier this morning." She glanced up at me, looking tired herself. "It is still morning, isn't it?"

"For a few more minutes. Has she eaten anything? Perhaps that would help."

Kate rose to her feet, covering a yawn with her hand. "It did help," she said. "I managed to convince her to eat something about an hour ago. Before that, I feared she might choke on it."

"With both you and the nurse gone, is it possible someone came in and gave her too much laudanum?" Of course, the woman might have dosed herself. I moved to the table near the window where Nurse Plum kept a glass, a pitcher and a bottle of laudanum. I picked up the bottle. Pulling back the heavy draperies to let in some light, I could see the level in the brown glass bottle had barely moved since the last time I checked it.

Kate had come up beside me. "I noticed that, too, but if someone is drugging her, wouldn't it make sense that they'd have their own supply of laudanum? They must have given it to her earlier last night."

She had a point. Laudanum was easy enough to obtain. "Did you check on her when you came home last night?"

"I did." She glanced at me in confusion. "How did you know I was out last night?"

"I was in the audience at the Lyric Theatre. You were quite good as Miss Daisy Chain, but you must see that now I question your performance as Katherine Stover."

She parted her lips to speak, then stopped herself and eyed me warily. "You don't for a moment believe I would hurt her?" She threw a glance toward her aunt.

"I don't want to believe that, but you are making it very difficult to trust you." I placed the bottle back on the table and held up my index finger. "You stole Lord Peter's journal from Jonathon."

"You know why I did that."

"I know what you told me, and for all I know, that story was simply to make me suspicious of the Ashleys." I held up a second finger, then added a third, as two more offenses came to me at once. "You lied to me about Mr. Montague, and you are practicing a deceit on your aunt and her stepchildren. The very people who have taken you in."

She looked genuinely shocked. "I am doing no such thing."

"Indeed?" I cast a glance at Lady Winstead and lowered my voice, though since she was snoring, it was unlikely she'd hear us. "Does anyone in the family know you're an actress? Does Lady Winstead know?"

"Oh, that. I suppose I am deceiving them, but there's no harm in it, and they're unlikely to ever find out. No one in the theater knows I'm Katherine Stover, either. I work under a different name."

"I managed to find out."

She moved a step closer to me. "I don't perform every night. I am only an understudy. If one of the chorines can't make a performance, I go on in her place. As for the Ashleys . . ." She released a little snort. "It's not difficult to deceive them. They pay little attention to anything that does not directly involve themselves. Yesterday was only my second performance, anyway, so the chances that anyone else saw me and would recognize me later—"

"Are still not insignificant, but that's a different problem." I held up a hand to stop the conversation from going astray. "Right now, the only reason I find the Ashleys more suspicious than you is that Lady Winstead's"—I searched for the right term—"let's call them health problems began before you arrived." I shrugged. "And her missing jewelry."

"Well, that's rather meager encouragement, but does that mean you will work with me to help my aunt?"

"It does, and to begin, you cannot leave her alone at night

again. Whoever is drugging her has little opportunity during the day, when the servants are about and when Nurse Plum is here." I paused. "Unless, of course, she is our culprit. But at night, I fear Lady Winstead is fair game."

"I understand," she said. "When I came home last night and saw my aunt like this, I knew I could not keep leaving her alone." She reached out and took my hand. "My acting doesn't change anything I've told you. I still believe someone is drugging her and stealing from her. I worry that they will try to kill her. I've already sent a note to the manager to tell him I won't be available for at least a few weeks."

"A few weeks should do." Then I recalled her presentation and the reason I was here. I seated myself at the table and indicated she should take the other chair. "Lady Winstead is my primary concern, but I am ostensibly here to oversee your presentation. Do you intend to continue acting afterward? Is this a career you've chosen? I don't mean to be cruel, but as your sponsor, I am introducing you as a part of the upper crust. You cannot have a career."

At least not so publicly.

She groaned, cradling her forehead in her hands. "This was all meant to be so much easier. I had hoped to have this conversation with my aunt when I arrived here. I understand she may have aspirations for me, but high society is not something I ever aspired to. I love acting, and you said yourself I am reasonably good at it. I would like to pursue it and hoped to gain her approval, but since I arrived, she has not been well enough to fully comprehend anything I tell her." She raised her head and swiped away a few stray tears. "My aunt is my only family. She has grandiose plans for me. I wish to let her down easily and, hopefully, to maintain good relations with her."

Well, of course. After all, it would be difficult to claim an inheritance if Lady Winstead disowned her. And now I was being cruel, or at least unfair. As George had pointed out, Kate was simply working for her living. There was nothing wrong, or even unusual, in her hope of a financial gift from her only relative.

Unless she intended to murder her for it.

And I still didn't know if that was her intention. I might have one eye on the Ashleys, but the other was still on Kate.

"We have two weeks before the queen's drawing room," she said. "With me caring for my aunt, perhaps she will recover, I can explain everything to her, and we can dispense with the society nonsense. If she will not accept my career choice, then perhaps I can find some way to take the role she has set out for me and involve myself in the theater in some other capacity. Perhaps as a patron of the arts."

Either this was a very good performance or she was sincere. I felt rather sorry for her. If she married into the aristocracy, she was unlikely to ever be involved with the theater. Still, I had to keep in mind that she might be lying to me and remember George's advice to keep her on my side.

"If someone in this house came in here last night to drug Lady Winstead, then you have chosen a poor hiding place for the journal."

She frowned, as if confused. "The journal?"

"I propose you let me take it home. I know the person investigating on behalf of the British Museum, and I promise to at least attempt to enlist their aid in Lady Winstead's case. It would help if I could give them the journal."

She gave me a wry smile. "I assume it would also help in convincing you that I'm trustworthy."

"Perhaps," I said.

When Kate went to the bureau, I moved to the side of Lady Winstead's bed. Her color already seemed to have improved since I arrived. I reached across the bed, took her hand, and was relieved to find it warm. "I think she really means to help you," I whispered. When her eyes opened and connected with my gaze, I leaned closer. "Did someone come into your room last night? Did they give you laudanum?"

There was no recognition in her gaze, and within seconds her eyes closed. "Good girl," she said, her voice barely discernible.

So much for that tactic. I straightened and saw Kate staring at me, a look of confusion on her face.

"The journal's gone," she said.

Chapter Ten

⌐≈⌐

We had no time to search. Our appointment with Madame Celeste was fixed, and now Fiona would be waiting for us, too. But we couldn't leave Lady Winstead alone with a family who might be trying to kill her.

"The dressmaker will have to wait for another day," Kate said, raising her arms helplessly.

"Just because the nurse isn't in this room doesn't mean she isn't in the house." There was a bellpull by the table. I rang, hoping Fuller would respond to my call. Meanwhile, I rummaged through the other drawers in the bureau while Kate paced the room.

"It must have been the viscount who found it. Wouldn't you agree? Do you think it was he who drugged my aunt?"

"We'll find out about the former soon enough," I said and closed the last drawer. George was right. I should have insisted on taking the journal home when I had the chance. "If the viscount found the journal, I would assume he'd hand it over to the British Museum. Determining if he drugged your aunt could take more investigation."

Fuller arrived in the doorway. "How may I help you, ma'am?" I moved out to the hallway and inquired about Nurse Plum. "I'm afraid she's still not here," he said.

"Is there any way to contact her?" My mind was planning ahead even as I asked the question. Someone had to stay with Lady Winstead, but I could go on to Madame Celeste's myself, meet with Fiona, and make a new appointment for Kate. Lord Jonathon wouldn't be happy with Kate for putting off the visit, and as it was, we weren't giving Madame Celeste much time to make the gown, but I couldn't think of another choice.

As if my thoughts had conjured the man himself, Jonathon approached from the other end of the hallway with Vi Ashley.

"Something amiss with Lady Winstead again?" Vi had a copy of the *Lady* in her hand and used the thin periodical to point into the room.

"I'm afraid there's something amiss with Nurse Plum. She hasn't arrived yet. Kate and I have an appointment, but we are hesitant to leave Lady Winstead alone." I decided not to mention last night's possible drugging.

Jonathon waved a hand. "If that's all, Violet can sit with her." He turned to glare at her when she made a small noise of disgust. "Nurse Plum is generally reliable," he said. "I'm sure she'll be here soon. Besides, you have your reading material to pass the time."

With a sigh, Vi stepped around me and walked into the room. "He's right. The two of you shouldn't miss your appointment."

Satisfied that his work was done, Jonathon inclined his head in my direction and descended the stairs.

I turned an inquiring glance at Fuller, who still waited by the door. "I'll have a note sent to Nurse Plum's home," he said before heading for the baize door and the servants' stairway at the end of the hall.

Jonathon might believe he had solved our problems, but whether she was our culprit or not, I wouldn't leave a potted plant in Violet Ashley's care. This arrangement would not do. I stepped back into the bedroom, where Vi had already seated herself in the bedside chair and was flipping through her magazine.

"Fuller is sending a message to Nurse Plum," I said. "I'm certain she will arrive shortly." I stepped up next to Kate, who glanced from Vi to me and back, looking anything but comfortable with the arrangement.

"I'm not—"

I stopped whatever Kate was about to say with a nudge and a shake of my head. "Wait," I whispered.

With a scowl, Vi closed her magazine and glanced up at the two of us. "Is he gone?" she asked.

"Lord Jonathon?" I widened my eyes in the hope of looking innocent. "Yes, he just went downstairs—to his office, I assume."

"Good." Vi came to her feet and crossed to the door. "As if I have time to watch an old woman sleep." She opened the door a crack and peeked out before turning back to us. "Ta-ta, ladies," she said and slipped out of the room.

Kate's mouth drooped open as she watched her go. "You knew she wouldn't stay. How?"

"Good deeds aren't really part of Vi's nature," I said.

"I can't say I'm sorry she's gone, but we're still left with no one to watch over my aunt."

That wasn't entirely true. We did have someone, though I hated to ask her. I heaved a sigh and held up a finger. "Give me a moment."

Sometimes I wondered why Bridget put up with me. I've asked her to lie for me and spy for me, and after leaving her waiting in the carriage for thirty minutes, I enlisted her aid in sitting with Lady Winstead for me. As usual, she agreed graciously. I truly didn't know what I'd do without her.

With Bridget on duty, Kate and I were free to leave. My fingers were crossed that upon our return, no one would even realize she'd been there instead of Vi. Meanwhile, we had to rush to get to our appointment on time.

Madame Celeste had come to my attention roughly a year ago, when I needed a new wardrobe and had little to spend. She had managed to transform several of my old gowns into fashionable creations any woman would be proud to wear, and had charged me a mere pittance for her labors. I liked to return the favor by bringing in well-funded customers. Madame was perhaps in her mid-fifties, with a rounded figure and dark hair that was graying at the temples in a suspiciously artistic way. She was a Frenchwoman who had lived in England enough decades to have nearly lost her accent, but knew it lent her a certain cachet in her chosen field.

She greeted us and drew us into her antechamber/office/fitting room off the general shop area, where I found Fiona awaiting us. I introduced Kate to Fiona and Madame, who set about measuring her right away. Fiona eyed Kate with interest while Madame pelted us with questions.

"When is the presentation to be? Is the young lady married or single? Will we be needing anything beside the presentation gown? I have a gold silk that would be oh, so perfect with the mademoiselle's complexion!"

"Yes, we will be needing a few gowns in addition to the presentation gown," I said, taking a seat along one wall of the small room.

Fiona settled in next to me. "I'm not so sure gold would work for her, Madame. I think some shade of violet would be better. Something with bluish undertones."

I couldn't have disagreed more. In fact, the suggestion was utter rubbish.

Madame clapped her hands to her cheeks and gasped. "Never blue," she said. "Warm tones only."

I cut a glance to Fiona, who gazed through narrowed eyes at Kate, tapping a gloved finger against pursed lips. "I'm just not sure gold would be the thing. Perhaps if I saw her in the color."

With a flick of her wrist, Madame snapped her measuring tape free of Kate's waist and draped it around her own neck. Then she turned on her heel and left the room, presumably to retrieve the fabric.

"What was that all about?" I asked Fiona.

But she was on her feet, moving toward Kate until they were practically nose to nose. "I know you," she said, her eyes alight with excitement. "You are Daisy Chain from *Florodora.*"

Kate covered her mouth with her hands and glanced at me for help.

I groaned.

Fiona ignored us both and bounced on her toes in excitement. "I can't believe I know a *Florodora* girl. You must be thrilled to be part of such a wonderful production."

Fiona turned to me, full of dimples and smiles. I gave up the fleeting hope of convincing her she was mistaken. I put a finger to my lips and stepped closer to them so we could speak quietly.

"How do you know?" I asked her.

"I saw the play, of course." She took hold of Kate's hand. "And you were quite delightful, my dear."

Kate chewed on a fingernail. "I'm sorry, Frances. I suppose there's no reason to go forward with this appointment."

Fiona's smile disappeared. "Whatever are you talking about?" She turned to me. "What is she talking about? Why would you no longer have use for a new gown?"

Was she serious? "Why? Because it's not just a new gown. I brought Miss Stover here for a presentation gown. For a presentation to the queen."

"What an honor, my dear!" Fiona clasped her hands together at her breast. "I knew Her Majesty adored the theater, but such a distinction is rare indeed. Is she acknowledging the entire cast?"

"You misunderstand, Fiona. Miss Stover's presentation is meant to be part of one of the queen's drawing rooms. She is being presented as a daughter of a country gentleman and the niece of Viscountess Winstead. Her Majesty will be given to believe that Miss Stover"—I scowled as I tried to recall the exact phrase—"wears the white flower of a blameless life."

"Oh." Fiona let her hands fall to her sides. "I suppose since I recognized her, you fear others will, as well, and that someone will reveal to the queen that Miss Stover is an actress."

"Exactly. The queen may love the theater, but I suspect she'd very much resent such a deception. It's too large a risk."

Fiona gave Kate a speculative glance. "I don't suppose you'd consider giving up your career as an actor," she said.

"I have given it up."

This was becoming ridiculous. "You have given it up temporarily. If anyone recognizes you, they will check with the theater. Someone there will give you away." The despair in her eyes broke my heart. And took me by surprise.

"I thought life as an idle aristocrat wasn't what you wanted, anyway?" I said.

"It isn't." She blotted her eyes with a handkerchief. "But my aunt wanted it so badly for me. At least she wanted the presentation. I hate that I'll disappoint her." She lowered the handkerchief and gazed at me. "May I be honest?"

What kind of question was that? In my opinion, honesty was far past due. "Kate, if I haven't made it abundantly clear, I'd very much prefer that you be honest with me."

"My aunt was always kind to my father and me, but it wasn't until he passed that she began taking an interest in my future.

Prior to that, I had no reason to believe that she would. I assumed I'd have to support myself."

"Of course you did, you poor dear." Fiona turned her lost kitten gaze my way. "She was an orphan, Frances."

"I am not unsympathetic to her plight, Fiona."

"I'm not trying to play upon your sympathies," Kate said.

Oh, heaven forbid!

"I just want you to understand my choices. Our home wasn't far from Plymouth, where I managed to get roles in local theater productions. I never used my own name, because the people in our village would have expected me to be at home, mourning my father. When my aunt offered her assistance, she made it plain that she expected me to have a presentation and take part in society. But I wanted this role so badly, and since no one ever recognized me from my prior performances, I thought I could get away with it. I'm afraid if she learns I'm not eligible for a presentation, her disappointment will cause her to withdraw her assistance."

Fiona looked at me as if I'd just kicked a dog. "You don't want to be the cause of a rift between Miss Stover and her aunt, do you?"

Had she taken leave of her senses? "Neither do I want to deceive the queen. Besides, I suspect Lady Winstead will forget about that disappointment if we concentrate on her recovery." I turned to Kate. "She'll be grateful that you took care of her."

"What is wrong with Lady Winstead? Apart from being rather crotchety, that is?" Fiona asked.

"Well, I doubt being poisoned puts anyone in a good mood." Kate placed her hands on her hips.

Fiona took a step back. "Poison? Who is poisoning her?"

I squeezed Kate's fingers, making her glance my way, and made a cutting gesture, hoping she would understand and drop this conversation.

Instead, she stared blankly at me. "Oh. I assumed you told her," she said.

For heaven's sake, had she no understanding of discretion? "I did not."

She frowned in confusion. "But she's your friend. I just assumed . . ."

Fiona glared daggers. "Yes, Frances. I am your friend."

"You are my very dear friend, Fiona, which is why I expect you to understand that when I'm told something in confidence, I keep it confidential, as I have done many times for you."

She looked somewhat mollified. "I suppose that's to your credit. But I'm sure you told George."

"Well, he is part of the investigation—" And now I'd just betrayed George's involvement. I massaged my throbbing head. "We must drop this topic immediately. Too much has been revealed to too many already. Madame Celeste will be back—"

"She is already here." Madame's voice sang out as she opened the door.

I bit my tongue to avoid wailing in frustration.

Madame gave me a smile as she moved between Fiona and Kate, carrying her fabric. "You must know by now, Mrs. Hazelton, that if I repeated anything I heard during the course of my work, I would very soon have no work." She glanced at me before opening the length of the gold silk. "I intend to forget this conversation as soon as I make one observation."

All three of us raised our brows in question.

"If Lady Winstead is unwell and confined to home, and the other Ashleys are in mourning and unable to go out in society, how will any of them know if you and Miss Stover actually arrive at the queen's drawing room or not?"

Fiona glanced at me, her eyes filled with wonder. "You can send your regrets to the Lord Chamberlain, tell the Ashleys you're going to the palace, but instead you come to my house.

You'd want to be sure to take your own carriage, so their groom or footman doesn't find out."

Lovely. Now I was meant to deceive the entire family. Well, more than I already was. "There's usually a notice in the court circular about the presentations," I said, knowing this was a feeble protest.

"None of them will look for it," Kate said. "Even if they did, I can rant about the journalist who left me off the list."

Madame Celeste returned to her business as if she had not suggested this insanity. She draped the silk over Kate's shoulders and invited us to look. "It's perfect," she said. "If you buy nothing else, you must have something made of this silk."

Chapter Eleven

⤸

Fiona insisted on returning to Ashley House with us and sent her own carriage on home. Kate agreed that we might just as well let Fiona in on the entire story, since she'd heard so many pieces of it and since she could indeed be trusted to keep the details to herself. Now the question was, Where to begin? I told her of Kate's concern, which I shared, about Lady Winstead and the possibility that someone in the family was keeping her drugged with laudanum, possibly with the intent to kill her. Then I moved on to the journal—a subject I had to handle carefully. I explained its contents and that it was meant to be given over to the British Museum but had gone missing.

"Kate and I had seen the journal in Lady Winstead's room, but it is no longer there."

Fiona wasted no time delivering her opinion. "You can't leave poor Kate . . . May I call you Kate?" At Kate's nod, Fiona continued. "You can't leave her to protect her aunt and find this journal on her own. Preparing Kate for her presentation is your excuse to be in the house, so I don't see the harm in conducting the ruse. Surely, you can't be worried about playing a small deceit upon the Ashleys." Her lips formed a grimace, clearly displaying her opinion of the family.

Actually, I was embarrassed by how little lying to the Ashleys bothered me. Particularly since Jonathon had been so rude and insulting. I was more concerned with recovering the journal for George. Then there was the problem of Lady Winstead. If I gave up on even pretending Kate planned to go forward with her presentation, I'd be giving up on Lady Winstead, too—leaving her with less protection from the Ashleys. And worse, I'd have to tell Lady Esther I'd done so.

That was a truly daunting prospect!

"You are right, Fiona. Kate and I will continue as if her presentation is drawing near. At least for now." I directed my attention to Kate. "If nothing else, that will give you more time to search for the journal." I turned back to Fiona. "You should be aware that we are not meant to know it's missing."

"How do you know it's missing?" she asked with a raised brow.

"I'd rather not go into that at the moment." Never, if I could help it. "But I do know Lord Jonathon suspects Kate of taking it, as well as Nurse Plum."

"Was it just the two of us he suspected?" Kate asked.

I gave the question some thought. "Perhaps not, but everyone else in the house is family or trusted servants. It's understandable he'd suspect the outsiders."

"The nurse strikes me as a very likely suspect," Fiona said. "Surely, she knew who Lord Peter was, and it's equally certain this journal would be easily identifiable as his work. Presuming she didn't know about the bequest to the British Museum, why wouldn't she take one look at it and see it as worth a pretty penny? You say it was in Lady Winstead's bureau drawer, so she might assume no one would miss it."

The creaking of the carriage springs filled the silence while I considered the possibility that Nurse Plum was our thief, and gazed out the window at the hustle and bustle on the street. A carriage beside us pulled forward, revealing the greengrocer's wagon next to the curb. Men and women walked along the pavement, dashed in and out of shops, or peered through the windows, just going about their normal days. I wish I had more normal days.

"If Jonathon suspected Nurse Plum of stealing the journal," Kate said, "wouldn't he be more concerned by her tardiness?"

With a scuff of wheels, we turned a corner, leaving the businesses behind and entering the residential neighborhood of the Ashleys.

Fiona heaved a sigh, and I dragged my gaze from the window. "She is missing," Fiona said. "The journal is missing. Do you really think that's a coincidence?"

"We don't know that she is missing," I said. "Only that she was behind schedule."

Fiona glanced out the window. "I suppose we're about to find out. We've arrived."

"That was fast." Kate stared out the window while the carriage settled. She curled her fingers into a fist. Working up the fortitude to enter the house? "I suppose the two of you are eager to be off?"

"And never find out if the intrepid Nurse Plum is missing or not?" Fiona looked aghast. "Of course I'll come in."

"You've forgotten the family is in mourning," I said.

"That's right. I suppose I must wait here." Fiona looked crestfallen. "But you can go in," she said to me. "I still wish to know about the nurse."

"I'll come in to check on Lady Winstead and collect Bridget," I told Kate, even though I, too, wanted to know if Nurse Plum had arrived yet.

My spine stiffened when we reached the door. Sympathy pulled at my emotions for this woman without a friend in the house save the one she hoped to protect. I glanced at Kate when she pulled her shoulders back. Of course, she could be the one drugging Lady Winstead. What a muddle.

Fuller met us in the hall, but from the cacophony of voices, it was clear that everyone was gathered in the drawing room. Kate and I shared a glance and ventured forth. When we entered the room, I saw that I was incorrect. It was only the three gentlemen.

"I don't wish to intrude," I said, still in the doorway, with Kate at my shoulder. "I am, however, curious to learn if Nurse Plum has arrived."

Lord Jonathon came to his feet and motioned us inside, which led me to believe things were not as they should be. I followed Kate into the room and took a seat next to Si. She remained on her feet, weaving her fingers together.

"I take it there's a problem with Nurse Plum," I said.

"She never arrived," Jonathon said. "We've contacted the agency to find out what happened to her nearly an hour ago, and we've yet to hear from them."

"How is Lady Winstead faring?" She was the patient, after all.

"Vi's been with her all morning," Si said, making Kate smirk, "so I assume she is well." He tsked and shook his head. "This is a task Vi has little time or taste for. I'm certain it brings up memories of nursing her mother in her last days, and Mrs. Godfrey was not as difficult a patient as our stepmother. I hope this agency will send another nurse tomorrow if Nurse Plum is indisposed and unable to come."

"I'd be happy to take care of my aunt," Kate said. "She really is no trouble, and it's the least I can do to repay her kindness to me."

"That will do for a day or two." Jonathon clasped his hands behind his back and took a broad stance. "But this is really a job for a nurse, someone who can look after her all the time."

"Perhaps it's time we considered a sanatorium," Si suggested.

After Hetty's explanation of Nelly Bly's research into such a facility, I felt suddenly ill at the thought of Lady Winstead locked up and possibly mistreated.

Kate blanched. "I can provide care for her around the clock. There truly is no need to move her to some institution, where she will be friendless. Here she has family and her familiar things."

Jonathon began shaking his head before she finished speaking. "Very thoughtful, Katherine, but you will not have time for such work."

"Whatever do you mean? What is taking up my time?"

"The very thing your aunt wanted you to do," he said. "Making your curtsy to the queen, then finding a suitable husband."

Kate gave him a look of impatience. "That can wait."

"It most certainly cannot wait," Jonathon countered. "Do you suppose Mrs. Hazelton is at your beck and call? Is she expected to cancel your presentation and arrange another audience with the queen?"

"I honestly believe my aunt would prefer having me to take care of her than spending my time finding a husband."

"Can't agree with you there," Si said. "She's quite the traditionalist."

"I do agree with Kate on one point," Andrew said, causing us all to look at him in surprise. "A sanatorium is a cold place. Lady Winstead is not out of her head. She would feel the absence of the familiar and of family. However little she cares for us, she is family. I'd be in favor of hiring a new nurse."

"Before you do any of those things," I said, "it might be best to wait until you know if Nurse Plum is able to return to work soon. You may find there is no real problem, just a temporary issue. Did Fuller receive a reply to the message he sent her?"

Jonathon's brows shot up. "Fuller sent her a message?" He moved to the bellpull and gave it a tug. "I wasn't even aware we knew where she lived."

"While we wait for Fuller," he continued, holding up his index finger, "there is another issue you are not aware of. My father's journal has been stolen. With Nurse Plum missing, of course my suspicions turn to her. I'm willing to wager she has it in her possession and plans to sell it to the highest bidder."

Si looked at him as if he were crazy. "Father's journal? Who would want it but the British Museum? If she's fool enough to contact them for money, they are more likely to set the police on her than to pay up."

Jonathon frowned. "There could be any number of publishers who would be interested in obtaining it. Father was an explorer of some renown."

"If she has taken it, it's no longer our problem, is it?" Andrew said. "Let the museum handle it from here. Though I suppose we wouldn't want her back in the house once she's stolen from us." He shrugged. "In that case we could hire a new nurse."

I was beginning to consider seventeen-year-old Andrew as the most sensible person in the family. The nurse may well have stolen the journal, but this conversation was giving me a headache.

A tap sounded at the door, and Fuller stepped inside.

"Ah, Fuller," Jonathon said, approaching the butler. "Have you heard from Nurse Plum in response to your message?"

"I'm afraid the boy was unable to deliver the message, my lord. No one was at home."

Jonathon clasped his hands behind his back and surveyed the rest of us. "There, you see? It's just as I said."

Before any further discussion could ensue, I came to my feet. "I'm afraid I must return home," I said. "And I'd like to look in on Lady Winstead. Kate, will you walk me up?"

"Of course."

Fuller stepped out to the entry hall with us. I stopped him before he could return to his duties.

"Would you be so kind as to write down the nurse's address for me?"

"Yes, madam. I'll have it for you when you leave."

He left the entry hall with my thanks, and Kate and I went up the stairs at a trot.

"Do you think Simon is right and Vi really has been sitting with Lady Winstead all morning?" she asked.

"I find that hard to believe. It's more likely that Jonathon told Si he left Vi with their stepmother, and he simply assumed she stayed there." Still, I crossed my fingers when I pushed open the door, and breathed easier when I found only Bridget with Lady Winstead.

Bridget reported that Lady Winstead had slept fitfully, waking every fifteen minutes or so to growl something unintelligible at her, then falling back asleep.

Her ladyship's color seemed improved, and her breathing sounded regular, so Bridget and I took our leave. The footman at the front door handed me a folded note card with Nurse Plum's address.

I had completely forgotten that Fiona waited in the carriage. When Jack, our driver, opened the door, I started at the sight of her, smiling and eager, as if she were having the jolliest of adventures. She slid across the seat, and Bridget and I climbed inside.

"I have one more stop to make. Shall we take you home first?" I said.

"Heavens no. I assume this has something to do with the nurse? Still not shown up? Do you plan to call on her?"

"I do."

"Then, by all means, I'd love to accompany you."

I gave the nurse's address to Jack, and he closed the door. I had Fiona updated before we even pulled away from the curb.

"That is far less intriguing than I'd expected," she said. "The woman is probably unwell and unable to answer the door. But

I'm still glad I'm going. This gives me a chance to apologize for encouraging Kate in her stage career."

I waved a hand. "Her career choices are hers to make as far as I'm concerned. But that choice means she'll have to forgo her presentation. I doubt she cares, but only hates to disappoint her aunt."

"You should bring her to my party."

I gave her a long look. "You recognized her. I recognized her. How will you feel if one of your guests points her out as a *Florodora* girl? How will she feel?"

Fiona tsked. "Should that highly unlikely event occur, I will make it clear I knew already and no one had better dare insult her in my home. As for Kate, it is a far safer venue than the queen's drawing room."

She made a good point. "I'll extend the invitation. A look at society might help her decide which future she prefers."

"Lady Winstead never took a great role in society," Fiona mused. "Why would she wish that on her niece?"

"I have no idea, and I'm afraid the woman is in no position to explain it to me. Perhaps it's time I report in to Lady Esther. I had hoped to provide her with more information, but she may well be able to tell me something about Lady Winstead's intentions toward her niece."

Fiona gave me a sidelong look. "Will you tell her Kate wants to be an actress?"

"I'm not sure about that part."

"She might actually make a better marriage as a *Florodora* girl than as a debutante, you know. Each one of the *Florodora* girls from the American production married millionaires."

I turned to her in surprise. "Married them?"

Her smile beamed. "The men were reportedly overwhelmed by their beauty."

"I'm not sure that sentiment would translate to marriage within the British aristocracy."

"True. They often offer a completely different situation. But she could always go to New York and take her chances there." Fiona glanced out the window. "It almost seems as though we are headed that far ourselves. We've just crossed the Thames. Where does this woman live?"

"In Lambeth. As for Miss Stover, I'd prefer she stay where she is until we learn more about her aunt's condition. Is Lady Winstead simply ill, or is someone making her so?"

Fiona's mouth popped open in surprise. "You surely don't suspect Kate has anything to do with that, do you?"

"I suspect all of them, including Nurse Plum. Lady Winstead is clearly under the influence of laudanum. Each one of them has had the opportunity to provide her with a lethal dose, and I'm beginning to think someone is trying to do just that. The problem is that I can't watch over her all the time."

Bridget let out a fretful squeak.

"Don't worry, Bridget," I said. "I wouldn't do that to you." She looked skeptical.

"At least not a second time."

"What could the nurse have to gain from drugging Lady Winstead?" Fiona asked.

"Possibly a payment from someone in the family."

She recoiled. "That's a horrible thought."

I silently dwelt on that thought until the carriage rocked to a stop.

"Shall I come with you?" Fiona asked.

"It should take only a moment to learn if she is well and intends to return to her work," I said, wishing I'd given this more thought. "Though I'd hoped to look around for the journal, that's as likely to happen as her confessing that she's trying to murder her patient."

Fiona sighed. "Fine. I'll wait here with Bridget, then."

I stepped out on the street, in front of a tidy row of single-bay houses, which I suspected were divided into flats. Many flats. I found the correct address, climbed the steps, and pushed through the common door into a dimly lit foyer filled with doors. Muffled voices, clatter, and the aroma of an unidentifiable dinner indicated that life went on behind them. My decision about which flat might belong to Nurse Plum was easily made when I saw the stocky, blue-coated constable posted at an open door along the back wall. It looked as though Nurse Plum had a good reason for her tardiness.

The constable stiffened as I approached him.

"I'm looking for Nurse Plum," I said. "Is this her flat?"

He tipped his head to the side. "Do you have some business with her, ma'am?"

"I'm here to check on her welfare."

I heard a shuffle just inside the flat. "Is that you, Frances?"

If I was surprised to find the police at the nurse's home, I was even more surprised to find George there. He poked his head through the doorway. "I'm afraid your welfare call is a bit belated. Nurse Plum has been murdered."

Chapter Twelve

George and I returned to the carriage to inform Fiona that poor Nurse Plum was no longer missing and to send her and Bridget home. I would stay on with George. The carriage pulled away, and we walked back to the nurse's flat. My attention was caught by the squealing of two small boys swinging on a rope slung over the crossbars of the lamppost, while two more bounced on their toes nearby, awaiting their turns. Amid death, life goes on.

And I was bursting with curiosity.

"I assume your presence here has something to do with the journal," I said to George, "but how did you know to come here? How did you know Nurse Plum had been murdered?"

He linked his fingers with mine and brought my hand to his lips. "I love that I can still impress you with my mastery of intrigue and"—he thought a moment—"general sneakiness."

"My dear, you have no equal in general sneakiness, but I shall be even more impressed once I learn the details."

"Unlikely, but I'll tell you, anyway. I instructed one of my police contacts to inform me of any case he came across that involved the Ashleys. Rather simple really."

Hm, that was simple. "Is your contact Delaney?" Delaney was Inspector Delaney with the Metropolitan Police, in the Chelsea Division. He began our acquaintance by investigating me when I first moved to London just over a year ago. He's become far less suspicious and more accepting of me, considering I've been somehow relevant to many of his investigations since. Not all, of course, but more than I care to count.

George scoffed. "Delaney's far too busy to cater to the likes of me, but the members of the constabulary are more accommodating." He took my arm when we ascended the steps to the door. "Anyway, my contact put me in touch with the detective handling this case, and he's given me leave to search for the journal once they've cleared the scene."

"What does that involve?"

"Once they've recorded or taken all the evidence they can find in relation to the crime, I will be free to search."

"They'll do that quickly?"

He opened the outer door, and we entered the vestibule. "One can hope," he said. "I have nowhere else to look at this point except the Ashley home itself, so I might just as well wait around. They will, of course, watch my every move to ensure I take nothing else."

"Have they told you what happened?"

George led me past the constable into an open room with low ceilings that served as kitchen and sitting and dining rooms. All could be taken in with one glance. It was comfortably furnished, and everything seemed to be in its place. A doorway on the far wall had to lead to a bedroom. I was pleased to note the body of Nurse Plum was not in sight.

As if reading my mind, George squeezed my fingers. "They've already removed her body," he said. "And as to what happened, I arrived only a few minutes ahead of you and hadn't the chance to inquire." He turned to the constable guarding the door. "Are you able to enlighten us, my good man?"

The constable straightened and cleared his throat, with his

lips compressed, his chin jutted forward, giving him something of a bulldog appearance. "Neighbor across the hall noticed her door wasn't closed this morning. No answer to his knock, so he pushes it open and peeks in. Sees her on the floor and calls for us. Well, what are we to gather from that? No blood. No mess. And her just lying there." He leaned closer to us. "Looked like natural causes to me, but not to the detective inspector."

He glanced toward the wall, behind which, I assumed, the detective inspector was searching the bedroom. "He notices there's two teacups on the table, and one of them smells a bit of alcohol. Laudanum, he says. That's enough for him to ask the coroner to take a good look. Which he does. Turns out she's been given a big dose of the stuff through a needle. Found a mark on her arm." He pointed to the inside of his own arm. "Sneaky devil injected it into her arm, can you imagine? To us, it looked like she had a heart attack or something."

"That is rather tricky," George agreed. "The killer must have given her a bit of laudanum in the tea, so she'd be too relaxed to put up a fight when he injected her. Did she live here alone?" George continued while I cringed at the thought of poor Nurse Plum.

The constable shook his head. "No sign of anyone else living here."

"Have you had a chance to speak with the other neighbors?"

"That's what we'll do soon as they're done in there." He tipped his head toward the wall. "And as soon as you're done and we've locked up."

"I'm happy to get started out here if you'd like to follow me around."

The constable waved George on, and he began searching through the nurse's shelves and cubbies, lifting cushions from the furniture and running a hand along the crevices. They both stepped into the bedroom while I watched the door. The way the constable was rushing George along, I had a feeling we'd be back at another time.

When George emerged, he was accompanied by two more policemen, one of them in plain clothes—likely the detective inspector. He approached me.

"D. I. Reed, ma'am," he said by way of introduction. "I understand the woman's employment was in Mayfair."

"She was a nurse for Lady Winstead," I said. "There was a great deal of concern when she didn't report for work this morning."

"Oh, I'm sure they were terribly concerned." The sarcasm dripped from his voice. I supposed he was right. The Ashleys were far more concerned about how her absence affected their lives. I didn't contradict him.

Reed had already turned away from me and spoke to the other officer. "We've asked the Chelsea precinct to interview the employers. Sounds like that part of town is where she spent most of her time, anyway. You can get started interviewing the neighbors here."

The officer left the flat, and Reed turned to George. "You all right, then?"

George nodded. "I didn't find what I was looking for, so I'll be on my way and let you gentlemen close up here." He gestured for me to go first, and we left the building.

"What now?" I asked once we were outside on the pavement. The children had gone elsewhere to play, possibly due to the clouds gathering overhead.

George pulled his watch from his waistcoat pocket. "It's just gone four. Did you want to tell the Ashleys what happened to the nurse?"

"I suppose I ought to inform them. Aside from Kate, I don't believe they're much for caretaking. They may kill Lady Winstead accidentally if they don't get another nurse in soon."

"We can find a cab in the next block over," he said, offering his arm.

I took it, and we walked up the quiet street. "In your search for the journal, you didn't happen to see anything that might be Lady Winstead's jewelry, did you?"

"Ah, yes. Miss Stover's claims that her aunt's jewelry is missing. I saw nothing of the sort. If it truly is missing, I doubt Nurse Plum took it."

"She was already away from the house when Lady Winstead had her bad spell last night. Do you suppose that means she's not the culprit?"

He gave me a wry smile. "The fact that Nurse Plum is now dead leads me to believe that not only is she not the culprit, but she also knew who is."

We found a cab at the corner. George dropped me at the Ashley residence, and he went on to the Chelsea precinct, in the hope of speaking with Delaney. If he ended up involved in this case, George wanted to alert him to the missing journal, the possible drugging of Lady Winstead, and her missing jewelry.

When Fuller let me into the house, I saw that George should have stayed with me. Inspector Delaney was already here and was arguing with Lord Jonathon.

"My stepmother is unwell, and I won't have you bothering her."

Jonathon's voice carried from the drawing room when Vi Ashley came out to the entry hall to greet me.

"I'm here to give you the bad news," I told her, "but it seems as though you've already heard."

She lifted her gaze heavenward. "Yes, we are all in an uproar here. Jonathon is outraged that the police are questioning us about the nurse. Kate is insisting she will take over the nursing duties. She's up with Lady Winstead now if you wish to speak with her."

"I don't want to take her away from her aunt."

"Give it a moment and you won't be. It appears this police inspector wants to search our stepmother's rooms, and I'm sure he won't allow Kate to stay there while he does. Do come in."

On our way into the drawing room, we passed Lord Jonathon and Delaney exiting the room. Jonathon stopped when he caught sight of me.

"Mrs. Hazelton. It appears we now know what kept Nurse Plum from her duties."

"Yes, I heard."

Delaney's bushy gray-streaked eyebrows lifted slightly, showing his momentary surprise upon seeing me here, but he merely nodded and gave no indication that he knew me. Following his lead, I did the same.

"If you'll excuse me," Lord Jonathon continued, "the inspector seems to think Lady Winstead's room will turn up some information about the woman."

"I'm sure he's correct," I said. "After all, Nurse Plum spent a good deal of time there. All of us may know more about the woman than we imagine we do."

Delaney's gaze sharpened on me before he glanced at Jonathon, and the two men moved on. I hoped he understood that I had more to tell him, but even if he didn't take my meaning, I could always contact him later.

Vi applied a slight pressure on my arm, and I followed her into the drawing room, where Si Ashley fiddled with a pipe by the fireplace.

"What I could possibly know about the nurse?" she mused, guiding me toward a comfortably cushioned chair near her husband. She seated herself on the sofa, then glanced at Si. "I wouldn't light that in here if I were you. Your brother will have your head."

He slipped the pipe into his coat pocket and joined Vi on the sofa.

"How long had Nurse Plum been caring for your step-mother?" I asked, glancing from one to the other.

Si tipped his head and glanced at his wife. "A few months at least, don't you think?"

She frowned. "It wasn't long after we moved in."

"Vi and I gave up our place in January, shortly after Father passed," Si said. "Our stepmother was having spells even then, and after putting up with Father's illness, it didn't seem fair that Jonathon should have to care for her, too."

"You moved in with Lord Jonathon to take care of your stepmother?" If that was the case, these two had gone through a significant change in character in the year or two since I'd seen them last. But then I recalled Vi's determination not to sit with Lady Winstead today. This was probably a story for the general public. Their true reason for moving here was more likely financial.

Vi smiled at me. "Not like the good old days anymore. Now we have responsibilities. Seeing to it that Lady Winstead has everything she needs is one of them. After all, we might have children one day."

The two statements seemed unrelated, until I realized Vi hoped to win favor with Lady Winstead so she'd leave them something in her will. I suppose as the oldest, Jonathon inherited a majority of any wealth, along with the entailed property and the title. A second son with no fortune of his own often pinned his financial hopes on some other relation.

Vi released a wistful sigh. "We certainly had fun in the old days, didn't we?"

"The old days?" Si laughed. "They weren't that long ago, my dear. I do miss Reggie, though," he said, looking at me. "I recall that house party . . . not sure where it was, but that American heiress played a ukulele every night for five nights, and it drove you so mad you finally hid the instrument."

Both of them burst into chortles and giggles over what must have been a highly entertaining prank.

"You'd remember her name, Frances," Si continued. "Reggie insisted you give it back to her, but you refused." Si noticed my stony expression and allowed his laughter to run down. "Surely, you remember?"

"I'm afraid that wasn't me."

Vi choked back a laugh, perhaps finally remembering that Reggie had almost never attended house parties with his own wife, so the woman in question had likely been the wife of someone else. It didn't sound like something Alicia Stoke-Whitney would do. I wondered if Reggie had cheated on his favourite paramour.

Si came to his feet. "Yes. Well. I guess I'll have that smoke, after all." With a shallow bow to me, he left the room.

Vi remained in her seat, twisting her bracelets. "Forgive us, Frances. I only now remember what a cad Reggie had been."

Yet knowing that had never stopped her from associating with him or allowing him to entertain them—with the money from my dowry. Bygones, I supposed. If I held a grudge against everyone who had ever joined my late husband in his revelries, I'd be at odds with half of London.

I retrieved the thread of our previous conversation. "It sounds as though Nurse Plum joined the household around February."

Vi's expression relaxed. "Or late January."

"How did you find her? Through an agency?"

Voices in the entry hall caught our attention. "She'll be fine." That sounded like Andrew Ashley. "Come into the drawing room. Let me pour you a sherry."

We hadn't long to wait in curiosity. Andrew and Kate entered almost immediately, he looking his usual jovial self, she quite distraught. Both looked surprised to see us.

"I've just heard the sad news about Nurse Plum," Andrew said. With a hand under Kate's elbow, he guided her over to us. "And they've evicted poor Kate from Grandmama's room, so I'm consoling her with sherry. May I pour a glass for you ladies?"

We both declined, and he moved across the room for the sherry.

Kate took a seat next to Vi, who patted her hand. "We were just discussing Nurse Plum's history with this household. Do either of you remember how Jonathon found her?"

"She was Lord Peter's nurse," Kate said. "I remember meeting her at his funeral, along with that Dr. Waldschmidt."

"Was he Lord Peter's doctor?" I asked.

"Heavens, I've no idea," Vi said. She turned to Kate, who shook her head and took the glass Andrew held out. "Do you know?" she asked him.

"I believe he was," the young man replied.

I made a mental note of the doctor's name in case we needed to speak with him. "Was the nurse living in when she cared for Lord Peter?"

"I was away at school," Andrew said. "When I came home for the Christmas holiday, she seemed to be here all the time, but I wasn't really paying attention. You would know, Kate. You were visiting when Grandfather died."

Kate nodded. "I believe she lived in, but as Andrew said, Lord Peter died a day or two after I arrived. Nurse Plum would have left at that time. Now that you mention it, it seems odd that Lord Jonathon would have asked her to come back to care for my aunt. I would always associate her with his father's death."

Andrew laughed. "If he thought that way, perhaps he ought to ask you to leave."

Kate turned sharply toward him. "What do you mean by that?"

"That was quite rude, Andrew," Vi added. "You should apologize to Kate."

"I'm only pointing out the obvious," he said. "First, she was caring for her father, who died. Several months later, she was visiting us when Grandfather died. Now you've been here a week, and while Grandmama is still with us, her nurse has died. What do you say to that, Kate? Are you cursed?" Andrew grinned impishly. He was clearly jesting, but his humor was macabre and so highly offensive even Vi didn't find it amusing.

Kate, her eyes red and damp, set her glass on the table and fled the room.

"That was cruel, Andrew," Vi said. "Go and apologize to her."

I held up my hand to stop him while I came to my feet. "Let me speak with her," I said. I was sure Andrew would do more harm than good.

"I was just bamming her," he said. "I'm sorry. I meant no harm." He was indeed young enough to be that stupid, but Vi took him to task regardless.

I left the two of them in the drawing room and went in search of Kate, whom I found in the library, just on the other side of the wall.

Tears streamed down her cheeks, but she raised her hand when I approached. "I'll be fine. I know he's just a foolish boy and his words shouldn't hurt me." She drew a shaky breath. "He has too much time on his hands and nothing to do with it."

"Why didn't he return to school after Lord Peter's funeral?" I asked.

She gave me a guarded look. "I'm not supposed to know, but Lord Jonathon hasn't been paying the school's fees. Andrew isn't welcome back until his father settles his bill." She heaved a sigh. "Quite a family, aren't they? If it weren't for my aunt, I'd love to just leave this house and its occupants forever."

I handed her a handkerchief to wipe her tears. "Take heart," I said. "I'm sorry it took Nurse Plum's death to get the police to come here, but now they have. Inspector Delaney is one of the best. If you have any opportunity to speak with him alone, tell him about your suspicions regarding the theft of your aunt's jewelry and that you believe someone is drugging her. This is your best chance."

Her expression turned hopeful. "Should I go to him now?"

"You won't be able to speak freely while Jonathon is with him," I said. "Wait for a chance to get Delaney alone. Meanwhile, try to ignore Andrew's taunts."

Disregarding my own advice, I considered Andrew's words. Kate was in attendance when her father died and when Lord Peter died. She was also close by when the possible attempts on Lady Winstead's life were made. Perhaps I should focus more on Kate.

Then I considered Andrew himself. He had nothing to do but get into mischief. He was no less suspicious than Kate. I sighed. All of them were suspects.

Chapter Thirteen

I arrived home at the same time my brother-in-law's carriage dropped my daughter, Rose, at the door. In the entry hall, she gave me a short summary of her day while Jarvis collected our outerwear. Nanny hovered over her charge, ready to rush her off to the nursery, so I gave her a hug and kiss and told her I'd see her at dinner.

Which would be in about an hour. This day had simply disappeared.

I found George upstairs, dressed for dinner and ready to go down. "Delaney wasn't at his office, so I came home early."

"He wasn't at his office, because he had already started his investigation with the Ashleys." I rang for Bridget while George digested this information. "He was surprised to see me there," I added. "But he didn't acknowledge knowing me, so I followed suit."

George leaned back against the bedpost while I unpinned my hat. "How did it seem to be going?" he asked.

"Jonathon Ashley was acting like the typical aristocrat. He didn't want his family disturbed by questions from the police.

He did, however, give in and allowed Delaney upstairs to search Lady Winstead's room and perhaps the nurse's, too. I don't know if Lady Winstead was up to answering questions, but I'm very eager to learn if he found the journal."

"Yes, that's one reason I'd hoped to speak with him before he approached the Ashleys. If he didn't find it in this search, he may not get another chance."

"You are probably right about that. Jonathon was not happy to have him there. I did give Delaney a veiled hint that I had information for him, so he may call on us soon."

Bridget arrived then, and I joined her in the dressing room. In a mere ten minutes, she had me refreshed and suitably dressed for dinner. George and I went down to the drawing room for a glass of sherry and to wait for Rose. We'd recently made this change to have Rose dine with us unless we were entertaining. She enjoyed it and thought we were indulging her, but in truth, she was growing up so quickly, and between her schedule of studies and activities and our schedules, we saw little of her throughout the day. This was one way to ensure we'd spend some time together as a family.

When Rose arrived, we moved into the dining room, and all—well, most—formality was forgotten. With just the three of us, we sat at one end of the long oval table—Rose at the end and George and I across from one another. A single candle replaced the bulky candelabra, and it felt quite cozy. It also made it easier for Jarvis and Frederick to serve.

Once we were all dipping into our soup, I recalled that Rose had had her lessons today. "Do you know what Mr. Barry plans to do when Martin joins his brother at school this fall?" I asked her. Mr. Barry was Martin's tutor.

Her brow creased in thought. "I guess he'll find another boy to teach."

"Girls are taught by tutors, as well, dear. Just take yourself, for example. Would you be interested in continuing your studies with him if he is not already engaged elsewhere?"

Rose had just taken a forkful of potato, so I was grateful she merely shrugged and bobbed her head. I took that to mean she wasn't particularly attached to Mr. Barry.

"A tutor like Mr. Barry is generally employed to prepare children"—George cast me a wary glance—"usually boys, for school. Rose may already have learned everything he's qualified to teach." He gave Rose a warm smile. "For someone as bright as you, my dear Rosie, a well-educated governess might be a better choice, though I'm not certain where we'd house her."

"We don't have the space," I agreed, "but your sister came up with an excellent scheme this morning. Grace's governess is leaving, and she suggested we join forces to hire another. The candidate would live in with Fiona, and Rose and Grace could study together."

"I'd like that," Rose said, bouncing in her seat.

"I can make no promises," I cautioned her. "This is just a possibility." I turned to George. "If you are agreeable to the plan, Fiona and I will make a list of qualifications, determine a salary, and contact an employment agency."

George's gaze traveled from Rose to me. "What sort of curriculum do you envision?"

A good question. I sat back to allow Frederick to remove my soup bowl. "Well, I'd like someone who can give the girls a firm grasp of history, geography, mathematics, and literature."

"That sounds basic enough," George said.

"I'd also like you to learn at least one other language, to make travel easier when you are older," I added, with a glance at Rose, who frowned.

"When I went to France with Grandmama, she didn't speak French."

"And she had a frustrating time trying to communicate, didn't she?" I knew very well that was true because my mother had complained at length that the French didn't speak English.

Rose admitted that was so.

"Languages aren't very difficult to learn when you are young, dear. You may enjoy it. We'll also have to try music, art, and dance as you get older. I'm sure you'll enjoy one of those."

"That's quite a lot of instructors, don't you think?" George's brow furrowed as he glanced from Rose to me.

"It is," I agreed. "But it may be a matter of just a few lessons. Rose may not have an ear for music or be able to draw a straight line."

Rose pulled a face.

"You may also have Aunt Hetty's financial genius. I want you to try different subjects, but I won't push you to pursue anything you simply despise."

That seemed to relieve her mind. George also relaxed a bit more now that he knew that Rose's, and any future children's, studies would neither bankrupt us nor force us to rely on my father unduly.

He turned to Rose. "Is there something in particular you'd like to study?"

"Egyptian," she said, without a second thought.

George and I stared. "Might take a bit of work finding an Egyptian instructor," he said.

"What brought on this interest?" I asked.

"Lady Winstead has been to Egypt. She told me some stories about the pyramids and deserts, and I want to go there some-day. Are you going to the Ashleys again soon? May I visit Lady Winstead when you do?"

All my thoughts came to a full stop. While I mistrusted nearly everyone in that family, I always felt perfectly safe there.

Surely, Rose would be fine. "You may come with me, but if Lady Winstead is not up to company, you would have to stay by my side."

George agreed with the arrangement and asked Rose to share some of those Egyptian stories, which she did with delight. In fact, she became so animated, she entertained us throughout our dinner. Just as we finished and sent her up to the nursery, Jarvis informed us Delaney had called and awaited us in the drawing room.

"You're working late, Inspector," I said as we entered the room.

Delaney, looking spare in his shapeless brown suit, unfolded himself from his seat, took George's extended hand, then bobbed his gray-streaked head to me. "I was eager to satisfy my curiosity, ma'am. Since seeing you at the Ashley home, I've heard the two of you were also at the home of the deceased nurse. Would you mind telling me what your connection is to the Ashley family? And, of course, if you've had any interactions with Margery Plum."

The name took me by surprise. "I've only ever heard her called Nurse Plum," I said, guiding Delaney to a chair. "It's as if she didn't have a given name."

We all took a seat, and I explained the evolution of my role with the Ashleys, from Lady Winstead's original request to sponsor her niece, to Lady Esther's request to find out what was happening to her friend, to Miss Stover's claim that her family was not only harming the viscountess but also stealing from her. "I'd had very little interaction with the nurse, but I have been in the room when she attended Lady Winstead. She seemed competent and dedicated to her patient." I gave him a close look. "Do you believe her murder had something to do with her employment?"

"At this point, I have no idea. What is your opinion of Lady

Esther and Miss Stover's concerns? Have they any merit? Viscount Winstead took the lady from the room when I arrived to search it. She was in a wheeled chair. Is she unable to walk?"

"A few days ago, she was unable to sit in that chair. Yet yesterday she got herself out of her bed and into her chair and carried on a conversation with me. She seemed weak and tired, but that could very well be due to an overdose of laudanum."

Delaney rubbed the back of his neck. "People have been known to indulge themselves with laudanum."

"She had a nurse who would likely put a stop to that if she wanted to keep her job."

"That depends upon who is paying her," George said, lifting his brows.

Delaney gave him a sharp look. "It sounds as though you think the family might have a hand in this. Anyone in particular?"

"I haven't dealt with any of the Ashleys enough to venture a guess," George replied. "But if they are overmedicating Lady Winstead, I wonder if the nurse knew about it, and if that is what led to her present condition."

"Possible." Delaney turned to me. "Have you any suspect in mind?"

"All of them."

"Including Miss Katherine Stover?"

"While you were upstairs with the viscount, I had a conversation with Andrew and Vi Ashley. Andrew was teasing Miss Stover, rather cruelly I thought, about bringing death wherever she goes."

Delaney raised his brows, urging me to continue.

"First, her father died while she was caring for him. Then while she was visiting the family, the late viscount died. This time she's been in the house only a week and the nurse ended up dead. As I said, it was cruel, but it made me wonder about her motive. She'd been nursing her father for quite some time. Perhaps she wanted her freedom, or simply just to see him at peace. As for Lady Winstead, Kate may be hoping for an inheritance. If she was attempting to kill Lady Winstead, the nurse may have been in her way."

I raised a finger and continued. "The flaw in the Kate Stover theory is that Lady Winstead's health improved when Kate spent the night in her room—as if her presence prevented the culprit from drugging her aunt. And I can't think of any reason for her to murder Lord Peter." I laughed ruefully. "Though I have no evidence to accuse her, I can't completely exonerate her, either. On the other hand, if someone in the Ashley family is drugging Lady Winstead, is it possible they did the same to Lord Peter and accidentally killed him?"

"You mean did they accidentally give him too much?" Delaney rolled the idea around in his mind. "What do you know of his death?"

I looked at George, who shrugged. "Only that he was ill for some time. I assumed he succumbed to whatever it was."

"If, at the time, there was no reason to attribute his death to anything other than natural causes, no one would have ordered an autopsy." Delaney leaned forward in his chair. "What reason would they have had for drugging him? Or killing him, for that matter? Not all overdoses are accidental."

"I'm afraid I don't know anything about their relationship with Lord Peter," I said. "It's just the fact of Nurse Plum treating both husband and wife that has me wondering."

"Lady Esther might have more information," George said to me. "If you're willing to share your suspicions with her."

I gave that a little thought while Delaney watched me. "She did ask me to investigate," I said. "I don't want to alarm her, but Hazelton is right. She could provide a wealth of information. She and Lady Winstead are longtime friends."

"Why did her friend ask you to investigate?" Delaney asked. "What was she worried about?"

I told him how Lady Esther had described the change in her friend's letters over the past few months and how the Ashleys had turned her away at the door when she called on Lady Winstead. "She said the viscountess had made plans to travel to the Continent during her mourning period—off by herself. Lady Winstead had told her that once she was settled somewhere, she'd invite Lady Esther to visit. It wasn't many days later that she was too ill for visitors, according to her family. Lady Esther, like Miss Stover, is concerned someone is drugging her."

"It sounds to me that you suspect Miss Stover in the potential overdosing," Delaney said.

"They are all suspects in my mind. But, as I said, I can think of no reason Miss Stover would want to harm the old viscount."

"And the others?"

"My aunt mentioned cases of this nature in which the children are a bit too eager to spend their future inheritance and the parent is holding too tightly to the purse strings. I have no idea if that is the case with the Ashleys, but I suppose it's possible."

Delaney frowned. "You said Miss Stover suspected someone in the family of stealing from the woman. Did Lady Esther ever mention theft?"

"No. I can ask her, but since she hasn't seen Lady Winstead, I doubt she'd know about the theft. But Miss Stover can show you the letter Lady Winstead sent to her in which she said someone had stolen her jewelry. And Lady Esther should be able to give me more information about the family and whether money was an issue. I doubt it, since Lady Winstead would have brought quite a fortune into the marriage."

"With the old viscount deceased, wouldn't his son have inherited any fortune along with the title?" Delaney gave me a close look. "That is how it works, isn't it?"

"Generally, yes," I said. "Since you are investigating a murder that might be connected to the family, you ought to be able to question the Ashleys' solicitor, isn't that right?"

"I'm not so sure that would help," George said. "I had a difficult enough time just convincing him to verify that Lord Peter meant to leave the journal to the museum."

Delaney had pulled out his notebook and was scribbling notes. "Solicitors are rather sticky about confidential information. I'd need further evidence to obtain a warrant. Either way, to ask those questions now would alert the family and possibly end my chances of questioning them in the future. And I'm certain I'll have more questions for them as the investigation moves along." He glanced up from his notes. "I'll still take that solicitor's name if you have it."

George took Delaney's notebook and wrote it down.

"I'm beginning to think I need a notebook of my own," I said. "I must ask Lady Esther about the Ashley children and Lord Peter, find out what she may know of Miss Stover, the potential theft, and how finances are settled in the family. Is that it?"

Delaney's eyebrows drew together in one fuzzy line, and his compressed lips twisted to one side, telling me he was not happy with my involvement, though he knew it was the most efficient way to gain the information we needed.

"Would Lady Esther know the financial matters of the Ashleys?" George looked skeptical.

"She was the Fiona of her day," I said, causing him to laugh and Delaney to give me a curious look. "Somehow, they both manage to know everything. This particular detail may have escaped her notice, but maybe not."

"Anything you can find out about those matters would be

helpful, particularly the theft. I didn't have an opportunity to speak with Miss Stover, but Viscount Winstead never mentioned anything about missing jewelry, though he did mention a journal of his father's. He believed the nurse may have taken it." He turned to George. "Does that have anything to do with your search of the nurse's home? Is that the same journal you spoke of?"

"It is," he replied. "It's the property of the British Museum, given to them in the late Lord Peter's will. The journal itemizes the artifacts he collected on his expeditions and donated to the museum. It's a very important part of the collection. Lord Jonathon held on to it until the museum forced the issue. He agreed to turn it over, but somehow, it's gone missing. They've brought me in to investigate and, hopefully, retrieve it."

"Interesting. You also thought the nurse had taken it?" Delaney asked.

"I thought it was worth a look, particularly since she was murdered. But if she did take it, I couldn't find it."

"Maybe the murderer took it," I said.

George lifted a brow. "Or she never had it in the first place."

This was not the first time I cursed myself for not finding a way to bring that journal home. I was grateful George didn't mention that Kate had been responsible for the original theft of the journal. I didn't want to believe she had anything to do with the nurse's murder, but there was one more thing Delaney ought to know about her.

"Do you intend to return to the Ashleys' and question the rest of the family?" I asked.

Delaney nodded. "We should have a time of death for Nurse Plum in the morning. There was little point in inquiring as to their whereabouts until I knew the time of death. The two of you have given me a few more lines of questioning to take." He came to his feet. "I'll keep an eye out for that journal, but I'll need someone from the household to report the missing jewelry or I'll have no idea what to look for."

"If possible, you should try to speak with Miss Stover alone. There are things she would not want the rest of her family to know, so she won't speak freely if there is a chance they'll overhear."

George looked at me. "With a hint like that, you might just as well tell Delaney yourself. It's highly unlikely Winstead will leave Delaney alone with Miss Stover."

"It feels as though I'm revealing a confidence."

Delaney waited.

"Fine. Miss Stover is an actress. She has a role as an understudy for the musical *Florodora*. The Ashleys don't know about it. When she's needed, she slips out of the house, goes to the theater to play her role, then sneaks back home. She did this last night. When she returned and checked on her aunt, the woman was unconscious."

Delaney continued writing in his book. "Anything else?"

"She knows where Nurse Plum lived."

"So there you have it, Delaney," George said. "We have an elderly woman who may be drugged, adult stepchildren who may be doing the drugging and may have murdered their father, and an actress who also might be a murderess. You couldn't ask for a more interesting family. Which reminds me, did Nurse Plum leave behind a family of her own or any suspicious friends?"

"No husband or children. Any family she has is still in Leicester. A neighbor said she visited them for two weeks every year. We're still working on interviewing neighbors. If there are any friends to uncover, we hope they can lead us in that direction. I'll dig into her employment tomorrow." Delaney pocketed his notebook. "I'm curious to find if there are any mysterious deaths among her previous patients. One more thing related to the Ashley family . . . Assuming the viscount-ess was being drugged, if the nurse wasn't the one giving her too much laudanum, then it's likely to continue."

I shuddered. "That's precisely what I'm afraid of."

Chapter Fourteen

❧

By the time Delaney left, it was too late to send a note to Lady Esther—at least if good manners were to be observed. But it had been three days since she'd seen her friend collapse, and I knew she was eager to hear anything I might have learned. George and I were hoping she could provide us with some information, as well, so to the devil with good manners. I sent the message, anyway, and asked her to call on me at her earliest convenience.

While we dressed the following morning, George grumbled that I'd left my request too vague. "Morning calls don't usually happen until afternoon," he said. "You ought to have requested she come at ten."

"Lady Esther doesn't follow society rules. And considering her concern for Lady Winstead, she'll be very anxious by now. I'll be lucky if she doesn't call before nine." I had finished brushing the tangles from my hair and had tied it back with a ribbon when he stepped up and flicked his fingers toward the small gilt-edged clock on my dressing table.

"It's nine o'clock now."

"Then consider yourself lucky she's not pounding her walking stick outside our door, demanding to be let in here," I said. "Let's go down. I'd at least like to have coffee before she arrives."

He followed me down the stairs, our footsteps muted by the carpet. "I was hoping to hear from her before I left."

"Where are you going so early?" I asked.

When we reached the main floor, we turned toward the back of the house and headed to the breakfast room. I took a seat at the table while George poured us each a cup of coffee.

"I'll start at the Chelsea precinct and see where that leads me," he said. The tantalizing aroma of coffee preceded him to the table, where he placed the cups and took the chair beside me. "Delaney likely has the time of death for the nurse, as well as the results of the interviews of the neighbors by now," he continued.

"Do you still think the nurse had something to do with the missing journal?"

He frowned. "Since it was hidden in Lady Winstead's room, I think the nurse is a good suspect. The Ashleys would look rather suspicious if caught rummaging through Lady Winstead's belongings. Particularly if they don't visit her often."

I lifted my hands, palms up. "That's what Kate claimed."

He sighed. "She would be the next suspect on my list. After all, she took it in the first place. Once you discovered it, she may simply have hidden it somewhere else."

"Why?"

"The same reason as the nurse, I suppose," he said. "She may see it as a source of money."

I gazed up at the ceiling, thinking. "If any of the Ashleys took the journal, I would assume they'd just return it to Jonathon. Should I ask Lady Winstead if her stepchildren have been lurking around her room?"

"No. Delaney will be interviewing them. Let him find out. I don't want the family to decide you are too curious."

I was saved a reply by the entrance of Jarvis—Lady Esther had arrived. Since she was not someone I'd invite to the breakfast table, I told him we'd meet her in the drawing room and gulped the rest of my coffee.

Rather than waiting for us in a comfortable chair, we found Lady Esther putting her walking stick to good use by pacing behind the sofa. She stopped upon seeing us. "Well," she said. "What have you learned?"

I invited her to take a seat on the sofa. George and I took the chairs facing her.

"Would you care for tea, ma'am?" he asked.

"No." She tapped the floor once with her stick. "What I want is information. Is Augusta being drugged?"

George opened his mouth to speak. I knew his legal brain would make him dance around the answer. That would only aggravate the poor woman.

I touched his hand to stop him and met Lady Esther's gaze. "Though I haven't seen it for myself, it is possible your suspicions are correct. It appears that Lady Winstead takes laudanum frequently, if not daily. That may be her choice, but occasionally she takes too much, and I am quite certain that isn't her choice."

"It's that nurse, isn't it?" Lady Esther gripped the handle of her walking stick. I waited for her to start her furious tapping, but she seemed to think better of it.

This time George stopped me from speaking. "Are you referring to Nurse Plum? What makes you suspect her?"

She huffed. "It's not like the Ashleys to do their own dirty work. They'd hire someone else to handle it for them. Is she the same nurse who tended Peter and likely sent him to his grave?"

I stared at the woman. "I just learned yesterday that she is the same nurse, but what makes you think she sent Lord Peter to his grave?"

"Augusta mentioned it herself—at her husband's funeral. She had no proof, of course, and admittedly she was emotional." She arranged both hands atop her stick and leaned forward. "However, if someone is drugging Augusta, what can we do about it?"

"That's a bit tricky," I said.

"If it were easy," she said, "I wouldn't need the two of you."

"We've discussed some of our concerns with the police," George began.

She waved a hand. "Bah! What can they do?"

I was rather surprised to hear her dismiss the police so abruptly, but George seemed to have been expecting it. "Apparently, you haven't heard that Nurse Plum has been murdered," he said.

She narrowed her eyes. "Indeed? By whom?"

"They don't know, which is why the police were quite receptive to the information we provided. Unfortunately, there's a great deal about the family we couldn't tell the inspector."

"That is where you could help us," I added. "And in doing so, we would likely be helping Lady Winstead, as well."

"Am I to understand that the police suspect one of the Ashley family of murdering the nurse? Why would they do such a thing?"

"Didn't you just suggest one of the Ashleys was responsible for the nurse drugging Lady Winstead?" I asked.

Her pursed lips showed her impatience with me. "I did more than suggest it, my dear, and you are making my point. If they coerced or paid her to do so, why murder her? They'd have to begin again with a new nurse." She tsked.

Obviously, she had a poor opinion of the Ashleys. Not only did they have murderous inclinations, but they were also lazy into the bargain. "Lady Esther, you know the family better than we do. Would you mind answering our questions so we can have a better idea of Lady Winstead's situation?"

"Yes, yes. Go ahead. I suppose the police are insisting on evidence."

"They are rather finicky about such things," George said.

She harrumphed, as if she thought the police were wasting her time. I might feel the same if a close friend of mine were in Lady Winstead's place.

George nodded at me to begin.

"Earlier you implied Nurse Plum had something to do with Lord Peter's death. Hadn't he been ill for some time? Was his death unexpected?"

"You have it exactly right," she said. "Late in the autumn he became ill with a cold or some such and canceled his travel plans. Two weeks later, when he hadn't recovered, I learned he had a nurse attending him. Augusta was worried about him, but when the doctor visited, he assured her Peter would recover. He was as surprised as anyone when Peter developed pneumonia. I daresay it was less than a month later, right around the Christmas holiday, that the poor man died."

"And you believe the nurse hastened his death?" I asked.

Her expression hardened. "Somebody did. Peter was a healthy man with a zest for life. There was no reason a trifling cold should turn into pneumonia." She gave us a scowl. "Yes, he was old, but so am I. Seeing me today, would you not be surprised to learn next week that I had pneumonia? And the following month that I was dead? That's rather how this played out. Somebody hastened his death. The nurse was there, supposedly caring for him."

Frankly, her example didn't sound at all beyond the bounds of belief to my mind. "But the nurse wouldn't have murdered him on her own," I said. "Who would have been controlling her, whether it be through money or coercion, as you suggested?"

"For all of Peter's patriotism and love of country, he didn't necessarily feel any duty toward his title or the estate. Or his children, for that matter. Expeditions are very expensive. He received some grants, but they were only supplemental. He provided most of the funding himself. Thus, he was spending their inheritance."

"But he'd been doing so for years," George noted. "If money was the motive, why wait until then to kill him?"

"Peter didn't spend a great deal of time at home—certainly not with his children. This may have been their only chance. Particularly once he became ill. It's also possible that his children had only recently learned how much of his fortune he was spending."

"But didn't he gain a great deal by marrying Lady Winstead?" I asked. "I understand she has a large fortune."

Lady Esther's expression tightened so much her hairline moved forward. "Indeed, she does. And it belongs to her. Lord Peter received a dowry. Nothing more. Augusta's first husband tied everything up nicely—to protect her. Peter married a rich widow, but he never had control of her money."

"A shrewd move on the first husband's part," I said. "Do the Ashleys know?"

"I couldn't say." The airy wave of her hand said she could not care less.

George and I exchanged a look. "If they know they have no claim to Lady Winstead's fortune, it seems to me that they'd do their best to make sure she lives a long and healthy life," I said to him. "Wouldn't you think?"

"Long, yes, but not necessarily healthy," he replied. "Remember what your aunt said?"

Lady Esther leaned forward as I told her about the "control through laudanum" theory. "But I'm not sure that applies in this case," I said. "How would they have access to Lady Winstead's fortune? If she had no intention of leaving it to them, she would hardly allow them to draw from her accounts."

"Augusta and I employ the same solicitor. He acts as her agent in financial matters," Lady Esther said. "I shall pay him a call and find out if she has granted any of the Ashley children access to her accounts."

George looked doubtful. "Her solicitor is hardly likely to discuss such confidential matters with you."

I shook my head at his folly. Personally, I felt the older woman capable of coercing anyone into giving up their secrets, but more importantly, it didn't do to contradict her or question her abilities.

She pinned him with a withering look and drew her lips back from her teeth in a caricature of a smile that made the hair on my arms stand up. "Well, now," she said, "I shall look at that as a challenge."

"Hardly a challenge for you, ma'am," I said, throwing George a quelling glare. He simply looked amused.

"Perhaps," he added, "you could inquire about Miss Stover, as well."

I still wasn't sure how I felt about Kate as a suspect. She was deceiving the Ashleys, but I rather believed she'd have told Lady Winstead the truth about her career if the woman had been capable of carrying on a conversation. But then I recalled her lies and her theft of the journal. I could not trust her. "Are you acquainted with Miss Stover?" I asked Lady Esther.

"I know Augusta is fond of her, but I met her only the one time with you. What is your concern about her?"

"She hasn't been entirely honest with me."

George's smothered laugh emerged as a snort. I gave him a dark look and returned my attention to Lady Esther.

"So, you'd like to know if she has any reason to want her aunt dead," she said. "Is that correct?"

"I wouldn't have phrased it that way, but yes, if you can find out if she has an inheritance coming, that would be helpful. There is one piece of information she passed along to me that I do have confidence in. Lady Winstead believes some of her jewelry has been stolen."

Lady Esther heaved a sigh. "That would be one way to get money out of her if the Ashleys don't have access to her accounts. Are the police looking into this claim?"

"Not yet, and possibly not ever," George said. "Lady Winstead made her claim in a letter to Miss Stover. No one in the family, including Lady Winstead, made such a claim to the police."

"The police haven't yet spoken to Lady Winstead in relation to Nurse Plum's murder," I said. "If they are able to do so, the stolen jewelry may come up."

"If the jewelry went missing before Miss Stover arrived, that exonerates her from that crime." She frowned. "A good thing, since I can't vouch for her. One thing I can tell you is that Augusta never cared for, or trusted, Peter's children. I know she left them nothing in her will. I also know that when she wasn't wearing it, she kept her jewelry in a vault at her bank. She would not have locked it up in the family safe."

Goodness, she really didn't trust them.

"However, there was a set she wore quite frequently. Necklace, earrings, and bracelet. Made up of sapphires and diamonds. If anything was stolen, those are the most likely pieces as she might not have had an opportunity to return them to the bank between events."

"My understanding is that she kept those pieces locked in her dressing table," I said.

"And now they are gone?" She let out a tsk. "Perhaps the police can look wherever one looks for such things."

"I doubt the police will, but I might be able to do so," George said.

"I would appreciate it. Augusta is my friend and a good woman. She did nothing to deserve this treatment." She paused. "Well, she hated those children and made no secret of it, but that's still no excuse."

"Why did she dislike them so?" he asked.

Lady Esther flapped a hand. "She thought them useless, and of course, it's true. She is from a different class, remember. She felt people should not be handed money simply because of their birth. They ought to do something to earn it." She took note of the clock on the mantel and came stiffly to her feet. "I must be on my way. I will meet with Augusta's solicitor and see what I can find out. Is there anything further I can tell you?"

George rang for Lady Esther's coat. I stepped to her side.

"Do you happen to know anything about a Dr. Waldschmidt?" I asked. "I understand he was treating Lord Peter before the Ashleys brought the nurse on."

"Indeed, the man is also Lady Winstead's physician. Smart of you to think of him. I know only that he has offices on Harley Street."

"Excellent. We will pay him a call. This has been very helpful, Lady Esther. Thank you for all your information."

"I'm glad someone is finally looking into things." She narrowed her eyes. "Is there anything else I should know?"

I hesitated, considering what to say. "I believe Lady Winstead would like to see you. With Kate in the house and my coming and going, I doubt Lord Jonathon could turn you away."

She lowered her gaze and shook her head. "I fear that would make her stepchildren suspicious. In truth, I ought not to have gone with you the first time. If I show up repeatedly, they may wonder if you and I are in cahoots. It's safer for Augusta if I stay away."

It was a shame she felt she must keep herself from her friend, but she may have the right of it. For myself, I couldn't repress a little thrill at being in cahoots with the likes of Lady Esther.

After Lady Esther had gone, George and I returned to the breakfast room and took our seats at the table. The food was barely warm, but the coffee was still hot. I poured us each another cup, handed one to George, and posed a question. "If you had to make a guess as to what is going on in the Ashley household, considering what we've learned so far, what would it be?"

George stared out the window at the back garden. We'd had some rain in the night, and cherry blossoms littered the lawn with festive pink petals. The branches of the tree hung low with the weight of the wet flowers. He spoke without turning around. "I think one of Lord Peter's children—I'd suspect Lord Jonathon—took advantage of a slight illness to murder his father and put an end to his rampant spending."

"Expeditions don't come cheaply, do they?"

"Not at all. Jonathon may have convinced himself that he was doing it for future generations of Ashleys." George turned to me. "In a sense, he was probably right. Though given some thought, I'm sure he could have found a better way."

"Vi and Si had the same motive to do Lord Peter in," I said. "Si has no prospects of his own. If the family coffers dry up, they'd have nothing to live on. Andrew Ashley, though young, seems the most sensible of the family, but I cannot discount him as a suspect, either. I'm sure he'd like to return to school and complete his education."

"And Miss Stover?"

"She was in the Ashley home at the time, but I don't have a motive for her. She and Lord Peter seemed to have had little to do with one another."

George leaned back in his chair and stared up at the ceiling. "How to learn if they got along? The only people you could ask are the other suspects. Not very reliable sources."

"It's not just did they get along, but was there a disagreement or some source of animosity? Alternatively, would Kate have had something to gain from his death? It seems so unlikely."

"Didn't you mention a maid in the Ashleys' employ who was following Miss Stover around?"

"Aggie. I've never had a chance to speak with her alone, but I'm sure she'd be biased toward the Ashleys." I shrugged. "Perhaps Lady Esther will learn something from Lady Winstead's solicitor. Let's put Lord Peter's death aside. It might have been due to natural causes, anyway. What do you suppose is going on in that house?"

He raised his brows. "You are better situated to hypothesize than I."

I sat back and stared into my cup before answering. "I do believe someone is drugging Lady Winstead. Nurse Plum must have been going along with it, but with the two episodes her patient had in the past few days, perhaps she became frightened. After all, Lady Winstead was in her care. Maybe she threatened the malefactor—said she'd quit or, worse, that she'd go to the police. Either way, she had to be silenced. That leads me to believe it was a family member."

"Ah, but which one?"

"That's the question, isn't it? And does that person want Lady Winstead sedated or dead?"

George took a sip of his coffee. Neither of us had much interest in breakfast. "Based on Lady Esther's knowledge," he began, "Lady Winstead won't be leaving money to any of the Ashleys in her will, so there's no advantage to killing her. Thus, my answer is that the overdoses were accidental, and they only want her sedated. Much easier to spend her money that way. But there's another question. What can we do about it?"

I raised my hands helplessly. "They are her family. How are we to prove they're drugging her against her will and that she is not medicating herself?"

"I'm not sure we can. But if we can prove they're stealing from her . . ."

"Or that one of them killed Lord Peter." I began to see his line of thinking.

His gaze sharpened. "Exactly. Would you be willing to pay a call on Dr. Waldschmidt and see what he recalls about Lord Peter's illness?"

"I have an engagement in the afternoon, but I could squeeze it in earlier—assuming he can see me. Why? What will you be doing?"

"I'll be looking for some stolen sapphires and diamonds."

"So we need to prove theft or murder in order to help Lady Winstead?"

He lifted his cup. "Unless you want to kidnap the woman and keep her here until she's free from the effects of laudanum?"

The thought made me cringe. "Rose would love it, but let's save that as a plan of last resort, shall we?"

Chapter Fifteen

As luck would have it, Aunt Hetty called on me shortly after George left for his sleuthing. I met her in the entry hall and explained my plans to call on Lady Winstead's physician and ask him some questions.

"Would you care to accompany me?" I asked.

"I don't mind, but how do you know he'll see you?"

"I was just about to telephone his office and find out."

Hetty's eyes rounded. "You plan to use the telephone? I thought you kept it for decorative purposes only."

I smiled. When I first learned that George possessed a telephone, I imagined he used it all the time. The reality was very different. I sighed. "Yes, yes. Mother has already told me London lags behind New York regarding the telephone exchanges."

Hetty tutted. "Your mother makes everything a competition."

"Actually, I believe that's part of the problem. The city is cooperating with the company rather than competing." I shook my head. "And something about underground wires. All I can say with any certainty is that the subscription is very expensive and few people in town bother."

"Indeed? Then how do you know the doctor has a telephone?"

"I'm about to find out. Do you care to join me?" I waved a hand to the library, and Hetty preceded me inside.

The telephone awaited on George's desk. I sat in his chair and gestured Hetty to the one I'd been using across the desk. "You might wish to be seated. This often takes a great deal of time." I turned the crank on the base of the telephone and placed the handset to my ear. The crank turned easily, so I knew the operator's line was not engaged.

"Now we wait," I said.

Hetty frowned. "Why must you wait?"

"We're on the post office exchange. I hear our service is better than the National Telephone Company, but the post office can be rather busy, so we wait."

"I see. By the way, did you say the doctor's name is Waldschmidt?"

"I did. Do you know him?"

"I've seen him myself. He's a fine doctor."

"Are you unwell?" Aunt Hetty was always so vibrant. I couldn't imagine her ill.

"Just a slight fever and some chills," she said with an airy wave of her hand. "It was a few weeks ago, and I'm quite fit now."

"The doctor didn't by chance prescribe laudanum, did he?"

She gave me a knowing look. "Ah, you want to find out if he's involved in this scheme. He didn't advise anything like that for me, and he was recommended to me by your friend Lady Fiona." She paused and chuckled. "Actually, she's your sister-in-law now, isn't she? Perhaps she can tell you more about the doctor."

"Fiona does seem to know everything about everyone, but for now, I just wish to ask him about Nurse Plum."

Hetty glanced at the telephone. "What's in that box?" she asked, pointing to the varnished maple box the telephone sat upon.

"The battery, and yes, I know American telephones don't need . . . Oh, hello, Mr. Otting," I said to the exchange operator, who had come to the line.

"Hello, Mrs. Hazelton," he replied. "What number would you like?"

"I'm afraid I don't know. I'm sure the exchange is Holborn, though. I'm trying to contact the office of Dr. David Waldschmidt."

"Oh! I hope everyone there is well?"

"We are indeed. Thank you for asking." I ought to have realized he'd be alarmed at the thought of my telephoning a doctor. Sometimes it was much easier to send a message with a servant.

"That's fine, then," he said. The line went silent while Mr. Otting found the doctor's line and connected me. Then suddenly he said, "You're through." With a click, he left the call, and I was speaking over the ever-present buzzing noise to Dr. Waldschmidt's receptionist.

"Good morning," I said, being careful to speak up and enunciate each word. "This is Miss Price. I'm the personal secretary for the Countess of Harleigh."

Hetty gasped at my audacity.

"Lady Harleigh would like to speak with the doctor on a sensitive matter and wonders if he has a moment for her this morning?"

Of course, a moment was found in the doctor's schedule. I replaced the handset and turned the crank to disengage from the exchange. "He will see us in thirty minutes," I announced.

"Well, well. It seems there is an advantage to using the telephone, Miss Price. Or are you Lady Harleigh now?"

"Dr. Waldschmidt has no real reason to speak with me about Lady Winstead. I'm hoping rank will buy me a few answers, but I don't expect much." I came to my feet. "Shall we go? I'll have Jarvis send for a cab."

Instead, Hetty offered the use of her new carriage, and I accepted gladly since the sky was dull and the air quite chilly. Not a day to wait on the pavement for a cab. Instead, we were able to settle into the comparative warmth of the carriage's plush interior.

"What was your impression of the doctor?" I asked once we were on our way. "Did you go to his office?"

"No, he called on me. He seemed efficient, gave me some powders. Whether they actually helped or the fever ran its course, I'll never know. But he has a good manner. I felt confident in his ability."

The drive to the doctor's office was short. A glance out the window told me we were on the northern end of Harley Street, surrounded as we were by narrow, elegant, Georgian-style town houses. The newer, more flamboyant buildings were to the south end of the street. We found the correct address as well as a brass plate bearing his name and a sign that instructed us to walk in.

A sturdy woman in a drab bluish-gray two-piece sat behind a desk next to the entrance. Her hair was firmly pulled into a knot at the nape of her neck. I approached and explained our purpose in calling on the doctor.

"Ah, yes," she said. "Dr. Waldschmidt is in with his final patient for the day. He'll be off to the hospital after that, so you've caught him at the perfect time. If you don't mind taking a seat and waiting for him, it should only be a moment." She indicated a line of wooden chairs along one wall of the room. Hetty and I dutifully each took a seat.

Within five minutes the door at the back of the reception area opened and a middle-aged man emerged. I lifted a brow at the receptionist, but she shook her head and wished the man a good day as he exited. Then she came to her feet. "Allow me to inform the doctor you are here, Lady Harleigh," she said, then disappeared through the door herself.

I straightened my collar and sleeves, then glanced at the closed door. "Does it seem like it's taking him a while to decide whether or not to see us?"

"It's been a matter of seconds," Hetty said. "Don't make yourself nervous." She nodded to the door when the reception-ist reappeared.

"The doctor has a few minutes for you now, my lady," she said.

Only a few minutes? The man was already preparing me for disappointment. Hetty and I rose and stepped into his small but brightly lit office. Another door off to the side might have led to an examining room, for there was no medical equipment in here, only a desk, two chairs for visitors or patients, and a wall of books behind it.

Dr Waldschmidt surprised me by having a very pleasant, almost friendly countenance, with a wide mouth and lines that indicated he used it to smile or laugh frequently. He removed a pair of spectacles and stood when we entered the room, revealing a lanky, angular form. I'd have put him somewhere in his fifties if not for his completely white hair. I immediately sensed that I could trust him, then berated myself. My instincts were not always on point. Either way, I decided it was best to be straightforward.

"We are here about Nurse Plum," I said after introductions were made. "I hope I'm not bringing you the first news of her death."

The big man seemed to deflate a bit and shook his head. "I heard of it yesterday. Such a tragedy." He invited us to be seated and returned to his own chair.

"I believe you worked with her in relation to Lord Peter, the late Viscount Winstead," I said.

"And many more patients," he replied. "I knew Margery,

Nurse Plum, that is, before I opened my own practice. We worked at Westminster Hospital together. Hers was always the first name that came to mind whenever one of my patients required a private nurse. She'd been in private nursing for at least a decade now."

"Was your recommendation due to her skills or her manner?" Hetty asked.

"I can honestly say both. She was a highly skilled nurse with a no-nonsense manner. That's what's needed when dealing with someone in their own home, otherwise they will order the nurse around and take over their own care." He raised his hands palms up. "What is the point of that?"

"Are you aware Nurse Plum was murdered?" I asked.

His expression showed his distress. "I did hear about that. You aren't suggesting one of her patients murdered her?"

"Not at all. I would imagine anyone who required her services would be too ill to carry out such an activity." I narrowed my gaze. "But perhaps a family member who did not care for her methods."

He sputtered a bit. "I believe she's always delivered her care with professionalism. If a family member doesn't approve, they are always free to dismiss her. I hardly think murder would be necessary."

That was a good point. I'd have to try another tack. "Have the two of you crossed paths professionally since your first recommendation?" I asked.

"Oh, yes. If she is working with one of my patients, she occasionally needs to consult with me."

"Did she ever consult with you about Lady Winstead?"

"Lady Winstead?" He emphasized the title. "I wasn't aware she required a nurse. I haven't seen her since Lord Peter's funeral. Obviously, that wasn't in a professional capacity." He took a glance at his pocket watch. I was losing his attention.

"Nurse Plum had been caring for Lady Winstead almost

since the funeral. The police have a theory that her work there may have led to her death."

Fine, it was my theory, but that is the reason Delaney was put on the case.

"I appreciate that you'd rather not speak ill of a colleague," I continued, "but the police are looking into two matters in relation to her murder. One is the theft of a valuable item from the house. The other relates to Lady Winstead's laudanum and the possibility of addiction and overdose."

The doctor lowered his gaze to his desk, where his fingers toyed with his spectacles. "You are correct, my lady. I would not normally discuss anything regarding a patient with someone who is not responsible for their care."

"But Lady Winstead was not your patient," Hetty reminded him.

"That is one reason I'm willing to answer you. The other is preserving Nurse Plum's good name. She—"

"Yes?"

Dr. Waldschmidt pressed his fist against his lips. Perhaps simply choosing his words with care or consulting his conscience.

"Are you well, Doctor?" I asked.

He came to his feet and rested his hands on the back of his chair. "There was an incident many years ago. Nurse Plum was accused of theft and dismissed, but her guilt was assumed, never proven. However, having such a blot on her record, I should think that would make her even less likely to abscond with something that didn't belong to her."

I understood the doctor's defense of Nurse Plum, but it could be just as true that she'd stolen many times and been caught only once.

"As to the issue of the misuse of laudanum, I truly can't imagine it." We must have looked less than convinced, for he continued. "Private nursing is a significantly better position than nursing in a hospital. Margery Plum had been doing this long enough that she would not have risked losing her position or reputation. She would not have wanted to go back to a type of work that is more like drudgery."

Dash it all, that made sense. Nurse Plum could easily have been replaced if she displeased her patient or whoever paid her wages and, once dismissed, might have been less likely to obtain similar employment. We'd reached the moment when I simply had to ask the question I'd been avoiding. "What if the family wanted her to do it?"

His expression turned to one of shock. He ran a hand through his hair as he glanced between Hetty and me, then drew a calming breath. "I won't pretend to misunderstand you, but I'd have no way of knowing that answer. As you pointed out, Lady Winstead wasn't my patient." He narrowed his eyes. "And I must ask why you would believe such a thing of the Ashleys?"

"There is no love lost between Lady Winstead and her stepchildren."

He scowled. "I recall dealing with Lady Winstead when I treated Lord Peter, and I'd find it hard to believe there was anything but ambivalence between her and *all* other humans. She is hardly a warm and caring woman." He held up a hand. "Yes, I understand I am making your case. I refuse to speculate about the Ashleys, but if a plan existed to keep Lady Winstead drugged, I believe it more likely Nurse Plum would have walked away from the job than to have done an injury to someone under her care."

I was surprised by the doctor's goodwill in indulging our questions and truly hated to antagonize him, but his response led me to another question. "Then I suppose it's impossible for you to believe she might have done something to harm Lord Peter, either?"

"The viscount was my patient, and I will not discuss his care with you other than to say in my estimation, he died of natural causes." He pushed himself away from the chair. "Now, if there's nothing else?"

"You have been very kind in indulging my inquiries, Doctor, and I am exceedingly grateful." I rose to my feet and extended my hand. He looked relieved as he shook it and turned to Hetty to do the same.

He walked us to the door, where I turned back to face him. "There is just one more question, now that I think about it. It requires only your opinion."

He compressed his lips but indicated I should continue.

"With Nurse Plum gone, the family is considering moving Lady Winstead to a sanatorium."

"That is rather a surprise, but surely that isn't your question."

"No. You mentioned you saw Lady Winstead at her husband's funeral. In your opinion, was there any reason she should have been prescribed laudanum at that time?"

His pause was long enough for me to wonder if he would refuse to answer, but I didn't look away. Finally, he shook his head. "She was quite in control of herself. I would not have recommended it."

"You should consider that even if the doctor didn't recommend laudanum, plenty of people simply take it upon themselves to use it—and use it liberally. Every household has a leftover bottle of the stuff from a prior illness or headache or toothache."

We were back in Hetty's carriage, heading home. Her comment had me gaping in surprise. "You were the one who told us about those poor old women drugged senseless," I said, "while their offspring squandered their fortunes."

"And that does happen, but surely you know that people,

usually women, often abuse the drug with no assistance from anyone else?"

I held up a gloved finger. "Those women you speak of are often trying to escape pain or, worse, the world. Lady Winstead's idea of escape was to travel. I feel quite confident she is not responsible for her own condition. I'm less confident about her late husband's cause of death."

"The doctor said he died of natural causes."

"At least it looked natural enough that he saw no reason to investigate further. I'm very curious to hear what Lady Esther finds out from the solicitor."

Hetty stared. "Surely, he won't tell her anything about his client?"

I released a mirthless laugh. "You don't know how persuasive Lady Esther can be."

Hetty looked disgusted and let out a tsk.

"Come now, Hetty. The solicitor may be concerned about Lady Winstead, too. Even if he tells Lady Esther nothing but that, she may be able to convince him to go to the police with his concerns."

The carriage swayed as it took a corner, causing us to do the same and bump the brims of our hats together. Hetty adjusted hers, then leveled her gaze at me. "I could understand his suspicion if the children are withdrawing funds from her accounts."

"I'd be surprised if they were authorized to do that, but they may have come to him inquiring how they can legally go about accessing them. Perhaps it would require that Lady Winstead be institutionalized."

"I see what you mean," she said. "He may already be concerned for his client. If a friend of hers comes along expressing her worries, he might be persuaded to do something about it. You mentioned someone in the family suggested moving her to a sanatorium."

"Either Si or Andrew did just yesterday, but Lord Jonathon didn't seem to take to the idea and wants to hire a new nurse. I'm afraid Lady Winstead's chances depend a great deal on the next nurse they hire. Now that we've spoken to Dr. Waldschmidt, don't you find it strange that the family hired a nurse without ever consulting him?"

"I think that means you are correct," Hetty said. "Someone in that family is up to no good, but that still leaves us with the question, Which one?" She placed a hand on my arm. "What if Lady Winstead's solicitor has heard nothing from the Ashleys?"

"If the family hasn't raised any suspicions, we will just have to keep investigating. It doesn't mean they are innocent."

"You and Hazelton have quite a difficult task with this case." We had arrived at home and alighted from the carriage. "Would you care to join me for tea?" Hetty asked once we were on the pavement.

"Thank you, but another time, I'm afraid. I must deliver an invitation to Miss Stover."

"Would that be for Lady Fiona's birthday party?"

"It is," I said. "I ought to have told her about it yesterday, but then we learned of Nurse Plum's death. Fiona is eager to have her attend, and I think it will give her a little taste of society. She already has an idea what it is like to make her living on the stage. This will allow her to understand what her other option involves."

"It's good to know one's options. You ought to inquire if the Ashleys possess a telephone."

"A good idea, but as you saw, sometimes it's easier to pay a call."

"Feel free to use the carriage."

"Thank you. I must go inside first, but I shall."

She turned to go up the steps to her door, then glanced at me over her shoulder. "I wonder, though, if Miss Stover will feel comfortable leaving the house for a full evening."

I headed for my own door. "I'll soon find out."

Even though I warned her this was to be a quick visit to the Ashleys' home, Rose chose to come with me. I regretted it almost immediately. Si Ashley was passing through the hall when the butler opened the door to us.

"Frances, my dear! How good to see you. Come in. Come in." Fuller moved behind the door as Si ushered us into the foyer. "Ah, you've brought your daughter, as well. Delighted, my dear." He instructed Fuller to arrange for tea, then shepherded us into the drawing room, as if he were a corgi.

"We've stopped by only to ask how Lady Winstead is faring today and to extend an invitation to Miss Stover. I don't mean to impose on your time, Si."

He led us over to the tea table, and I had no choice but to seat myself. I took the sofa, and Rose sat in the chair next to me.

"Frances, please," he said. "It's no imposition at all. Jonathon and Vi are off doing some sort of family business, and I find myself at loose ends."

"You could always pick up a book if you have no other way of entertaining yourself." The voice had come from Andrew Ashley, who had been tucked away in the far corner of the room with a book of his own. He came to his feet and inserted a scrap of paper to mark his place.

"I do like a man who practices what he preaches." I smiled and indicated the book.

Si threw his nephew a look of annoyance. "Just because I prefer the company of actual people to books," he said, "doesn't mean I don't read."

Andrew crossed the room, clearly planning to join us, since he had left the book behind. I repressed a sigh. This might take some time. He seated himself in the chair opposite mine and glanced at his uncle. "It does indicate you haven't the means to entertain yourself. Whenever Aunt Vi is gone, you are either at your club or"—he cast a glance at Rose—"at loose ends, as you said."

Or enjoying the company of some other woman, I thought. Andrew had to know about his uncle's amours, but I appreciated him not mentioning them in front of Rose. I ought to take her visiting with me more often. It could be a good way of avoiding some of the more unsavory gossip.

Si seated himself on my other side. "I reckon you're right about that. I enjoy having people about. It makes life much livelier."

I thought Andrew had meant to imply that Si was poor company even for himself, but fortunately, Si had chosen to take the comment without the offense in which it was given. That might be why, regardless of how shiftless he was, he managed to maintain his friendships.

I wondered how Andrew would turn out. Between his self-absorbed grandfather, his sanctimonious father, and his feckless uncle, it was difficult to say in whose footsteps he'd follow. Perhaps he'd forge his own path. One could hope.

"To what do we owe the pleasure of your company today, ma'am?" he asked. "Or did Uncle Si simply waylay you on your way to visit Kate?"

I chuckled. "We are here to pay a call on Kate and Lady Winstead. Have either of you seen the viscountess today? Is she well?" I had hoped to make this a short call but resigned myself to spending a few extra minutes with these two and wondered what information they might be willing to impart.

"Kate would know that best," Si replied. "When the maid brings the tea, I'll have her inform Kate that you're here."

"I think she might decide to forgo the experience of a presentation in order to provide constant care for her aunt," Andrew said. "She rarely leaves Grandmama's room."

"Yes, well, we know your father won't allow that." Si gestured for the maid, who had just entered with the tea service, to lay everything out onto the table. "I don't know why not. Better she takes care of the woman than us." He threw me a sheepish glance, as if he regretted his words. "She does just as well as the nurse, and she's Lady Winstead's only blood relation, you see. It seems appropriate to me."

"I suppose my father feels a sense of obligation to his stepmother," Andrew said. "And I'm not sure he quite trusts Kate. He's already contacted the service to request another nurse."

"Nonsense. Kate's just the sort of girl Lady Winstead needs." Si stopped the maid as she was about to leave. "Let Miss Stover know she has a caller."

The maid turned to me. "She's not likely to leave Lady Winstead, but I'd be happy to take you up to her, if you like, ma'am."

"Yes, thank you," I said just as both men voiced a negative response. I gave them a smile and came to my feet. Rose was already halfway to the door. Bless her. "Thank you both for entertaining us while we waited."

I stepped quickly over to the maid before either of them could stop me. I hated to be rude, but I couldn't deny there was something about this family that simply put me off. Hetty was right. Telephoning would have been better. I turned before leaving the room and addressed Si. "By the way, do you keep a telephone in the house?"

"Horrible contraption," Si said with a grimace. "My stepmother insisted upon having one, though no one uses it."

I nodded and followed the maid and Rose out to the hall and up the stairs. We stopped at the doorway to the dowager's room. The maid announced me, and Kate scurried from her chair by the bed.

"Frances, I'm so glad you're here." With a smile for Rose,

she took me by the arm and led me toward the chair she'd just vacated.

"How is your aunt, dear?" I glanced automatically to the bed, expecting to see her sleeping.

Instead, she was sitting up, holding out a hand to Rose, and greeting her with a smile. When she turned her gaze on me, I took a step back in surprise. Those hazy eyes looked as lucid as I'd ever seen them.

Chapter Sixteen

❧

"Lady Winstead," I said. "You look . . . well." I struggled to keep the surprise from my voice but had only slight success.

The older woman narrowed her eyes, the soft wrinkles surrounding them folding in on themselves. "Lady Harleigh, is it? Thank you for bringing Lady Rose to see me. Tell me, is my niece ready for her presentation?"

I took a steadying breath so I wouldn't babble an unintelligible response. There was still a bit of slow drawling to her speech. Her expression was not as animated as I recalled from the past. And she was in bed, so who knew how steady she'd be on her feet. Despite all that, she still looked significantly better than I'd seen her over the past few days.

"Kate is not quite ready yet, but the queen's drawing room is almost two weeks off. I'm sure we will both be prepared in time."

"Very good. With any luck, I won't be locked up by then."

"Heavens, would anyone consider such a move?"

"There have been whispers among the Ashleys," Kate said, "but it will go no further if I have anything to say about it." She stood next to me, the bottle of laudanum in her hand.

"That won't help matters," I told her, glancing from the bottle to the patient. "Lady Winstead, do you actually need this medication? Are you in pain?"

Kate stepped closer, refusing to cede any ground. "I've done some research on this and learned it could be harmful to stop the laudanum all at once. I read it might be too much of a shock to her body and that it was best to wean her off slowly. Nurse Plum's notes read a teaspoon a day."

I gave her a look of disbelief, and she pulled a small book from her pocket and handed it to me. Heavens, the nurse had kept a record of her patient's care. It noted everything—when Lady Winstead took her meals, got out of bed, visited the garden for fresh air, and had her one teaspoon of laudanum per day. From what I'd witnessed of Lady Winstead, it was hard to believe she stopped at one.

I leafed through the pages, looking for evidence of a crime. Finding nothing incriminating, I handed the book back to Kate and returned my attention to Lady Winstead. "Are you in any pain?" I repeated.

"It helps me to sleep," she said, sounding aggrieved.

"Then perhaps it would be best to hold that until the evening," I said, eyeing the bottle. "Otherwise, she may require more later."

"That makes sense." Kate moved to return the bottle to the bedside table.

"Is there somewhere it could be locked up?" I asked. "Or at least put out of sight? I'd hate for someone else to come in and give Lady Winstead additional medication she doesn't need." I widened my eyes, and Kate took the hint.

"I'll find somewhere else to keep it," she said, and taking the bottle, she headed for the dressing room.

"Nurse Plum is the only one to handle the laudanum." Lady Winstead drawled the last word, losing a syllable and dragging out the vowels.

I seated myself in the chair. "Nurse Plum hasn't been here

for two days. Someone else must have brought your medication. Do you remember who it was?" Could it really be this easy?

She shook her head. "It was always Nurse Plum."

Not so easy, then. I was about to ask if Lady Winstead trusted her niece, but Kate returned to the room and waved me over to the door.

"Rose, will you stay and visit with Lady Winstead while I speak to Miss Stover?"

Rose readily agreed, and I followed Kate to her room next door.

"What is it?" I asked.

She stood with her hands folded at her waist. Her back was straight, and her expression determined. "I'd like to remove my aunt from this house," she said in a low voice. "I can't help feeling she's in danger here. She can stay with me in a hotel until I can find other accommodations for us."

Removing Lady Winstead from this house might be the best solution—unless Kate was the one drugging her. Then it might mean the woman's demise. Of course, there were practical issues to consider, as well. "How do you intend to get her out of the house without a trio of Ashleys blocking your way?"

"I hoped that with your support and your carriage, we would win the day. It's not as if they want to care for her."

"Neither do they want to be seen throwing her out on the street, which is what it would appear to be to their friends and neighbors. It is also very likely that Lady Winstead is paying for the running of the household. That alone would induce the family to fight you for her." It dawned on me that Kate had drawn me away from Lady Winstead for this conversation. "Your aunt is more coherent today. Have you discussed your plan with her?"

Kate glanced away. "She does not understand her situation. When I suggested I take her away, she became very agitated—

shouting and refusing to leave." Kate's jaw was clenched so tightly, her lips barely moved. "I hoped with the help of you and your husband, we could sneak her out."

"I will not involve Hazelton in a kidnapping plot." I placed a hand on her shoulder before she could deny the truth. "That is what it would appear to be. Particularly if she is shouting that she wishes to remain here. This is her home. Her family has been caring for her. You would likely be arrested, and your aunt returned here—all the worse off because she would not have you to protect her."

"I must do something."

"Continue as you are. Give it a little time. If your aunt continues to recover, she will likely reconsider leaving."

"If Lord Jonathon doesn't lock her up somewhere."

"Let us hope we can prevent that."

We returned to Lady Winstead's room, where Rose was up on the bed, with the older woman's arm around her. They were reading together.

"That's enough for now," she told Rose when we entered the room.

Rose obediently scooted off the bed and walked across the room to replace the book on a shelf. I'd hoped to speak more with Lady Winstead, but by then she looked as if she'd prefer to drift off than to answer questions. I had to take some relief in the fact that she appeared much better now the nurse was gone, but I was concerned her condition could easily deteriorate with more laudanum.

When the older woman's eyes closed, I told Kate about the invitation to Fiona's birthday celebration.

"I don't know—" she began.

"I thought I'd find you here." Vi appeared in the doorway. "And Frances too. How lovely, but it seems all this company has been too much for Lady Winstead."

"Indeed, she just dozed off," I said. "Rose and I really ought to be leaving. You'll consider the ball, Kate?"

"A ball?" Vi sighed with envy, then glanced at Kate. "What is there to consider?"

"It's tomorrow, and I hate to leave Aunt Augusta alone."

"Ah, but you won't be. The agency is sending a new nurse over tomorrow afternoon. She will be here to care for Lady Winstead all evening. Heavens, someone in this house should be out enjoying themselves. It feels as if we've been in mourning forever. You must go."

Kate made no reply, but I knew better than to take that as acceptance. She meant simply to defer the argument until I was gone. I took my leave of them both and, taking Rose by the hand, stepped into the hallway, almost tripping over Aggie, who was nearly hidden behind the stack of linens she carried.

"Gracious, Aggie! You needn't hover in the doorway," Vi said, stepping into the hall. "Go on in. I'm sure Lady Winstead needs something."

The maid lowered her head and slipped into the room.

Vi let out a tsk. "I'll see you to the door, Frances."

We arrived home just in time for Rose to change for her riding lesson. Graham would send the carriage for her, so I was free to prepare for my afternoon. In fact, I had only a short time before Fiona called for me on the way to Cornelia Dawson's drawing room entertainment. Wishing I'd sent my regrets rather than acceptance, I met Bridget in my dressing room, where I changed into something a bit more sophisticated for an afternoon call. Once she had neatened my hair and settled my hat, I went downstairs just in time for Fiona's arrival. Jarvis answered the door, helped me with my cloak, then came outside and handed us into Fiona's carriage. Sometimes it was lovely to have a butler.

As I seated myself, I picked up a leather-bound diary that had been left on the seat. "What is this, Fiona?"

"I've been noting my requirements for a governess," she said. "Look through them and add anything you think necessary. I'll contact an employment agency next week. We might even consider taking an ad in one of the newspapers."

I scanned Fiona's entries while listening to the clomp of the carriage horses. After the past few dreary days, there was actual sunlight streaming through the window, making the task easier. I agreed with most of her requirements and added a few of my own. The carriage had just arrived at the Dawson town house when Fiona recalled her invitation to Miss Stover.

"Did you invite her? Will she be coming?"

"She was very hesitant when I extended the invitation," I said. "I'm afraid she won't want to leave her aunt alone with the Ashleys."

The carriage door opened, and a groom assisted us down to the pavement. I leaned in closer to my friend as we strolled up the walk to Cornelia's door. "She actually suggested kidnapping Lady Winstead and hiding her away in a hotel until she recovered."

Fiona grimaced. "That's dedication."

"Or a crime," I countered.

"Her intent isn't criminal, Frances. She wants to protect her aunt."

"I think what she wants to protect is her inheritance."

"She wouldn't be the first."

I had no chance to reply, because the door opened, and we were swept into the house by our hostess herself. Cornelia was always one of the brightest lights of the social season. If one examined her features, she was not a great beauty. She had a nice-enough figure, and her hair was a light brown, her nose straight, eyes blue, and chin pointed. But there was a vivacity about her that made her attractive to everyone. I had attended many of her literary evenings, which always included the authors and a great deal of stimulating conversation. Since this was more a theatrical afternoon, I wasn't quite sure what to expect.

Dawson House was about the size of mine but with a larger drawing room. Under normal circumstances, it was cluttered with furnishings, but because the performers were actually enacting scenes from various plays, everything that could be moved was against a wall to make a stage area in the center of the room. The guests numbered about two dozen and were scattered in small groupings about the perimeter. Cornelia waved a footman over with glasses of wine and another with a tray of canapés. Fiona and I mingled with the other guests long enough for me to wonder if there was to be any entertainment. Then a buzz of anticipation stirred the air.

"The next scene is about to start," Cornelia called out to us, excitement glowing in her eyes.

We found three seats along the wall just as the performance began. Rather than *Florodora*, it was a scene from Shakespeare's *The Taming of the Shrew*.

"This is rather different, isn't it?" Fiona whispered.

I didn't respond, as I was distracted by the actor playing the role of Petruchio. At first, he looked only vaguely familiar, but as he spoke, I realized this was Mr. Montague, Kate's so-called old friend from home. Well, I supposed that much could be true. She may have simply neglected to mention he was also an actor. But hadn't she said he was only visiting London on business?

I shifted closer to Fiona and tipped my head toward her shoulder. "I don't recall seeing him in *Florodora*. Do you?"

"He played Gilfain, the villain. I'm not surprised you don't recognize him. He was gray-haired, bearded, and well padded."

Heavens! The transformation was astonishing. Gilfain was

meant to be American, so Mr. Montague must have altered his voice when mimicking the accent.

Deep in my thoughts, I barely noticed Cornelia lean forward across Fiona, but I could hardly ignore the touch on my arm. I looked into her beaming face.

"Isn't he wonderful?" she asked.

"Do you mean Petruchio?" I had the feeling she wasn't referring to his acting ability. "Yes, he is quite good."

"He and I are old friends." She gave me a wink. "He is so much better than good."

Fiona had a smile in place but rolled her eyes when she turned to me. "You know by 'old friends,' she means lovers," she muttered close to my ear.

I scowled. "Of course I know that."

"And by 'good'—"

"Stop it, Fiona. I'm aware of what she means. What I want to know is how long they've been together."

She drew back and studied me. "Why?"

Cornelia had returned her attention to the scene. Nevertheless, I drew Fiona close enough to whisper, "I met him a few days ago and was told he had only recently arrived in London from Devon. For business."

"Devon, you say?" Fiona let none of her surprise show in her expression, but her fingers tightened on my wrist. "Isn't that where Miss Stover is from?"

"I'll tell you what I know later," I said. "Just ask her."

"That won't be necessary. I know they've been together for quite some time." She casually checked to see that Cornelia was paying us no heed and turned back to me. "It's rumored he fathered one of her children."

Cornelia's youngest child was at least five years old. Theirs was an arrangement of some standing.

"Do you plan to speak with him?" she asked.

I considered the possibility. The only thing I still needed to ask was about his relationship with Kate. With Cornelia by his side, this was neither the time nor the place. "Not today," I said.

"Excellent. We'll leave as soon as this scene is over, and you must tell me everything on the way home."

The scene seemed to go on forever, but it finally ended. Several of the female guests gathered around Mr. Montague, as if drawn by the magnetic pull of his charms. Cornelia barely acknowledged our farewells as she stormed away to put an end to their fawning.

Once in her carriage, Fiona wasted no time in satisfying her curiosity. "Is Miss Stover in love with him?" she asked. "Will you tell her about Cornelia?"

I told her the circumstances under which I had met Mr. Montague. "It was Kate who lied about him. First, she said he was a friend of Lady Winstead and had called to visit her. When I didn't believe her, he became an old friend from home." I shook my head in frustration. "I'm afraid Kate is not to be trusted. Perhaps I shouldn't bring her to your birthday gala, after all."

"Now, now. Don't be so hasty." Fiona patted my arm.

I gawked at her. "You have already mentioned her to some gentleman, who is now eager to meet her, haven't you?"

"Perhaps I have, but I still think you are too quick to judge."

"Quick to judge?"

"Her prevarication is understandable in this case," she added when I took offense. "If I heard you correctly, you met Mr. Montague before you learned Miss Stover was an actress." At my nod, she continued. "How was she to explain her friendship with an actor without revealing that she was an actress?"

"So, to maintain one lie, she had to tell me another." I folded my arms over my chest. "Somehow that doesn't make me more inclined to trust her."

"I see." Her lips curled up in a wicked smile. "Then you've

never found yourself in a similar situation? The Ashleys, for example. I suppose they know exactly what you're doing?"

There was no arguing against that point. "Tell me, Fiona, in this situation, am I the pot or the kettle?"

"Frances, you are my dearest friend." Her eyes softened. "If I can't point out the truth, who can?"

"Yes, yes. You are right. Still, I wonder if Kate will tell me the truth about Mr. Montague now that I know about her acting."

"Do you suppose she's in love with him?"

"She may be, but considering his arrangement with Cornelia, I hope not."

She gave me a knowing look. "I believe you're fond of Miss Stover."

"That doesn't mean I trust her."

I arrived at home to find Hetty and Gilliam in our drawing room, seated around the tea table with George. The scene reminded me that only that morning we'd met with Dr. Waldschmidt. It felt more like days ago. I handed my wrap to Jarvis and moved toward George, who greeted me with a smile and a cup of tea when I joined them.

"Good to see you, Gilliam," I said, taking a seat. "Has Hetty told you both about our visit with the doctor?"

"I told them about our less than resounding success," Hetty said. "The doctor could see no evil in either the nurse or the Ashleys."

I took a sip of tea. "Hetty describes it well. We might just as well continue thinking as we did before speaking with him."

"That means someone, and we don't know who, is drugging Lady Winstead," George said.

"Nurse Plum was definitely giving her laudanum. Miss Stover found the log where the nurse recorded the details of the care she'd rendered."

"It was the nurse?" Hetty looked surprised.

I raised my brows. "If only it were that easy. According to her logs, the nurse was giving her ladyship one teaspoon of laudanum a day. I believe that's all Miss Stover has given her, and you should have seen how alert the woman was today."

"Do you believe the nurse was lying?" Hetty asked.

"In a manner of speaking, yes. She may not have given Lady Winstead more laudanum than she stated, but someone did. It's impossible to believe the nurse didn't recognize the symptoms, so I still think someone in the house was paying her either to drug Lady Winstead herself or to turn a blind eye while they did."

"Then I trust you don't believe it will end with the death of the nurse?" George leaned back in his chair, looking thoughtful.

"I do not. Though I cautioned Miss Stover to keep the laudanum hidden away, it would be easy enough for anyone to obtain another bottle."

"What if she is the culprit?" George always seemed to pin down the very thing that troubled me.

"Then Lady Winstead is truly in danger. I don't recall if I told you this, but on one occasion when I called at Ashley House, I found Kate entertaining a gentleman alone in the drawing room. A visiting neighbor from Devon, she called him."

"Was that untrue?" Hetty asked.

"Definitely. I learned he is a fellow actor, currently performing in *Florodora*. I saw him today at Cornelia Dawson's theatrical afternoon. Cornelia and he have a very cozy relationship."

Gilliam smothered a laugh, drawing our attention. "That must be Henry Montague," he said. "Fairly talented actor, but rather a shady character, I'm told."

"Do you know him personally, Gilliam?" I asked.

"I've met him. He auditioned for me a few months ago. Sally warned me he'd be trouble, but he wasn't right for the role, anyway." Sally Cooper was the outspoken and irrepressible actress who was directing Gilliam's latest production.

"I have my own suspicions," I said, "but what sort of trouble did Sally mean?"

"He's a handsome devil with charm to spare. Sally doubts he'd ever do anything to upset the arrangement he has with Mrs. Dawson, but he'd still lead the young actresses a merry chase and have them at each other's throats." Gilliam shrugged. "In other words, he likes the attention."

George leaned forward, placing his forearms on his thighs, and tilted his head toward me. "Did you get the sense that this man and Miss Stover were involved romantically?"

"I did. When I walked in on them, they were standing very close. He was holding her hand, though she called it a mere handshake. It could have been innocent, but they jumped apart upon hearing me enter, as if they didn't want anyone to see them together."

Hetty scowled. "Do you suppose he's playing Miss Stover for a fool? He must know she's related to a very wealthy woman—and an elderly woman at that."

"I hadn't considered that . . . until now," I said. "Today she asked me to help her spirit Lady Winstead away. She wants to move her to a hotel, where she can stay with her and see to her recovery. I wonder if Mr. Montague might have suggested that scheme?"

"What did you tell her when she asked for your help?" George asked.

"I told her no, but it didn't matter, because Lady Winstead rejected the idea herself." I raised my cup to my lips before I realized the tea had gone cold, and placed the cup back on the table. "It seems Lady Winstead became anxious at the thought of leaving her home, though she may change her mind as she regains her health. Kate seemed to see the truth of what I said, but I'd say she was still determined. I just don't know if she's trying to protect her aunt or harm her."

"She'll require some watching," George said. "Speaking of

hidden away, you didn't happen to come across the journal, did you?"

My shoulders sagged. "It didn't occur to me to look, but in my defense, I wouldn't have had the opportunity. Either Kate or Rose was with me all the time."

"I hesitate to file my report with the museum. What do I tell them? Miss Stover admits to taking it, but it's no longer where she hid it." He frowned. "Have you seen any signs that Viscount Winstead is actively searching the house for it?"

"Not unless he has the servants looking. That maid Aggie turns up at the oddest times, but I'm inclined to think she's spying on Kate as opposed to searching for anything." I lifted my shoulders. "Other than her, no one else seems to be paying attention to anything going on in that house."

George leaned back in his seat. "I still have a day or two before I must give them a report. If you have an opportunity to look around Lady Winstead's room or Miss Stover's, that would be helpful, but do not attempt any of the other family rooms. I don't want the Ashleys to become suspicious of you."

"Well, we know it isn't at Nurse Plum's home, at least."

"I'm not so certain of that. I checked all the obvious places she might have hidden something—drawers, cabinets, under the bed. But with the constable following me around, I didn't check behind cabinets or tap on floors or walls, looking for a place she might hide something valuable. I'll have to return sometime after the police are finished and before the landlord leases it again."

"George, what was this Hetty told me about some jewelry you were looking for today?" Gilliam poured himself another cup of tea.

"Something we suspect was stolen from Lady Winstead," George said. "I visited jewelers and pawnshops, looking for sapphires and diamonds or anyone who fit the descriptions of one of the Ashleys and who might have come in and asked questions about selling such jewelry."

"The way you describe your day, it sounds as if it didn't go any better than mine," I said.

He saluted me with his cup. "You are correct. Since I couldn't give much of a description of the pieces, and I had no idea when they might have been brought in, I gave up looking for the jewels and just started asking about the family. No one I spoke to recalled having done any business with them."

"A jeweler who turns a blind eye to shady business—and a man trying to sell an expensive necklace sounds rather shady—isn't likely to admit anything to you," Gilliam said. "However, I'd imagine such a jeweler would prefer to do such business with someone they know. They'd see a toff like the viscount as nothing but trouble."

George rubbed his chin. "That's a good point. But where else would a toff go if he needed to sell an expensive piece of jewelry?"

"If he's smart, he wouldn't sell the piece itself. He'd sell only the stones," Gilliam said. He lifted his brows, and George leaned in. "If he's very smart, he'll replace the stones with fakes and return the fake piece to its usual place. Then he can sell the stones by themselves. Or he can have the jeweler do it for him. Meanwhile, the owner may never realize the jewels are fake."

"That would be an excellent plan," George agreed. "I haven't dealt much with jewelry, stolen or otherwise. I'd assume Lord Jonathon wouldn't know much more than I. How would he find such a jeweler?"

"I don't see how that would be a strange request to make of any jeweler," Hetty said. "If one is traveling, one may want to bring some favorite pieces along. Unfortunately, one must always worry about the risk of theft. The solution is to have a piece made with false stones."

"But in that situation, the customer is only making a copy, not removing the real stones," I said. "That's the suspicious part."

"I'm not sure what pretense he might use," Gilliam said,

"but I know several jewelers who make paste jewelry for the theater. We often need elaborate pieces for productions, and we certainly aren't going to pay for the real thing. They are proper businesses, so if they did work with someone looking to remove stones from a piece, they'd want some sort of proof of ownership. However, they could very easily fashion a copy. Once he had that, the viscount needn't worry about damaging the setting. He could simply remove the stones himself."

"Goodness, Gilliam, I had no idea you were so cunning." Hetty glanced at him in such a way that it was clear she found this more attractive than alarming.

George chuckled. "But one wonders if Lord Jonathon is that cunning."

"Or Si Ashley," I added. "He's always short of funds. Or Andrew Ashley. We know nothing about him."

"Or Miss Stover." George studied me over his cup. "She is the one with the theatrical background, after all."

"She is," I said. "And I still don't know if she's trustworthy. In addition to Kate's revelation today, I also learned that the viscount is set against her caring for her aunt. I don't know if that means he fears she'd harm Lady Winstead, but his son, Andrew, has made some remarks, supposedly in jest, that people have a tendency to die around Kate." I glanced at my companions, who all seemed to be waiting for me to continue. "Is it possible this is all due to Kate? Lord Peter's death, the nurse, and even Lady Winstead?"

"She did steal the journal," George said. "Though she came up with an explanation for you, that doesn't mean her story was true."

"We've witnessed her skill on the stage," Gilliam said. "I'd say she's a fairly good actress."

I poured myself a fresh cup of tea, wishing it had the jolt of a thick cup of coffee, and set about collecting my thoughts. "She couldn't have stolen the jewelry. Lady Winstead remarked on

the missing pieces in a letter to Kate over a month ago. Kate
was still in Devon then. I can't imagine any reason why she'd
steal the journal other than the one she gave me. It's obviously
written by Lord Peter about his expeditions. As we observed
with Nurse Plum, Kate would have a difficult time selling it." I
paused. "Though Jonathon mentioned there might be publishers who would be willing to buy it."

"We can't completely rule her out," George said.

"I agree, but much of this happened before she joined the
household. She was there when Lord Peter died, but he became
ill at least two weeks prior to her arrival. Lady Esther claimed
the family refused to let her see Lady Winstead back in January, well before Miss Stover arrived in town. If everything is related—Lord Peter's death, the missing journal, Nurse Plum's
murder, and the drugging of Lady Winstead—I'm having trouble assigning all the blame to Miss Stover."

Hetty narrowed her eyes. "It may well be one of the Ashleys who is keeping Lady Winstead drugged, but it could be
Miss Stover who gave her the extra doses that might have
killed her. Does she expect to inherit something from her
aunt?"

My head spun from all the possibilities. "I never thought I'd
be saying this, but poor Lady Winstead. If what we assume is
actually true, she's being attacked from every side. Some want
to keep her drugged but alive, so they can have access to her
money. Another may want to kill her for an inheritance. Lady
Esther should be able to shed some light on her friend's financial settlements. In fact, I'm surprised she hasn't called already."

I glanced at Gilliam and George. "Perhaps the two of you
might call on some of the jewelers Gilliam spoke of. If Kate visited one of them, asking to have a costume piece made, I'm certain they'd remember dealing with her. It would be unusual for
a young woman to take care of such business herself."

"I could spare a few hours tomorrow if you're game, Hazelton," Gilliam said.

George agreed readily. "I'd appreciate the assistance. What would be really helpful would be to have someone installed in the house who could keep an eye on all our suspects and Lady Winstead, too."

My head jerked up as George uttered the very words that I'd been thinking. "That would be helpful indeed," I said. "I therefore volunteer for the task."

Chapter Seventeen

"Are you quite serious?" George came to his feet and stared at me as if he thought I'd lost my mind. "At least one person in that house is very dangerous. The only reason I'm not worried about you now is that you don't spend much time there. This is a terrible idea. I won't hear of it."

I stared at him, open mouthed. His response was completely unexpected, and I didn't know quite how to react. Fortunately, Hetty spoke, allowing me a moment to put my thoughts into some sort of order.

"It's not a bad idea at all, Hazelton," she said. "In fact, you just said it would be good to have someone in the house. And if one person is good, two must be even better."

I drew in a sharp gasp. "Aunt Hetty, do you think to accompany me?"

She spread her hands. "Why not?"

"Because it's a terrible idea," George repeated. "You'd be putting yourselves in danger."

"Oh, I don't think so, George," I said. "They trust me. I actually have a purpose in that house. I can easily tell them Kate needs intensive tutoring before her presentation, and they will believe me. I can keep an eye out for the journal much easier if I'm living there. At the same time, I can watch them all interact with Lady Winstead."

George had his hands on his hips, prepared to fight me on this. "What if they stop trusting you? What if they become suspicious of your motives?"

"Then I suppose they will ask me to leave. There is truly no need for them to do anything more. Lady Winstead has requested my assistance, and the family agreed. Should they decide they no longer want it, they have only to say so. Once asked to leave, I would have to comply, though, and that means leaving you there on your own, Hetty."

Gilliam shook his head. "I don't care for the sound of that. And why would they ask you to leave but allow Hetty to stay? What is her excuse for being there?"

"The new nurse," Hetty and I said in unison.

Both men stared in confusion.

"Hear me out," Hetty said. "Frances said the Ashleys have requested another nurse to care for Lady Winstead. I suggest we cancel that request and I go as that nurse."

Gilliam sputtered a protest, but George seemed to be considering the idea. "Wouldn't the Ashleys know you?" he asked at last.

"I don't recall ever meeting them," she replied.

George turned to me and raised a brow.

I scoured my memory. "Jonathon Ashley may have attended some of the same events we did last spring, when Lily made her debut, but I don't remember introducing Hetty to him. I didn't see Si and Vi at all last year, and Andrew would have been away at school."

"So, Jonathon Ashley might know you by sight." Gilliam chose to note the one negative.

"If so, you can be sure he won't remember me. Nobody notices women of my age. We are invisible to the general population. I can do all the snooping necessary." She waved a hand at me. "Frances doesn't even have to come."

"I won't let you stay there by yourself," I said. "We'll do this together. Even George must admit there is safety in numbers."

"Must I?" he said, his brows raised nearly to his hairline. "Don't you suppose the Ashleys will find it odd that you are moving into their home when your own is only a fifteen-minute ride away?"

I had to concede that to be true. "The only one likely to question it would be Lord Jonathon, but I've managed to talk my way around men like him before."

George gave me a look of deep scrutiny. "Yes, you do seem quite adept at that."

I released a tinkling laugh as I touched his shoulder. "You're far too clever, darling. I would never attempt that with you."

"Huh." His eyes narrowed. "Of course not."

"In fact, I can tell the family that Lady Winstead requested that I move in. She won't dispute my claim."

"That's an excellent idea, Frances," Hetty said.

Gilliam came to his feet and stood by George. "They're doing this, aren't they?"

George heaved a sigh. "It appears so." He slipped into the seat beside me and took my hands. "What you said about the Ashleys is true. They can simply ask you to leave, but remember this. You can't expect that someone who feels trapped—or, worse, caught—to act within reasonable parameters."

He looked so concerned, I almost relented. I knew how I would worry if the shoe were on the other foot. Regardless, I would not have stopped him. "I'll be careful. I promise."

"Wait just a minute." Gilliam looked well and truly confused. "How do you propose to manage this switch, Hetty for a real nurse, that is?"

"One of us will have to contact the agency," Hetty said. "You could do it, Gilliam. Say you're Jonathon Ashley's secretary and cancel the job."

"Do you even know which agency they used?"

"I do," George said. "I saw it on Nurse Plum's paperwork when I searched her home. This could work, but do you both feel comfortable enough to see this through?" He glanced at Hetty. "Do you know anything about nursing?"

"Nothing beyond the usual home remedies, I'm afraid. But I do know when to call in a doctor. I won't let any harm come to Lady Winstead."

"Dr. Waldschmidt said he didn't know why she had a nurse in the first place," I said. Suddenly I wasn't so certain of this plan, after all. "Perhaps we ought to check with him before we move you in. I'd hate to endanger her health."

"Are you suggesting we take him into our confidence?" George looked aghast.

That was precisely what I had been thinking, but I was loath to admit it now. "I simply thought we could inquire as to her health."

"But we did that earlier today," Hetty said. "He told us he'd never examined her."

"That's right. Since they simply hired a nurse without consulting a doctor first, it's unlikely Nurse Plum was doing anything more than dosing her with laudanum. I think we'll be fine."

"I'm still not in favor of this plan." Gilliam glanced between Hetty and me.

"Oh, dear. And I was counting on you to help us, Herbert." Hetty's voice was smooth and low. "I'll need some sort of uniform, won't I? I was hoping you had something at the theater that might work for me."

Gilliam stared upward, probably reviewing his costume racks in his mind. "It is rather like playing a role, isn't it?"

"Exactly." Hetty was nearly purring.

George glanced at the clock. "It's almost six. If we're to do this, we ought to call the agency soon."

"I think it an excellent idea," I said.

"I'm certainly in favor of pursuing it." Hetty grinned at me.

Gilliam shook his head. "I doubt there's any way of talking you out of it, so I suppose I'll go along."

"My sentiments exactly," George said. "Let's hope this works."

The following morning Hetty met with Gilliam at his theater to rummage through costumes and props for the proper attire and accessories that would convince the Ashleys she was indeed a nurse. Meanwhile, I received a message from Dr. Waldschmidt. He asked that I call at his office at my earliest convenience.

The agency had informed George that it was too late to cancel Nurse Carmichael, but if we didn't need her, we should simply send her home. She would arrive at Ashley House at two o'clock this afternoon, so we were free to call on Dr. Waldschmidt at once. This time there were two patients in his waiting room when George and I arrived. We explained our business to the receptionist, who was just a little confused that I was Mrs. Hazelton today. She slipped into the doctor's office to inform him, and we took our seats. I was next to a woman holding a child of about two years of age in her lap. Though the woman wore a coat over her dress, it was clear she was his nanny. The child's clothing was worth twice what her coat must have cost.

"Is the little one unwell?" I asked, wondering what kind of parent sent their child with the nanny to see a doctor.

"No, ma'am. He's just fine. His mother's been feeling poorly, so I've come to get her medicine."

I wondered if the medicine in question was laudanum. The other patient was a middle-aged man across from us, reading a newspaper while he waited. I didn't have a chance to wonder about him, though, since the receptionist returned and told us the doctor would see us now. Though I felt a bit guilty jumping ahead in the queue, I was relieved our wait had been brief.

Dr. Waldschmidt met us at the door to his office. "Thank you for coming," he said, closing the door behind us.

I introduced George, and at the doctor's invitation, we seated ourselves in his guest chairs while he leaned back against his desk.

"I've been thinking about our conversation ever since you left yesterday, and feeling that I rather let Lady Winstead down."

"In what way?" I asked.

The doctor's hands were restless. He clasped them, unclasped them, then finally rested them on the desk behind him. "She is not my patient, but I've observed her closely enough to have answered your questions. I didn't want to become involved in any sort of family dispute, but my first duty is to render assistance. I apologize for rebuffing your inquiry."

Well, this was interesting. I hadn't expected the doctor to welcome our questions yesterday, but if he was willing to assist us further, I'd accept wholeheartedly.

George must have been of the same mind. "Was there something you neglected to tell the ladies yesterday?"

The doctor drew in a breath. "I should have mentioned that Lady Winstead also questioned the nature of her husband's death."

That was not what I'd expected him to say.

George pursed his lips and studied the doctor for a moment. "To be clear. When did she pose the question, and to whom?"

"She very quietly and discreetly pulled me aside at the funeral and asked if I had found anything suspicious about his death."

"And?" I urged.

"I answered her honestly. Considering his age, and the extent of his illness, death was always a possibility, but I had fully expected him to recover. It was clear she didn't like my answer, but since she didn't press me further, I thought the matter was closed. I still have no reason to suspect his death was anything but natural, but it's possible Lady Winstead did."

I glanced from George to the doctor. "If Lady Winstead suspected foul play, you may not be the only person she consulted about his death. What if she mentioned it to someone in the family—someone who did hasten Lord Peter's death? That would explain why she is being drugged with laudanum."

"We still don't know that anyone did hasten his death." George glanced at the doctor. "Do we?"

He wagged his head. "Not without a proper autopsy, I'm afraid."

George raised a hand before I could ask the question. "We could never gain permission for an autopsy with such speculation as this. Our first order of business is to stop Lady Winstead's laudanum, however she is receiving it."

"That can be both tricky and time-consuming." Dr. Waldschmidt folded his arms over his chest. "If she is addicted to laudanum, you'll have to wean her off the stuff. If you take it away altogether, she may suffer withdrawal symptoms. That will, of course, alarm the family, and your mission will be for nothing."

He went on to explain precisely how much and how frequently we should administer the laudanum. "And make sure you keep it locked up. Not just for fear of someone else giving it to her, but that she will medicate herself."

We left him with a better sense of the task ahead of us and his promise to come immediately if we needed his help.

George wanted to make a quick stop at Nurse Plum's flat since the police had finished with it. Jack dropped us off on the corner and walked the horses around the block, where the buildings were of a more commercial nature and where he would look less conspicuous waiting for us. George easily got us through the front door to the communal hallway. It took a few minutes longer for him to pick the lock to Nurse Plum's door, but we managed to gain access before anyone emerged from the surrounding flats.

"Are we looking for the journal?" I asked once we were safely inside.

George had already moved to the bedroom, so I followed him. "We're looking for a hiding place. Somewhere she could store small things—documents, money, jewelry." He threw me a glance. "And yes, I'm hoping we find the journal."

I left him with the bedroom and moved to the small kitchen. There was a worktable with a center drawer, which was partially open. In it, I found nothing but cutlery and kitchen tools. I pulled one of the chairs away from the table to examine a shelf that ran along the wall behind the stove. I opened each of the canisters and checked inside and under the stove. I looked behind all the items on the pantry shelves and under the shelves. The sink held a pot of murky water. I found nothing underneath it. I was just scanning the room to see if there was any corner I'd missed when George joined me.

"Anything?" he asked.

"Not a thing." I sighed and pushed the drawer in the table closed again. It slid back out about two inches. Odd. I pushed once more. It opened. "Maybe I *have* found something," I said.

He pulled the drawer all the way out and set it on top of the table; then, crouching down, he reached into the opening. "I believe you're right." His arm disappeared past the elbow. His head, near the side of the table, jerked. His face contorted. "Something's got me, Frances. Help!"

"For goodness' sake, George. We haven't time for pranks. Pull your arm back out of there."

Instead, his arm slid deeper into the opening, and his eyes seemed to bulge.

"Are you really stuck on something?"

When his only reply was a choking noise, my heart began to pound as I realized something was truly wrong. I crouched alongside him, and after wrapping my arms around his chest, I pulled with all my strength. His arm came free, and we both tumbled to the floor, with him landing on top of me.

My heart still raced. "Are you all right, darling?"

When he turned his face to me, he wore the most annoying grin. "Heh, heh, heh!"

With a gasp, I pushed him off me and came to my feet. "You," I said, shaking my finger, "need to stop this nonsense!"

He heaved a sigh and pushed himself up. "You used to laugh at my jokes."

"They used to be funny," I snapped. "Besides, this is not the time. Now, what did you find behind the drawer?"

"Not the journal," he said. He reached back into the opening and removed a fistful of envelopes, then placed them on the table.

They were plain paper envelopes, sealed, but slit open. Each one contained a two-pound note and nothing else. There were a dozen envelopes. One per week, perhaps? If this represented Nurse Plum's wages, she was paid about three times more than the average nurse.

"There's nothing written on the envelopes, either." Even I could hear the fatigue in my voice. "Why can we never find one obvious clue? One clue that clearly indicates the person in question has done something wrong? Instead of the journal, we find this. This money could indicate someone was paying her to drug Lady Winstead or to turn a blind eye while they drugged her, or it could be completely innocent." I let my hands drop to my sides and turned to George. "Why?"

He opened his arms. I leaned willingly against him while he stroked my back. "It's damnably frustrating, I know."

"I don't think you do." My words were muffled as I spoke them against his shoulder. His chuckle rumbled through his chest. "And don't laugh at me."

"I'm not laughing at you, but at the situation. And only because it's one I've been in before. I can't tell you how many times I've been on a case and asked myself if there is even a crime for me to investigate."

"It's so frustrating."

"Indeed. But for my purposes, the British Museum would like their journal, and for yours, Lady Esther would like some peace of mind. We agreed to help them, and therefore, we must soldier on."

I heaved a sigh, pushed away from him, and waved a hand at the envelopes. "What do we even do with these?"

"Turn them over to Delaney," he said. "Or rather, stuff them back in the opening and tell Delaney where to find them."

"The last time I did that was with the journal, and it disappeared before I could turn it over to you. I like your first statement better. The inspector had to know you'd be back to have another look around. He can't fault you for that if you bring him potential evidence." I huffed. "Evidence of what, I don't know."

"That would work best if I left you out of the story and told him I found them myself. I have authorization to be here, whereas you do not. Could get sticky if I report that you found them."

I waved a hand. "Then by all means, let my accomplishments be lost to history."

George made a derisive noise, which made me laugh, as I think it was meant to do.

"We have to draw some conclusion to this investigation before I lose my mind," I said. "I'm actually glad I'll be staying at the Ashley home, where I can observe everyone with my own eyes and find out if anything untoward is actually happening."

George collected the envelopes from the table and stuffed them in his pockets. "I wish I felt the same, but I am relieved Hetty will be there with you. And I think we do know something is happening there. We simply don't know who is at the bottom of it. So, don't let your guard down with them, like you just did with me."

"I have no intention of doing that. As for you, it was your face that fooled me. How did you make your eyes bulge like that?"

He grinned. "I refuse to divulge my secret. You might try it on me someday."

With a chuckle, I glanced around the kitchen. "Are we off, then?"

"One more stop before I give you up to the Ashleys." His tone was a bit stiff. He was not joking. It took a moment for me to realize he was actually distraught, and I understood why.

I took his hand and linked our fingers, then brought his knuckles up to my lips. "It will be our first night apart," I said.

"I shan't sleep a wink, you know."

"For worrying about me?"

He pulled me toward him with our linked hands. "That, too, but I've grown used to your snoring sending me off to sleep."

I gasped. "I do not snore!"

"You needn't upset yourself. It's a dainty little gnashing noise. Like a kitten with a stuffy nose."

The cheek! "Oh, is it really? A far cry from yours, which makes the walls rattle."

He preened. "My dear, you can hardly expect me to make some mewling little sound. A man of my stature must have a manly snore."

"You have certainly accomplished that," I said. Laughing, I cradled his face in my hands. "I shall miss your manly snores."

"Then be sure to return to them—and to me—as soon as possible."

Chapter Eighteen

~≈~

We had one final stop to make before I took myself off to the Ashleys'. It was half past twelve when we stepped into Lady Esther's drawing room. It was a bright room, enjoying a sunny exposure from the two front windows and furnished sparsely with fine pieces. A Jacobean tea table took pride of place in the center of the room, accompanied by a settee and several chairs of the same style.

Lady Esther was seated off to the side of the room, in a Queen Anne chair that could easily have accommodated two people of her size. It was the only chair in the vicinity, making me wonder if George and I were meant to stand for the entirety of our visit. After assuring her we had no immediate news of Lady Winstead, she wrapped a gnarled hand around the head of her walking stick and rose to her feet.

"Let us make ourselves comfortable, and you can tell me what you do know." She gestured with her stick to the tea table. The chairs looked anything but comfortable, but at least we were allowed to sit. We briefly explained our plan to move myself and Hetty into the Ashley household.

"This is precisely the type of thing I was hoping you would do," she said. "The very thing I would do if I were able." Her lips curved upward in approval. It made her look almost friendly. "How may I help?"

"The Ashleys requested a new nurse for Lady Winstead," I told her. "We need to stop her from reporting for work at two o'clock today."

Her smile turned wicked. I'd have sworn the temperature dropped.

"We also need to provide her with something to do and pay her well enough to keep her from contacting the agency or the Ashley family," George added.

"Of course," she said. "A satisfied employee is unlikely to make trouble. We'll intercept her and bring her here. I doubt she can tell the difference between one curmudgeonly old woman and another." She raised her brows, as if seeking consensus.

As if I'd rise to that bait.

"Indeed, every person has his own unique way of being a curmudgeon, wouldn't you say?" George's eyes were so full of mischief, even Lady Esther laughed. Goodness, I think she was actually enjoying herself.

"I know we must move swiftly," she said, "but I believe we have time for a cup of tea, and I have some news for you."

We waited quietly and patiently while she rang for the maid. The moment she sent the girl off for tea, we pounced.

I spoke first. "You saw Lady Winstead's solicitor, didn't you?"

Her self-satisfied smile was answer enough. "The Ashley family will receive nothing from her upon her death."

"Does that mean her fortune didn't become Lord Peter's upon their marriage?" I asked.

"It does," she said, holding up a finger. "But I have learned more . . . much more."

I cast a glance at George, who looked as eager as I felt, then turned back to Lady Esther, who preened just a bit before continuing.

"Peter Ashley had almost beggared the estate before meeting Augusta. Her late husband's bank held the mortgage on the Ashley town house."

George shook his head in disgust. "I assume all his money went toward his expeditions to Egypt?"

"You assume correctly," she said. "Upon their marriage, Augusta took over the mortgage on the house in town and gave Peter an annual allowance. A very generous one, but the fortune her first husband amassed never fell under her new husband's control." She leaned forward over her walking stick, as if sharing a secret. "I always knew Augusta was an astute woman."

"So, that means the new viscount already has everything he can expect to inherit," George said.

"Which amounts to an estate that is not performing well, a house in town with a mortgage to pay, and whatever small sum Peter may have had upon his death." She narrowed one eye. "I cannot be certain Jonathon knows that is the case, but I would assume his father would have informed him of the fact."

"Have any of the Ashleys ever asked the solicitor about any potential inheritance?" I asked.

"He managed to talk around that question, I'm afraid. Though he, too, believed Lord Peter would have explained the family financial situation to his heir. They should all know by now that Peter had little to bequeath them, but it's difficult to know if Jonathon informed his brother and son that any money Augusta brought to the family with her marriage to their father will not remain in the family after her death."

"They all need to find some other way to support themselves," I said. "I don't suppose he mentioned whether the Ashleys have been withdrawing money from her accounts?"

"They have not," she replied. "Indeed, they cannot."

"Then perhaps Miss Stover's accusation that someone in the family stole Lady Winstead's jewelry is correct," I said.

"I'm afraid this situation is very much as your aunt described." George returned his cup to the tray and began his usual pacing behind our chairs, his arms clasped behind his back. "They need to keep her alive and paying the bills. I assume the household expenses are paid by the solicitor from her account?"

Lady Esther nodded.

"So, alive, paying the bills, and with no energy or will to get on with a life of her own." He let out a tsk.

"Certainly not a life that doesn't include them," I added.

"But there has been at least one mistake," he said. "At least one time where they gave her too much laudanum. The last thing they want is for her to die. Then they'd lose everything."

"It's happened more than once," I said. "Either the person was very careless or someone does want to kill her. Why do you suppose the nurse was murdered?"

George turned to look at me. "Perhaps she wanted more money."

"More money?" Lady Esther glanced between the two of us. "Do you mean more than her wages? Or was someone paying her for something nefarious?"

"We don't really know," I said. "Someone paid her several installments of two pounds each, which to a woman of her means would have been a goodly sum. If it was one of the Ashleys, I would suspect it was either to turn a blind eye or to drug Lady Winstead."

"But you don't know who made the payments, do you?" she asked.

I shook my head.

"What of Miss Stover?" George asked.

"I don't believe she has enough money," I said.

He waved a hand. "No, I mean with regard to drugging

Lady Winstead. I said there'd been at least one mistake, but what if it was Miss Stover intentionally giving her aunt too much?"

"I'm still not certain I see her as a murderer, but it is possible. She must assume she'll inherit something upon Lady Winstead's death." I glanced at Lady Esther. "Will she? And would she know about it?"

Lady Esther pursed her lips. "Unfortunately, the solicitor was not that forthcoming. As her only living blood relative, Miss Stover no doubt has expectations, but unless Augusta has told her, she'd only be able to guess at the amount. And for all I know, Augusta's will leaves everything to a home for feral kittens. She's never discussed it with me."

George frowned. "We may not know for certain where Lady Winstead left her fortune, but Miss Stover is a likely candidate, wouldn't you think?"

"Jonathon Ashley thinks so," I said. "He asked her to marry him when she first arrived in London. Considering his financial situation, I can't imagine him making such an offer unless he believed her to be an heiress."

Lady Esther's face took on an expression of horror. "I presume she turned him down."

"Oh, yes," I said.

"Smart girl."

"But definitely a suspect," George said.

"I can't disagree," I said. "But with both Hetty and me on hand, I think we can keep Lady Winstead from harm, whether it comes from the Ashleys or Kate Stover. However, I do believe we should be going, or the real nurse will arrive there first."

George and Lady Esther took her carriage to redirect the agency's nurse to Lady Esther's home. I couldn't imagine what they planned to do, but knew there were no two people better capable of such subterfuge. I returned home in our carriage and found that Bridget had finished packing our bags and was ready to leave for the Ashleys. I had some subterfuge of my own to work on that family. I hoped I hadn't become too rusty.

If Fuller was surprised to see me with my maid and our bags, he made no show of it. For my part, I simply acted as though I was expected, and fortunately, Lord Jonathon was away from home until later that afternoon. What was the poor butler to do?

He apologized that a room had not been made ready for me and took all responsibility for the oversight upon himself. I accepted gracefully.

"It's no trouble at all, Fuller. I'm here, after all, to work with Miss Stover. I assume she's with Lady Winstead?"

"Indeed, she is, ma'am. We expect the new nurse this afternoon, but since she has yet to arrive, Miss Stover has been tending to Lady Winstead."

"Then perhaps my maid can go downstairs for a cup of tea, and I'll go up and check on the dowager."

"I'll take you up myself, ma'am."

Fuller instructed a young footman to take Bridget to the servants' lounge; then he escorted me upstairs. As expected, Kate was at Lady Winstead's bedside. But the lady herself was upright in bed and listening to the young woman read. The maid, Aggie, sat in the far corner, sewing. She stood when we entered the room.

Fuller signaled for her to come with him, then gave me a shallow bow. "I shall have Aggie prepare your room as swiftly as possible," he said, then backed out of the room, with Aggie following.

"Good afternoon, Frances," Kate said. Her brow was furrowed in confusion. "Are you staying here?"

Well, now. This was something George and I hadn't discussed. If Kate was a suspect, how much should I tell her? Since

Lady Winstead, who was watching me closely at the moment, seemed to move in and out of lucidity, did I want to frighten her by explaining how dire her situation might be? On the other hand, just how complicated did I want to make my lie?

"Lady Winstead and I discussed this yesterday," I lied. "In order to ensure you'd be ready for your presentation, and still allow for the time you like to devote to her, we thought it best if I moved in."

At least that was the same story I planned to tell the family. Lady Winstead didn't so much as twitch or wink or offer any acknowledgment of my words. Kate, on the other hand, wagged her head, as if she completely understood some underlying meaning to my statement. I assumed she thought I meant to help her watch over her aunt. And in a way, she was correct, so my story was accepted.

"I'm afraid we were a bit too eager," I added, "and neglected to gain Lord Jonathon's approval of our plan."

Miss Stover smiled. "Aunt Augusta has been feeling much better." She glanced at the older woman, who did indeed seem almost alert. "I very much doubt she'll back down to Lord Jonathon."

"No, indeed." Lady Winstead's voice was quiet but stronger. "You are very welcome here, Frances."

I approached her and was about to express my delight at her continued recovery, but Fuller returned at that moment and addressed me.

"His lordship has come home," he said, "and would like you to join him for tea in the drawing room."

Bother. I'd hoped to be moved in before facing Jonathon. "Of course," I said.

Lady Winstead took my hand. I could feel her icy fingers even through my gloves. Apparently, she wasn't completely well yet. When I turned, she was looking up at me. "Stand firm," she said.

I gave her fingers a squeeze. "I shall."

Jonathon Ashley awaited me in the drawing room. His eyes were hooded, and his expression was guarded, but his fingers drumming on the arm of his chair gave away his anxiety. He didn't want me here, and the only reason I could think of was that I interfered with his plans. Of course, those plans might not involve Lady Winstead, but I'd soon find out.

"Lord Jonathon," I said as I entered the room.

He came to his feet and indicated a chair across from his. "Ah, Mrs. Hazelton. How good of you to join me."

I took the seat and smiled pleasantly. "I almost never refuse afternoon tea. Shall I pour?"

He glanced at the low table filled with cups, plates, a pot of tea, and a tray of delicacies as if he'd forgotten it was there. "Um, certainly. Please do."

Since I was already reaching for the pot, there was little else he could say. I busied myself with the tea things while he fidgeted, clearly wondering how to bring up the subject of my invasion of his home. He took the cup I offered and cleared his throat.

"Fuller has informed me that he's made up a room for you."

"Ah, excellent. I'm sure my maid is moving my things there as we speak." I gave him a smile. "You needn't apologize, sir. The wait was insignificant."

He drew back with a frown. "I had no intention—"

"Of course not. You'd never intentionally hold up our progress." I gave him a knowing look. "After all, you did indicate you wanted Kate to make a splash this season."

This time he looked completely baffled. "I said no such thing."

"Perhaps not in so many words." I poured tea into my cup, then glanced up at him. "But you did say you wanted her . . . How did you put that? Oh yes, you wanted her out of this house as soon as possible."

He actually looked embarrassed. "I don't believe I phrased it quite so baldly as that."

"Oh, I recall it with perfect clarity. Out of this house, you said, and as soon as possible."

"Well, perhaps I said something of that nature."

I squeezed a wedge of lemon over my cup. "And you made it quite clear that you expected me to handle that task."

"And so I do, but I don't believe a splash, as you call it, is at all necessary. It sounds rather expensive."

"Lady Winstead has authorized all our expenses, so you needn't concern yourself."

"Lady Winstead—"

"Is quite in agreement with you about Kate."

He tipped his head to the side. "Am I to understand she wants Kate out of the house?"

"No, no. I was referring to Kate's entrée to society. Lady Winstead understands the benefit of causing a sensation."

His frown deepened. "A sensation? Why is that necessary? And just what is the benefit?"

"Why, suitors, of course. Many of them. Kate will have her pick."

"I suppose that is a benefit."

"Indeed, it is, but she is far from ready." I leaned in and lowered my voice. "She needs quite a bit of polish, you know."

"Yes. Well, would it not have been just as easy to apply this polish at your home, madam?"

I had been choosing between a scone or sponge cake and glanced up at him with a look of innocence. "You mean, have her move into my home?"

"Is that a possibility?" His expression was hopeful.

"I'm afraid not. Kate is far too concerned with her aunt's health. She truly hates to leave her alone, which is why Lady Winstead and I devised this plan. While she keeps her aunt company, we can both tutor her."

I could see he was losing patience with me and the whole situation. "If my stepmother is able to tutor her, why does she require your help? I hadn't noticed that Kate is so without manners or style that she needs two of you."

"Perhaps not, but Lady Winstead does tire easily. Also, there's the problem of her being homebound and all of you still in mourning." I sighed. "None of you are able to escort Kate to the balls and events that every young lady must attend in order to meet the right sort of gentlemen. Like the ball we are attending this evening."

He set his cup down and glanced at me sharply. "I thought you said you planned to see only to her presentation?"

I waved a hand. "Well, Lady Winstead entreated me so charmingly." I almost laughed at his expression of astonishment.

"I find it hard to believe my stepmother is lucid to the point of exhibiting civility, let alone charm."

"You do her a disservice, sir. She seems to improve daily." I lifted my shoulders in a casual shrug. "But if you prefer to wait until you are available to escort her, I'm sure your stepmother can be persuaded."

"No, no," he said, clearly flustered. "I appreciate you're taking her under your wing, so to speak. Perhaps after a time—a few days or so—we can reassess this arrangement. I'm sure you'd prefer to remain in your own home, after all."

I tipped my head, as if the thought hadn't occurred to me. These living arrangements had better not last beyond a few days, or I'd likely lose my mind. "An excellent notion," I said.

"I also don't think it's quite the thing for Kate to spend so much of her time with an invalid. We are to have a new nurse this afternoon. Let us hope she is more trustworthy than Nurse Plum. Then Kate may confidently go about her business."

I agreed, absently wondering where Hetty was. It was well after two o'clock. But I needn't have worried. Fuller knocked, then stepped into the drawing room.

"Excuse me, my lord, but the new nurse has arrived, along with a Dr. Gilliam."

Dr. Gilliam?

Chapter Nineteen

⟨≈⟩

If I was surprised to see Gilliam in the entry hall with Aunt
Hetty, the viscount seemed completely taken aback. Fortunately, that meant he took no notice of me when I followed
him out of the drawing room to see the pair for myself.

The change in Gilliam was subtle. His suit looked a bit worn
and didn't fit him as well as his usual clothing. The bag he carried was the only thing that identified him as a doctor. Hetty,
on the other hand, looked the image of Florence Nightingale.
She wore a blue-checked cotton dress with white collar and
cuffs, a white apron that crisscrossed over the bodice and held a
variety of mysterious instruments at the waistband. A white
cap covered most of her hair.

Lord Jonathon ignored her and strode up to Gilliam, his
hands folded behind his back. "Doctor?" he said. "I never
asked for a doctor. How did this happen?"

Gilliam removed his bowler. "I'm afraid it's routine when a
new nurse is assigned to a patient, my lord."

Jonathon turned to Hetty. "You are the new nurse, I take it?"

Hetty cast her gaze downward as she dipped a slight curtsy.
"Yes, my lord. I am Nurse Chase."

"Egad! You're American."

Gilliam stepped between Hetty and Jonathon. "The records at the agency indicate Lady Winstead hasn't been seen by a physician in over a year. An exam is a protection both for the patient and the agency. I want to be sure that Lady Winstead needs nothing more than the general day-to-day care our nurses provide. I'm sure that is your aim, as well, sir, is it not?"

"What sort of exam?" Jonathon asked.

"A general one, sir." Gilliam played the doctor well enough to convince me. "We'll see that she's hydrated, not suffering from any obvious disease, check her breathing and her heart."

"You assume she has one," the viscount muttered. "All right then. Might as well get on with it. I'll take you up myself."

Gilliam gave him a pleasant smile and stepped aside to allow the viscount to precede him up the stairs. Hetty followed, carrying a leather bag, which I assumed held her clothing for her stay. Neither man attempted to carry it for her. I trailed behind her, hoping Jonathon would continue to disregard me.

When our little caravan arrived at Lady Winstead's room, Kate stood in the doorway, determined to stop us from entering. "She's just gone off to sleep," she said. "I'd prefer not to wake her."

"I'm afraid that's unavoidable," Jonathon said. "Unless the doctor is willing to return at another time?"

Gilliam shook his head. "I won't be able to leave Nurse Chase until I've examined the patient."

The viscount gestured to the door. "Then by all means, go ahead."

Gilliam and Hetty passed through the doorway, but when Jonathon made as if to follow, Gilliam blocked his way. "I'd prefer to see the patient alone, sir. If you don't mind."

Jonathon squared his shoulders and looked Gilliam up and down. "I ruddy well do mind."

"It's to protect her modesty, sir," Gilliam said in a calm, doctorly tone. "I'm sure you understand."

Before Gilliam could close the door, Kate stepped forward. "I will not have two strangers poking and prodding my aunt without someone in the room with her." She pushed right past Gilliam and into the room.

He heaved a sigh and closed the door, leaving us to wait in the hallway. Bother! I'd thought Gilliam's idea ingenious, particularly since even Aggie was occupied with preparing my room. Alone, they could speak freely with Lady Winstead. Perhaps even remove her from the house if she'd willingly leave. But with Kate hovering over her aunt, they would have to continue their charade. An opportunity missed. It wasn't ideal, but it couldn't be helped. At least Hetty would have a chance to earn Kate's trust.

Our wait wasn't long, though Jonathon paced up and down the hallway the entire time. He was clearly anxious, but why? Now that I knew he needed to keep Lady Winstead alive, why would he worry about a doctor examining her? Perhaps she really was ill, and he hoped to hide it? Or was he just concerned the doctor would take the laudanum away?

"You are concerned about your stepmother, after all, Viscount," I said. "And all the while I thought you all despised her."

He made a small, derisive noise. "Quite the reverse, I assure you. She has nothing but contempt for me, or the aristocracy in general—considers us all out of touch and rather useless. Makes me wonder how she found any value in my father. But somehow, she did."

"Lord Peter made some very important historical discoveries."

"He enjoyed travel and adventure. Any discoveries he made were completely by chance."

His expression darkened when he spoke of Lord Peter, and this led me to believe I'd misjudged his feelings about his father and stepmother. He might be disappointed by Lady Winstead, but it was Lord Peter he despised.

Whatever his concern, his relief was obvious when Gilliam

opened the door and joined us in the hallway without Hetty. "I'm not entirely sure Lady Winstead is in need of a nurse," he said. "If she has been ill, she is clearly recovering, though still weak, I'll allow. I've given Nurse Chase instructions as to her diet and routine." He lowered his voice to a whisper and leaned toward Jonathon. "I suspect the lady has relied overmuch on laudanum."

The viscount raised a brow. "Indeed?"

"It can dull the senses when a loss becomes too heavy, but then one becomes dependent upon it. Nurse Chase will work on that. Slowly bring her dosage down."

A muscle pulsed in Jonathon's jaw. "Very well. Anything else I should know?"

"I leave her in Nurse Chase's competent hands. She knows how to contact me should she have questions." Gilliam gave the viscount a shallow bow. "I bid you good day, sir."

I placed my hand on Jonathon's sleeve. "I'm sure you want to check on Lady Winstead. I'll see the doctor out."

Gilliam moved down the hallway before Jonathon could respond. With a swish of my skirts, I turned and followed him. I caught up with him midway down the stairs. "I don't suppose you were able to speak privately with Lady Winstead?" I kept my voice low.

He pulled a face. "Hetty tried to distract Miss Stover, but she was quite determined to remain at her aunt's side." He chuckled. "I put on the best show I could, but I suspect Lady Winstead wonders just what sort of doctor I am."

"It was a brilliant idea, Gilliam. It just didn't work out," I said. "We shall be dining in a few hours, and unless Miss Stover insists on sitting with Lady Winstead, Hetty should have some time alone with her then. At the very latest, this evening, since Miss Stover and I shall be out."

"Hopefully none of the other Ashleys will be crowding her room."

"They visit her rarely, if at all." I whispered the last, since we'd reached the entry hall and Fuller waited at the door. I gave Gilliam my hand and thanked him for his time, wishing I were walking out that door with him.

Dinner with the Ashleys was both an interesting and enlightening experience. I joined them in the drawing room about ten minutes ahead of the scheduled dinner hour, and just as we were about to adjourn to the dining room, Hetty brought Lady Winstead in, in her wheeled chair. The expressions of shock on every Ashley face told me she had not been expected.

Though she still looked as if she ought to be in bed, someone had taken some trouble with her appearance. Her white hair had been brushed, plaited, and wound around the crown of her head. Her gown was suitable for evening. She'd even bothered to wear earrings and a bracelet—a simple design with jet stones, so of no great value.

"Egad," Jonathon muttered. "What is she doing here?"

Vi recovered first and rushed to Lady Winstead's chair. "How delightful to have you join us for dinner," she said, stopping Hetty mid-stride. "We were about to go in—unless, of course, you'd care for something to drink?"

Lady Winstead gave her a withering look. "I doubt that would be advisable, Violet." She twisted around to speak to Hetty. "You heard her, I assume? No point standing around here. Take me to the dining room."

Without so much as a grumble, Hetty wheeled the chair around and out to the hallway, while Vi directed her to the dining room. Si and Jonathon hurried to accompany her. Andrew watched them fawn over the older woman with a sad shake of his head, then offered Kate and me his escort.

"Ladies, I suggest you fortify yourselves early in the meal, for you will soon lose your appetites."

We each took an arm and proceeded to the dining room,

where we found Fuller rearranging the table settings so that
Lady Winstead was at the easily accessible head. This included
moving Lord Jonathon to the opposite side. It was absolutely
amazing how these people who had barely noticed her exis-
tence a few hours ago fell over each other in an effort to make
her comfortable. I had to applaud Hetty for keeping her com-
posure. She stood against the wall, in the event Lady Winstead
needed her.

Finally, the adjustments were made, everyone was seated,
and the footmen served the soup course.

"You are looking much improved, ma'am," Jonathon observed after an uncomfortable silence of several minutes.

Lady Winstead huffed. "I'm quite certain I look as though
I'd been dragged behind a carriage for several miles, so don't
bother with your niceties. I decided I felt well enough to come
down and have a look at all of you, and I barely gave Aggie
time to get me dressed." Her eyes rolled upward. "I don't even
want to think what my hair must be doing, but I look well
enough to dine in my own home, I suppose."

"I am delighted to see you down here with us, Aunt Augusta." Kate, at Lady Winstead's right hand, smiled as if she
truly meant the words.

"And the doctor thought this was advisable?" Jonathon ignored his soup and glowered, as if he were planning to have a
sharp word with Gilliam if she answered in the affirmative.

Lady Winstead grimaced. "Doctors. What do they know?"

"Medicine," Si said between slurps of soup. "I should think
they know about medicine. That's why we called him in, I assume."

"We didn't call him in," Jonathon said, eyeing Hetty momentarily before turning his gaze back to Lady Winstead. "He
simply showed up with the new nurse. Apparently, the service
sends a doctor to check on patients when a nurse is changed."

"How Peter ever fathered you is beyond me," Lady Winstead said. Her voice shook as she spoke, as did her hands. She quickly tucked them into her lap, but it was clear, at least to me, that she'd be unable to hold a knife or fork. The woman was using all her strength to sit through this meal.

"You speak as if Nurse Plum went on holiday," she continued. "The poor woman was murdered, and none of you care two figs. You're more concerned with the inconvenience to yourselves." She followed up this condemnation with a bout of coughing.

Jonathon looked away. Andrew glared. Si and Vi continued to enjoy their soup. I simply stared at Lady Winstead in amazement. She was surviving this dinner on determination alone.

Kate patted her aunt's hand. "Please don't distress yourself, Aunt Augusta."

Or anyone else, I thought. If someone in this family had been drugging Lady Winstead, I didn't want her outburst to cause a retaliation of some sort. But she ignored Kate's advice.

"They are not worth it," she said. "Useless, every one of you."

"Amazing, then, that you found any value in our father," Jonathon muttered. "We are his sons, after all, and live our lives in a similar manner." He lifted his head and stared at Lady Winstead. "But that's not entirely true. His father left him the means with which to run the estate. Ours frittered it away on travel."

Point to Jonathon, I thought. *Estates do not run themselves.*

Lady Winstead forbore answering while the footmen cleared the first course and brought the next. She showed the first sign of weakness as she waved the food away. Unfortunate since when she wasn't eating, she continued to criticize her stepchildren, with barbs so sharp it was a wonder they weren't diving under the table for cover. For the most part, they ignored her, but eventually Andrew could hear no more.

"Perhaps you've forgotten Nurse Plum didn't arrive here by magic or royal decree," he said. "My father brought her on when you were ill. It sickens me to see that this is how you thank him for his kindness."

"You make a good point, young man." The strain of dining in company showed on her face. "I shall devise a suitable way to express my gratitude." She waved Hetty to her side. "Take me up to my room," she said.

Hetty did as she was bidden, taking one of the footmen with her to help Lady Winstead up the stairs. Dinner may not have ended, but a heaviness had settled over the table and dampened all interest in food.

Vi spoke up for the first time this evening. "I'm sorry you had to hear that, Frances." She threw a glance at Jonathon and Andrew. "I find it better to ignore her than engage with her."

"How could I not engage with her?" Andrew threw his napkin on the table. "She was insulting all of us." He turned to Kate. "Except you, of course, though Lord only knows how she considers you to be useful. You live just as the rest of us."

"That's enough, Andrew." Jonathon's voice was like a whiplash. "Kate is a guest in our home, and you will speak to her with respect. Violet is correct. None of us should have lowered ourselves to arguing at the table. In front of our guests." He gazed at me, then Kate. "Please forgive our poor manners."

What does one say to that? I forced a smile.

"Perhaps it's time to proceed to the drawing room for tea," Vi suggested.

"I'm afraid Kate and I must excuse ourselves so that we can dress for the evening."

Kate gave me a grateful look, clearly prepared to follow my lead, as I came to my feet. The gentlemen at the table also stood.

Jonathon cleared his throat and forced a smile of his own. "Of course. I hope you ladies have an enjoyable evening."

I was quite sure it would be better than theirs. Kate and I climbed the stairs together.

"That was a most unpleasant experience," she whispered.

"It's a relief to hear they don't behave like that at every meal."

"The family? They often trade barbs among each other, but I've never seen them point so many at Lady Winstead."

"She did seem intent on provoking them. Have you never seen your aunt in that humor?"

"No, but that doesn't mean it hasn't happened before. Since I arrived, she's stayed in her room, and they have avoided her. And she's been unwell. My prior visits were before Lord Peter died. He would never have allowed them to speak to her in that manner." She paused before reaching the landing. "I don't recall them speaking to each other much at all."

"Well. Just our luck they chose tonight to begin. I was surprised by Lady Winstead's reasonably good health. She seems even better than when I first arrived this afternoon."

We ambled on to our bedchambers. "It's just for show," Kate said. "She is better than yesterday, but I believe she needed to prove to them she was well. I'd be willing to bet she had to grit her teeth just to sit at the table that long. I'm sure that didn't improve her mood."

Clearly not. I left Kate at her door and rang for Bridget the moment I entered my room. We had lingered a bit too long at the table and would have to hurry. George was set to call for us in an hour.

Bridget arrived swiftly, as usual, and had me transformed in little more than thirty minutes. I stood before the mirror, pulling on my gloves, while she brought my reticule.

"Do you have a gift for Lady Fiona, ma'am? I didn't see anything in our luggage."

"Mr. Hazelton will bring it." I turned away from the mirror. "This could be a very late night, Bridget, but there's no need to wait up for me. You've had a long day."

"I thought I might stay here most of the evening, anyway, in case your aunt needs me. I can catch up on my sewing or some such."

"That's very kind of you, and now that you mention it, I ought to check on her before I leave. Lady Winstead was in a particularly ill humor this evening. I suppose I would be, too, if someone were trying to drug me against my will. Still, Hetty might be having a difficult time."

Thinking Lady Winstead might have tired herself, I trod quietly up to her door and peered inside. I was right. Lady Winstead was in bed and asleep. Hetty, however, leaned, as if exhausted, against the bureau. She glanced up when I hissed, and motioned me into the room.

"You needn't concern yourself with waking her. She's likely to sleep like the dead."

"That might not be the best word to use in this situation." I followed her over to the low cushioned bench fitted below the window. Hetty sank into one side of it.

"I wouldn't be surprised if it's a word used quite frequently around her ladyship, along with *murder, strangle, bludgeon*." She waved a hand. "I realize I volunteered for this position, but that woman is a terror. I completely understand why her family might want to keep her drugged. This"—she gestured toward the sleeping woman—"is the only time she's tolerable."

"Come now, I know she's unpleasant, but she can't be that bad."

Hetty gasped. "Not that bad? Did you hear how she spoke to the Ashleys at dinner? Well, she'd been speaking to me like that all afternoon. She's chastised me for being too slow, too sloppy, for not anticipating her needs, for anticipating her needs, but most of all, for not giving her more laudanum." Hetty massaged her temple. "I assume that was the real problem. She's addicted to the stuff, and abstinence has turned her into a witch."

"I assume you gave her some to help her sleep?"

"I gave her a dose to give myself some peace, but yes, it has the additional benefit of helping her sleep."

"Would you mind searching the room for Lord Peter's journal?"

"I will, but I'd better do it soon, while she's sleeping heavily. Otherwise, she may wake and accuse me of stealing from her." She shook her head. "The woman is truly impossible, Frances."

I took the seat next to her and squeezed her arm. "With luck, we'll solve this case quickly and get you back home. I know Lady Winstead must be an unpleasant patient."

Hetty raised her brows. "My dear, she takes unpleasant to new heights, or should I say lows? If I have to spend much more time with her, Delaney may be arresting me for murder."

Chapter Twenty

～

I left Hetty searching Lady Winstead's chamber and found Kate in hers. Aggie was just handing Kate her gloves. Kate turned as I walked in, and I must say she looked lovely. I was used to seeing her in rather dowdy clothing, with her hair styled simply, if at all. This was quite the transformation. Madame Celeste had restyled her gown so that it clung to her figure in all the right places; the gold color complemented her complexion and turned her hazel eyes to a warm brown. Someone, I suppose it must have been Aggie, had woven pearls into her coiffure, and they seemed to glow amid the dark waves.

"What is wrong?" she asked. "Why are you staring at me?"

"There is nothing at all wrong. I'm staring because I've never seen you looking so fine." I gave her a nod of approval. "You are quite lovely. Aggie, you have my compliments." Indeed, I was shocked to see Aggie had managed this look. I'd been certain she was nothing more than a spy for the viscount.

The little maid beamed.

Kate turned back to the mirror, patting her hair. I took her by the hand and pulled her away. "It's perfect. Don't fuss with it."

Kate thanked Aggie, then took up her reticule and followed me downstairs, where we found George in conversation with Si and Vi in the drawing room. Considering how lovely my companion was, I was gratified that when we entered the room, George's smile was only for me. He came to his feet and took my breath away in the same moment. I loved seeing him in evening clothes, particularly with his newly broadened shoulders. He took my hand and brought it to his lips, pulling me closer than we might normally stand in the presence of others.

"I missed you," he whispered, and I completely forgot that anyone else was in the room.

"Oh, how I envy you both." Vi's voice brought me back to the here and now. "Eight more months before we'll be out in company."

"Buck up, old girl," Si said. "There's that dinner tomorrow."

Vi glanced up with a sour expression. "We're dining with Jonathon and Si's crusty old uncle and his family tomorrow. Hardly what I'd call an occasion, but at least we'll be let out of the house." She eyed my gown, pale blue and dripping with beading, then brushed her hand across her black wool skirt. Vi had once been a favorite of the Prince of Wales. It must be killing her to go through a full year of mourning, but at least she wasn't doing it alone.

I gave her a sympathetic smile and turned to introduce George to Kate, and with no further ado, we departed. George assisted us into the carriage, and once we were on our way, we made polite conversation. Though I was privy to both his investigation and Kate's career onstage, neither of them knew what I'd told the other. Best to avoid either topic. Kate might expect me to confide in my husband, but that didn't mean she'd be pleased to hear evidence that I'd done so.

As we rode through the damp streets, we had rather used up the topic of the weather when I recalled it was Fiona's birthday. "Did you remember to bring her gift?" I asked. A quick glance told me it wasn't in the carriage.

He huffed. "I dropped it off on my way to fetch you. What on earth is it? The package was enormous."

"What does Fiona love more than anything else?"

"Her husband. Her children?" He snapped his fingers. "I know. Her brother."

"That last one is an excellent idea," I said. "Keep teasing and I'll pop you in a box and send you to your sister."

Kate laughed, and George pretended to look chagrined. "You wouldn't?"

"Of course not. She'd much rather have a hat."

George pronounced it the perfect gift, and before we knew it, we had arrived. Judging from the number of carriages and even a few automobiles, Fiona had managed quite a crowd for so early in the season.

"Heavens," Kate said, gazing out the window as the carriage inched its way to the front entrance.

I smiled. "This should be a lovely first ball for you. Lady Fiona invites such lively people. There is always good conversation and eager dancers at her affairs."

She made a strangled little noise in response.

I exchanged a glance with George and took her hand. "You are not nervous, are you?" I asked.

We had finally reached the front of the house, and Jack stopped the carriage. George climbed out and turned to assist us, but Kate still clung to my hand. "What if someone recognizes me?"

"Then you are well and truly caught, and your decision about going through with the presentation to the queen will have been decided for you."

"Aunt Augusta will be so disappointed in me."

"Lady Winstead seems so much more clearheaded, you should explain your career to her soon whether anyone here recognizes you or not. And as to that, no one will expect to see an actress here tonight, so even if someone thinks they know your face, it's unlikely they'd be able to place you."

She brightened. "That's true. People see what they expect to see."

"Exactly. In addition, everyone here will be a friend of Fiona's. Even if someone recognizes you, they wouldn't make an issue of it and embarrass their hostess." I held on to her hand, as she would have left the carriage. "However, if anyone is so bold as to tell you they recognize you, deny it. Then tell me immediately."

George poked his head through the open door and raised his brows. "Am I to attend this party alone?"

We stepped down to the pavement and up to the Nashes' door. Fiona and Robert waited in the white-paneled entry hall, where a glittering chandelier hung from a soaring ceiling. Fiona bestowed a grand smile on us as we joined them inside.

"Many happy returns of the day, my dear sister," George said.

Fiona made as if to kiss the air next to his cheek, but he swept an arm around her and drew her in for a hug. She smacked him on the shoulder when he let her go.

"Silly. You'll crush my gown." Her grin belied her words.

"Your gown be damned. It's that coiffure that has me worried. If it ever came down, it could take out two or three bystanders."

Indeed, Fiona's hair and the feathers tucked into it could rival Marie Antionette's for complication of style.

"I assure you it would hold up in a stiff wind," Robert said, grinning at his wife.

"As if you two know anything about style." Fiona held out her gloved hands to me; a beautiful new opal and diamond bracelet dangled from her wrist. "Frances, my dear, your husband must learn to keep his critiques to himself."

I took her extended hands and, leaning in, kissed her cheek. "Happy birthday, dearest. I must say, you had years to train your brother before leaving him in my care. You should accept some of the blame for his manners."

George sighed. "It's as if I weren't even here."

Robert, as tall as George but stouter, slapped him on the arm. "Then it's the perfect moment to escape. Come, let me introduce you to one of the finest malt whiskeys I've come across in years."

George looked perfectly amenable to the idea, but Fiona stopped them both with a look. "Before you introduce George to anything, allow me to introduce Miss Stover to you."

Her husband dutifully welcomed Kate to his home, then turned to greet the new arrivals coming through the door.

We would have moved on, but Fiona was loath to release Kate. "Mr. Applebee," she said to one of the new guests, "you must meet Miss Stover."

Upon spotting Kate, Mr. Applebee looked more than eager to make her acquaintance. She was a lovely woman, after all. It took only a moment for Fiona to produce a dance card for her and get the young man's name affixed to it. I had just reached out to Kate when the door opened to a new influx of guests, including a few single gentlemen who Fiona felt simply must meet her.

George and I were clearly unnecessary, and it took little persuasion on his part to convince me to move out of Fiona's orbit.

"I hope your sister knows what she's doing," I whispered to him as we nodded and smiled our way through the crowd in the entry hall. "What if one of those men recognizes Kate from the theater?"

He lifted a brow. "What was it you just told Miss Stover? Something along the lines of, no one would expect to see an actress here, so they won't?"

"Something like that, but that was before Fiona brought her to the attention of every male in the house under fifty."

"Give her time, my dear. I'm sure she'll include the older men, too." He grinned. "You know how she is when she sets her mind to something."

I tsked. "Like a dog with a bone. I hope Kate can manage them."

"You may as well leave her to Fiona now." He took my arm and urged me forward. "Let's find a glass of wine and a quiet spot. I'll tell you how I spent my day if you will do the same."

I agreed readily as we meandered through the drawing room, and I finally took note of my surroundings. The room had been completely transformed from its usual state. The partition that usually separated this room from a smaller sitting room had been removed, as had the normal furnishings. Chairs stood along the walls, with a few small tables scattered among them. The rugs were also gone, leaving polished wood underfoot that reflected the glowing chandeliers overhead. Footmen wove their way through the seventy or so guests, with trays of delicacies and drinks.

"Heavens," I said, "this was a great deal of work for Fiona on the occasion of her own birthday."

"She lives for this type of thing." George snagged two glasses of champagne from a passing footman and handed one to me. "If she couldn't entertain, I do believe she'd go into a decline."

"I suspect you are right." I nodded at some acquaintance as George and I moved through the crowd. We kept moving toward the back of the room until we found the door to the garden. "It's dry outside," I noted. "Shall we try it?"

George agreed, and we slipped through the door. The slight nip in the air would assure our privacy.

"I'm afraid we'll have to stand very close to stay warm," I said.

He smiled. "Those were my exact thoughts." We spent the next few minutes keeping very warm indeed.

Finally, I took a reluctant step back. "If we are ever to rejoin the party, I suppose we should compare our notes." I gave him a brief summary of my day at the Ashley home. George laughed when he heard Gilliam had accompanied Hetty as a doctor.

"I knew he was more worried about her than he let on."

"It was really quite brilliant," I said. "He insisted on seeing Lady Winstead privately, with only Hetty in attendance. If their plan had worked, they could have told her they were there to help."

"But for Miss Stover."

"Exactly. She pushed her way in before any of us could stop her."

"What is your assessment of her?"

"She seems like a lovely young woman who might be drugging her aunt in order to claim her inheritance." I told him about dinner with the Ashleys.

George snickered. "It sounds like Lady Winstead is shaking off the effects of the drug and returning to her usual charming self."

"She hasn't completely recovered. It definitely took all her inner resources just to remain at the table as long as she did. But my hope is that she'll stay lucid enough for Hetty and me to explain the danger she's in and that she'll allow us to remove her from the house."

"Will Hetty give her more laudanum?"

"Lady Winstead insists she needs it, and you may recall the doctor indicated she should be weaned off the drug gradually. Besides, I don't know how long Hetty can stand her without the laudanum. She is quite a terror."

"If anyone can handle a terror, it's your aunt."

"That's true enough," I said. "Now tell me what progress you made, before we succumb to the chill."

"I paid a call on several jewelers Gilliam recommended. Now I know why he couldn't join me himself, but fortunately, using his name gave the proprietors some confidence in me."

"Did you find Lady Winstead's necklace?"

"No, but I did find the jeweler who made the copy. He recognized my description of Jonathon Ashley. It seems he brought in a set—necklace, bracelet, and earrings of sapphires and diamonds. The jeweler was commissioned to replicate each piece with false stones, which he did. Ashley returned to collect both fake and real jewelry a week ago."

"I assume the name Jonathon used was also fake."

George nodded. "Not that it matters, but it shows he understood the illegality of his actions. It's likely he still has both sets of jewelry in his possession. Is there any chance of my gaining entrance to the house to search for them?"

"A very good chance. You may have heard Vi mention the family will be dining out tomorrow evening. Kate and I have nothing planned. I don't think it would be considered strange if you called on me at their home while I'm in residence."

"Hopefully, the servants will retire early and there will be no one about to have an opinion of my calling on you."

"Have you told Delaney what you learned about Jonathon Ashley and Lady Winstead's jewelry?"

"I let him know when I stopped by his precinct to deliver the envelopes we found at Nurse Plum's lodging. He's not sure what to make of that, either." He paused for a moment. "Now that I think of it, I was able to give Delaney a good description of the jewelry. He'll surely pay a call on the jeweler himself to confirm that the man was Viscount Winstead, but once he does, there's nothing stopping him from conducting his own search of the house. Perhaps there's no need for me to snoop around myself."

"Well, I have no objection to your calling on me regardless."

He gave me a sly glance. "Why, Mrs. Hazelton, am I to understand that you might possibly miss me?"

"Oh, George. It hasn't even been a full day yet."

"What?" He held me at arm's length, looking completely outraged as I laughed.

I took a step toward him and pulled him close. "But I'm certain I shan't sleep a wink without your snoring."

"Ha, you teasing baggage! If it's noise you crave, we should go back inside. It sounds as though they've started the dancing." He stepped back, but I held fast to his arm until he met my eyes.

"Yes, I've missed you," I said.

He released an exaggerated sigh. "Finally. You do understand that my pride is entirely under your stewardship. If I must pry compliments out of you like a bad tooth, I'm in danger of losing all my confidence."

"You?" I stared in amazement and a significant amount of disbelief.

"It could happen."

I smothered my laughter behind my hand. "Very well. I shall take care to both nurture and regulate your pride. Now, shall we go inside?"

George was right. The dancing had begun. And Fiona had been successful in partnering Kate with Mr. Applebee. In fact, I wouldn't be a bit surprised if her dance card was completely filled.

Fiona quickly stepped up to claim George as a partner, leaving the young man she'd been dancing with no choice but to offer his hand and lead me out to the floor. That would have been fine except the man in question was Daniel Grayson, who had once courted my sister. Since her marriage to Leo, Mr. Grayson had seemed to resent me for not pushing her in his direction, something I would not have done, since I believed he was shopping for an heiress.

We had barely danced two steps when he mentioned he'd heard Miss Stover had arrived with me. "How well do you know her?" he asked.

Well enough to know she did not have the fortune he sought, unless something happened to Lady Winstead, that is. "I met her only a few days ago, so not well at all, but she seems like a lovely woman."

His frown deepened the lines between his brows. "Do you know for a fact that she is Lady Winstead's niece?"

His words gave me a chill, but I kept my smile in place. "What a strange question. Lady Winstead does indeed claim Miss Stover as her niece. Why do you ask?"

"I don't quite know how to say this." He took a quick glance over his shoulder. "I think someone is playing a trick."

I frowned. "What are you trying to say?"

"I've never met Miss Stover, but I can say with assurance that the woman dancing with Mr. Applebee is an actress." Noting my surprise, he gave me a smirk. "I saw her onstage not a week ago. She sang and danced in the chorus. A *Florodora* girl, they're called. She's a beautiful woman, but she cannot be Miss Stover."

Now what? This was exactly what I had been afraid of. I was a fool to bring her here, but now I had no choice but to brazen it out. "I can verify with all certainty that is Miss Stover. Lady Winstead and all the Ashleys have claimed her. Your memory must be playing the trick. The theater is dark, and the actors use face powder and rouge and such things. You would have seen her from a distance." I shook my head. "You must be mistaken."

His hand tightened on mine as he pursed his lips. "I am not wrong. I have a keen eye for a face. That woman has won your trust by false means. Perhaps she intends only to fool society, or perhaps she is a thief. I am shocked that you are not at this moment warning Lady Fiona. Are you not her friend?"

I was too angry to panic. How dare he question my actions! "My friendship with Lady Fiona is not at issue. What is, is your confidence in that keen eye of yours."

He sputtered a few words, but I didn't back down.

"Your trust in your perception has you calling the dowager

Lady Winstead, Lord Jonathon, the rest of the Ashley family, and me all fools. Do you honestly believe Lady Winstead wouldn't know her own niece?"

His eyes darkened as he scowled. "From what I understand, Lady Winstead's faculties aren't what they once were. I tell you I know her to be an actress. Perhaps I will confront her myself if you don't wish to do anything about it."

Just as panic threatened to rise, I spotted Lady Esther holding court with some elderly gentlemen across the room. "Before you speak to Miss Stover, you had best tell your theory to Lady Esther. She and Miss Stover are quite close."

At the mention of Lady Esther, his determination faltered. I could see hesitation in his eyes and couldn't resist pushing my point. "Surely you don't mean to question her faculties?"

"I . . . No, of course not," he said just as the music came to an end.

As the other couples left the dance floor, we stood facing one another. "Come," I said. "We shall speak to Lady Esther now."

Unsurprisingly, Grayson found a reason to make himself scarce. I hoped I had the gravitas of a Lady Esther one day. Still, since I didn't know if Grayson would keep his mouth shut on the matter of Kate, I thought I'd better warn Lady Esther.

I made a circuit of the room, so as not to look too obvious. Besides, I wanted to keep an eye on Kate and another eye on anyone who might be observing her. By the time I found myself at Lady Esther's side, she'd seen me coming and dismissed her companions.

"You look as though there's trouble afoot," she said, inching closer.

The musicians played once more, covering our conversation. I kept my expression pleasant when I replied, "There may well be. Have I ever mentioned that Miss Stover is employed as an actress?"

She blinked and moved her head back a fraction of an inch.

That she allowed any change to her countenance at all indicated that she was very shocked indeed. "No, my dear. You missed that small detail."

"She's been on the stage in London only twice. It seemed unnecessary to tell you."

"I assume it's become necessary?"

I explained that Daniel Grayson had recognized her from the play. Counting Fiona and myself, he was the third person in the house to have done so. "Apparently, all her dances are spoken for, otherwise I might simply extract her from this company. Have you any advice?"

"Let me consider the matter while you tell me how my friend is faring and if you managed to install the new nurse in the household."

"Lady Winstead seems to be improving. She seems less vague and foggy. She is, however, quite irritable. I assume that is due to her addiction."

Lady Esther was absently watching Kate. "No, that's just Augusta. I believe Lord Peter used to call her cantankerous—said it was part of her charm."

Goodness, love truly was blind. "Whatever it's called, our fictitious nurse is already regretting her offer of assistance. By the way, what have you done with the real nurse?"

"Blindfolded her, took her for a long carriage ride, and dropped her off on a dodgy back street in the city." She glanced calmly at my stunned expression. "She is currently ensconced in my library, eating French bonbons and reading novels. You needn't worry. Her lips are sealed, though I don't know how I shall ever get her out of my house."

"Ah, bribery, then."

"Indeed. It was the most dependable tool at my disposal."

"And what of Miss Stover?"

"I think Miss Stover is in need of the protection of an older woman whose position in society is unimpeachable."

I was inclined to agree. "One who strikes fear in the hearts of the younger set and in men of any age."

She chuckled and flapped a hand. "You flatter me."

"Not a bit. With your support, she could withstand the scandal of discovery. No one would have the nerve to insult her. At least not tonight. Who wouldn't want such protection?"

She gave me a sidelong glance. "You are far too clever to need it yourself. But should the occasion ever arise, I assure you, you would have it."

"Thank you, Lady Esther."

"Fine. Fine. Now, before you go digging up some trouble for yourself, why don't we have a chat with Miss Stover?"

Chapter Twenty-one

~

Fiona's birthday gala carried on throughout the night and into the early hours of the morning. After joining Kate across the room and gathering a fair number of guests into our circle—witnesses, if you will—Lady Esther made it obvious that she thought Miss Stover a delightful, charming and, most importantly, proper young lady. If anyone dared to cast a verbal barb her way, it would take only one stern glare from the matron to dampen their insults into harmless puffs of hot air.

George delivered Kate and me to the Ashleys' home just as the staff were waking and beginning their morning duties. I hated to let him drive away, but his reminder that he'd be back that very evening made the parting easier.

We let ourselves in with the key Lord Jonathon had given me. Apparently, he still didn't trust Kate enough to award her a key of her own. I locked the door behind us, and we crept up the stairs, knowing the family would still be abed. On the landing, Kate squeezed my fingers before turning left to her room. Mine was to the right, just past Lady Winstead's. As I tiptoed by her room, I heard voices behind the closed door and paused to listen. Though I couldn't make out the words, I recognized Hetty's voice and another sound. Was that a growl?

I waited. There it was again—not a growl but a snarl. Aggie would never attempt to snarl at Aunt Hetty. I slumped. It must be Lady Winstead. Dear heavens, it was five o'clock in the morning. Why was she even awake? I placed my hand on the doorknob and waited just another moment. Hetty was an adult and no shrinking violet, either. But she had been dealing with Lady Winstead all day. And it was five in the morning.

Crash!

That decided me. I turned the knob and pushed open the door. "What is going on in here?" I asked, my voice a stage whisper.

Nothing could have prepared me for what was going on in there.

Near the bed Hetty stood in her nightclothes, water dripping from her hair, face, and collar, her eyes and mouth wide open in shock. Her hands, fisted at her sides, shook, as if she were struggling to keep them from strangling someone. It didn't take much imagination to know who. I turned my gaze to see Lady Winstead cowering in bed, clutching the comforter to her chest, one hand flung out to ward off . . . Hetty?

Oh, dear! I quickly glanced back at my aunt, who had given up the struggle with her better nature and was, indeed, reaching for the old woman.

"Hetty, no!"

Her head snapped around, and she held up a hand of warning to me. "Watch your step, Frances. The old beast has smashed the water glass on the floor."

The room was lit only by the lamp on the bedside table, but from its glow, I could see shards of glass scattered across the floor.

Hetty swiped some water from her forehead, then dropped

her arm to her side, shaking her head at the woman in the bed. Her fury seemed to have dissolved into exhaustion.

I picked my way over to her as the door popped open and Kate rushed into the room. She froze and assessed the room when we cautioned her about the broken glass.

"What happened?" she asked while she carefully stepped to her aunt's bedside.

"She tried to poison me!" Lady Winstead looked much braver now that Kate and I were in the room. She had dropped the protection of the comforter and pointed a crooked, accusing finger at Hetty.

"It was only water," Hetty said. Leaning close to me, she muttered into my ear, "Poison would take far too long."

I asked Kate to comfort her aunt, then put an arm around Hetty and led her to the bench under the window across the room—as far away from the broken glass and Lady Winstead as possible.

"Honestly, Frances," she said in a lower voice. "A few days ago, I was astonished to learn her stepchildren may have wanted to do her in. Now I don't know how they have put up with her for so long."

I pulled a handkerchief from my reticule and handed it to her. Standing over her seated figure, I allowed her to mop her face before asking once more, "What happened? Why is she even awake at this hour?"

"It's her addiction, I suppose," Hetty said. "I think she had been given more than a teaspoon of laudanum a day previously. That's all I gave her, mixed in a glass of water, before getting her settled in bed last night. It must have worn off, and she woke in the most unpleasant humor. Ranting about her discomfort. She wanted to be up. She wanted breakfast and tea. When I sat her up, she started coughing, so I tried to give her some water." She threw Lady Winstead a glare. "She took the glass and threw the contents in my face."

I gasped.

Hetty gestured to herself. "Once the water hit me, I jumped away before she could bash me with the glass, so she threw it on the floor instead. After dealing with her yesterday, then dragging myself out of bed to tend to her, well, a glass of water in the face was the last straw. Thank heavens you came in before I strangled her."

"You would never have done such a thing," I said.

"Don't be so sure."

"Why don't you go back to bed? I'll try to settle her down for a few more hours at least."

Hetty shook her head. "I'm up now, and she's not likely to go back to sleep. You, on the other hand, have yet to go to bed. Nor has Miss Stover." She came to her feet. "I've calmed down. You go on."

"Don't leave me alone with her," Lady Winstead said in a raspy voice while clinging to Kate.

Hetty rolled her eyes and walked over to the bellpull. "I might as well ring for some breakfast for her. I'm sure the kitchen servants are up by now. At least we can have tea."

I approached the bed slowly, but Lady Winstead didn't seem at all afraid of me. "Why did you think Nurse Chase wanted to poison you?" I seated myself on the edge of her bed, wishing Kate weren't there, so I could explain to Lady Winstead that Hetty was an ally.

The older woman shook her head. "The water. I thought it was drugged."

"I understand why you might think that since that's how you take your laudanum, but most of the time, a glass of water is simply a glass of water." I lifted the pitcher from the table and gave it a sniff. "I don't smell any laudanum in here, so you should feel safe to drink this—once we replace your glass, that is."

"Let me make you more comfortable, Aunt," Kate said, fluffing the pillows.

Lady Winstead did seem to be tiring. Maybe breakfast could wait. Particularly since I wanted to ask her some questions.

"Lady Winstead, was Nurse Plum the only one to give you your medication?"

She nodded.

"No one else in the family ever tried to give you a dose?"

"They don't come here," she said. "Only Kate. And only the nurse gives me my medicine. She had that scent." She wrinkled her nose.

Nurse Plum had always smelled of lemon and bergamot. A very common scent among the middle classes, but I thought it unusual for a nurse to wear a fragrance at all. She was shut in with her patient round the clock, which, now that I thought about it, might be the very reason she wore it—to counter the smells of a sickroom. It wasn't an objectionable fragrance, unless, of course, you were Lady Winstead, who objected to everything.

But Nurse Plum had been gone for two days. Kate had given her the laudanum that first day, and Hetty had yesterday. Her memories must be swirling together. Perhaps I was wasting my time. Her eyelids drooped. Both—no, all four of us—needed sleep. A maid tapped on the door in answer to Hetty's call. While she and the maid spoke, I took Kate's hand and sent her out the door to her own bed. When the maid had left, I turned back to Hetty.

"She looks as though she might sleep again," I said. "I'm sorry about dragging you into this scheme."

"It was my foolishness for volunteering. I completely underestimated how much work it would be to care for someone in her condition. The maid will bring a broom, tea, and toast in about an hour. I can't count on her sleeping any longer than that."

"I'm off to bed, then. Hopefully, you'll get some sleep, as well."

"Before you go," she said, "I heard some of your conversation. I wouldn't put too much stock in her belief that only the nurse administered her medication. As foggy as she gets sometimes, how would she know?"

I nodded and headed to my room. Frankly, I suspected her fogginess was precisely what the culprit counted on.

It was noon before Bridget even attempted to wake me. I could hardly be blamed for resisting, since her inducement was nothing more than the same tea and toast Hetty had ordered for Lady Winstead. I truly wanted to go home to my coffee, but needs must.

Bridget had no revelations for me. With the exception of the late Lord Peter's valet, the staff had all remained after his death. They weren't particularly fond of the new viscount, but they had nothing good to say about Lady Winstead, either. Of Lord Peter, they particularly enjoyed the fact that he had traveled so frequently. None of them knew much about Nurse Plum. She had kept mostly to herself, taken her meals with Lady Winstead, and slept in a small room just off the lady's dressing room. Difficult to get to know someone under those circumstances.

After completing my toilette, I ventured down the hall to check on Hetty and Lady Winstead. Both were dozing. I had a feeling Lady Winstead hadn't been as close to sleep as I'd thought when I left her early this morning. Well, the best way to help her and to remove Hetty and myself from this madhouse would be to find out who was drugging her. Time to snoop around. Though this room might hold some important secrets, I had no intention of disturbing the sleeping Cerberus, Lady Winstead.

I ventured down to the main floor, which was very quiet. I found both the drawing room and library empty. The viscount had an office toward the back of the house, but I couldn't think of an excuse for being there if I were caught. When I wandered back to the entry hall, Andrew descended the stairs.

He spied me and manufactured a smile. Perhaps he, too, wondered if my presence here was necessary. "Are you looking for someone, madam?"

"I was," I said. "But it seems Kate is still abed, and everyone else is"—I raised my hands and gestured to the surrounding rooms—"somewhere else. Kate will be up soon, and we'll continue our lessons. In the meantime, I suppose I'll read a book."

"You ladies must have had a very late night for her to still be sleeping." As he crossed the hall, he pocketed a pair of gloves he'd been carrying. "I'm on my way out myself but can always spare time for a cup of tea if you'd like to join me?"

"I'd like that very much."

He gestured toward the drawing room, followed me inside, then stopped to ring for a servant before seating himself next to me on a sofa near the tea table. "What did you think of our quiet family dinner last night?" he asked.

I grimaced. "Awkward doesn't quite begin to describe it."

"We are in agreement there. I'm sorry you were exposed to that exhibit. I don't know why she stays here, to be honest with you. She can't stand the lot of us, and I'm sure my grandfather left her financially set. I thought it our duty to care for her while she was ill, but if she's recovered, perhaps she'll find a place of her own—and leave us in peace."

A maid came in then in answer to the bell. I studied him while he ordered tea, then returned his attention to me. "Surely, you must find it strange that I am here instead of at school," he said. "The fact that you haven't asked me about it means someone has already explained that I am not allowed back until my tuition is paid up. And the woman who refuses to pay it does not hesitate to pay for gowns and fripperies for Kate."

"Do you think it Lady Winstead's responsibility, then, to pay for your education?"

He had the grace to look discomfited. "I suppose not, but if she truly has no affection or sense of duty to this family, why does she stay?"

Was he truly unaware that someone in the family was drugging Lady Winstead? Or was he hoping to find out what I knew . . . or suspected?

"I understand it had been Lady Winstead's intention to leave shortly after Lord Peter was laid to rest," I said.

Andrew raised his brows. "She planned to leave?"

"Yes. To the Continent."

Our tea arrived, and we each poured our own. Andrew asked a few questions about Fiona's party but soon turned the conversation back to Lady Winstead.

"Well, all I can say is it's a pity she changed her mind about leaving," he said between sips of tea.

"I'm not sure it was her mind that was changed, but her circumstances. She's hardly in any condition to search for a new place to live now."

"Perhaps she must go to a sanatorium for a cure."

"I doubt a cure can be found at such a place."

He drained his cup and returned it to the tray. "Perhaps not, but we should not be stuck with her for the rest of our lives."

He came to his feet before I could react to his cold assessment. "I'm so sorry to leave you to your own devices, but I must be off, or I shall be late for my appointment."

I waved away his apology. "I'm quite content to be on my own."

With a bow, he strode out to the entry hall. I sank back into the cushions when I heard the front door close. I was coming to find that Andrew, who had seemed so charming, was quite callous. He had made cruel jokes about Kate and seemed all in favor of locking up his late grandfather's wife. Perhaps he didn't realize that people who entered a sanatorium rarely left it, but frankly, it sounded as if he didn't care.

I relaxed for a while with my tea, wondering what Rose and

George were doing and wishing I were at home with them. A twinge of guilt reminded me that I ought to check on Hetty or find Kate. Before I could do either, the doorbell rang and Fuller admitted Inspector Delaney. He asked to see Viscount Winstead. When Fuller left him in the hall to see if Lord Jonathon was at home, I slipped out of the drawing room.

Delaney, in his ill-fitting brown suit, looked as out of place in this gilded hall as a bear, yet it seemed to have no effect on his confidence. "Inspector," I said as I crossed the marble floor. "I'm surprised to see you here. Has something new developed?"

Delaney drew his bushy brows together. "I must say I'm a bit concerned to see you here, ma'am. When your husband told me you'd installed yourself in this house, I thought he must be joking."

I moved closer to him and lowered my voice. "Someone has to watch out for Lady Winstead. Besides, no one here has any reason to harm me."

"I wouldn't be too sure of that. There's been a development in the Nurse Plum case."

"Something that involves Lord Jonathon?"

He gave me a sharp look. "What makes you say that?"

"I heard you request to speak with him just now."

"One of the neighbors reported seeing a doctor call on Nurse Plum on her afternoon off—on the day she died."

"Dr. Waldschmidt?"

"No. I met the good doctor earlier this morning. He can prove he was elsewhere. Besides, he doesn't fit the description from the neighbor."

"You have a description?" Thank heaven! This might end right here and now.

Delaney frowned. "He didn't see the caller's face."

My spirits deflated.

"He was, however, able to provide the approximate height

and build of the man, describe his clothing as very fine, and recollect that he carried a small bag that could be a medical bag."

"Hmm. The clothing doesn't match the profession."

My observation was rewarded with a smile. "Yes, that bit was helpful and made me think of the viscount, who is the right build and has very fine clothing. I'm here to inquire about his whereabouts that day. You didn't happen to see him, did you?"

Everything seemed to point to Jonathon. The thought made my stomach churn. "No," I said at last. "I wasn't here until the next day, and by that time they were all concerned that Nurse Plum was late. Or at least they seemed to be. By the way, have you had a chance to speak to the jeweler about Lady Winstead's jewels?"

"I have an officer calling on him right now." He rubbed his chin. "It's probably time I asked the viscount what he knows about that, too."

I heard footsteps down the hallway and assumed it was Fuller and the viscount. "I'd rather he not see me chatting with you, Inspector." I slipped into the library, which shared a wall with the drawing room, and closed the door just as I heard Jonathon's footsteps in the entry hall.

Chapter Twenty-two

◈

I was well concealed from Jonathon's view when I heard him greet Inspector Delaney. With any luck, they'd go into the drawing room for their discussion, but on the off chance they came in here, I quickly pulled a book from a shelf and settled myself in one of the comfortable armchairs scattered about the room.

"Your case has become something of a nuisance to my household." The viscount's voice competed with the tapping of their shoes against the marble. "I can give you only ten minutes."

"I suppose that will have to do," Delaney replied.

The next thing I heard was the drawing room doors close.

After dropping my book on the chair, I crossed to the shared wall. Sadly, the only sounds that penetrated were incoherent murmurings. Bother! These walls were sturdier than I'd expected. I'd have to wait until the next time I saw Delaney to learn what Lord Jonathon had to say.

"I? You want to know where *I* was?"

Or maybe not. At least not as long as Jonathon continued shouting at such a volume. I fully expected him to have some sort of alibi for the time the nurse was murdered, whether he'd done it or not. I wondered if Delaney planned to ask about the two-pound notes we'd found.

When I heard more murmuring, probably Delaney calmly repeating his question, it occurred to me nothing was stopping me from listening at the doors. I'd heard them close, and no one was in the entry hall. Why not?

I crept out to the hall and took the few steps over to the drawing room door. This was a little better.

"And what if I did? My stepmother gave my late wife that jewelry. It was mine to do with as I please. Who are you to investigate my actions?"

That sounded like a brazen lie to me. Jonathon's wife had died years ago, and Lady Esther claimed Lady Winstead had worn that jewelry frequently and much more recently.

"It was suggested that the jewelry was stolen, my lord." Delaney's voice was low and calm. "And the jeweler himself thought the transaction a bit suspicious. There's no need for concern. I'm sure Lady Winstead will confirm that she gave the pieces to your late wife. Perhaps you could take me up to her now."

There was a pause, and I wondered if I should hurry back to the library. Then I heard Jonathon sputter, "You wish to speak with her? Now? I'm afraid that's impossible. She's far too ill to be disturbed."

"Is that so?" Delaney drew the words out; his inflection indicated concern. "What is it that ails her? My mother-in-law has had every sort of malady an elderly woman could suffer. I can recommend a good physician."

"I'm afraid her illness is not that simple. She seems to be wasting away from grief since my father died."

"Hmm, I'm sorry to hear that, for her own sake, of course, but for yours, as well. You see, if she can't confirm your statement that she gave the jewelry to you, we'll have to act on another statement that it was stolen." He tsked. "That could become troublesome."

"She gave it to my late wife, and how could that be a problem? My stepmother certainly didn't file a complaint with the police. Who else could have a concern in the matter?"

"Well, her solicitor would want to act on her behalf or on behalf of her heirs if, heaven forbid, she should fail to recover her health. If someone else thinks they are entitled to the jewelry, you might have a fight on your hands."

"But I do expect her to recover."

"Jolly good. I hope you are correct in your assessment."

"Of course, she has good days and bad days. I'm sure in a few days she'll be well enough to speak with you, Inspector. Now, if you have nothing else to discuss, I'm afraid there's much I need to be doing."

I didn't think even Delaney would get any more from Jonathon at that point. Since I had no desire to be caught with my ear to the door, I rushed back to the library, picked up the discarded book, and managed to seat myself just as the men emerged from the drawing room. I didn't bother to close the library door behind me and easily heard them cross the hall to the front door.

"I wouldn't worry about the jewels, my good man," Lord Jonathon said. "Lady Winstead will surely be up and about soon." He snapped his fingers. "Perhaps she can send you a note explaining the situation?"

"I'd much prefer to see her in person, sir."

Jonathon opened the door. "I'll be sure to let you know when you can expect that meeting. Good day."

Delaney bid him good day, and I heard the door close behind him, then a weary sigh and some heavy footsteps. They seemed to be coming this way, so I applied myself to my book. I looked up when I sensed someone at the doorway.

"Lord Jonathon. Is there something I can do for you?"

He took a step forward. "You can tell me what the devil you're doing in here. Were you listening to my conversation?"

I straightened my spine and sat a little taller. "I beg your pardon? I assumed this was one of the public rooms of the house."

"It is, but one must wonder what brings you here alone, when it's my understanding your purpose in the house is to tutor Kate in all the details of proper deportment." He made a show of looking around the room. "Yet I don't see her."

I closed the book and placed it on my lap. "You are correct in that I'm here to make myself more available to Kate. However, we had a very late night, and she is still abed. Further, I'd like to point out that I am not in your employment, sir. I have accepted this task as a favor to Lady Winstead and because I like Kate. And I am not one for half measures, so your implication that I am shirking my duties is insulting."

He studied me through narrowed eyes, but I refused to look away and simply tipped my head to the side. "If I recall correctly, it is your wish to have the young lady off your hands. It appears that I am moving things in that direction rather quickly. She was very well received at Lady Fiona's ball."

"You will have my eternal gratitude when I see the results for myself. In the meantime, I suppose I'll have to keep an eye out for you lurking in the background."

I came to my feet, prepared to give him a scathing reply, but defense came from an unexpected source.

"For heaven's sake, Jonathon, leave off." Si strode into the room and to my defense. "You rate your conversations far too highly if you believe Frances has any interest in them. Besides, unless you were speaking right in this room, she'd never hear anything. Do you have any idea how thick these walls are?"

Jonathon glared at his brother. "None at all," he said. "But if you have such an interest in the structure of old homes, perhaps you can find yourself employment in the building trade and begin supporting yourself." He gave me a stiff bow. "Good day, Mrs. Hazelton. I wish you Godspeed with your endeavor."

Before I could respond, he turned on his heel and stalked out of the room. I held my tongue until I could no longer hear his steps on the floor. Then I turned to Si. "Thank you for your defense."

He indicated I should be seated, then took the chair next to mine. "I'm quite sure you had no need of my assistance, but every now and then it pleases me to poke a hole in my brother's puffed-up pride. I beg you to forgive his bad manners."

"He's seemed very nervous for the past few days. Do you suppose he's concerned for Lady Winstead?"

Si laughed. "Jonathon? Oh, I think not. You shouldn't waste your concern on her, either. As mean as she is, she'll outlive us all."

"What a horrible thing to say! And inaccurate, I must add. Mean people die every day." That wasn't exactly what I meant to say. "She made your father happy. Surely, you must see some good in her for that."

"Unlike Jonathon, my father was of a happy nature, and no, I will not give her credit for his disposition." He leaned toward me over the arm of the chair and narrowed his pale eyes. "It's easy for you to take the moral high ground. You don't live with her. Well, you do at the moment, but it's only temporary. You saw how she was at dinner last night. Until she began nursing herself with laudanum, that was a nightly performance."

"Performance? That's an odd thing to call her behavior."

"Ah, but you've been privy to only one evening of it. Sometimes she is far more dramatic, and yes, I believe it's at least partially for show."

"For what purpose?"

He grinned. "To make us grovel, perhaps? I'll admit, I haven't come up with a reason yet. I suppose it's possible she actually hates us as much as she appears to do, but why? We've done nothing to her. And if she hates us, why does she stay here?

This is no longer her husband's house." He sat back in his chair. "Therefore, I believe her entire attitude is for show."

"You've given this a bit of thought." Si seemed unaware that Lady Winstead still held a mortgage on this house. It didn't make it her house, but it wasn't fully Jonathon's, either. I also noticed he believed Lady Winstead was to blame for her own addiction. "Perhaps her moods relate to whether or not she's had her laudanum. I understand it can be very difficult to stop once one has been using it regularly."

"I don't think she ever took it before my father died, and I can tell you she was still difficult to deal with even then. As for Jonathon, he was likely just rattled about the police inspector still nosing around here. I ran into the man just now as I came home, and he stopped to question me."

That made me take a good look at Si. He was about the same size as Jonathon and also wore fine clothes. "Why, whatever would he question you about?" I tipped my head to the side and tried to look as if I couldn't imagine Si stepping a toe out of line.

He grinned. "The man wanted to know where I was when Nurse Plum was killed."

I huffed. "Such impertinence. Did you even bother to answer him?"

"Why not? I was most likely at my club, so that's what I told him."

Most likely? "Excellent. Then there will be witnesses to confirm your claim."

Si stared at me, open mouthed. "Do you mean to say, he'd go to my club and ask?"

I confirmed that Delaney would do exactly that, then excused myself and went upstairs to the dowager's room. Lady Winstead was dozing when I entered. Hetty enjoyed a cup of tea at the window seat. I declined her offer of a cup and took the chair next to her to inform her of Delaney's visit.

"I managed to speak with him for a few minutes while Fuller

was fetching the viscount. It appears a doctor, or someone who looked like one, visited Nurse Plum the day she was murdered."

Hetty blinked. "How does one look like a doctor?"

"This one carried a medical bag. The witness told the police it was a doctor, but Delaney thought the description of the visitor fit Lord Jonathon."

"Does Inspector Delaney think the viscount murdered Nurse Plum?"

I held up a hand. "I wouldn't go that far. Delaney is interested in him, enough to inquire as to his whereabouts when Nurse Plum was murdered."

"Even if he has no alibi, doesn't Delaney still have to prove it was him visiting the nurse? And what if he had some other reason for doing so? It seems to me that requires quite a bit of evidence before the police can make an accusation. Does Delaney have it?"

"The inspector is still working on determining whom the evidence implicates, but he knows Jonathon is the one who commissioned the copy of Lady Winstead's jewelry."

Hetty let out a tsk and shook her head.

"Delaney brought up the jewelry in his questioning with Jonathon, so all in all, Jonathon must be feeling very nervous about now. We still haven't found the missing journal, and Delaney is questioning him in relation to a murder and a theft that Jonathon would have thought was well hidden. I think we should keep a close watch over him. With all this pressure, there's no telling how he'll react."

"You two are speaking far too quietly. I've managed to hear only a few words."

Hetty and I turned as one toward the bed.

Lady Winstead, as clear-eyed as I'd ever seen her, sat on the edge of the bed, leaning forward, as if to hear better. "Well, go on, then," she said. "What does the policeman suspect? Did Jonathon kill Nurse Plum? Is he trying to kill me?"

"You look awfully bright-eyed for someone addicted to lau-danum." Hetty came slowly to her feet as she spoke, her voice thick with suspicion. "A few days without Nurse Plum and you're back to normal?"

A sense of dread tickled the back of my neck. Not the fear of someone in the Ashley family drugging and harming Lady Winstead, but the pure certainty that the elderly woman was about to reveal something so egregious that I might not want to hold Hetty back from pummeling her.

Hetty strode up to the bed, her hands clenched into fists. "You've been faking all this time, haven't you?"

Chapter Twenty-Three

⁓

Hetty's face reddened as she loomed over the elderly woman. "How dare you!" she said.

"How dare I?" Lady Winstead tipped her head back for the sole purpose of looking down her nose at Hetty. "You forget yourself, Nurse," she said.

I rushed to my aunt's side before she could do something she might come to regret, then turned to Lady Winstead. "She is not a nurse. This is my aunt, Mrs. Chesney. Lady Esther thought you needed our help. I'm no longer so sure of that, and I do think you owe us an explanation."

She leaned back against the pillows. "Yes, Esther has been concerned about me. I suppose I must explain, though I don't know what the two of you are so upset about." She looked us up and down, as if she were the aggrieved party.

"You don't—" Hetty's hands shook with the effort she exerted to hold herself in check. She let out a squeal that sounded like steam escaping a teakettle. "After all you put us through, you are not even in danger."

Lady Winstead struck the mattress with her fist. "I most certainly am in danger. I'm just not as vulnerable as you had assumed. Or as my stepchildren had assumed. Thank heaven! But it wasn't so long ago that I was. I fought my way free of that wretched drug even while that nurse eagerly pushed it upon me." She turned to Hetty and raised her chin. "So if I'm a bit out of temper from time to time, you'll simply have to understand."

"Out of temper?" Hetty scoffed. "You threw a veritable tantrum. And you threw water at me."

If Hetty thought she had any chance of an apology, she didn't know Lady Winstead. Taking a seat at the foot of the bed, I intervened. "Are you saying that you were being drugged and you did succumb to the laudanum initially?"

"Exactly. I was bereft when Peter died—and angry. I thought I did a reasonably good job of keeping that anger to myself. I didn't want Peter's children to know I suspected one of them of killing him."

The thought of Lady Winstead successfully keeping anger to herself was impossible to imagine. I parted my lips to comment, but she held up a hand to stop me.

"Yes, yes, Peter was ill, but it was a minor fever. The doctor told me he expected him to be fine in a few days . . . a week at the most. He just needed rest. Which was why I didn't think it odd when he slept so much over the following days. Now I believe that's when someone started dosing him with laudanum."

I raised a brow. "Someone, meaning one of his children?"

"Hard to believe, isn't it? Their own father. Drugging me, I understand. I'm the outsider, the interloper. They would prefer that I was gone."

"But they need your money."

Hetty held up a hand. "Let's get to that in a moment and go back to Lord Peter's death. When was Nurse Plum called in?"

"After the first week of his illness, I called for Dr. Waldschmidt to look in on Peter again. He wasn't recovering as expected." She raised her hands helplessly. "I just felt something was wrong. Though he didn't say anything about it to me, looking back, I believe the doctor suspected something, too. However, he's in a position where making such an accusation could cost him his practice. Instead, he suggested we bring in a nurse to provide proper care. He still felt that Peter would make a recovery as long as someone kept an eye on his medications."

"I think I know what happened then," Hetty said. "Someone bribed Nurse Plum to take over their dirty work."

"I have no proof," Lady Winstead said, "but that is what I suspect. Nurse Doom cared for him for another two weeks, through the Christmas holiday. Kate was here at that time, and she suggested that I call in another doctor. I should have listened to her, but Peter's children had confidence in Dr. Waldschmidt. He had a good reputation. They convinced me they saw improvement in their father—that recovery was just around the corner." She shook her head slowly, her eyes full of regret. "Instead, his end was what awaited him around that corner."

"I spoke to Dr. Waldschmidt," I said. "He told me that you asked him if Lord Peter's death was at all suspicious."

She nodded. "I was simply in shock at first. It wasn't until the funeral that I began to wonder why he became so ill. Why the children had been so confident he'd recover. Why the doctor suggested we hire a nurse. At that point, I couldn't have imagined his own children had a part in his death, but some instinct told me not to discuss his illness with them—just a vague sense of distrust. The doctor was the only one left to ask." She let out a tsk. "He refused to consider anything but natural causes. He was very sympathetic, but . . ."

"Not particularly helpful," I suggested.

"Not at all."

"What happened after the funeral?" I asked. "Lady Esther told me you were contemplating travel to the Continent. When

did your plans change? How did you come to start using laudanum?"

"The day after the funeral, I knew I couldn't face the thought
of living here with Peter's children. Kate had left for home already, so I had a good idea of what my life would be like, and I
didn't like it. I had a good fortune. I didn't have to stay here, so
I decided to forgive the mortgage loan, give up all claim to this
house, and wash my hands of this family."

She sighed. "It was at breakfast that I dropped a few hints
that I would both travel and seek out a new home. Jonathon,
Andrew, Simon, and Violet were all there, and they responded
benignly, which is what I'd expected. By evening, I began feeling groggy. I slept like the dead and woke up the following
morning with my mind in a fog."

"Heavens," Hetty said. "They didn't waste any time, did
they?"

She shook her head. "One day rolled into the next. Afterward, I realized I was drugged like that for more than a month.
Nurse Plum had been hired to care for me, and I didn't even
know it."

It was no more than what I'd suspected, but hearing the
story from her own lips made it all the more horrifying. "How
did you manage to stop?"

"Aggie helped me."

"Aggie?"

"She knew right away something was wrong with me. Once
Nurse Plum came to care for me, she went to the police and
told them what she suspected. But when she added that the
family had hired a nurse, supposedly to take care of me, they
didn't even bother writing a report. Just sent her on her way.
When she returned home, she was determined to keep me from
taking more laudanum."

"That must have been risky for her," Hetty said.

"And here I thought she was just spying for Jonathon," I said. "She kept following Kate around."

"She was following you, hoping to enlist your aid, but it seems she never saw you alone."

That was true. Someone else was always there. "You are fortunate to have such a loyal servant," I said.

"Indeed, I am lucky my stepchildren never sacked her," Lady Winstead added. "She'd been my lady's maid, but in my condition, there was little for her to do. She took on more upstairs maid work but always had some excuse to visit my room. No one really paid much attention to her. On Nurse Plum's afternoon off, they'd leave Aggie in charge of me. She found the bottle of laudanum and diluted it by half."

"Good for her!" Hetty said, clearly forgetting her recent desire to strangle Lady Winstead.

"Oh, yes. I believe the woman saved my life. A few days later she had the chance to speak with me alone. I was somewhat more cognizant at the time, enough for her to make me understand that the nurse was drugging me. The very thought outraged me. And I'll admit, with less laudanum, I was easily stirred to outrage. But Aggie thought it best to play along until I was off the stuff completely."

The woman was astonishing.

"How on earth did you manage to fool them?" I asked. "Particularly the nurse?"

She waved a hand. "The hardest part for me was staying calm. I knew if they saw me agitated or angry, they'd only give me more of the drug. As long as I kept myself under control, they became careless. The nurse trusted me to drink my drug-laced water every evening and didn't watch to make sure I did so. She also slept like the dead. Her own room was just through the dressing room, but once she'd retired there, nothing would disturb her. Aggie would join me then, and we'd make plans, talk, read, whatever it took to keep me awake all night, so I could be convincingly groggy the following day."

"When I came here to meet Kate, you didn't appear to be acting. Were you?"

Her eyes widened. "Not at all. There have been a few episodes where someone managed to give me something. I assume it's more laudanum, but in a dose large enough to simply overpower me." She wrinkled her nose. "I can usually taste it, but that time it was in the tea. It must have been. One moment I was conversing with Kate, and the next, everything was a blur."

I brought the scene to mind. "I wonder if you were drugged to put on a sort of display for me, so I'd be witness to your weakened condition. Was anyone visiting the other times it had happened?"

"To the best of my recollection, there were only two other times. The most recent was the day Nurse Plum was killed. The other was about two weeks ago, at dinner. You may be correct that the time you saw me was meant to make you see how ill I was. But since they need me alive to keep paying for everything, it might simply have been a mistake."

"Good heavens," Hetty said. "Why are you still living in this house?"

"My thoughts exactly," I said. "You had Aggie to assist you. Why did you not leave here and go to the police?"

"I haven't enough proof. I need to catch red-handed whoever is doing this."

I understood her desire all too well. "Lady Winstead, if you actually caught the culprit red-handed, the likelihood that they would allow you to leave this house and report them to the police is nonexistent. You ought to have a care for your own life and get out of here before someone makes another mistake and you don't survive. You could go to Lady Esther. She is more than willing to help you."

"Esther has helped. She encouraged me to contact you."

I narrowed my eyes. "Are you saying you two were communicating?"

"Through Aggie. She's the only one in the house I could

trust, and thank heaven, she's very clever. She's been able to sneak out and take messages back and forth between me and Esther—my only contact with the outside world. I know she's been concerned about me."

"One would think Lady Esther might have been more forthright with me. How could she send me into this situation without all the available information?" In truth, I was highly irritated that both these elderly women were more cunning than I was. Years of practice, I supposed.

"That is my fault, too. I didn't know if I could trust you at first, so I couldn't give away my only method of communicating with Esther. I know I'm being stubborn in staying here, but I'm not foolish enough to cut off all my ties with the outside world. Esther also has advised me to leave, but I must do something to bring Peter's killer to justice—whoever it is."

"That seems to be a tripping point. We don't know who it is." I pondered the little we did know. "Jonathon has had a copy made of some of your jewelry. I can only assume he plans to sell the real stones. Did you give his late wife any of your jewelry?"

"Absolutely not. The poor wretch had already taken the family jewelry into her possession before Peter and I married. Mine disappeared only a month ago or so."

"There's a chance we may get to the bottom of that tonight." I explained to both Hetty and Lady Winstead about George coming by to search for Lady Winstead's jewels. "We first learned they were missing through Kate," I said. "She can't be involved in controlling you through laudanum, since she wasn't here when it began, but there is a chance she gave you what you consider the accidental doses. Do you trust her?"

She gave me a sad look. "I wish I could, but with everything going on, there are only three people in this house I trust, Aggie and now the two of you."

I glanced at Hetty, who leaned heavily against the bedpost,

exhaustion from caring for Lady Winstead and a virtually sleep-
less night apparent from the shadows under her eyes. I stood
up and gave her my seat. "If you knew to trust me," I asked
Lady Winstead, "why didn't you say anything to me sooner?"

"I never had an opportunity to speak with you alone. Neither did Aggie, though heaven knows she tried."

I sighed. "Yes, she did try."

"As for you." She glanced at Hetty. "I didn't know until just
a few minutes ago that you were also an ally." She snapped her
fingers. "That's a thought. Why don't you offer to carry on
where Nurse Plum left off?"

Hetty's eyes widened as she shrank away. "Are you suggesting I offer to drug you?"

"It's worth a try, don't you think?"

"That could become rather tricky," I said. "To whom does
she make the offer? If she approaches the wrong person, Hetty
could find herself in prison."

"And I'd rather not suffer Nurse Plum's fate, either. Thank
you very much."

I turned from Hetty to Lady Winstead. "I'm afraid the best
thing we can do is to get you out of here before one of your
family does you any more harm."

She raised her hands in what might have been surrender. "I
know, I know. Let us at least wait until your husband has a
chance to search for the jewelry. That could answer many questions."

"The journal, too," I added. "He plans to come tonight, while
the family are out, but I'll stop at home this afternoon to tell
him about this new development."

"Why would your husband look for a journal in this house?"
Lady Winstead asked, then narrowed her eyes. "Are you referring to Peter's journal?"

Heavens, I'd forgotten Lady Winstead wouldn't know about
the missing journal. Or would she? Suddenly, it dawned on me

what might have happened to it. "He is searching for the journal Lord Peter bequeathed to the British Museum." I raised a brow. "My guess is that you moved it from Kate's hiding place."

She smiled. "You and Kate were acting suspiciously about something in that drawer the other day. Once you were gone, I checked it and found Peter's journal. Your daughter and I have been reading from it."

I released a sigh. "Of course you have. Where is it now?"

"Well, if Lady Rose were of a greedy nature, it would be in her possession. I asked her to take it home, but she refused. I did not wish to involve her by explaining it would be safer outside this house."

"I appreciate that. Is it still in this room?"

"It is." After sitting up, she swung her legs over the side of the bed. She wobbled a bit and took hold of my arm as she stood. "I spend so much time in that blasted bed, I have a hard time finding my land legs."

"Why not just tell me where it is so I may fetch it?" I suggested.

She released my arm and pointed to the mattress. "It's just under there."

My fingers brushed the book's spine as soon as I slipped my hand under the thick feather ticking. I pulled the journal out, relieved to finally have it in my possession again. "May I take this to my husband? He will be sure it gets to the British Museum."

Lady Winstead had both hands against her lower spine as she stretched backward. "Of course," she said. "By the way, did Kate say why she hid it?"

"She claimed to have been worried about you. It seems when you wrote her, you were completely lucid—and you mentioned the missing jewelry. When she arrived here and saw you, she was understandably surprised. According to her, she knew the journal was important and hoped its theft would bring the police to the house so she could show them that someone was drugging you."

She heaved a sigh. "That may be true. I did tell her I thought someone had stolen my jewelry, but I don't know if bringing the police here would have helped."

"That's what we've learned. Tell me, Lady Winstead, is Kate your sole heir? Lady Esther tells me the Ashley family will inherit nothing from you."

She looked affronted. "I wonder how Esther found that out."

I kept my silence. It was best if Lady Esther enlightened her about that.

"Esther isn't exactly correct," she continued. "Jonathon Ashley will receive the deed to this house, and that's hardly insignificant."

"That's right. You mentioned something about that earlier. You made Lord Peter a loan, I take it? Did he use this house as collateral? I understand that's a personal question, but it would certainly give Jonathon a motive."

She chuckled. "If only it were that simple. This house is actually how Peter and I met. He and my first husband, Thomas, were friends . . . Well, they were friendly, at least. Thomas held the mortgage on this house, or rather his bank did. Frankly, the house isn't worth much more than the loan. When Thomas died, Peter came to see me and asked if I could take over the loan rather than let it go with the new owners of the bank—for the sake of his friendship with my husband."

"That's a very large request," Hetty said.

Lady Winstead padded in bare feet across the rug and back, swinging her arms at each turn, as if to get her blood flowing. "It definitely was, but Thomas left me very well off, and I had an interest in the bank. I assumed—correctly, it turned out— that Peter was lax in making his payments. The bank would have taken the collateral—this house—and sent Peter and his family packing. He and I met every month so he could explain why his payment would be late yet again. He was rather pathetic, but I still found him charming." She smiled at the memory. "And endearing. And exciting. He was such an adventurer."

She wiped a tear from her cheek. "Whatever it was, I fell in love with him. He never paid another penny on that loan, but it was understood I'd renounce any claim to the house when the time came."

"That's kind of you," I said. Embarrassed that I sounded so surprised, I turned away from her and placed the journal on the bedside table.

Lady Winstead took no notice. "Regardless of how useless I find them, it wasn't their fault their father was irresponsible. But they'll receive nothing more than the house."

"And Kate?" I prompted.

"Kate is not my sole heir, but she will find herself very well off when I'm gone. However, it's not as if she knows that."

I almost laughed. "You may not have told her in so many words, but she has reason to believe herself to be your heir. You've made it plain you dislike your stepchildren, and you have no children of your own. I'm confident she suspects she'll inherit a substantial fortune." I thought of Kate, her handsome actor friend, and her sudden desire to spirit her aunt off to some hiding place and "care" for her.

Lady Winstead returned to the bedside and faced me. "I suppose you're right, but what of it?"

"That gives her quite a motive to murder you."

Chapter Twenty-Four

Lady Winstead looked as if she were about to argue, but before she could respond, there was a gentle knock at the door. With a speed I'd never seen her exhibit, she was back in bed and wearing her dazed expression by the time I reached the door.

Hetty jumped to her feet and smoothed all evidence of her prior occupation from the coverlet. After moving a chair to the bedside, she took a seat, snatched a book from the bedside table, and began reading in a low voice.

I opened the door to find Kate wearing a look of surprise. "I wasn't expecting to find you here, Mrs. Hazelton," she said as she slipped into the room.

"You were still abed this morning, so I thought I'd check on Lady Winstead."

"That's my intention, too." She stepped over to the bed, where Hetty closed her book and stepped out of the way. "How are you this morning, Aunt?" Kate asked.

Lady Winstead gave her a blank look, then seemed to recognize her and placed her hand on Kate's cheek. My goodness, Lady Winstead could give acting lessons to her niece.

Kate took her aunt's hand, then glanced at me. "She looks better, don't you think?"

If only she knew how much better. "Yes," I said in a bright voice. "I thought so, too." My gaze took in Hetty and Lady Winstead and—oh, heavens—the journal! That was the book Hetty had been reading from and now held pressed against her chest. I took hold of Kate's arm and turned her toward me and away from the journal. I supposed I could just tell her I'd found it, but at this point I wasn't sure if that was wise.

"In fact, Lady Winstead is in such good hands, I don't think we should linger and distract her. Why don't you come to the drawing room with me? There's something I've been meaning to discuss with you, and we may as well talk over tea."

I gave her little choice, since I nearly yanked her out of the room. I glanced inside as I pulled the door closed, to see both ladies watching to make sure we left. Bother! Now I'd have to find a way to slip back in there without Kate to pick up the journal.

I put it out of my mind and tried to focus on Kate's recitation of her evening. She chatted on and on while we descended the stairs, crossed the hall, and entered the drawing room, where we seated ourselves on opposite ends of the sofa. Clearly, she had quite enjoyed herself at Fiona's birthday celebration. It sounded as if the gaiety, the society, and probably the wealth of the other guests had lured her into at least an interest in joining polite society. However, I knew the theater had its own allure, particularly when it came in the shape of handsome leading men. I wondered which would win in the end.

After about twenty minutes of detailing the attributes of her dance partners, Kate stopped herself mid-sentence. "I'm sorry, Frances. You said there was something you wished to discuss with me?"

Considering that people kept appearing unexpectedly—and inconveniently—in this house, I moved closer to Kate so I could speak softly. "I must ask you about your relationship with Mr. Montague."

She looked at me with some surprise, and I anticipated her denial. I held up a hand. "Before you tell me he's returned to Devon, I know he's an actor and that he has a role in *Florodora*."

Her lips parted, but she made no sound.

I waited.

"I'm sorry I misled you," she said at last. "At that time, you didn't know I was an actress. I was still hoping to keep that my secret."

"I understand," I said, pleased that I'd had this conversation with Fiona first, or I might not be so understanding. "But what of Mr. Montague?"

She shook her head and peered a little closer at me. "What of him?"

"Are the two of you involved romantically?"

Her eyes grew wide. "Absolutely not! He was only bringing me my lines for that evening."

"The way you both jumped apart when I walked in on you led me to believe there might be something between you."

"He is a notorious flirt," she said. "And I'll admit he's very handsome, but I could never take him seriously. Everyone knows he's involved with Cornelia Dawson." She sucked in her breath. "I shouldn't have said that."

"It's fine." I placed a hand over hers. "I'm relieved to hear you know about . . . them."

She leaned toward me. "They do not keep it a secret."

Perhaps it was relief or the stress of the past few days, but I found the whole idea absurdly humorous and giggled like a child. My giggles infected Kate, and it took us a few moments to pull ourselves together. Vi Ashley chose that moment to wander into the room in her usual languid manner. She paused when she spotted us, then slid into the chair next to Kate.

"It looks as though you two had an enjoyable evening," she said with a grudging tone. "You don't realize how difficult it is to be stuck in this house with no company except three dull men and a ranting old woman." She gave us both a look of suffering. "How I envy you."

As if neither of us had ever been in mourning. Obviously, Vi did not feel the loss of Lord Peter. But then, why should she? The man was out of the country for most of the years she'd been married to Si. It was not as if he had been a part of their lives. I decided not to judge her. She had to be chafing against her enforced solitude.

"It will soon be six months, Vi. In half mourning you will be able to visit friends again. In fact, aren't you all dining with friends tonight?"

"Family," she said. "Boring family, but you are right. It is a start." She forced a smile. "Shall we have tea?"

I took the opportunity to excuse myself. I simply had to get home to see George and give him the latest news before he left on some other business. Leaving the ladies in the drawing room, I stopped in at Lady Winstead's room, which was much easier than I'd anticipated since Kate was occupied. I took the journal and told Hetty I'd be gone for an hour or two.

"You are coming back, aren't you?" She looked quite panic-stricken.

"Of course. I'd never leave you to deal with this family on your own." I gave her a hug and went to my own room to find a bag large enough to hide the journal. Bridget was seated at the writing desk with a book. She glanced up when I came in.

"Can I do something for you, ma'am?"

"I'm going home—"

"Oh, thank goodness!" Even if she hadn't said a word, the look of relief on Bridget's face spoke volumes. "I'll have us packed in a jiff."

I caught her arm as she passed me on her way to the dressing room. "We're not moving back home. At least not yet. I just need to pay a call on Mr. Hazelton." I ushered her back to the chair and seated myself on the end of the bed. "You sound like Aunt Hetty, but I know why she's so eager to leave. Why are you?"

"It's an awkward household, ma'am. Some of the staff are here from the old days . . . Lord Peter's servants. Others were hired by the current viscount. Since Lord Peter died, they've been trying to get the upper hand, because they work for the new Viscount Winstead. A few more came here with Mr. and Mrs. Ashley, and they act like they're better than the others, because their master and mistress are friends with the Prince of Wales. They expect to be treated like visiting servants, the way I am. And one came with Lady Winstead." She wrinkled her nose. "Everyone belowstairs despises her."

"Would Lady Winstead's servant be Aggie?"

"She is, and you may recall she's quite the sly little thing. I can see why none of the other servants trust her."

"I've recently been given to understand that she does a very good job of taking care of Lady Winstead. I'll tell you the whole story another time, but I'm now more inclined to sympathize with Aggie rather than suspect her of any wrongdoing. Is it just that the animosity makes you uncomfortable, or are any of the staff making trouble for you?"

"I suppose just the former, but I won't be sorry to leave here."

"Hopefully, we'll be doing that very soon. For now, I just need to get this journal to Mr. Hazelton and give him some information. I don't want anyone seeing me leave with it. Have I a bag large enough to carry it?"

She twisted her lips while she eyed the book. "I don't think you do, ma'am, but I have one. You'd look strange carrying it, but I could go with you."

She looked so comically hopeful that I agreed. "We have to leave immediately," I said. "And we'll be coming right back."

Her eagerness for our departure overwhelmed her concern for our return, and she produced an appropriate bag—she was correct about me looking foolish carrying it myself—and we set off. We had one of the footmen find a cab for us and were almost out of the house without incident when Jonathon Ashley emerged from the library and caught sight of us in the hall.

"Hallo. Are you leaving us, Mrs. Hazelton?"

Bother! Another person trying to rid himself of my presence. "Only briefly, sir," I said. "My husband informed me of a stack of invitations at home that require my attention. It strikes me that I might be able to include Kate among our party in a few instances. You seemed rather eager that she have every opportunity to meet potential suitors, after all."

"Indeed." He narrowed his eyes as he scrutinized me. "How much longer shall we be enjoying your company?"

"Not long, I think. Kate should be prepared for society soon. With the family dining away from home, she and I can work on the judicious consumption of wine at a dinner party." I leaned in to speak in confidence. "Last night the footman was a bit too quick to refill her glass."

He blinked in surprise. "She wasn't—"

"Tipsy? Just a tiny bit, but no harm was done. This exercise will prevent any future faux pas."

"Very well, then. We appreciate your dedication to your task and are grateful to your husband in allowing you to stay with us. How is Hazelton keeping himself occupied in your absence?"

Sometimes Winstead was such a typical man . . . thanking George for my work. Or was there some other purpose in his question? Did he know George was involved in the search for his father's journal? He'd never expect George to confide in me.

"He's been spending some time at the British Museum, I believe." I watched his face for any sign of reassurance or, alternatively, panic, but it remained as bland as usual.

"Has he? How very interesting."

"I'm not sure he finds it so. He's said very little about whatever task has taken him there." I shrugged. "But then, I don't provide details of what Miss Stover and I are doing, either."

We both chuckled at the absurdity of a husband and wife having any interest in one another's activities. Finally, the footman returned with the cab, and Bridget and I could escape.

When we arrived home, I sent Bridget downstairs for a cup of tea and found George and Rose at the card table in the drawing room. A chessboard lay on the surface between them. I heard George's deep voice, followed by a trill of giggles from Rose.

"Goodness, I've never known a game of chess to bring out such cheer," I said, dropping Bridget's market bag on the sofa as I walked toward them.

"Mummy!" Rose scooted out of her chair and into my arms. George slipped up behind her and embraced us both.

"Giving up already, are you?" he whispered in my ear.

"You know me better than that," I replied.

We finally came apart and Rose and I took seats at the tea table. I leaned back into the sofa and stretched my arms overhead, while George poured us a glass of something—I didn't even care what. It was so good to be home, temporarily or not.

I pulled the journal from the market bag. "In addition to seeing my two loves, I have some business to take care of." I dangled the journal in the air. "You may give this to the British Museum."

George's eyes shone with pride as he set our glasses on the tea table and took the journal from me. "Good work, Frances. How did you find it?"

I shifted my gaze to Rose. "Lady Winstead handed it over. It turns out she and Rose have been reading it."

He seated himself next to Rose. "Right under our noses all the time, eh? With you and Rosie on my team, I feel quite at leisure to put up my feet and hand off my assignments to you."

Rose beamed, though it was clear she wasn't exactly following the conversation.

I leaned toward her, as if sharing a confidence. "I'm afraid I must deliver some other news to Georgie now, and it might be best if you were not in the room." I lowered my voice. "He's apt to start yelling."

She giggled. "Georgie doesn't yell."

"You've just never heard it. And it's best if you don't." After assuring her I'd be home for good soon, she left us, and I met George's expectant gaze.

"Is this about Lady Winstead?" he asked. "It sounds as though she's vastly improved."

"Ah, yes. About that." I drew a bracing breath, hardly believing what I was about to tell him. "Lady Winstead has been faking her drugged state. At least for the most part."

He dropped the journal to his lap. "Are you joking? Do you mean none of this was ever necessary?"

"Well, it was necessary if you were to obtain the journal. She felt it was necessary to flush out the person who killed Lord Peter, which is very likely the same person who murdered Nurse Plum and attempted to drug Lady Winstead."

I explained to him how she found herself under the influence of laudanum until her maid helped her break her addiction. When I got to the part where she enlisted Lady Esther's aid to bring me into the household to find out who was trying to murder her, George exploded and jumped to his feet.

"The gall of that woman!" Flinging his arms about, he paced across the rug, stopping here and there to send me a pointed look. "Why has she stayed there? And what is she thinking to bring other innocent people into that house when clearly some skulduggery is afoot? You shouldn't even go back. Send Bridget there to collect your things and your aunt, and let Lady Winstead work this out for herself. Apparently, she's lucid enough to do so."

I twisted around to better see him. "She believes whoever is attempting to drug her also killed Lord Peter with an overdose of laudanum. She wants to catch that person and have them arrested. If she simply puts her stepchildren out on the street, she'll never have the proof she needs."

"I am all in favor of bringing a murderer to justice, but using herself as bait to catch one is a step too far. She is putting herself, you, and your aunt at risk. She brought you into this situation under false pretenses. When you thought she was drugged and could not act on her own behalf, it was understandable, but she is not helpless."

"I do not disagree with you. She has been very high-handed and dishonest with me, but I'd like to remind you this person murdered the man she loved and very likely Nurse Plum. I wouldn't be surprised to learn that it was Jonathon Ashley. He might even have killed his father to keep him from spending any more of his inheritance."

"Be that as it may, he should know by now that he'll receive nothing upon Lady Winstead's death, so he has no reason to kill her. If he's our culprit, and because he's stolen her jewelry, I suspect he is, killing his father was an accident. Thus, the heavy doses given to Lady Winstead were also accidental, and she can evict them from the house without concern that the viscount will come back to kill her." He brushed his hands together, as if our work were done.

"An accident is always possible, but I think it unlikely here. Jonathon needs Lady Winstead's money, and he is not one for risks. He hired a nurse to care for her, just as he did for his father. Don't you think that was meant to ensure they were given the correct dosage only to remain sedated? He must be determined to keep Lady Winstead alive, knowing that with her death, he loses everything."

George stopped his pacing. "If you don't think the overdoses were accidental, you must believe someone else is trying to kill her."

"I'm not certain, but it's a good possibility. Jonathon may know he needs her alive, but does Si or Andrew? On the other side of the family, Miss Stover must be aware she'll inherit a fortune. Perhaps not everything, but at least a tidy sum. Yes, I think there's a very good chance the heavy doses were not an accident."

George clucked his tongue in disgust. "The whole family seem worse than vultures. Whatever it takes to get at her fortune."

"And yet you balk at accepting a gift of money from my father."

He froze mid-step and cocked his head. "Are you planning to drug your father, or simply changing the subject?"

I ignored the comment and pressed on. "Fiona thinks you are worried you'll end up like your aunt Julia."

He stared in astonishment. "Aunt Julia? My aunt? The woman who is gadding about the Continent without a care in the world? Imagine the horror of ending up like her."

"She meant the version of your aunt who was something of a prisoner in your house."

"Fiona thought that? I suppose Father did have some control over her—" He cut himself off. Leaning over the back of the sofa, he let his gaze lock with mine. "I do not for even a moment believe you would use your father's money as some sort of leverage or control over me."

"Thank you for that."

"I just have to reconcile my new access to money with the fact that I've done nothing to earn it. I simply married a woman of means."

I placed my hand on his cheek. "You poor dear."

He laughed. "I promise you I will come to terms with this." He took my hand in his and straightened up. "Now, back to Miss Stover as one of our vultures. How might she have managed to murder the nurse?"

"Delaney told me a doctor was seen calling on Nurse Plum before she was killed. Kate knows people from the theater, and she knows where the nurse lived."

He had been prepared to speak and snapped his mouth shut. With a sigh, he clasped his hands behind his back and resumed his pacing, this time along the carpet in front of me. "I don't like this, Frances. The risk is not worth the reward in this case."

"I'm about to surprise you and say I completely agree."

He paused and snapped his head around. "Somehow I think there's more."

"There is. Tonight the risk is very much reduced. All the Ashleys will be dining with friends, leaving only Kate at home. Only one suspect. Thus Hetty, Lady Winstead, and I will outnumber her. Bridget and I will return to the Ashley home, and I shall give Lady Winstead notice that we will leave tomorrow. That includes Hetty, of course. Meanwhile, you will call on me this evening as planned to search for the jewelry."

"Winstead has as much as admitted to having it." George rubbed his chin. "That ought to be enough for Delaney to arrest him on charges of theft."

"He told Delaney Lady Winstead gave the jewelry to his wife. Lady Winstead disputes that, but she hasn't spoken to Delaney. I still think you ought to search. Remember, Lady Winstead found the journal for you."

He heaved a sigh. "But whether I find the jewelry or not, this ends tonight?"

"Definitely. As you said, Delaney will probably arrest Jonathon for theft once Lady Winstead refutes his claim that she gave the jewelry to him. Then it's up to her to decide what she wants to do about the rest of the family. If I were her, I'd make them all aware of the details of her will. As for finding the killer, that will have to be up to Delaney and the police this time."

He furrowed his brow as he considered my plan. "If Delaney makes the arrest tonight, there's no reason for you to stay there."

"I suppose you're right. Very well, Hetty and I shall leave tonight if Delaney makes an arrest." I lifted a brow and held out my hand. "Are we agreed?"

"Agreed." George took my hand and gave it one swift pump, then pulled me to my feet and into his embrace. "I will see you this evening. Please don't do anything dangerous in the meantime."

After our discussion, George had some rather romantic notions, and as a result, I stayed much longer at home than I'd originally anticipated. After I said good-bye to Rose, it was time to leave.

George walked me to the carriage, and Bridget and I were off. She was far less excited to return to the Ashleys' than she had been to leave, but she brightened when I told her we'd be leaving the next day at the latest.

Once we arrived, I stopped in Lady Winstead's room to see how she and Hetty were faring. Lady Winstead was napping. Her skin seemed to have more color than this morning, though it might just be the contrast to her white hair draping over the white coverlet. Her snore was certainly hearty.

The noise didn't seem to bother Hetty, who was at the table, reading. She put aside her book when I joined her. I quickly told her about George coming this evening to conduct his own search for the jewelry and that no matter what we found, we'd be leaving by tomorrow.

Hetty looked concerned. "Are we simply going to leave her to the mercy of her family?"

"She holds all the power in this family. She could easily cast them out of the house, including Kate. Or she could leave herself. I do feel badly that we won't find Lord Peter's killer, but we have no real proof that he was murdered."

"What about the nurse, poor dear?"

"The police are working on that case. Delaney doesn't need our assistance, and before you give Nurse Plum too much sympathy, remember she was taking money to drug Lady Winstead with laudanum."

"Oh, yes. I'd forgotten." She sighed. "There are no innocents here, are there?"

"Not even Lady Winstead, so please be careful."

By the time I returned to my room, Bridget was ready to help me change for dinner. Just as she finished tidying my hair, Fuller knocked at the door and informed me that Lady Winstead was dining in her room, and asked if I would care to have my dinner on a tray in mine.

I agreed to the suggestion, but when the tray arrived, I had the footman deliver it to Lady Winstead's room. I followed him there, intending to inform her of my plans while we shared a meal, hoping food would make her more amenable.

Hetty responded to our knock. Lady Winstead was out of bed and seated in her wheeled chair at the small table across the room. I instructed the footman to unload the tray on her table. As soon as he'd completed his task, Hetty closed the door behind him.

"Well, isn't this cozy," she said as we moved to the table. "You take the chair, Frances. I'll use the window seat." She slipped around the back of the table. "Has the family left for their engagement yet?" she asked.

"I heard them leave about twenty minutes ago." I turned to Lady Winstead. "The servants must be sitting down to their dinner by now, and my husband should arrive shortly. I'll take him first to Lord Jonathon's office. That would be the ideal place to hide something."

"Ideal because there's a safe in there." Lady Winstead lifted her nose. "How will your husband get inside?"

I waved a hand. "You needn't worry about that. He's very resourceful."

"I don't understand why he's looking for my jewelry. I thought it was the journal he was after."

"The journal was his first objective. He's grateful you gave it to him and would like to help us. If he finds the real stones, along with the paste necklace, Jonathon will have some explaining to do to the Metropolitan Police. Inspector Delaney spoke with the jeweler who made the paste items for him, and with your statement that the jewelry was taken from your locked dressing table, that ought to be enough to arrest him and charge him with the theft."

I began my meal just as Lady Winstead pushed her plate away. "You know that isn't the arrest I was hoping for."

"Yes, I do. But since laudanum played a role in Nurse Plum's murder, I think the police will take action if you tell them someone in this house has been keeping you drugged with the same drug. Let the police handle it from here. You are taking too much of a risk."

She pursed her lips and stared at me, then finally heaved a sigh. "Perhaps you are right. I didn't realize laudanum was involved with Nurse Plum's murder. It would stand to reason we were both victims of the same person."

"Then we are all leaving tonight. I think that calls for a toast." Hetty glanced around. "Didn't the footman bring up a bottle of wine?"

"No, but check the decanter," Lady Winstead said. "It's on the dresser over there."

Hetty retrieved the decanter and glasses. After setting them on the table, she poured wine for the three of us.

"What happens if Hazelton doesn't find the jewels?" Lady Winstead asked.

"I'm afraid Aunt Hetty and I will still leave. I'd suggest that you do the same. Perhaps you could go to Lady Esther and contact Inspector Delaney from the safety of her home. Then I suppose you must decide what to do about those in your family who are not trying to kill you. Will you let them stay here, do you think? And what about Kate? I'm sure she'd prefer to be with you rather than the Ashleys."

"Assuming she isn't the one drugging you," Hetty added. "Where is she, by the way? Surely she didn't go with the rest of them?"

"I doubt they'd invite her," Lady Winstead said.

I hadn't seen Kate since late this morning and wondered if she was back onstage or at least back with her actor friends. I turned to Lady Winstead as she reached for her glass. "There's something you ought to know about Kate," I began.

She glanced at me and held the glass under her nose, swirling the contents. "Something's off with this." She took a small sip, then spat it back into the glass. "Don't drink that," she said, her voice full of outrage. "It's laced with laudanum."

I took the glass from her fingers and gave it a careful sniff. "It smells like . . ." I shrugged. "Alcohol."

"Like too much alcohol," she replied. "This is my favorite wine. It's not meant to smell or taste like this. There is a great deal of laudanum in here."

Hetty stared. "For heaven's sake, was it someone's intention to kill us all?"

"Not likely," I said. "I had planned to dine in my room. You are Lady Winstead's nurse. They wouldn't expect you to be drinking wine with her. No, I'm afraid this was meant for you alone," I said to the viscountess. "How long has the decanter been here?"

"I noticed it there this afternoon."

"No," Hetty said. "There was a decanter of wine on this table yesterday. Isn't this the same one?"

"I haven't been drinking wine," Lady Winstead said. "Kate took the one that was here yesterday, so someone must have brought this one in today. Perhaps you stepped out," she said to Hetty, "while I was napping."

"I never left the room," Hetty said.

"But you took a nap, too," I reminded her. "Someone might have slipped in here without you hearing."

"I should have known," Lady Winstead said. "Even in my sleep, I smelled that lemon and bergamot. Someone came in then."

Lemon and bergamot. "That scent belonged to Nurse Plum, Lady Winstead. She hasn't been here for three days."

"Nevertheless, I tell you I smelled it."

Hetty wrung her hands. "I can't believe there was a chance to actually catch the culprit in the act, and I missed it. I'm a terrible spy."

The whole situation bothered me. I tossed my napkin on the table and came to my feet. "I want to check on Kate," I said. Her room was just a few steps down the hall. It shared a wall with this one. She could have brought in the tainted wine while Lady Winstead was sleeping.

I rapped on the closed door.

No answer. I tried the handle. It turned easily, so I pushed the door open as quietly as I could. The room was dim. If Kate was gone, she hadn't left a lamp burning. A thought struck me. If Kate was gone, I might just as well have a look around. The arrangement of the room was similar to that of her aunt's room next door. A bureau near the door. A large bed with two bedside tables were to this side of the room, with an open space between the bed and a small table near the window.

Except, as I stepped farther into the room, I noticed the open space wasn't empty. Sprawled facedown across the rug lay Kate, a decanter of wine and an empty glass on the table beside her.

Chapter Twenty-five

❧

Finding a dead body never gets any easier. I wish I could stop my propensity to do so. I took a steadying breath and sank to my knees next to Kate. She lay sprawled on her stomach, one arm out to her side, as if she'd tried to break her fall. I took that wrist and felt for her pulse.

And found one! It wasn't the strongest pulse I'd ever felt, but it existed. I scampered to my feet and scanned the room for the bellpull, then gave up when I heard voices outside the door, and rushed out to the hallway.

It was empty. Yet I still heard voices. Someone had to be in the entry hall below. I bent over the railing. "Hallo!"

The two men below looked up and were apparently surprised to see a woman hanging over the banister, waving her arms.

"Frances, is that you?"

George! Thank heaven. The other man was Fuller. "I need both of you up here right away." I pushed away from the banister and saw Aggie running down the hall toward me.

"What's happened, ma'am?" She stopped when she reached

me, but clearly wanted to get around me. "Lady Winstead rang for me. Is she all right?"

"She's fine," Hetty said from Lady Winstead's doorway. "We heard the commotion in Miss Stover's room and thought you might need help, Frances."

Just then George and Fuller barreled up the stairs. I took Aggie by the arm and led them all into Kate's room. "I fear Miss Stover is in grave danger."

The little maid gazed down at the body in horror. George moved around us to Kate.

"She still has a pulse," I was quick to add. "I suspect she's had too much laudanum." I turned to Aggie. "Tell us what we should do."

She looked at me in confusion. "Why was Miss Stover taking laudanum?"

"I don't believe she did so intentionally." I pointed to the table where the empty glass and decanter stood.

"Why would someone do that to Miss Stover?" Fuller asked from the doorway.

Ignoring him, Aggie snapped around to face me. "That wine is from her ladyship's room. She didn't drink it, so Miss Stover took it, thinking she'd have a glass later."

"I'm aware," I said, "there is a second decanter in Lady Winstead's room—also full of laudanum."

Aggie frowned in confusion. "Someone must have brought it up this afternoon. Did her ladyship drink it?"

"No, and she's fine, but please tell me how we can help Miss Stover."

"I have no idea. I've never seen her ladyship this sozzled. When they managed to slip her the drug, I'd just keep an eye on her while she slept it off. Miss Stover doesn't look like she's sleeping."

George was on his knees next to Kate, lifting her eyelids.

"We should call a doctor immediately," I said.

"I'm not sure there's time for that," he said. "St. George's Hospital isn't far from here." He called the butler over. "Help me get her in my carriage, and I'll take her there now."

Unconscious, Miss Stover could provide no assistance and simply hung between the men as they walked her down the hall to the stairs.

"Aggie, go with Mr. Hazelton. You know Miss Stover, and I'm sure they'll have questions at the hospital," I said.

"I can answer them, ma'am." She followed along behind them.

George paused at the door and looked up at me. "It's time for you to leave—all of you. Before the Ashleys return."

"I want to telephone Delaney first, but I couldn't agree more."

"This is not an argument you can allow her to win," he added, referring to Lady Winstead. "For all of your safety, you must leave here."

I waved my hands to shoo him out the door as I came down the stairs. "Go quickly, before you drop her." In truth, I felt confident that Kate was in the best of hands. I felt far less confident in my own task—convincing Lady Winstead to leave. So, if at all possible, I wanted Inspector Delaney here before the family returned home from their evening out.

A clearly unsettled Fuller returned and informed me that Lady Winstead had indeed had a telephone installed in the house. He took me to a small cubby under the stairs so that I could telephone the police. While I waited for my connection, I instructed him to send Bridget up to Lady Winstead's room. Despite all the horrors of this evening, Delaney's voice when he answered brought me some assurance.

I explained about the drugged wine, Hazelton's arrival, Miss Stover's trip to the hospital, and my intention of packing a small bag and moving myself, Hetty, and Lady Winstead to accommodations more suitable to living through the night. He thought the idea a fine one, cautioned me to preserve the wine in its current state, and assured me he was on his way. With that task completed, I went upstairs to convince Lady Winstead it was indeed time to go.

When I entered, she waited in her wheeled chair in the center of the room. Hetty stood behind her.

"Thank heaven Hazelton was here to take Kate to the hospital," Hetty said.

"Aggie has gone with him," I told them. "In light of this latest incident, I've contacted the police. Inspector Delaney will be here as soon as he possibly can."

Lady Winstead heaved a sigh. "I must agree that it was indeed necessary to contact them. It's terribly unnerving that someone in this house wants so badly to see me dead. Even more so that poor Kate has suffered because I wouldn't act."

Hetty placed a hand on her shoulder. "At least this would indicate that Miss Stover wasn't the party responsible for drugging you."

"I feel guilty that I ever thought she was," Lady Winstead admitted.

My own suspicions about Kate had come and gone in rotation. Just as I was certain she could have had nothing to do with drugging her aunt, Lady Winstead had mentioned smelling lemon and bergamot—the fragrance Nurse Plum had worn. It was the type of thing an actress would have noticed. And thinking her aunt was heavily under the influence of laudanum, Kate might have worn that fragrance and slipped in here to drug the wine, assuming Lady Winstead would say it was the nurse, and everyone would disregard her words as laudanum-induced rambling.

But there was no denying that Lady Winstead believed she had smelled that fragrance this afternoon. If it wasn't Kate, then who? With the family gone, now was the perfect time to search. For what, I wasn't sure. Something that smelled like Nurse Plum.

Before I began any search, I had to deliver one more unwelcome command. "I don't think you should wait here to speak with Inspector Delaney. It's unlikely he'll arrest anyone tonight, which means you aren't safe in this house."

"Oh, I don't wish to leave," she said. "How am I any less safe now than yesterday?"

"You weren't entirely safe yesterday, either, but you did have one advantage. Whoever was drugging you thought he was dealing with someone insensible. Even if you could accuse him, who would believe you? Now that we've brought the police into this business, you will have to make a statement and won't be able to pretend any longer. That person will know that you know what they've been doing, and that you intend to have them arrested."

"The cat is out of the bag," Hetty said. "I would prefer to see you throw them out of the house, but for now, it's safer if you leave."

Lady Winstead gave her reluctant agreement. "I won't argue with you, but it pains me that I'll never know who killed my Peter."

"Wouldn't it be the same person who drugged you?"

"I assume so, but once I leave, will we ever find out?"

"There's one thing I can do before we leave." I said. "Hetty, since Aggie is with Kate, would you mind packing a bag for Lady Winstead? Bridget will be up soon to help you. I want to do a quick search of the upstairs rooms before the police get here."

"Or before the family come home," Hetty added.

"I'd say we have two hours or more before we can expect them. We should be long gone by then." I headed for the door.

Lady Winstead wheeled herself along behind me. I turned in the hallway.

"Please stay here, ma'am. I simply wish to make a quick search of the rooms."

She made a shooing motion. "Yes, yes. I would only slow

you down." She didn't move back into the room, but I had to trust that she wouldn't follow me. I really did need to get this done quickly.

The family rooms were on the other side of the stairs from mine and Lady Winstead's. The first door I came to was Si and Vi's. I paused outside the door and listened for any sound behind it. Just because Si and Vi were out for the evening didn't mean one of their servants wouldn't be inside.

I pushed the door open slowly and stepped in. After a quick scan of the room, I crossed to the dressing room, which it appeared they shared, and found nothing but clothing and shoes. Back in the bedchamber were two bureaus and a wardrobe, and Vi had a dressing table pushed against the wall in a corner. Nothing there but what might be expected—hairpins, a brush and comb, some lip pomade. Terribly unsatisfying, but there were still the bureaus.

Tackling the first one, I pushed aside shifts and stockings, looking for who knew what. When I came across a packet of letters, I paused, my hand hovering just above it. But I wouldn't get another chance, would I? I opened the first letter and scanned it quickly—and in confusion. It was from a Mr. Jenkins from Jenkins and Son, but it was addressed to a Mrs. Godfrey. I glanced at the first paragraph, and my eyes crossed. I had no time to decipher the legal language, but something about that name sounded familiar.

I almost returned the letters to the drawer, then hesitated and stuffed them in my pocket. This might be nothing, but Hetty would understand the contents. I'd ask her to look at them. I found nothing incriminating in the remaining drawers.

The bureau and wardrobe for Si bore even less fruit. Other than items of clothing, I found only a calling card or two and a theater program—not for *Florodora*, thank goodness. This time I had started with the bottom drawer and moved up. When I'd finished with the top drawer and pushed it closed, it caught on something. I pulled it back out and stuck my hand inside, feeling around over the back of the drawer and the frame. My fingers closed around a book of some sort with a soft cover. A little maneuvering brought it forward. An account book.

A quick examination made it clear that Si and Vi hadn't moved here to share the work of caring for his father. It was definitely a lack of funds that had them giving up their own residence and living off Jonathon, who in turn lived off Lady Winstead. Though interesting, this was hardly the evidence I'd been hoping to find. I stuffed the account book in the back of the drawer and closed it. Onward.

The next room, if I wasn't mistaken, belonged to Jonathon. Pressing my ear to the door, I could hear someone moving around inside. No point doing battle with his valet. I'd move on to Andrew's room for now. Perhaps Jonathon's room would be empty when I returned.

There were no sounds emanating from the young man's room, so I cautiously opened the door and peeked inside. The gas lamp was turned low, making it difficult to see. It also made it unlikely anyone was in here, so I entered slowly, allowing my eyes to adjust. As they did, I scanned the room. A desk was placed under the window on the far wall. The surface was clear except for a stack of books on one side. If they were Andrew's textbooks, it didn't look as if he'd opened them since the Christmas holiday.

A bureau, a large canopied bed, and two bedside tables filled the rest of the room. I started my search with the dressing room. After turning up the overhead light in the small room, I looked behind garments hung along the walls, rummaged to the backs of shelves and, using a stool, checked the top shelves, too. Upon climbing down, I replaced the stool and noticed there'd been something tucked behind it—clothing, it seemed.

Lifting the pile from the floor, I immediately caught the scent of lemon and bergamot. I gave the clothes a shake, and they took the form of a skirt and shirtwaist. Given the scent and their size, the clothing must have belonged to Nurse Plum. Andrew would have had to walk through Lady Winstead's room undetected to get to Nurse Plum's room. Not an impossible feat, but risky given that Kate, Aggie, and Nurse Plum herself had often attended to Lady Winstead. The only other way he could have obtained her clothing was if he'd been at her house. Chances were that if he'd been at her home, he'd gone there to murder her.

I searched the floor behind rows of shoes. If he'd killed her, wouldn't he have a bottle of laudanum in his possession, too? Feeling pressed for time, I swept my hand along the floor in the dark corner. I heard a rattle as my fingers brush against something smooth. I wrapped two fingers around the short neck of the bottle and pulled it out. Laudanum, of course.

After pushing myself up from the awkward position, I wrapped the bottle in the clothing and moved back into the bedroom, confused. Andrew must have murdered Nurse Plum, but would he have been the one paying her to drug Lady Winstead? Surely if someone of his tender years had made her such an offer, she would have refused and at least told his father. Or was I just determined to see Jonathon as the culprit?

No matter. That was for Delaney to sort out. I returned to Lady Winstead's room with the clothing and laudanum. Hetty and Bridget were packing a small bag. Lady Winstead sat in her chair, worrying the ends of a shawl.

"Lady Winstead, is this what you smelled this afternoon while you rested?"

She turned her attention to me and leaned away as soon as she caught the scent of the clothing, waving a hand before her face. "Yes, that's it exactly."

Hetty had moved closer. "Good heavens, Frances. Tell me those aren't what I think they are. Where did you find them?"

"I believe these are Nurse Plum's clothes. I found them in Andrew's room."

"Andrew?" Lady Winstead looked dumbfounded. "Why, he's little more than an adolescent."

"He also had this." I held up the bottle of laudanum. "This isn't necessarily proof that he murdered Nurse Plum, but it looks very much as if he slipped in here this afternoon to bring you more drugged wine."

"Then was it he who killed Peter?" She shook her head. "This is such a shock. You are right, Frances. I must leave this house immediately."

"This should be everything you need to do so." Hetty indicated the bag Bridget was struggling to close. "I'll go to the back room and gather my things."

"Wait, Hetty." I pulled the letters from my pocket. "I found these in Vi's room, but I don't know what they are. Would you review them?"

She took the letters to the table to read, and I considered our next step. "I'll have a footman fetch a cab for us." Before I made a move, I heard someone in the entry hall, followed by the sound of the front door closing.

Someone leaving? Or had the Ashleys come home?

Chapter Twenty-six

"Maybe it's Inspector Delaney," Bridget whispered.

"He wouldn't have simply walked in." At least I didn't think so. "Get yourselves ready to leave, and I'll see who it is." I handed the garments and bottle to Lady Winstead since she was closest to me. She turned her head away, but took them. "Even if it is the family," I continued, "Delaney will be here shortly. We will leave according to plan."

With that, I headed out toward the stairs. Whoever was in the entry caught sight of me first.

"Frances. Whatever has happened here?"

I blew out a breath. Vi Ashley.

She approached the stairway. "Fuller sent a message over saying Kate had become ill. That she had been taken to the hospital. I volunteered to come home and see what happened. Is Lady Winstead well?"

I made my way down to the landing. The relief I felt at seeing only Vi in the hall made me realize how nervous I'd been. With any luck, I could convince her to return to her dinner party. "We had a bit of a fright this evening, Vi. Lady Winstead is well, but I found Miss Stover unconscious on the floor of her room." I gave her my most innocent expression. "I have no idea what was wrong with her, but Hazelton was here, so he took her to the hospital."

She placed a hand on the banister and gazed up at me through narrowed eyes. "Why was your husband here?"

"He arrived right when I found Miss Stover, so I pulled him into service immediately. I didn't have a chance to ask him." I shrugged. "Perhaps he simply missed me."

"Of course." She raised her brows. "But you have no idea what happened to Kate? Have you checked her room for signs of poison or anything?"

"Poison?" I'd been counting on Vi to be disinterested, as usual. This was not going at all as I'd hoped. "How would she have come into contact with poison?"

Vi pushed past me and climbed the stairs. "One never knows, but we ought to look."

I followed up the stairs behind her, then pulled up short when she stopped abruptly. I looked around her to see that Lady Winstead had wheeled herself down the hall to the top of the stairs, still holding the nurse's clothing.

Vi glanced at me over her shoulder. "It looks as though you've done some investigating already." She waved a hand at Lady Winstead. "Those are Nurse Plum's clothes, aren't they?" She turned back to me. "Where did you find them?"

"In Andrew's room."

She widened her eyes. "Do you think Andrew murdered her?"

I stared at her in amazement. Unless Vi had the nose of a hound, she couldn't possibly smell the nurse's cologne from where she stood, yet she'd seen a pile of fabric on Lady Winstead's lap and somehow she knew it was Nurse Plum's clothes. And I had the sense she had known before asking that I'd found them in Andrew's room. Why had I ignored Vi as the culprit? She had cared for her own mother until her death. Her mother, Mrs. Godfrey. Would those letters tell us something? Was Vi the killer?

"Why did you think something had happened to Lady Winstead?" I asked.

Her expression turned blank. "What do you mean?"

"The butler sent you word that Kate had taken ill, but when you came in just now, you asked about Lady Winstead. What did you think had happened to her? And how did you recognize those clothes as Nurse Plum's?"

Trapped between me and Lady Winstead's chair, Vi leaned against the banister and glared at me. "I suppose I'm simply observant. Why are you interrogating me?"

"Did you kill Nurse Plum?"

Lady Winstead made a noise that sounded something like a growl. When Vi darted a glance at her, I drew my finger across my lips. I wasn't sure where this was going, but I thought it best if Vi still believed Lady Winstead was drugged insensible.

"Don't be ridiculous. You found her clothing in Andrew's room. If you were searching his dressing room, presumably you already had some suspicions of him."

"I never mentioned his dressing room. I said I searched his room."

"She searched your room, as well, Mrs. Ashley." Hetty had slipped out to the hallway and now stood behind Lady Winstead, holding the letters I'd given her. "Or should I say Mrs. Godfrey?"

Vi's posture stiffened. "Mrs. Godfrey was my mother. Those are just old papers that have nothing to do me." She lifted her chin. "Now take Lady Winstead back to her room this instant."

Hetty smirked. "I don't think I will," she said, much to my relief, since I had no interest in being left alone with Vi. "It's interesting," she continued, "that Mrs. Ada Godfrey, your late mother, is listed as a beneficiary to both Lord Peter and Lady Winstead on these insurance policies."

"That is interesting, Aunt Hetty," I said. "How do you explain that, Violet?"

"She's your aunt?" Vi's hands on the banister were trembling. She glanced at each of us in turn, but she had no exit.

"I can explain it," Hetty said, waving the insurance documents. "Vi must have been in possession of her late mother's certificate of birth or marriage, or some other identifying document. By carefully changing a date, she could present herself as Mrs. Ada Godfrey."

Vi's face glistened with perspiration. Her nerves were getting the best of her.

"Did you murder Lord Peter?" I asked. "And the times Lady Winstead was overdosed, that was you?"

"Of course not!" She let go of the banister and wrung her hands. "I simply took advantage of the situation. Jonathon had the nurse keep his father drugged. I knew it was just a matter of time, so I bought the insurance. Later, when I saw he was planning the same for Lady Winstead, I insured her life, as well."

Her revelation stunned me to silence, but Hetty had no such problem. "You bought insurance policies rather than report him to the police or at least ask him to stop?" she asked. "You are as cold-blooded as he."

"I suspect you also murdered Nurse Plum," I said. "Jonathon needed her to do his dirty work. He wouldn't have killed her."

Vi pointed to the clothes on Lady Winstead's lap. "You found those in Andrew's dressing room with a bottle of laudanum. Isn't that evidence that he killed her?"

I didn't believe her for a minute. "Andrew couldn't have done it. Delaney has verified his alibi for the time of her murder." I tipped my head to the side. "And how did you know about the laudanum I found?"

"I won't stand for any more of this." Enraged and frightened, Vi reached up to pull Lady Winstead from her chair and, I assumed, push her into me, with the intention of using that momentum to knock us both down the stairs to the marble floor below.

She hadn't counted on Lady Winstead being completely clearheaded.

And exceedingly angry.

When Vi touched her, Lady Winstead threw herself at the younger woman. Two steps below her and reaching upward, Vi was caught off guard and off-balance. The two of them would have tumbled down the length of the stairs had I not caught Lady Winstead by the arm and pulled her against me. Anchored as I was to the banister, we both remained standing while Vi slid, rolled, and tumbled down the staircase to sprawl across the floor in the entry hall.

Hetty and I settled a shaking Lady Winstead back in her chair just as the bell rang. I headed down the stairs. Vi was moving and groaning as I stepped around her. Fuller arrived and came to a shocked standstill just as he was about to tumble over her. I waved him away, opened the door, and was delighted to see Inspector Delaney on the other side of it.

He took in the scene with a glance, then looked me up and down. "I take it this is our culprit?" He waved a hand at Vi.

"She is one of them," I said. "I'm afraid it's a long story."

After assessing Vi for injury, Delaney's constable took her back to the precinct for further questioning. Lady Winstead was brought downstairs and she, Hetty, and I moved to Jonathon's office to explain what had happened and, at Lady Winstead's request, to check the safe for her jewelry.

The office was small and windowless, with a gaslight fixture overhead and a lamp on the desk, which took up most of the room. There was shelving with books behind the desk and two chairs in front of it. Delaney took the chair behind the desk. Hetty wheeled Lady Winstead up to the side of it, and she and I took the guest chairs. I began the long explanation of our evening. Delaney scribbled in his notebook diligently, only looking up when I mentioned the insurance policies; Vi's declaration that Jonathon was responsible, via Nurse Plum, for drugging both his father and stepmother; and her attempt to accuse Andrew of murdering Nurse Plum.

"She seemed to know too much about Andrew's hiding place, though," I added. "So, I fibbed a bit and told her you had already verified Andrew's alibi for the time of her death." I winced. "That's when she tried to push Lady Winstead down the stairs. We had her cornered, and I think she simply hoped to get away."

"Actually, all three of the Ashley men's alibis were verified— something that had me stymied until now. You say Violet Ashley used the name Ada Godfrey for the insurance policies?" At my nod, he continued. "We examined Margery Plum's appointment book. As it happens, she was expecting a visit from an Ada Godfrey on the day of her murder. I think we have enough evidence to charge Violet Ashley with murder."

"Murder of Nurse Plum, that is," Lady Winstead added. "You cannot charge her with my husband's murder?"

"Or Lady Winstead's attempted murder?" Hetty asked. "Or Miss Stover? Why, Violet Ashley has left victims everywhere we turn."

"She didn't intend to drug Miss Stover," I said. "The wine was meant for Lady Winstead."

Delaney cleared his throat, drawing out attention. "We shall keep investigating, but we don't have enough evidence to make those charges tonight. Give us a chance to question the suspect."

Lady Winstead sighed. "I suppose one life sentence is sufficient, but what about Jonathon and his role in all this?"

Unfortunately, without testimony from Nurse Plum, Delaney wasn't certain they could prove that Jonathon had drugged his father and stepmother. He suggested they begin with charging him with the theft of Lady Winstead's jewels. After finding the key to the safe, Lady Winstead identified the jewels inside as hers and confirmed she had never gifted them to anyone.

We were just finishing up when Fuller brought George into the office. "Looks like everything is under control once more," he observed.

"How did you leave Kate?" I asked.

"Awake and in good hands. Aggie is still with her."

I stepped over to him and drew him into a hug. "She'll be all right?"

"She should be fine," he said, releasing me. "And it appears things have progressed here while I was gone."

I gave him the gist of what Vi had done and attempted to do.

"And then Lady Winstead pushed her down the stairs?"

Lady Winstead chuckled at the suggestion.

"It didn't happen exactly that way," I said. "And Delaney arrived at precisely the right moment."

With Delaney's work here finished, it was time for all of us to leave.

"What will happen next?" Lady Winstead asked as we all moved into the entry hall.

"I am off now to find the viscount and arrest him for theft." Delaney popped his hat back on his head and pulled open the door just as Jonathon, Si, and Andrew arrived on the other side of it.

"Viscount Winstead. How convenient," Delaney said.

Jonathon glanced at all of us suspiciously. "What on earth is going on here?"

A rare smile slipped across Delaney's lips. "You, sir, are under arrest."

Chapter Twenty-seven

❦

Delaney left with Jonathon Ashley in custody, but we remained at the Ashleys' home for at least another hour. Si was entitled to some explanation, as was Andrew, who was stunned his own aunt had tried to implicate him in the business of murdering Nurse Plum. Both men seemed at a loss of what to do. Perhaps Vi and Lady Winstead were right: the Ashley men were helpless.

Though the culprits had been arrested, we thought it best for Lady Winstead to stay elsewhere until she decided what to do about the remaining Ashleys. Finally, we sent her off in her carriage to spend at least that night with Lady Esther.

It was nearing midnight when George, Hetty, Bridget, and I finally arrived back at our own homes. Knowing I'd never have to return to Ashley House again, I slept like a baby.

Two days later, I was summoned to Lady Esther's home, where I met Inspector Delaney coming down the walkway from that lady's door. He looked quite frazzled, and I believed I knew why.

"I assume Lady Esther had a few questions for you, Inspector."

"Both of them had questions," he said. "Some of which I ought not to have answered." He took a restorative breath. "I only wish I could hire those ladies to interrogate suspects." He tipped his hat, and we both went on our way.

Within minutes I joined Lady Esther, Lady Winstead, and Kate around Lady Esther's tea table. They were more than happy to share what they had learned.

At first, Jonathon and Vi had simply accused each other, but Nurse Plum's appointment book and the insurance policies were rather damning to Vi. After a bit of pressure, she confessed to murdering Lord Peter and Nurse Plum and attempting to murder Lady Winstead, as well. Jonathon was charged with theft and the false imprisonment of Lady Winstead.

"With the criminals in custody and Kate back at home," I said, "it seems everything has been wrapped up neatly."

"It was the strangest thing to wake up in hospital when the last thing I recalled was dining in my room," Kate said. "You may be relieved to hear that the experiences of the past week have led me to be honest with my aunt and tell her about my acting career or, more to the point, the acting career I hope to have."

Lady Winstead turned to me with a wondering look in her eyes. "I couldn't believe it when Kate told us she's a *Florodora* girl. We are attending this evening's performance. You and your husband should join us."

I declined the invitation and asked, "Then you do not mind that Kate has chosen a career over life as a gentlewoman?"

"Do you know, I find that I do not." She appeared surprised by her own reaction. "I'm still growing used to the idea, but Kate knows her own mind, and I shall be happy to help her advance in her chosen career."

"I shall be grateful for a place to live, Aunt. It won't be necessary to help fund my career."

I smiled at Kate. "Lady Fiona will be disappointed that her gala didn't convince you to take part in London society."

Her eyes shone with delight. "I enjoyed her birthday celebration immensely and will always be grateful to her and you for giving me that experience. But even if I hadn't chosen to pursue a career, I would not have had time for a London season. Aunt Augusta and I intend to travel."

"Indeed, we do." Lady Winstead spoke with more energy than I'd seen from her in a long time. "I only wish we could convince Esther to join us."

Lady Esther sighed. "I'm afraid I must return to the country. My husband is entitled to some of my attention, after all."

This was the opening I'd been waiting for. "Speaking of husbands, I have been wondering how much of Lord Peter's journal you've read, Lady Winstead."

She gave me a knowing look. "Your question leads me to believe you've had a chance to read it. Have you turned it over to the British Museum yet?"

"We must, of course, but I asked Hazelton to wait until you had been warned—if a warning is necessary?"

"I read most of it, and I understand why Jonathon didn't want anyone to see it," she said. "It does not show his father off to the best advantage."

"Do you think Jonathon held it back intentionally?"

"Oh, I do indeed, which is why he was beside himself when the dratted thing disappeared."

Lady Esther tapped her walking stick against the floor. "I don't understand you. Are you not speaking of Lord Peter's own journal? How could it show him to any disadvantage?"

A sly smile played about Lady Winstead's lips. "Peter had many faults, but deceit wasn't one of them. The journal reveals that he was not the great explorer everyone thought him to be."

"I don't understand." Kate placed her cup on the table and turned to her aunt. "What about all his discoveries?"

"The man responsible for them was Peter's companion and aide, Mr. Walter Fletcher, a penniless student Peter met on his very first trip."

"Well, that comes as a surprise," Lady Esther said. "Yet Peter was celebrated for those discoveries, and he accepted all the adulation. I'm very disappointed in him."

"Mr. Fletcher didn't care who got credit," Lady Winstead said, "as long as he could participate. And I suppose Peter was partially responsible for those discoveries since he funded or helped gain the funding for every expedition. And in the end, he is bringing the truth to light."

Still, the revelation that Lord Peter's fame and accomplishments truly belonged to another was rather scandalous. No wonder his son hadn't wanted the journal to be found.

"Did you know this all along, Lady Winstead?" I asked.

"Heavens, no. I only found out when I read the journal. Then yesterday I paid a call on Mr. Fletcher and told him what I knew—what was about to become common knowledge. He's a young man, and unless he receives the credit he's due, it's unlikely he'd obtain funding for any future expeditions. So, yes, your husband may hand that journal off to the British Museum. It's what Peter had wanted. They have my full permission to use it as they see fit."

Lady Winstead's lips spread into an unfamiliar smile. "And I will fund Mr. Fletcher's next expedition. In fact, I may just go on that trip with him."

With such a travel companion, poor Mr. Fletcher may find he was better off remaining anonymous.

I took my leave shortly after that exchange. Jarvis greeted me in the hall when I arrived at home.

"Is Mr. Hazelton in his library, Jarvis?" I asked as he took my coat.

"No, ma'am. He's in the drawing room, and he especially asked you to join him when you returned."

I entered the drawing room and found George lounging on the sofa. He looked up from the newspaper when he heard me. "How was your visit?"

I swept his feet off the sofa and took a seat beside him. "There was no need for a warning," I told him. "Lady Winstead was already aware that her husband was not the great explorer legend would have it."

"Excellent," he said, folding the paper and setting it aside. "I'll deliver the journal to the museum tomorrow and be done with this assignment."

"Mine is finished, as well." I paused for a moment as realization dawned. "In fact, I believe I've been sacked."

"It's your insolent behavior." George let out a tsk. "I always knew it would lead you to trouble."

I shoved him with my shoulder. "Kate and Lady Winstead plan to travel, so there will be no presentation. Therefore, no need for my services." I faced George. "And no gift of appreciation from Lady Winstead. That's rather disappointing."

"Disappointing? Why, it's an outrage!" George took to his feet. "You spent nearly a week working with the young woman— saw to it that she was properly attired, took her to a ball, probably saved her life, and Lady Winstead's, I might add. You deserve something for that."

"You'd think so, wouldn't you?" Now I was just a bit disgruntled.

"Lady Esther thought so." A smile broke across his face.

"She did? How do you know?"

"While you were still at the Ashleys' home, she asked me how she could best show her appreciation for all you've done for her friend."

My spirits rose. "That's something, though I think it would be more appropriate for her to show her regret for putting me in that horrible situation."

"Whatever her reason, her gift arrived while you were out." He grinned. "Would you care to see it?"

"Very much."

He took my hand and led me to the back of the room and to his library, where he pushed open the door and gestured for me to enter. Lady Esther's gift was impossible to miss—a beautiful, gleaming partners desk.

"It's perfect!" I ran my hands over the smooth surface and turned back to George. "What made you think of this?"

He lifted one shoulder. "Well, Jarvis may have given me a hint. He mentioned that swinging golf clubs is better done in the garden."

I couldn't help laughing. "He's an excellent butler."

"And he was right. We already share the desk. It might as well be built for that purpose. Besides, I've grown used to having you in here, and I'd miss seeing your face on the other side of the desk."

"I feel that I've already taken over so much of the house that this was your last refuge. You really don't mind sharing it with me?"

"I am happy to share everything I have with you."

"As am I, which leads me to the subject I've been hoping to discuss with you."

"Your father's gift of money?" He swung around and sat back against the desk.

I propped myself next to him. "And the likelihood of future gifts to come. It's just like this desk. It's ours. We share it."

He heaved a sigh. "It's not the money that bothered me, but more that it felt as though you don't really need me."

"As someone who has been needed only for her money, I can honestly say you wouldn't like it. Besides, as a third son, one would think you would have expected to marry a woman with a decent fortune."

"I suppose I did, but those anonymous women weren't you. Supporting you financially was just one aspect, and I have come to see that it isn't important. What I really want is to be a necessary part of your life, but you are so competent, so self-reliant. You ask so little of me, I fear you don't need me at all."

"And I thought I was asking too much. Think about it, George. Rose and I moved into your home. Your servants care for us. We use your carriage and horses. And that's not to mention the many wonderful things you bring to our lives."

I could see him resisting a smile. "For instance?"

"For instance?"

"Yes," He gave me a nudge. "Just what are these wonderful things I bring to your life?"

I had a feeling I knew where he was headed with this, but I was happy to play along. "Without you there'd be no magic in my life," I said.

He swept me with his gaze. "Magic, you say?"

"Yes, that mysterious element that just makes everything brighter and better."

"I bring that?"

"You do."

He gave me a sidelong glance. "Is that all?"

I couldn't hold back a bubble of laughter.

"Oh, now you laugh." But his own tone was full of amusement.

"Humor," I said between chortles. "You also bring humor to my life."

George was laughing along with me now. "Frances, my darling, beautiful, competent, intelligent wife. You excel in so many ways, but must I really pry even the smallest compliment from you?"

"I'm sorry. I'd completely forgotten your pride and self-confidence are in my hands."

"And I'd say you're basically wringing them right now."

I stifled my laughter and took his hand. "I never thought I was quite that stingy with my praise, but let me say from my heart, you are absolutely necessary to me. As necessary as breath."

His gaze softened. "Oh, that was good. I believe you, too. But I will need the occasional reminder."

"Goodness, I didn't realize your pride and self-confidence would require so much attention. I'll have to work on my compliments."

He grinned. "Don't worry. We have a whole lifetime to work on them."

I felt an answering smile tug at the corners of my lips. "Indeed, we do."

Acknowledgments

It's a pleasure to write the Countess of Harleigh mysteries. I'm grateful to my readers who enable me to continue writing them, librarians for putting them on their shelves, and book sellers for stocking and recommending them.

I am also grateful for the discerning eye of my critique partner, Mary Keliikoa; the editorial eye of Barb Goffman; and the support of Team M, with a particular acknowledgement to Ashley Winstead.

Special thanks to Luci Zahray, expert in all manner of poisons, for sharing your knowledge of laudanum, and to Sheryl Pacher, whose rough day at work inspired the character of Lady Winstead.

It's always a joy to work with my agent, Melissa Edwards, my editor John Scognamiglio, and the team at Kensington.

Lastly, thanks to my husband, Dan, for always being there. Love you!

Please turn the page for an exciting sneak peek of
Dianne Freeman's next Countess of Harleigh mystery
AN ART LOVER'S GUIDE TO PARIS AND MURDER,
coming soon wherever print and ebooks are sold!

Chapter One

~⚬~

July 1900

"We should go to Paris."

George, my husband, glanced up from his work to remove his reading glasses and send a frown across the polished walnut width of our partner's desk. It was fitted sideways against the back wall of the office in our townhome in Belgravia. Our chairs sat on either side of the window, so we both enjoyed the view of the back garden as we attended to our morning routine; one that I feared was becoming a bit mundane.

From my side of the broad desk, I handled matters such as our schedule, pending invitations, correspondence, and weekly menus suggested by our chef.

Exhilarating work it was not.

On his side, George read the newspapers and dealt with his own correspondence, like the letter he'd just set aside when our butler, Jarvis, brought in the tea tray. I'd noticed the letter had come from Paris.

"Thank you, Jarvis," I said as he placed the heavy, silver tray on the center of the desk, equidistant between us. "That's exactly what I need." The stocky butler, who looked more like a boxer, bowed and left us to it. I kept my gaze on the tray while I poured myself a cup.

George's chair creaked as he stretched his long frame up and backward, lacing his fingers behind his head. His lips turned upward at the corners, from a frown to something more like a smirk as he watched me attempt to look guileless. "Paris, you say? Should we? Why now?"

I relaxed enough to allow my spine to touch the back of my chair and lifted my cup toward my lips. "To visit the World Exposition, of course, or Exposition Universelle, as the French call it."

"Are they doing that again? Isn't it like the Great Exhibition Prince Albert held, in my father's day?"

"Exactly. In America, we call them World's Fairs. I can't believe you haven't heard of this one. Everyone is talking about it." I took a sip of my tea. "They say Paris is now the city of light quite literally, with buildings and streets illuminated at night. It must be breathtaking. People are traveling from every corner of the world to marvel at the display of art and industry collected in one place." I wagged my index finger at him. "You know you would enjoy it and it would be educational for Rose." Rose was my eight-year-old daughter.

George watched me, smirk still in place, completely unmoved.

"As for why now," I continued, "I believe I've waited long enough for a wedding trip. We were married in February. It is now July and here we are, still in London. Yes, we had good reasons for postponing our travel, but those reasons no longer exist, and it is well past time we go somewhere." Setting my cup on the desk, I crossed my arms and awaited his response.

George poured himself a cup of tea, gazing at me in assessment all the while. "Are you lying?"

It was my turn to smirk. "You tell me."

He eyed me while he stroked his beard—a recent addition to his handsome face that he had yet become used to. I, on the other hand, took to it very quickly. Somehow, the dark whiskers along his jaw made his eyes even greener and his lips all the more inviting. Gazing at him, I became so distracted I startled when he slapped his palm on the desk and took to his feet.

"All right, I'll admit I don't know." He leaned his hip against the desk next to my chair. "Are you lying?"

I held up my index finger and thumb just a fraction apart. "A bit. Though my statements are true, they aren't the reason I want to go to Paris."

"That's the best way to spin a tale. Keep it as truthful as possible. I must say you didn't give yourself away. I'm impressed."

My cheeks grew warm with his praise. "Thank you, darling, so I've passed the examination, have I?" George was something of an investigator. He'd worked for the Home Office for many years, even infiltrating criminal groups to uncover evidence of their illicit activity. He still accepted the occasional assignment from the government, but recently, we have been working on more personal investigations.

And yes, I did say "we."

I've assisted in George's investigations and tackled one or two of my own as well. Though I didn't have his expertise, I was learning. It was 1900, after all. Time for women to declare they could do more than decorate a man's arm or his table.

"You have most definitely passed," he said. "Not so much as a blush or twitch of those lovely blue eyes of yours." He cupped my chin with his palm and pressed a kiss against my lips. "Now," he said, propping a leg on the desk, "I'll take the truth, if you please. Why Paris? Why now?"

"Well, the part about our wedding trip is completely true. First, my family caused a delay in our plans. Then you had to heal from your injuries. I had thought we'd go somewhere after you recovered, but then you took an assignment, and quite honestly, I fear we've fallen into a routine and are on the verge of becoming dull."

George's mouth formed a grimace as I spoke. "Perhaps a little less truth would be better." He held up his hands as if measuring. "There must be a suitable place for me between perfect husband and dullard."

"I would never call you dull," I said. "But I do believe it's time we share some excitement. If I can't run off with you to some romantic hideaway, at least we can go somewhere interesting, entertaining, and enjoyable, where we can take Rose. Thus, the Paris Exposition. I might even get a look at my new niece."

My sister, Lily, married Leo Kendrick last October and almost immediately moved to France for Leo's business. She gave birth to a daughter early in May. Both sides of the family chose to ignore the timing. Leo's parents had met little Amelia Jane already. In fact, Patricia Kendrick, Leo's mother, had taken an apartment in Paris due to her work with the British Exposition Commission. Lily and Leo had left their home in Lille and moved in with her when the baby was due, so Lily would have the advantage of a Parisian doctor.

That was two months ago, however. Lily and her family had returned to their home, but even so, Lille was only a train ride away from Paris.

"I do miss my sister terribly," I continued. "It's very hard to hear how wonderful my niece is from Patricia Kendrick. She is a lovely woman, and yes, she's the child's grandmother, but she's still a third party. I'd like to see the baby for myself. In fact, Hetty might wish to come too." Hetty was my aunt. It was she who'd brought Lily to London from New York City over a year ago now. After Lily married, Hetty stayed in London, then took over the lease on my house when I married George.

George tipped his head, which caused a lock of dark hair to fall across his forehead. He swept it back. "This sounds as though you weren't lying to me at all."

"I already admitted part of what I'd said was true."

"And the other part?"

"That letter you received from France." I wiggled a finger toward his side of the desk.

"How did you know it was from France?"

"It has French postage. I have the power of vision." I gave him a wink. "Quite the detective, aren't I?"

"Is this a roundabout way of asking who is writing to me from France?"

I lifted my cup to my lips, realized the tea had gone cool, and set it back down, conscious of George's regard. "All right, I suspect the letter involves an assignment. If it does, I'd like to be part of it." I arched a brow. "Does it?"

"Not exactly an assignment. More of a request."

I waited for more. George stared silently at his hands. "Isn't that how it all works?" I prompted. "First, you receive a request. Once you accept, it becomes an assignment. Does it involve going to Paris and do you intend to accept?"

He released a heavy sigh. "It does, and I think I must."

His reaction and reply were not what I'd expected. George was always invigorated by a new case—excited and eager to get started. "This must be a disturbing case."

"It is . . . complicated. And confidential and potentially dangerous. The idea of making a holiday of it with Rose and your aunt along . . ." He shook his head. "That is not possible."

"Fine. Then you and I shall go alone. Once we've completed this investigation, they can join us, and then we'll have our holiday."

"Frances, this is somewhat personal."

Warning bells sounded in my head. "Too personal for your wife?" All manner of horrors crossed my mind as I rose to my feet and took a step toward him, putting us nose to nose. "George Hazelton, if there is another French woman out there declaring herself to be your wife, so help me I'll—"

"No!" George looked as though his life were passing before his eyes at the mention of events from last fall. He took me by the shoulders. "It's nothing like that. The letter is from my aunt Julia. It's of a confidential nature and I simply don't know how much of it she'd be willing to let me divulge to you."

My racing pulse slowed. "Is she in some sort of trouble?" I'd met Julia Hazelton years ago, when I made my London debut and became friends with George's sister, Fiona. Lady Julia had chaperoned us once or twice when Fiona's mother wasn't available. We always considered it a treat since she was only ten years older than us and far more indulgent than either of our mothers.

Lady Julia was the spinster aunt that all mothers warned their daughters they'd become if they didn't lower their standards and marry someone. From what I witnessed, hers didn't seem an unpleasant life. No worse than many of us who did marry, and far better than some.

I learned recently that Lady Julia had longed to travel and make her living painting, but for years the Earl of Hartfield, who was her brother and George's father, wouldn't allow it. Fiona thought her aunt Julia had been something of a prisoner in their home. George didn't see it quite so dramatically. Upon the old earl's death, George's brother inherited the title and set Lady Julia free, which is to say he gave her a generous allowance and told her she should do with it as she wished.

My understanding was that she had been living a nomadic life ever since. She'd managed to attain the ripe old age of thirty-eight without ever having to follow society's rules. She was a veritable advertisement for the joy of spinsterhood. I was surprised she'd written to George. "Is she passing through Paris?"

"She has been living there for the past seven years."

"For seven years?" Not so nomadic, then. "Wouldn't that have been when she left the family home?"

George gave me a mirthless smile when he saw awareness dawn in my eyes. "This is my dilemma. The rest of the family thinks she is traveling the world, and she has made it clear to me that she wishes to perpetuate that ruse. She has contacted me twice over the years, and I've helped her with matters of business." He ran a hand down my arm. "I'd love to have you with me, my love, but there are elements of her life she wishes to keep private."

"But if the point of your trip is to help her with confidential business matters, I can stay at our hotel while you work with her. Or I could find something else to do. It is Paris, after all. She needn't even know I'm there if you fear that will distress her."

"That's not exactly what I'm worried about." He stepped around to his side of the desk and picked up Lady Julia's letter. When he opened it, something fell to the desk—a small fragment of paper. George swept it up and handed it to me. "I don't think sharing this with you will breach any confidentiality."

It was a newspaper clipping from July eleventh—two days ago. I unfolded it to reveal a death notice. "Paul Ducasse," I read. "The artist?"

George indicated that I should continue reading.

The newsprint was small, and in French, so it took a moment to read. It was indeed Paul Ducasse, the artist, who had died—by accident, according to this. "It says he fell into the Seine and drowned on the evening of the tenth."

He held up the letter. "Aunt Julia thinks differently and would like me to investigate."

Ducasse must be of some importance to her if she wanted George to investigate his death. It appeared that Lady Julia had a few secrets. One of them involved a man—a dead man.

"So, you must see why it would be better if you don't accompany me." The confident tone with which George began the statement faltered when he caught my eye.

I smiled. "Must I?"

"Surely you don't want to become involved in this, Frances."

I tipped my head.

"Egad, I've no choice, have I? You're going with me."

I rested my palm against his cheek. "I'll start packing now."

Chapter Two

By the following afternoon, George and I were crossing the English Channel. When necessary, I can be the model of efficiency. Our need to depart quickly had made obtaining hotel lodgings impossible. I had heard more than twenty million people had already visited the exposition since it opened in April, and at least that many more were expected before it closed. Which meant George and I might have found ourselves on the street if not for Patricia Kendrick, my sister's mother-in-law.

Patricia was deeply involved with the British exhibit at the exposition, but was not currently occupying the apartment she leased in Paris. She'd returned to London last week for at least a month and suggested that George and I make use of her Paris apartment to visit the exposition and my sister, or to investigate a suspicious death.

She didn't say that last part in so many words, but I was confident she wouldn't mind.

Modern woman that I was, I used our telephone to contact her the moment I knew we were bound for Paris. She could not have been more accommodating. She sent the address and a set of keys with a footman within the hour and promised to notify the housekeeper in Paris of our arrival. My aunt, Hetty, was happy to take charge of Rose for a week or so. And just as willing to bring her along to Paris later.

And *voilà*! Here we were a little over a day later standing on the deck of the *Invictus* under a heavy sky. The cool sea air blew whisps of hair across my face. I lifted my hand to brush them aside, but George's fingers got there first and tucked the dark strands securely behind my ear.

He drew in a deep breath, clearly savoring the salty tang of the sea. "I knew it would be more enjoyable out here than in that tight cabin. Aren't you glad we came up on deck?"

"It's perfect," I replied, linking my arm with his and nestling into his side. We had come out on the covered deck almost an hour ago to watch our progress as we approached France. As we crept into the port of Calais, all sound was lost to the clamor of the coastal birds who screeched their objections at the steamer disturbing their pool. It's a shame we weren't traveling for pleasure, but with luck, that would come later—after Lady Julia's business.

I leaned against George's shoulder and watched the activity on the dock up ahead. There was no need to rush as we had Bridget and Blakely, my maid and George's valet, along to take care that our bags were loaded onto the right train and that a suitable compartment was made ready for us.

"Lady Harleigh, what a surprise."

I glanced to our left to see none other than Alicia Stoke-Whitney standing on the other side of a support beam. As always, I couldn't help but draw a contrast between us. Alicia looked like a fairy princess—pocket-sized, with a pointed chin and bright cheeks and eyes. Even her hair was a vivacious red, which completely matched her personality. I, on the other hand, was a few scant inches shorter than George's six feet, with dark brown hair, blue eyes, and a pert nose. The only time my cheeks were bright was when I pinched them.

Alicia had left England months ago, after her husband died,

intending to spend her mourning period on the Continent. Not that I thought she truly mourned her late husband, but that was beside the point. Mourning was a societal norm most widows followed. I had done so for my late husband and he was a complete rotter. In fact, he'd been in Alicia's bed when he died. I'd quite forgotten about that and the memory stung a bit, though I tried not to let it show. It was my late husband who'd broken our marriage vows, not Alicia. Since that time, she and I had become rather useful to one another.

Still, I did find it annoying that while the rest of us observed the formalities, she gadded about as she pleased. She'd clearly just come from England. And as clearly, she was in the company of a rather handsome man. He was only a bit taller than average, but everything else about him was distinctive. Thick, dark hair and moustache, piercing gray eyes, chiseled features, and broad shoulders. He looked to be in his early forties, which put him in the upper edges of Alicia's tastes. Her latest amours had been younger men.

George released a tsk that was audible only to me. Though I sympathized with his feelings, I was curious. "Hello, Alicia." I didn't bother correcting her use of my former title. I'd been Mrs. Hazelton since I married George. "I thought you'd forsaken England for the Continent."

She let out a tinkle of laughter and squeezed the gentleman's arm closer to her side. "I have certainly found much to love in France, but occasionally I must return to England for matters of business."

I wondered what business Mr. Dark and Handsome was helping her with. I shifted my gaze his way. Did Alicia intend to introduce him?

"Tell me, what brings you to France?" she asked. "Where are you staying?"

Hmm. Apparently, no introduction was forthcoming.

"The exposition, of course," I said. "You remember my

brother-in-law, Mr. Kendrick? His mother is a member of the British commission. We are staying at her home in Paris."

"Such a small world," she said. "I, too, am a member of the commission. I took my late husband's place. I don't believe I've worked with Mrs. Kendrick, though the name sounds familiar."

The steam whistle sounded, vibrating from my feet up through my spine and reminding us it was time to disembark. "We should go to our room and gather our belongings," George said, taking my arm.

Alicia smiled. "And we must be off as well. I'm sure we shall see each other again in Paris."

"Perhaps," I agreed, before George nearly dragged me through the door. "I'm coming," I said once we were out of their hearing. "Heavens, I know you don't care for Alicia, but you needn't run in your attempt to get away."

George darted a glance behind us and slowed his pace. "I simply didn't want to be trapped into providing any further information. I'd really prefer that no one know we're here until after we've taken care of Aunt Julia's business."

We'd reached our room to find that Bridget and Blakely had already removed every sign of our previous occupation. "We have a private compartment on the train," I assured him. "She'll never find us."

George gave me a bewitching smile. "That sounds rather like an invitation."

"I thought you were avoiding invitations at the moment."

"Not from you, my love. Never from you." He pulled me into his arms, and goodness! We nearly missed our train.

We arrived in Paris about four hours later. Upon disembarking the train, we found the Gare du Nord completely overrun with fellow travelers—some rushing across the platforms, heels ringing out on the metal grates, others waiting by stacks of baggage, each their own island within the flowing mass of people.

It was early evening, just after six. I suspected many of these people were returning home from their daily employment. The commuters scowled at the travelers who raised their voices to be heard over other voices, in every language imaginable. The noise echoed off the stone and metal structure and bombarded the ears like waves against the shore.

George gripped my hand so as not to lose track of me in the enormous building, and we stepped into the swirling mass. Bridget and Blakely had set out a good twenty minutes before us, so assuming we made it out of the station, they ought to have a cab waiting. I have never been so grateful for my height. I could see over most of the heads between us and the exit. When we finally made it out the doors, I expected to hear a *pop* like a cork released from its bottle.

"There's Bridget," George said. She stood on the back end of a cab waving her arms. Her fair Irish complexion was blotchy from the heat and her blonde curls had escaped her sedate bun.

"Blakely went on to the house with the luggage," she said as George and I climbed in. "And I got very lucky that this cabbie was willing to wait for you."

"Then hop in here with us and enjoy the fruits of your labor," I told her. "Heavens, I had no idea it would be so crowded."

"You were the one who said the entire world was traveling to Paris," George said. "I should think you would have been prepared for this."

I bumped against the back of the seat as the cab took off. "I suppose I thought the world had already been and gone. I hope it's just the station, but I fear we will be up against crowds everywhere."

We traveled along for thirty minutes or so when the carriage came to a standstill. I regarded the heavy traffic outside the window, wondering how long we'd be stuck here. We were south of the Opera House, approaching the Louvre. I consulted my 1896 Baedeker Guide. If it was correct, Rue St. Honoré, and the Kendricks' apartment, ought to be close at hand—assuming the carriage would move at some point.

"Why don't we walk?" I said, heaving a sigh of impatience. "We've been traveling long enough today and it's quite stifling in here."

"I'm game," George said. "Is the house nearby?"

A short consultation with our driver indicated it wasn't far at all.

"Shall we, then?" George said.

We left Bridget in the cab with our two small bags and payment for the driver. Then we picked our way around the multitude of carriages and even a few automobiles lined up on the broad boulevard. The sky was significantly brighter here than it had been on the coast, but without the breeze it was almost sultry, and we were still dressed for the channel crossing. I considered myself lucky when we arrived at the apartment before I'd completely wilted.

That is to say, we'd arrived at the entrance gate to the building. Suitable for a castle, the beautifully carved and ancient wood fit perfectly into an enormous arched opening in the stone wall. A knob was fitted into the side of the arch to ring the bell for the concierge. Before I could do so, Blakely opened one of the doors and stepped out. The valet was almost a head shorter than George, and the door he was manning was a good two Blakelys tall.

"Good to see you made it," George said as we followed the valet into the courtyard.

"I've been here just long enough to get your luggage brought in," he said. Neither the heat nor the exertion seemed to have had any effect on Blakely. His black suit and white shirt were just as crisp as when he'd left the house this morning. The pale skin that came along with his red hair was not even slightly flushed. I turned away with a sigh of envy and took notice of my surroundings.

"Why, it looks like a park in here," I said. A smallish park, anyway, enclosed on all sides with five-story buildings, the walls of which were covered with glossy green vines. The courtyard was paved with flagstones from the surrounding walls to a garden area in the center filled with showy mophead hydrangeas and fuzzy ferns. Small palm trees in pots lined the two long walls of the rectangular space and framed matching stairways that climbed up the opposing walls to outdoor landings on the first floor. It was blessedly cool and shady here. A refreshing change from the street.

"We left Bridget and our bags in the cab a few blocks away," I told Blakely. "She should be along shortly."

"Very good, ma'am," he said. "Then if you'll allow me to introduce the housekeeper, she can show you to your room, while I wait for Bridget."

"An excellent plan." We followed him up one of the stone stairways to the Kendricks' apartment that took up the first and second floor on this side of the building. Blakely pushed open the door at the top of the stairs and we preceded him inside.

I was familiar with the townhouses of my little area of London and the brownstones in New York City, but I had never been inside a Paris apartment. If pushed, I'd admit I expected them to be small, if not actually cramped. I was completely unprepared for such luxury as met me in the foyer. The ceiling soared up to the second floor where a softly glowing chandelier illuminated a railing around what must be a hallway above. The entry was paneled and painted a creamy white. It opened to a large salon and library on the right and a dining room on the left. A panel opposite the entry door slid open and a woman emerged.